EVA SCHMIDT

JILL MORNINGSTAR

With my deepest love, admiration and gratitude to Al, Leah and Ben.

Published through Opus Self-Publishing Services
Located at:
Politics and Prose Bookstore
5015 Connecticut Ave. NW
Washington, D.C. 20008
www.politics-prose.com / / (202) 364-1919

HISTORICAL NOTE

Of the characters in this novel, only Bertha Pappenheim, Joseph, Magda and Helge Goebbels, Wolf von Helldorf, Erik Hanussen, Edgar Mowrer and Victor Arlosoroff are historical figures. In the novel, I often paraphrase or include quotations from these figures as part of their fictional dialogues, speeches and letters.

Most of *Eva Schmidt* is set in the first nine months of 1933. Certain historical events referenced in the novel are written out of their chronological order to fit the arc of the story.

Bertha Pappenheim directed an orphanage in Frankfurt similar to the one in this novel, but she left the orphanage in 1907. Her continued work there, and the backgrounds of the children in the orphanage, as described in these pages, are fictional.

Eva Schmidt

JILL MORNINGSTAR

OPUS SELF-PUBLISHING
POLITICS AND PROSE BOOKSTORE
WASHINGTON, DC

PROLOGUE

Frankfurt, Germany, 1913

My story was told in three words, a quick whisper falling from a maid's yellowed lips. *Bastard. A Jew.* The old woman hadn't known where to put her hands after abandoning someone else's child. She let them float, waiting for the weight to return, then balled her oil-stained apron in her fingers and kneaded it like dough.

It was warm for March, and Frau Pappenheim held me, wrapped in a white sheet, on the stone steps of the Israelite Orphanage for Girls. "You work for the family?" she asked.

The woman nodded.

"Orthodox?"

The maid slid a simple cross back and forth along her gold chain. She nodded again.

Frau Pappenheim had no more questions because I came with no answers. I had no home because I'd never been born. I had no name because mothers didn't name air. With only blanks to fill, Frau Pappenheim took me into her orphanage, and welcomed me among her spiritual daughters. She named me Eva, after the woman born only to God, and Schmidt, after her mother, who was a Goldschmidt. I couldn't have been named Goldschmidt. The Goldschmidts were one of Frankfurt's most prominent Jewish families. Their story had no place for my three words. I lived my life so they would have no place in mine.

EXCEPTIONS

Berlin, 1933

1

EVA

I can't place you," the man said. The rich smell of his pipe made me want to curl up with my book, cheek against the worn leather of the library chair. We were the only two in the reading room and I'd felt him watching me. When he spoke, I let myself look at him. He had a fine face. I was 19 and he was older but not so much older that I wouldn't pay attention. His pointed nose tilted to the stilled fans. His clear, smooth skin was hardened by the light.

Frau Pappenheim's rules forbade speaking in libraries, or to strange men, so I only smiled at him in return.

"Don't worry," the man said. "I'm American. People interest me."

I'd always thought of myself as invisible to men with starched collars and silk ties. He saw me dumbstruck, and softened.

"I didn't mean to be rude. I'm Thad Cartwright. I work at the United States Embassy." He gestured to a stack of *Kriegsakademie* reports. His eyes were turquoise pools, big and inviting. When he smiled, they withdrew. "Who are you?"

"Eva Schmidt," I said.

"Pale skin, dark hair, blue eyes. If this were the United States, I'd say you were black Irish, but not in Berlin." He traced quick calculations against the heavy oak table with his forefinger. "Are you French?" He was comfortable not knowing the answer to his own question.

I wanted to be French and I wanted to say yes, but his bluntness compelled me to tell the truth. "I'm nothing."

"That's impossible."

"I have no parents."

He pushed back his chair. Its spindle legs scraped against the marble floor, and echoed under the vaulted ceiling as he rose to go. Before his words came out, I knew what he would say. *It was a pleasure to meet you . . . I'm late getting back to the office . . . I didn't mean to pry.* I looked down so I wouldn't see myself become small in his eyes, but his steps came toward me, instead of away.

"An orphan," he said. His gold cufflink flashed. I watched the graceful spread of his fingers and breathed their soapy smell as he lifted my chin. I could no longer avoid seeing his face. "It must free you."

I dodged the afternoon shadows on Mitte's side streets, not feeling the cold through my thinned soles. The happy hum Thad Cartwright had planted in me made me smile at strange things: an accounting firm's handbill, the mud-splattered side of a bus, and a man sweeping snow melt from the sidewalk. I didn't want to go to my night job at Karnevalklub. I wanted to be from nowhere. I wanted to be free. I loved that the strange American thought I could be.

What I wished I could have told him unfolded in my mind. I was raised by a crusader, although Frau Pappenheim called herself a social worker. She had founded several organizations dedicated to the improvement of Jewish women and girls. Something in her needed us to be successful. We needed to prove to men we had brains, gentiles we had grace and her powerful relatives she was a force in her own right.

In the orphanage, she demanded *bildung! Sittlichkeit!* Education! Respectability!

I'd done everything she asked. Her curt corrections molded my language into *hochdeutsch,* German as it is written, German as is correct. I recited Schiller, Heine and Goethe from memory. I learned English because she wanted me to, and quit piano because I knew I would never be good enough to impress her. Her praise— *Poignant example, Eva . . . Well-rendered argument*—could hold me for hours. It made me better than I was.

But better than I was wasn't enough. My truth cropped up like crabgrass, ugly nubs she couldn't polish over. I was an illegitimate orphan living among *Ostjuden* girls. They were Eastern Jews, victims of the Tsar, who despite their Yiddish language and ways, were whom the orphanage was about. When I read the Torah, it left no doubt about the differences between us. *A mamzer*, a bastard, *shall not enter into the assembly of the Lord. Even to the tenth generation shall none of his enter into the assembly of the Lord.*

Frau Pappenheim quietly assured me that the edict was not relevant to my case. She said, "One: a *mamzer* in Jewish law does not mean the same thing as a bastard in Germany. *Mamzer* only refers to those either born of incest, or of the union between a married woman and a man who is not her husband. Two: even if you are a *mamzer*, which is unlikely, there is no practical effect because there is no evidence of it. Three: even if there is evidence of it, which I am certain there is not, the only repercussion would be that you and your descendants would have to marry other *mamzers*, or Reform Jews. Four: the stigma you face will be social, not halakhic. That is why I teach you the way I do. That is why you must keep studying the way you do. Do you understand?" I nodded, and she replied, "Good. This is the last we will speak of it."

It wasn't, however, the last time I heard of it. Rabbi Berger often alluded to it from the *bimah*, the pulpit. "Our families, whole and pure, are the one thing Gentiles can't deny us. When you commit improper sexual acts, when you violate the sanctity of marriage, you sin against EVERY GERMAN JEW. EVERY GERMAN JEW is tarred by your disgrace."

My spiritual mother's fairy tales, published under a man's name, struck me even harder than the words of our leader and of our God. Her writing gave life to a de-limbed doll, a jammed coffee grinder, and a singed scrap of lace. The objects were abandoned to the mildewed shelves of a junk shop, a deformed and useless hodgepodge. But, behind their battered veneers, lay histories filled with love and tragedy.

To suggest that beneath our coats of dust, we were more than defective old things was kind. Like all good trash, we once belonged to someone. The *Ostjuden* girls' eyes lit up as they imagined themselves a dented thimble or a disassembled music box. That was because these fairy tales were written for them. They'd stumbled into the orphanage with matted hair and matte eyes. Their hundreds of words telling of dead mothers and shattered glass made our teachers cry, and brought understanding to Frau Pappenheim's stern face.

At night, when I lay against my flattened pillow, searching for shapes in the ceiling cracks, and I heard the Eastern girls' tears, I wanted their reason to cry. My sadness came only from my shame, so I never cried. I'd spent every one of my days in the junk shop. I had no past from which to derive value, and I hated Frau Pappenheim's tales.

My spiritual mother never treated me differently than the other girls. She forbade gossip, and when she heard it, it was punished.

But she couldn't protect me from the silence that dropped on my chest like a cement block when the teachers skipped my turn during lessons on the family tree, or when we had to present the dead for whom we were named, and my past held no dead for me.

Nor could she protect me when the girls crowded together at meals to speak Yiddish. Frau Pappenheim called Yiddish 'the Jewish women's language,' but that too, I wasn't born into. I couldn't feel its roundness or capture its swing. 'German is better,' the girls would say, if I broke into their babbling, bouncing conversations. When they did take the time to translate, a hundred raucous words boiled down to, 'her sister snuck out,' or 'my brother ate nothing but bread.' Sometimes, my friends offered little more than 'I wouldn't know how to say it so you'd understand.' I had little choice but to fade out, or rush off, as if I had something more important to do.

More important was *Bildung! Sittlichkeit!* I worked harder and read more than anyone else. I did anything I could to uproot my crabgrass. When I was 17, I was rewarded for my efforts. I was chosen to recite Beer-Hoffman's *Lullaby for Mirjam* at an assembly to honor Felix Warburg, Frau Pappenheim's cousin from America who was one of the orphanage's most generous donors. In her announcement, she said, "We will honor a young woman for her mastery of the German language and literature. Her name is Eva Schmidt." She said more, but I stopped listening. I could feel nothing beyond my pride.

We were to bring no traces of our pasts to the assembly with the great man. *Education! Respectability!* ruled the day. We were not to speak with our hands, or otherwise show emotion. Yiddish was forbidden. Unlike my friends, who held tight to their memories, I was the product of my spiritual mother's mind, and she had created me for this moment.

I held my shoulders back and my abdomen tight. Tilting my chin slightly upward, I declared the words meant to anchor us firmly within our people's history and faith. *Deep within us runs our forefathers' blood. Onto the future, it rolls like a flood. All are within us. Who says he's alone? You are their life and their life is your own.*

My nerves pricked at my cheeks and neck, but I knew I'd done excellent work because when I stepped back, Herr Warburg sliced the air with his hands. His thick mustache hid the movement of his lips, but I heard him say, "What a terrible waste."

His four words banged in my head. No more fine tuning could undo my three: *Bastard. A Jew.* It was then I decided to go.

"I'm leaving," I'd told Frau Pappenheim not long after. Two words. My breath collapsed with their weight. It was not how I meant to say it. The gentle lines I'd practiced dropped away. I owed her so much more. My spiritual mother's mold had left me misshapen and bruised, but she was the only person I'd ever loved. She always insisted we speak for ourselves, that she would presume nothing about us. Every silent second I let pass was a failure, and I said, too loudly, "I'm moving to Berlin!"

She flicked the air with the back of her hand. "You're not ready. You have another year of schooling."

"I am ready!" I demanded. My throat dried to gravel. "I'm not like the other girls. I'm not freshened-up junk hoping to be found. I want to be new. I've never been new."

Frau Pappenheim ran a pen between her thumb and forefinger. "If you want to get out a bit, fine. But stay in Frankfurt. Continue the work."

I didn't understand. "What work?"

"Yours and mine." She pulled a pamphlet out of her desk and dropped it in front of me. "When you're not studying, you can work at the Neu Isenburg House." The Neu Isenburg House was another of Frau Pappenheim's projects. It was a home for fallen women.

Its mission was to 'extricate' a young, unmarried mother from 'the filthy corner to which her needs have chased her, and prevent her from becoming saleable market goods.'

"You'll care for the children while their mothers take classes. What a marvelous example you'll set." She reached for her phone to set it up. She didn't need to say what I knew she thought. *Because you are one of them.*

"I couldn't live," I replied, but it came out choked. I focused on her roll of tape, which was stuck with bits of fuzz and dust. It was unlike her to keep something she could no longer use.

"I see," she said. Her voice was high, surprised. She hung up the phone, but mislaid it. That was also unlike her. "Allow me to think." There was a ripple beneath her words. By the time I recognized it as regret, she seized control.

"I don't raise junk, Eva." A metallic beep droned from the telephone.

"I didn't mean that. I'm so grateful. Of course, that's not what I meant."

She reset the phone, and held up her hands in passive surrender, moving neither toward me, nor away. "You are different from the rest. You've been with me since you were born." Her face warmed with the memory. The ripple returned. "You can go. I raised you to go."

Frau Pappenheim's hands bounced with the movement of the train. She had accompanied me to Berlin. Or rather, she'd brought me with her. She was giving the plenary address at the League of Jewish Women's Conference on White Slavery. In the guise of practicing her speech, I assumed she was delivering a warning.

"The Alfonse, the scum procurer, crawls out of the *shtetl*'s muck. With silk stockings and fake gold, with vows of jobs and running water in Buenos Aires or New York, he shines his way into a poor girl's trust. His deception spews like a hacking cough, but words are all it takes. The promise of something is better than the guarantee of nothing in the Pale."

I leaned my face against the rattling window, and hummed to make my voice shake with its vibrations. I'd never been on a train. I'd never seen the world move so fast.

My spiritual mother's crackled whispers wove in and out of my consciousness. Frau Pappenheim already had found me a job as an apprentice to Herr Max Perlstein, a garment maker on Oranienburgerstrasse. She'd vouched for me to the landlady of a near-derelict building a few blocks away, and paid my deposit. She'd worked as fast as a train to get me started. It was what I wanted. I didn't want warnings.

"The Alfonse targets the religious girl." She paused, and her fountain pen scratched out more words. "Because she doesn't know what she's done until he's abandoned her to her bloody sheets, beyond redemption." More scratching. "She succumbs to the trade again and again as punishment. She knows the Alfonse is the only one who will have her, the only one she deserves."

Just as I started to fade, my spiritual mother's fingers pressed into my palm. "Eva," she said. These words were meant for me, alone. "A girl is always complicit in the crimes against her, whether it is her fault or not, whether the blame lies in her mind, or in the minds of others. She is trapped forever in shame's sick hold."

A wave of dusty, smelly air gushed at me as I stepped from the train. It stung my eyes and lingered on my skin. Passengers trudged toward the exit in a gloomy slog. I thought they should have been happy. They were in Berlin.

Painted signs directed us: *MIND THE GAP! SLIPPERY WHEN WET! GUARD YOUR BELONGINGS!* Frau Pappenheim added to the demands: *Don't stop for strangers! Take my hand!*

On Potsdamer Platz, lampposts stood as tall as buildings. Book stalls and racks of indecent postcards lined the plaza. A legless veteran in a wooden cart rolled past the Maybachs and Mercedes idling in front of Kempinski Haus. A woman with short hair and a very short skirt rode a motorbike, legs astride. Another breezed by us in shoes with straps, her toes and ankles bare to the world.

My white blouse was buttoned to my neck. My skirt hung to the tops of my boots. Thick, scratchy tights puddled at my ankles. It wasn't the armor for Berlin-Mitte.

Frau Pappenheim had our driver take us to Unter den Linden. Brandenburg Gate, the Palace of the Crown Prince, and the green domed Cathedral on Museumsinsel all made clear why she had so much faith in our country. Her pride radiated from the up-angle of her jaw, as if what she saw was better, even, than she'd remembered.

She wrapped her knuckle against the car window as we passed the cavernous *Staatsbibliothek.* "The public library belongs to you. You will always be welcome there."

She knocked again when we reached the iron gates of the French Embassy on Pariserplatz. "This, and the charms of those in its employ, should be met with skepticism." The driver laughed, so I laughed, even though I didn't know what she meant.

Unter den Linden's beauty faded block by block as we moved north on Friedrichstrasse, under the birdcage train station and across the Spree. Frau Pappenheim told the driver to pull over. We were in a jungle of neon and dirt. Daytime drunks cowered at the feet of jeweled gangsters. Women, intent on seduction, were too thin or too fat. Runs in their stockings left pasty white bubbles in tracks up their legs.

The driver let the car idle. The hum grew louder as I waited for Frau Pappenheim to speak. "Freedom," she finally said, "has come too quickly for Germany. It has left Berlin with soft edges, made it slippery. You must watch every step." After a grueling pause, she directed the driver to an alley off Hirtenstrasse.

He stared at her in the mirror for too long, then grunted as he merged into the traffic, arm extended against the wheel.

Frau Pappenheim had taught us about Jews like Heine, Einstein, and the martyred Rathenau. She had written articles about the *shtetl*'s degrading poverty, and I knew the *Ostjuden* girls were not of this high German sort. Even so, my friends were once whole. Their stories were warmed with the smells of *Shabbos* and the surety of hands held, and foreheads kissed.

The fantasy evaporated on the alley off of Hirtenstrasse. Mouths with black holes where teeth should have been shouted at vendors. Mottled hands grabbed at raw chickens. Older children hawked shoelaces, used bottles and rags. Yiddish spilled from under faded awnings, and with it, the smells of soup and grime. The trash had been picked through for anything of value that could be used or resold on the streets. Torn posters advising of the *Moshiach*'s return were plastered on blackened buildings next to pictures of *Kibbutzniks* hoisting giant palm fronds onto their shoulders.

"Jews carry an unenviable burden of proof, and you, as an orphan, all the more so," Frau Pappenheim said. She held her hand toward the grandeur of Unter den Linden, and continued. "You must always assume when *They* look at you, *This* is what *They* see." She pointed back to the cluster of poverty and oddity in the alley as she said '*This*.' My feet grew hot in my boots. All I could think about was having shoes with straps.

"Through modesty, morality and love for country, you must demonstrate that you are not *This*. *They* will want you to fail.

Only the most thoughtful among *Them* will summon the will to distinguish you."

The sharp edge in her voice revealed better than any words why she gave her life to educating us in the extraordinary way she did. She couldn't be thought of like us, so her only option was to make us like her, who, aside from her proud faith, was almost exactly like *Them*.

"You gettin' out, Maam?" the driver barked in a heavy Berlin accent. Frau Pappenheim responded with the address of my flat, not far from where we were, but far enough. It was tangled in the alleys of Scheunenviertel, somewhere in the blur of Berlin's soft edges.

Leftover rain sat in the grooves between the cobblestones of my courtyard. Frau Pappenheim said goodbye under zigzagging clothes lines. She held my cheek to hers. "I'll miss you more than you can know, Eva." The same ripple I'd heard when I told her I was leaving vibrated in my ear.

I gasped from surprise. "I'll miss you, too." As was so often true, my words came out wrong. Four words never could tell our story. "Thank you," I added. Six words.

When she let go, she took my hand. Her eyes scanned the soot-stained buildings. "This will be temporary." Her words were an instruction, not an assertion of fact. I had never known her to lie, but I could find nothing in her face to indicate she believed what she said. Still, when her car drove away and I carried my few things up four aching flights to what amounted to little more than a closet, I floated.

2

EVA

Zara, my downstairs neighbor in Scheunenviertel, was a sight under Karnevalklub's flashing neon marquee. She was a dime-a-dance girl, and her sequin swing dress was dizzying under the light. I pointed to her hair, which was still in rag rollers.

"We were a waitress down at lunch. I had to cover three extra tables. You're lucky I'm dressed."

I followed her into the bathroom and helped her untie her rollers. When we finished, she swept her curls into a side twist and I sprayed them in place. "Good?" she asked, into the mirror.

"Great," I said. It was true. She was always beautiful, and when she put in even the slightest effort, she looked like she'd stepped off a Babelsberg movie set. She was Karnevalklub's top draw.

Zara got me my job at the *klub* when I needed to supplement my income from Herr Perlstein's shop. She said I was a shoo-in because the owner, Rudi Thun, unlike so many in our depressed economy, didn't mind managing people whose merits exceeded their responsibilities. I needed the money, but I also wanted to be with Zara. She was my first friend in Berlin.

Rudi was kind to me. He assigned me to the arcade. He said my diction and affect made customers pleased to pour *pfennigs* down the throats of metal boxes. He was my second friend in Berlin.

I searched the haze and found him at the end of the bar. His body lacked balance, with fat fingers and lips that were out of proportion to the rest of him. A French Army munitions blast hit his left side, leaving his shoulder sagging and his ear mangled and deaf.

"What can I do, Rudi?" I yelled to his right. The arcade's beeps and tinny barks were already giving me a headache. He nodded toward the Ladies. The Ladies were Nadya, the automated fortune teller, and *Can't-be-Wrong*, the Love-o-Meter. When they broke, I took over. At first, people handed me *pfennigs* in exchange for the machines' paper verdicts, but few accepted the paper and walked away. As a living being, they expected me to know more than machines, and I wanted to prove them right.

I black-lined my eyes and wrapped my hair in a flimsy, silk scarf I'd bought from a hawker. I became Salomé from Al-Andalus. A Gypsy Queen would not recite cold phrases from dog-eared slips of paper. To the tune of cascading guitar picks and stomping heels, I spoke from Salomé's heart. I was pleasantly surprised when the lovelorn, broken down and bored, came back again and again, asking for more.

I studied Edward Heron-Allen's *Palmistry: A Manual of Cheirosophy*. Nothing in it persuaded me that the palm controlled fate. Yet, when I looked into my own hand, I knew any fortune teller worth her salt would see a diviner's palm. My head line showed an intuitive mind prone to excessive worry. My life line, without the companion lines of family in Venus and community in Neptune, exposed my solitary existence, and its chained markings betrayed a wandering soul, ever in search of new beginnings.

This sort of basic outline, if presented with authority, could start a conversation. It was in this conversation that fortune telling's truth lies. The more people talked to me, the more I could reduce their personalities into a few key traits. When I put words to these traits, when people nodded, laughed, and even cried in affirmation, I understood them. From there, it was not difficult to predict, with some credibility, how their souls would fare in the face of life's challenges.

Divination was not what Frau Pappenheim had in mind when she taught me Schiller and tatting. To imagine her mortified judgment gave me moments of pause, but I told myself it was she who gave me my skills. Her books provided characters to study, her vocabulary, the words to parse. A good fortune teller edifies her subjects. She knows there is more strength in 'mournful' than in 'heartbroken,' in 'independent' than in 'alone.' Was I not just mastering the language my spiritual mother so deeply admired?

I reminded myself I hadn't come to Berlin to be someone else's low quality copy, aping a gentility that would never be mine. I preferred the bar's blinking haze, from which any sort of creature could emerge and reblend, whether a taxi driver, a court reporter, a housewife, or even a dreaded Nazi brownshirt. I dove into their fog, revealing myself only as much as I chose, and allowing myself, just as easily, to walk away.

The night was slow. Each time the door opened, my eyes skipped past our usual customers to look for Thad Cartwright. But these regulars were followed only by patches of cold air. I embarrassed myself thinking the American would come to Karnevalklub. I pictured his parallel life in the West End. At 9:30, he would walk into Ciro's attached to a fox-laden blond in the vein of Marlene Dietrich. He would decline a smoke from the pretty, if vapid, cigarette girl, but would get one for Marlene. The girl's smile would say she was available to him in theory, if not in practice. He would give her a charitable look and an excessive tip, then disappear. He didn't need to settle for a cigarette girl, never mind a bar room gypsy, as a companion.

Matthias Altmann, my third friend in Berlin, emerged from behind a black curtain where he did voice-overs and sound effects for peepshows. Cleavage, ruffled bloomers and partially clothed couples rolling around in the mud were the extent of the titillation. "I need Nadya," he said.

"Nadya's the one in the box. I'm Salomé."

"Then, I need you." Matthias was a law student at Berlin University, but he wanted most to be a screenwriter. He made coffee and mimeographed for Fritz Lang four times a week, paid only with the hope that one day the great director would bring him on. Matthias was dark all over. The tired circles under his eyes magnified the effect. It would have been too much if he weren't so quick to be kind. I always thought he was too sweet for the *lustmord* and *film noir* that dominated German cinema, but I knew better than to tell him that.

Matthias was my closest friend of the three I had. All I knew about him was that he was a Jew from Laupheim, and all he knew about me was I was an orphan from somewhere else. I often thought the pasts we kept from each other were what made us close.

On most nights, I listened to Matthias complain about Fritz, then worship him in rapid cycle, or prattle on about Ray and Tanguy and the writers he met when he took a work desk at Café Moka Efti. For his part, he walked me home at night, fended off the occasional barroom groper, and added just the right romantic touches to my daydreams of Salomé as an Andalusian bride, lulled by the saunter of an Arabian across sand.

Occasionally, I thought he was in love with me, but if he was, he kept it at a simmer. Mostly, I had his protection. For that, I sometimes believed I was in love with him, too.

"Did Fritz yell at you again?"

"What do you think?"

"Weak coffee?"

"Two typos on one page."

"Let me guess. He glared."

Matthias rolled his finger for me to go on.

"His face was so cold, you got a headache."

"My tongue could have stuck to it."

"Then?"

"He said to the room, 'Matthias is stupid' and spat the Ts like they were the slobbery detritus of sunflower seeds."

"If it helps, you're the smartest person I know."

"Fritz is the smartest person I know," he grumbled.

"Tell him you're taking your free labor to Carl Laemmle." Like Matthias, Carl Laemmle was also a Jew from Laupheim. He founded Universal Studios, and was exceptionally generous to people from his hometown.

"American cinema is commoditized *scheisse*."

"And what are your peep shows?"

"An authentic expression of the workingman's hopes and dreams!"

"Go back to the working man," I teased. "He needs you more than I do." I glanced at the door, and again, cursed my stupidity.

"Salomé, you're monitoring the door like you're expecting a Gypsy King." His eyes begged honesty, but I knew his scripts grew from what they got people to confess, so I weighed my words.

"I met an American today. I've never talked to one before. It was as strange as you would think."

"Why do you keep looking for him, then?" His mind ticked, already constructing my answer.

"I can't get him out of my mind."

A woman in a cashmere coat and ostrich shoes approached my table. Nobody so well put together had ever sought my advice. It wasn't her expensive clothes that most distinguished her from my usual customers, though. It was that her approach lacked deference. When she didn't remove her coat, as would have been proper, and set her purse on the table, rather than in her lap, I knew she wasn't wishing for something in her future, as most people did. She was expecting, even demanding it.

Without acknowledging me, she ripped a loose thread from my tablecloth and let it slide off the ends of her fingers onto the floor. It was an unnecessary reminder of my low station.

I chased down her gaze as she picked apart my workplace. "What brings you here?" I asked. "I don't think I've seen you here before."

"I'm certain you haven't." Her voice was sharp, like the installment seller who made his way through my building on Sunday nights.

"So, why today?"

"I've been cooped up. I needed to get out. Someone told me you're good."

I liked the compliment, but I didn't smile. I couldn't show weakness. When she opened her hand to me, she held her fingers tightly together. It was a sign of discomfort, and I liked that too. "You're waiting for something," I said. "What?"

"Aren't you supposed to know?"

"Details like that aren't in the palm. Don't believe people who say they are."

She flicked her hand toward Nadya's cartoon face. "I'd do better with the machine."

I put a coin in the slot. Nadya rattled, then spit out her paper. I handed it to the woman, but she didn't touch it, nodding for me to read it, instead. "Love will find its way to you," I recited.

"It's foolish. Suppose I have love. Suppose I don't want it."

"Tell me something you do want." This made her smile. Next to us, a Slav in a gray janitor's uniform started a baffle ball game. The machine banged as he leaned into it, putting too much force on its levers. It gave an angry belch, and the ball dropped into the well.

She looked from him to me, and asked, "How do you stand working here?" Then, as if reading the explanation in the smoky air, she said, "Times are bad."

"But I get to meet the nicest people." Only Salomé could talk back to her like that.

"Salomé is what you call yourself?" I nodded. "Well, Salomé, I may not be your typical customer, but you're not my typical gypsy, either." She laughed to herself. "Come to my house. My assistant will be in touch. I'll pay you for your time." She scribbled the name Trude Becher on the back of her fortune and handed it to me. I watched her with practiced indifference. I doubted I would hear from her again, though I was sure it would mean a good deal of money if I did. I'd never met a woman with an assistant before, and no one had ever asked me for a house call.

The Slav gave up his game and pushed his way into the bathroom. Its fluorescent light exposed her face like a camera flash, and in that instant, she looked like an angel.

3

HANS

Magda lost her baby over the new year and it almost killed her. Joseph was with our *führer*, 600 kilometers away, so he asked me to go to her. I will never erase that night from my mind. The doctor's cool face masked the madness of his words. Fever is too high, blood pressure, too low, heart rate, too fast. I fought back. Magda is too young, too beautiful. I still can't believe it was her, behind glass, washed in a fluorescent glare, skin a watery white.

Joseph's voice through the telephone shook in my ear as if he were next to me. "I am between life and death. I can't live without her." His words squeezed my throat, and I shook, too.

Usually, I resent being assigned to Magda. My women's work is a big joke around the office, especially with Friedrich Graff. Friedrich is my main rival for Joseph's favor. It seems that when he's sent to lay waste to a red printing press in Moabit, I end up going with Magda to fashion shows or *Bund Deutscher Mädel* luncheons. But that night, as I sat at her bedside, I didn't care.

There was a reason Joseph had sent a *Schutzstaffel* man with his lightning bolts and shining black shoes to get me from my mother's basement apartment on New Year's Eve. It was the same reason the SS man sat without flinching, on our sagging, cigarette-burned couch while I put on my suit and tie. It was why he pretended not to see the dirty dishes under the halo of our saloon lamp; and it was why he registered only respect as my catatonic father crushed bits of upturned tile under his rocking chair. The reason hung in the officer's voice when he commanded our driver to 'fly' to the hospital, and it stopped him in his tracks when the door to Magda's unit swung closed, and only I was allowed to enter. He was of no more use that night. Joseph Goebbels, Conqueror of Red Berlin, had turned to me. In his worst moment, he needed me.

That's why, when the rest of the office is buzzing about Hitler's secret negotiations with Franz Von Papen and Oskar von Hindenburg to form a new government, I'm sitting in a car, outside a Friedrichstrasse dive, waiting for Magda to finish with another gypsy. When the lady is depressed or anxious, she consults the stars. She's seen two since the miscarriage. They came to her sickbed. The dolt nanny, Ada, must have told her about this one. Only she could think Magda should show her face in a place where there is a Hungarian sot pissing into the opening of a downspout.

I'd told Magda I thought it was best for the gypsy to come to the apartment, as gypsies always do, but she shot me a wenchy glare, which said it wasn't mine 'to think best.' "If Auwi Wilhelm can spend the social season in a brown shirt, I can go to a bar."

My look said the Kaiser's son has more leeway to 'think best' than either of us, to which she scoffed, "I've been imprisoned in this damn bed for weeks. You're getting me out of here."

I explained that the Führer is in the middle of sensitive negotiations, and any violation of protocol could destroy all our efforts, but she interrupted. "Hansi, don't make me tell Joseph how tiresome I find you."

As always, she won out, which is why I'm here, tapping my fingers against the steering wheel, imagining gleeful clips from the bourgeois rags about Joseph Goebbels' voo-doo worshiping of a wife.

My work to-do list flashes like a siren in my brain. We have to work twice as hard as everyone else to get beyond the filter of the press. Joseph has three speeches tomorrow, and I haven't reviewed a single one. I have an opinion piece due by seven.

A whore with a ratty, fake fur peers through my windshield, and I'm not sure if it's a woman or a man. It's a woman, I decide. It's in her wrists as she pushes off the front of my car. I have no interest. I'm working. My watch's second hand taunts me.

Sooner than I expect, the door to the *klub* opens, and Magda appears. She's not fully recovered, and she looks jaundiced under the yellow light. Her lips purse. Things must have gone badly. She gets into the passenger seat and slams the door. I put both hands on the wheel, ready to take the blame for not predicting for her that this was a waste of time.

"How was it?" I ask.

"It was quite good," she says in her coy way. "I'll want to use her again."

4

EVA

Anticipation absorbed my focus. My mind skipped around the words until the black and white print blurred into a smear in my lap. I borrowed *Magic Mountain* from the library. I thought the American might have read it, and if he came back, we could discuss it. I wore my best blouse. It was blue silk and open at the neck, a gift from a woman for whom I'd worked through the night to finish a gown. My skirt's flared hem grazed my knees when I sat, and its wide belt accentuated my waist. I blushed at my boldness when I got dressed, but my male customers' appreciative stares convinced me I'd done well.

When hints of pipe smoke floated into the reading room, I didn't shift my gaze. Hands folded a fur-lined coat over the back of a chair. I debated whether to look up but he saved me from my dilemma, as a gentleman should. "An orphan who reads Thomas Mann. You remain a mystery."

"It's the best of his books."

"Have you read them all?"

I nodded.

"I'm impressed."

I tried not to smile too much. "Do you like him?"

"*Krimis* are as much as I can handle.*"*

I stopped myself from saying Frau Pappenheim forbade crime novels (*Good literature does not pander!*). I pointed to the sheaf of papers he was taking out of a leather portfolio. "All evidence to the contrary." Men take flattery literally, Zara always insisted. Though it was against my spiritual mother's dictates on transparency in human interaction, I wanted to indulge this handsome American. He was entirely comfortable with my praise.

A dusty old man with nothing to read but the exit sign cleared his throat. "We have to be quiet," I whispered, ashamed to have broken yet another of Frau Pappenheim's rules.

"Then I'll take you somewhere loud."

When he stood, he was different than I remembered. His hair was less blond, and while I had thought he was thin, he actually was skinny. It was considered unattractive in Germany. There were girls at the orphanage we called '*die puppen*' because they looked like marionettes. Their joints poked out from under their clothes and their limbs jerked as if pulled by strings. Each day, the nurse weighed them and forced them to eat the fatty skin off the top of cold soup.

Thad Cartwright was not a puppet. He was strong as he helped me on with my coat and his smile suggested good health. The way my heart leapt at his ease revealed too much to me of how deeply I wanted what he had to give.

Thad took his coffee black and ordered a Linzer torte after I did, but he didn't eat his. He asked if I was a student at the University. I was glad he thought I could have been, but I told him the truth. I wanted to get an honest measure of myself through his eyes.

"In the mornings, I assist a garment maker, Herr Perlstein, on Oranienburgerstrasse."

"And at other times of the day?"

His attentive calm opened me up. "It depends on the schedule. In the afternoons, I either go back to the shop, or I read here."

"Always Mann?"

"That's this week."

"You read fast."

"My teachers told me I read too fast to learn anything." I cringed. Talking about teachers made me sound like a schoolgirl.

"My aunt always read the last chapters of books before she bought them. She said she couldn't risk disappointment."

"I'm not that bad."

"There seems to be very little bad about you, in fact." He was as comfortable giving praise as he was taking it, but I was too flustered to respond with any grace. I beat back my flush by multiplying sevens in my head. He truly had turned me into a school girl.

"Now tell me, what do you do in the evenings?" he followed. It was a shockingly bold question.

"I work at Karnevalklub."

"A club? Are you a dancer?"

"I work in the arcade. I substitute for broken machines."

"People throw balls at you to win a stuffed crocodile?"

"My specialty is the fortune teller."

His eyes went wide. I couldn't believe how blue they could be. "Are you good?"

"Often," I said, aping Salomé's confidence.

"Do you tell people what they want to hear?"

"I'd put the machines out of business."

"So, you tell them what they don't want to hear?"

"Then I'd put myself out of business."

"What's left to tell?"

"Something they already know about themselves, but I make it sound interesting, even promising."

"Make me interesting."

"You're already interesting."

The American liked that. "So make me promising." The bones in his knuckles rolled as he gripped the handle of his mug. He didn't open his palm. Normally, if I started a reading by staring into someone's face, he would twitch, shift, and focus on anything but me. His discomfort would hide the reasons he'd come. But I didn't need Thad's palm. I'd been thinking about him for the past 24 hours, and my reading was already written. Even if it weren't, I knew there was nothing I could do to make him flinch.

I pretended to construct my words in the moment. I took a deep breath, closed my eyes, and when I opened them, I was Salomé. Unlike me, she could look straight at him, as was the trick of the trade, and not blink. She could speak without fear or doubt to this man who seemed to have everything.

"You work hard to know people. Not to make friends, but to understand them. So, if you sat at my table, I would say something like, 'You're successful at work. You have strong intuition. It makes people trust you. You'll get them to do what you need, and you'll get what you want.'"

"You make it sound self-serving."

"You have to strike a chord to be credible. If you were a real customer, I would say it so confidently, and so fast, you wouldn't have time to take offense before I moved on to something else. You only would remember the sounds of the chord, not what I'd actually said. The sounds are what's true for you, so you would believe me. I didn't say you were self-serving. That's what you heard."

"What did you intend to say?"

"It doesn't take an expert to read your ambition. It's in the way you enter the room, guide the conversation."

"To the degree you could call an assistant military attaché to a disarmed country ambitious, perhaps. My older brothers went into the family business. They said I could be general counsel one day, but the law seemed too tedious, don't you agree? The military and the diplomatic corps were the best of the rest for a youngest son from Princeton."

"You seem to like your work."

"My job isn't very different from yours."

"You're making fun of me!" I reddened again.

"Or striking a chord?" he laughed. "Let me finish. I'm attached to the diplomatic mission, but I'm not a diplomat. I gather information for the Army Military Intelligence Division. I track the armaments and actions of foreign militaries, and"—

"This makes you think we're similar?"

He held up his hand. "Fortune tellers get to know people to predict their behavior. Military attachés do the same, but we get to know national brains."

"What does Germany's brain tell you?"

"What it tells me, I shouldn't say. But what do I look for? Hundreds of things: religiosity, education, spending habits, class structure, the fact that your men willingly mutilate their bodies. . ."

"Not *my* men."

"No?"

"You haven't looked too far into Germany's national brain if you think *Junkers* with fencing scars would spend any time with orphans, shop girls or fake gypsies, never mind someone who is all three."

"You must know how much you undersell yourself." I swallowed more smiles. He continued, "The information tells us something about when, why and how a country will fight. That's important because it lets us"—he simulated a drum roll with his fingers—"prevent war."

He seemed surprised by his own enthusiasm. "As I say it, I see you've succeeded. I feel promising."

5

EVA

Thad came to the library three times over the next week. Things sorted in my mind by whether they were before, during or after our visits. Everything before was tinged with excitement, even suspense. Everything during was wrapped in light, and all that came after fell into a pit of disappointment. Matthias threw barbs my way. "How modern of you," he would say, "to count the minutes until you see your man."

The third time, Thad had a taxi waiting outside the triple arched entrance to the library. I couldn't tell him the ride we took to Kurfurstendammstrasse was only the 15th time I'd ever been in a car. The Ku'damm should have been miserable in winter. Patio umbrellas were folded and tied together. Iron chairs were stacked and chained on the empty sidewalk, and dead linden leaves scudded across the pavement with the wind. But for me, the destitution of the outside only made the cafés, with their steamed windows and trays of pastries, warm under glass, more enchanting.

He detected my excitement. "It thinks of itself as Paris or New York."

"You act like we're your poor cousins," I replied in English.

I could see his breath in the cold. "All this time, you've let me struggle through German, and you speak English?"

"You speak beautiful German. My English is barely conversational."

"Again, you underestimate yourself." He proceeded to test me in his language. "How did you learn English?"

"From a teacher?" I replied, ending the sentence with a question mark in the way Frau Pappenheim would have said made me seem simple.

"You must have gone to an excellent school."

"The head of our orphanage was very well educated. She said if we were her spiritual daughters, it was 'only appropriate' for us to learn English."

"Was she English or American?"

Tired of the exercise, I replied in German. "She spoke"—

"Stop," he interrupted. "I only hear English."

I couldn't resist him. "She was born in Vienna, but she spoke perfect English. She was from a wealthy family and was extremely well educated." Just this information was more than I'd ever revealed to anyone in Berlin about my childhood.

"The nuns are getting more sophisticated, aren't they?"

Everyone assumed I'd been raised in a convent, and I responded with a non-lie. "She called herself a social worker."

"In America, we would call her a socialist, not a social worker."

"*Sozialist?*" I mocked horror. "Never." Frau Pappenheim had five forbidden paths for us: America (*a country of bores, whores and inveterate materialists*), marrying a stupid husband (*the problem is self-evident*), Zionism (*had we not just been released from the ghetto?*), socialism (*immoral or amoral, but usually both, depending on the day*), and prostitution (*selling one's body for sex, marrying outside the faith and/or otherwise renouncing Judaism*).

"I suppose good Christians don't often fall in with Karl Marx," he murmured.

"Marx was a disgrace!" I announced, because it was what Frau Pappenheim always said. I shouldn't have said it. It was something a Jew with an ever-present burden of proof would have said. Gentiles had no call to distance themselves from their own.

If Thad was paying attention, he might have picked up on the tell, but he wasn't. Except for Herr Perlstein, I'd never told anyone in Berlin I was Jewish. I wasn't going to start with Thad Cartwright. I'd unloaded enough of my eccentricities on him for the time being. That bit of me could wait.

"You're lucky in some ways, Eva," Thad said. His dimple pierced his cheek. "You have no blueprint. You can be a Catholic or not, a Socialist or not, a gypsy or not, and no one's going to give a damn."

But could I be Jewish or not? I wondered.

"Whatever you are, let's go to Rosie's Cafe. Everyone speaks English there. You'll see what it's like to be an American or not!" He wrapped my scarf twice around my neck and I felt warm.

I'd imagined an American café to be boisterous. Frau Pappenheim told us that Americans were good at making money, but then made no good use of it because they had no taste. They assigned no value to anything difficult, or to anything that could not be bought and sold. One needed to look no farther than the motion picture industry to understand everything wrong with America. After all the films Matthias had taken me to, I imagined I was about to push through shuttered saloon doors into a menagerie of bawdy women and mud-splattered cowboys.

Between the gold, matte letters on the window, Rosie's café looked like any other with its black and white tiled floors, marble-topped tables, and waiters in black vests and ties. The cut glass on the door dazzled as we entered, but inside, the air was inert. The heat clung to us. There wasn't even the clink of cups against saucers to break the tension.

The bartender fiddled with the dials of a wireless. It crackled and squealed until it landed on a clear channel. There was no mistaking the voice, or the rhythmic chant of the crowd.

"It's Hitler. He's speaking from Wilhelmstrasse. Hindenburg appointed him Chancellor," the maître d' told us.

From behind the tin mesh of the speaker, the "*heils*," sustained and searing, pulsed through the café. My stomach dropped as if I'd walked off a high step thinking I was already on the ground.

I'd told myself Nazism was a temporary madness that would fail once rational people paid attention. Rational people would reject Nazi lies and violence because not lying and not killing defined what it meant to be rational. But even in my worst periods of denial, the Nazis lurked around corners and behind doors. Their anthems played in the background like the eerie music of a jack-in-the-box, and that day, the hideous clown had sprung loose.

"You look shocked," Thad said.

My eyes burned with each sound that spat from the throbbing box. My words fell out before I could think. "I'm heart broken."

With the face of someone who never had been heart broken, Thad shrugged. "At least he'll run out the Reds."

"The Reds! The Reds!" An American approached us. He shook Thad's hand. Then he turned to me. "They're all he ever talks about. It's decided. Hindenburg's mad. The Republic's mad, or dead, or mad and dead."

"Eva, this is Dan Levine. He writes for the Associated Press. He's paid to panic."

"Say it, Thad." He raised his arms like an orchestra conductor. "'The German character craves order. The pendulum will settle soon.'"

"And Thad would be correct, right, Eva?"

I wasn't ready to banter. Thad looked between the reporter and me, and with a wry smile said, "Thad is, in fact, correct."

Dan took the bill from his table and jammed it into Thad's suit pocket, announcing to the bartender and all assembled, "Drinks are on the optimist today." He put on his fedora and bid us a perfunctory goodbye.

A band of soused brownshirts, hanging on each other and immune to the cold, pushed through the doors, bellowing *Die Wacht Am Rhein*. One of them blocked Dan's path. My heart pounded. He sneered into Dan's face. *"Amerikaner?"*

"Gott sei dank," Thank God, Dan barked.

The brownshirt knocked Dan's hat to the ground and snapped, *"Amerikanische Schwanz,"* American prick. He grabbed at his crotch and thrust it toward the rest of us. His posse guffawed, repeating the gesture, then, backed out of the café, pawing at their leader.

Dan looked back to us. *"Der Vaterland* is in good hands."

"He'll get himself killed," I said to Thad.

"Levine has a chip on his shoulder. Give him another few months and he'll be calling on the new President to declare war. Roosevelt might be just radical enough to agree."

I pictured Zara's parents' living room, piled with their heavily carved furniture, waiting for the day they again could afford the space for two doily-capped sofas, four arm chairs, six alabaster sconces, and a curio cabinet filled with *kitsch*. I thought of Rudi's mangled ear, and the other shell-shocked and crippled who begged up and down Friedrichstrasse. I thought of Frau Koch, my widowed landlady, and her four angry children. "Another war is impossible," I insisted.

Thad was bemused. "War is always the most possible option."

When I only stared at him, he laughed under his breath. "As long as you're not a Communist or a Jew, you'll be fine."

Thad refused to let me go back to the *klub* alone. Our cab driver stopped before Potsdamerplatz saying he couldn't get past. We made our way on foot against the growing crowd. I was afraid to be seen walking away from the rally. Brownshirts assaulted people who turned their backs on them. That day, no one paid attention. They cared only for themselves and the one they'd come to see. Children bobbed and lolled on their fathers' shoulders. Bodies fed off each other, nourished by victory and belonging. They swarmed under snapping red and black flags to watch the brown torrent, wielding 20,000 sticks of fire, roar under their idol's window in the Chancellery. The smoke and flame cast an orange glow across the fronts of buildings, bathing people's faces in warmth. His black outline appeared above them and his arm shot out erect. Their fractured chants rose until nothing else could be heard.

The Berlin I had come to was a cold, indifferent city, a loose confederation of all types of humanity that indulged the best and worst of everything and everyone. People rose without question and fell without mercy. That was the deal we agreed to when we decided to live here. Having had nothing to lose, I'd never understood how many people hated it. Now, Berlin was theirs.

It was them, the followers, the watchers, not the snaking rows of brownshirts, who triggered my panic. Maybe one had offered me his seat on the bus, or another allowed me to take her measurements at Herr Perlstein's shop. They were normal Berliners, and their sense of relief, their unabashed satisfaction, echoed in my bones. They sang the Horst Wessel Song as one:

> *. . .Clear the streets for the brown battalion*
> *Clear the streets for the stormtrooper*
> *Millions are looking upon the swastika full of hope . . .*

Their bodies bumped and scraped against me. My breaths grew hoarse and fast. "I can barely breathe," I stammered. Thad's eyes reflected the torchlight. I clung to his arm so tightly it hurt. I was betraying too much fear to a man I hardly knew, but I needed his world, where these voices, this joy, this fire was far, far away.

The shadow of the mob hung dark over Karnevalklub. Nobody played the arcade. That beautiful Zara was downstairs, made-up, with her blond hair curled and piled on top of her head, meant no one was upstairs either. She and Matthias were at the bar, in front of bowls of pretzels and sweet mustard. They stared into steins stained with swill and dried foam. I joined their silence.

Matthias slid a pilsner down the bar to me. Frothy bubbles slipped down the sides of the glass, streaking the wood slab. I could see his ache. For the first time, I wanted to tell him the truth, that I was Jewish, that I ached too, that we were the same, and that we could take care of each other, but I was too close to tears to talk.

I decided not to tell anyone I was Jewish on my fourth Friday in Berlin. Since I'd arrived, I'd shed all my childhood rules. I wore my hair loose, and ran my fingers through it in public. I hemmed my skirts to just below the knee and gazed at my legs' reflections in store windows. I wore lip gloss that hinted at pink, mixed milk and meat, and even took measurements for male customers when Herr Perlstein wasn't there. On Fridays, I'd stood outside the black and gold-domed Neuesynagogue. I listened to its familiar chants, and said to myself as I walked past, 'Next week.'

On the fourth Friday, Herr Perlstein was tallying receipts on a wooden abacus. Its beads' taps and scrapes tingled in my inner ear. I liked Herr Perlstein. He'd taught me well, as if he wanted me to succeed, and when he wasn't teaching me, he left me alone. Even though he was Orthodox, he didn't seem to mind my slide toward godlessness. With Frau Pappenheim's shadow hanging over me, I studied his gestures for signs of contempt, but found none. He was content to let me be.

He said, "Fraulein Schmidt, Frau Perlstein and I hope you can join us for Shabbos tonight. She wants to meet you, as do my youngest girls, Sophie and Elke. They're close to your age. You'll like them." I knew from his conversations with friends that Sophie was the 'pretty one,' and Elke was the 'smart one,' and they both attended the Jewish Girls' School on Augustestrasse.

His attention took me by surprise, and my brain stalled. I'd relished every minute of my re-creation, and I lacked the confidence to step backward. Of all the choices I was making, one was not going to be to button my blouse back up to the neck, pull on my scratchy tights and braid my hair like a child's so I could sit, again the foundling, silent and grateful amidst Herr Perlstein's perfectly constituted family. I couldn't bear to watch him place his hands on each of his girls' heads to recite the blessing for daughters. *May God make you like Sarah, Rebecca, Rachel and Leah.* I could already see them sneaking glances at me, thinking how sad it was that no human would ever ask God to make me like anyone, at all.

I pulled at my shortened skirt and ran my hand down my loose hair. I could have found a hundred lies to get out of it, but his kindness grew my guilt to an absurd size, and I tripped over it. I stammered, "I'm not observing *Shabbos*, I mean, not that way, anymore. I don't want to intrude."

Herr Perlstein was distant, but he wasn't stupid. He pushed it no further. He nodded, smiled, and said, "You're welcome whenever you wish." He never spoke of it again.

I walked straight to the Neuesynagogue. Its three domes stood dominant, as if demanding my apology. Men in top hats and women in fine dresses mingled by the iron gates. *Gut Shabbos*, they said, with formal handshakes and kisses on the cheek. Children played between them. A little girl wrapped an arm around her mother's leg. Her cheeks were red and her hair was matted, as if she'd just woken up. When I looked at her, she buried her face in her mother's skirt, leaving space for a covert eye to monitor me. I waved, and her arm, stacked with fat rolls, reached for me. "You're pretty."

"Thank you," I said. "So are you."

"I'm four." She held up four fingers, and turned them side to side. "I'm 17."

"Is that a child or a grown up?"

"Closer to a grown up," I replied.

"Where's your baby?"

"I don't have one."

"So, where's your Mama?"

"I don't have that either."

"Do you have a Papa?"

I shook my head.

The girl's eyes grew wide. "How come?"

Her mother snatched her up. "Elisa! Don't be rude!" She turned to me. "Why would you say such sad things to a child? "

Perhaps she thought my parents were dead, but her tone was too close to that of our Frankfurt rabbi whose sermon was etched in my memory: *EVERY GERMAN JEW is tarred by your disgrace.*

I had no place among these lovely people. I was exhausted from being every Jew's disappointment. The only people I loved were Jews. The only things I believed in were Jewish. I wasn't ashamed of Judaism or of Jewish people. I was ashamed of myself as a Jew.

I crossed Monjibou Park and vowed before Museumsinslee's palaces, museums and cathedral that I would never become one of *Them*. Frau Pappenheim would never forgive me if I did, and I couldn't live outside of her heart. I never would stop believing I was a Jew. I just would stop telling people I was. It would be easy. Out of context, nobody ever guessed I was Jewish, not our Jewish customers, or even Paulina, the Hitler partisan who worked at the shop. It would be my secret. Not forever, but for the moment, until the rest of me could catch up.

Matthias clapped his hands, cutting through the fog. "Salomé!" he barked. "What's to become of us?"

Zara opened her palm to me. "Please, tell us."

I slammed my hand down on the bar. Warm beer splatted beneath it. I could take nothing from any of us, nothing from myself. Salomé was gone, and with her, every bit of intuition I ever thought I had.

Matthias's hand took mine. He guided me up to dance. I shook my head but he didn't stop. I leaned against him, letting his body move me. "I understand, Matthias," I said. I wanted to share his fear, but the truth I'd buried for so long sat like a hot rock in my throat, and I couldn't get it out.

"Shhh," he soothed. "It's okay."

I closed my eyes, losing my unspoken words to the darkness. Not until I heard heavier steps approach us, not until he shook Matthias's hand, not until I could smell his smell and feel the strength of his arm around my waist, did I open my eyes to see Thad. "Come," he said, pulling me against his hip, turning me from my friends. "Come with me."

The cold whipped down the street, and I felt cut by its edges. The songs were unrelenting. Tens of thousands of brownshirts barked the words:

When the soldier comes under fire

He feels courageous cheer
For when Jews' blood spurts from the knife
Good times are once more here.

I didn't speak until after we pushed through the revolving door into Thad's lobby, rode his elevator to the building's second highest floor and stood in his dark living room. Its thick walls muffled the outside noise, and when he switched on his light, I calmed down enough to take in his space.

"The truth is," he said, hanging our coats, "I spend very little time here. My secretary put it together." That much was clear given the uncomfortable Scandinavian furniture and the absence of art and photos that might have added character to the space.

He opened a rosewood bar cabinet and tonged ice into a glass, then filled it with Scotch. The cubes crackled as he poured. He handed it to me without asking me if I wanted it. I sipped and relished the burn in my throat.

"I shouldn't have left you earlier," he said, staring down at the Ku'damm. "You were upset."

I was shocked he'd put words to my feelings, and I blushed at the intimacy of it. I couldn't tell him I'd never been to a man's apartment except to deliver alterations to our best customers, but I was sure he could read it all over my face. "This is new to me," I said.

He pointed to a closed door in a hallway. "I'll sleep in my study. You can have the bedroom. I didn't want you to be alone."

His words touched my deepest fear. I'd never regretted leaving Frankfurt, but the adage about the tree falling in the forest and not making a sound had haunted me since. I feared I made no sound. I was in the dresses I sewed, the fortunes I told. But when they were done, I was gone. It left me cold, hovering above my life, wanting to know I could land with an earthshaking thud. That terrible night, Thad heard me.

He took my hand and led me into his room. He handed me an undershirt from his bureau, then stepped out so I could change. It hung halfway to my knees, soft and clean, brighter than white.

I opened the door. He was staring into his drink. I quickly tucked my unclipped hair behind my ears and asked, "Do you need anything from in here?"

His smile was not to be polite. It was in reaction to me. It told me I could sleep in this strange place, behind thick walls, where he never spent any time.

"I'm fine, Eva. Sleep well."

I closed the door and closed my eyes and didn't wake up until I heard the slow bubble of his coffee pot the next morning.

6

EVA

The swastika flags hung from lampposts and windows, a bitter reminder of the night before. Against the leafless trees and gray cityscape, the red, black and white were the only colors left. They commanded little attention. Cars still drove and people still moved briskly in and out of buildings. I still thought about Thad. Was it possible he was thinking about me?

At Herr Perlstein's shop, Paulina, the other assistant, sewed a seam into red velvet. She had braided her hair in the *volkisch* style, which I had to attribute to her führer's ascendence. The papers said Adolph Hitler rode to victory on the backs of women like Paulina. They sold their wedding rings and took food from their babies' mouths to donate to the Nazi party. In exchange, their idol vowed not to marry, leaving a spark of hope in each one of their hearts. Paulina was no exception. She thought Hitler was the most handsome man in Germany, which meant he was the most handsome man in the world.

"You must have come in early," I said, over the noisy grind of her machine.

"I've been here since seven. I needed to redo this skirt."

"But, Herr Perlstein said it was good."

She stopped the machine and sat tall in her chair, stretching her back. "He said it would do."

"That means it's good."

"That means I can do better! Meanwhile, you're late for you."

"It's not even nine," I protested.

"You get here between 8 and 8:24, not a second after. That's your way." She scanned the room, I assumed for Herr Perlstein, then leaned toward me. "Were you out late last night? There were some wonderful goings on, weren't there?"

"I can't stand mobs."

"Says the girl who works in a bar!" Paulina brought her hand to her chest, and opened her eyes wide. "Tell me you made off with a swastika man, at the very least!"

"Hush, Paulina!" It was my turn to scan for Herr Perlstein. I prayed he couldn't hear us.

"You're lucky to be single now, Eva. When I was your age, there was no stable of young men so ripe for the picking. We were lucky to find someone with both of his legs. My Werner was a real catch back then. Now he's up for something big. I count myself lucky. You should be so lucky." Paula never expressly said it, but I knew her Werner was a brownshirt.

When I didn't respond, she dug in, louder. "I'm just trying to look out for you, Dear. Something's changed in you lately. You're glowing. Is he handsome? Rich? I hope not. He'll only make a fool of you."

Paulina thrived on the currency of a good secret, and my romantic prospects were of particular interest. My education and style of speaking especially got under her skin. 'What are you playing at, putting yourself above us with the way you talk?' she'd asked when I started working at the shop. 'You'll insult the customers with your copy-catting. Do you expect they'll invite you to tea?' I did nothing to clarify my contradictions, so she spent hours scavenging for evidence of the ugliness she hoped lay beneath my skin.

"Tell me it's not that socialist law student you spend so much time with!"

"Shush, Paulina!" I snapped.

"As our new Chancellor says, we are to remain venerable women, not the pleasure and plaything of foreign races."

"He's not a foreign race or a swastika man. He's American. I'm sure you'd approve."

Herr Perlstein appeared in the doorway. It was only me he stared at through his thick glasses. His Adam's apple poked over his collar and I watched him swallow. Paulina looked between us. He kept staring, unconcerned by the hovering silence. He wanted me to stand up to her, to show some semblance of pride. As the seconds passed, a grayness settled around him, and he sank deeper into the floor.

"Ladies," he said, "keep your voices down. There's a customer."

7

HANS

Joseph starts slow, but the crowd in the *Sportpalast* moves with him. Its hum has a ring to it. Its focus is sharp. If I didn't know him so well, I would fear the crowd would devour him. His shoulders and hips are narrow. They sag beneath his double-breasted suit. His face is pale against the slick black of his hair. Another man, so little and part-crippled, would seem weak, but Joseph projects control.

His voice cuts through the audience, defying everything unimpressive about him. "Let them beware," he shouts. The people rise, anticipating a bold truth. Joseph knows what they want to hear and he puts their desire into words. "One day our patience will come to an end! The insolent Jews will have their lying mouths shut for them!"

Men and women *heil* and salute in ravenous agreement. They're experiencing the end of fear. Our leaders, who have no fear, who demolish the old rules about what can be said and thought, have released them from it. The thrill of freedom vibrates through the arena. I feel it in my fingers.

The Reichschancellor emerges from under a bough of arms extended in the Nazi salute. He is a plain-clothed king. Today, via radio, 20 million Germans in the Fatherland and beyond will hear the voice of Adolph Hitler for the first time since he took power. It is, as Joseph said, one of the greatest moments in the history of the world. I swell imagining German families across Europe huddled around their wireless sets, listening to what I can see and feel in front of me.

Our führer clasps his hands in front of him. He doesn't speak. He waits for the roar to wind down, his frown tucked beneath his mustache. It's almost silent. Still, he says nothing. What's he waiting for? A low rustle spreads in the crowd. *Stop talking!* I snap in my head. *Don't ruin it!* Hitler crosses his arms. He shifts his weight. Nervous coughs bark out. My muscles twitch when a few fools mutter. We're disappointing him, and I'm ashamed. Yet, the delay causes him no discomfort. All the discomfort is with us. His silence pierces. I vow to work harder for him, for Germany. At last, he spares us.

"Deutschland." His voice is a gentle gravel. He is our father, pulling us to safety from a frigid tide. He'll never let us drown. We are Deutschland, and we are his.

8

EVA

Three unexpected things lifted my mood. The first was petty, but I liked it. I received a letter from Frau Pappenheim dated January 26, four days before everything went wrong.

Dear Eva,

Frau Horwich passed away. Among her contributions, she established our library. A word or two from you about it would be a great comfort to Herr Horwich (Gartenstrasse 38). Enclosed, find formal stationery.

As to the talk of an agreement with the Nazis, don't be frightened. I have faith in our President. The Republic will hold.

Never forget you represent us all with your faith, your excellent work and your virtue.

I miss you. Your thoughtful letter meant a great deal to me.

As Always,
Frau Pappenheim

The day the letter was written, I would have wanted to shred the card she'd enclosed. Did she think I would write a condolence note on a paper bag? But most, I would have stewed over my 'thoughtful' letters, which withheld so much truth. I'd never told her I dressed improperly, ate uncleanly or worked in a *klub*. Worse, I'd never hinted I was hiding my faith, or that I hadn't told a soul in Berlin so much as her name. I knew she would see no difference between hiding and lying, or between hiding and rejecting. She would concede no freedom in my falsehoods. She would see only shame.

Still, on February fourth, my mental push and pull with her evaporated. Her week-old optimism documented for the first time in my memory that my spiritual mother was deeply and terribly wrong.

The second odd thing was that Trude Becher called me at the *klub.* She was the personal secretary to the beautiful woman who came to the bar the week before. She referred to the woman only as *Madam,* and said I was to meet her on February 20th at 4:00 at her Reichskanzlerplatz apartment. I knew this was an excellent address, and I hoped it would lead to more appointments that were higher paying than my hourly rate at the *klub.*

Later, my amazement over the first two events was eclipsed by Thad. He invited me to Giorgio's. I'd never been there, but I'd read about it. It was society page fodder—expensive, chic, a favorite of writers, actors and diplomats. Thrill and dread spilled inside me. I wanted so much to go, but I couldn't imagine how I could. I had nothing to wear. When I stumbled with my response, Thad laughed. "Borrow something."

Zara had a strapless something. She was more excited than I was, but she was not the one facing humiliation. I had the misfortune of making gowns for women who went to Giorgio's, and I knew well what I was missing. Zara's dress was five inches too long, so I had to baste and pin the hem, leaving bits of metal to tickle my calves with each step. It was too tight at the top, and my breasts made an awful show. "Men like that," Zara promised. "Between your décolletage and how the blue brings out your eyes, he won't notice anything else." She handed me a velvet-collared coat. "It used to be my mother's. It's old fashioned, but you can't wear yours."

The only things moving on the bouncer were his eyes, and I was sure if they caught mine, he wouldn't let me into the restaurant. With Thad, however, there was no problem. I fed off his confidence. He was well known to the captain and the coat check girl, who flicked back the tassel of her fez when she saw him. Her flirting, and Thad's comfort with it, made him more attractive to me. Frau Pappenheim would have chided that I was dizzied by the whirl of someone else's life, and she would have been right.

"You're popular," I mused.

"It helps to tip in dollars."

Giorgio, himself, welcomed Thad and opened the French doors to the dining room. What I saw was so apart from the upheavals of the past week, I could have been persuaded we'd traveled into my childhood fantasies of Paris. A glass fountain spouting mammoth crystal arches instead of water sprayed dizzying rainbows of light. The stained-glass ceiling soared two stories. Pedestals with vases of giant calla lilies stood sentry over candlelight. A twenty-piece swing band played *Dideldideldum* as if it were a careless summer night by the Halensee. I wouldn't have taken my eyes off the fountain all night but for the Negro woman in a silver, thigh length dress, playing the saxophone. She looked like a Nubian goddess. I had to conceal my shock at the sight of a woman playing a horn, never mind a saxophone. Perhaps it really was Paris.

"She's Collette Smith-Spire," Thad told me. "She's an American married to a French Jew." His voice brought me back. It was not an alternate universe, and it was not Paris. It was the Berlin of a month before, Weimar's Berlin, the city I had only read about in magazines, the city about which Paulina endlessly carped and from which Frau Pappenheim had tried to protect me. It was the Berlin of Fritz Lang, for whom Matthias made so many coffees and copies. It was what Zara imagined while she rumbaed at *Karneval Klub*. Mostly, it was a Berlin so loathsome to Nazism, it felt gloriously patriotic just to be there.

We were meeting Christopher Winslow, Thad's old friend from boarding school and Princeton University, who was in the consular section. He had already arrived when we got to the table, which was in a curtained alcove with a good view of the band. His hair and eyebrows were a startling white-blond, an effect accentuated by his ruddy skin. He was with a woman named Katharina von Steffens. She was one of the most elegant creatures I'd ever seen, with milky skin, strong arms and a small waist. Her chestnut hair was swept back in a *chignon*. She wore as many diamonds as a woman could wear and still be thought of as lovely. Her champagne-colored dress flowed effortlessly to the floor. Of course, only custom-made dresses fit that well. I laughed to think mine was custom-made, too, by Zara, with pins and tape I could only hope would hold through the night.

Thad made no show of the contrast between us, but my earlier confidence wilted as he kissed her cheeks, and she scolded him for our tardiness. "We don't become Italian, Darling, just because the restaurant is."

"You'll find it vulgar, Kat, but on occasion, I'm required to work into the evening."

"Your only flaw is you're dull, Thad," she replied. "Count the guns and go home. It's not more complicated than that."

Ignoring them, Christopher kissed my hand as a German would. A crested signet ring flashed from his finger. When Thad said something to him in English, he responded in German. Thad turned to me. "I should explain that despite tracing his lineage to the Mayflower and being a member of the Society of the Cincinnati, Christopher is a Germanophile of the first order." Christopher seemed too soft to be German. He looked overly fed and poorly exercised, without the discipline to earn the Mansur scars to which he apparently aspired.

"What else is there to be? Don't you agree, Eva?" Katharina asked. Her voice was cool, but not cold. I wanted her to like me, and not to notice my cleavage, which placed me more properly in a Friedrichstrasse dive than at Giorgio's.

"I won't argue," I said.

"Then why are you both here with Americans?" Thad asked.

"Pure rebellion. My mother asked that tonight. She made me promise to wash after mixing."

For my benefit, Thad said, "Frau von Steffens defines mixing as leaving Potsdam. She hasn't accepted an invitation in Berlin since the war."

"Not until the Kaiser is restored to his throne!" Christopher pronounced, raising his glass.

Katharina said, "She's boring."

"Only in Germany would it be considered mixing to step out with the grandson of a great American railroad baron," Thad replied.

"Americans only think about money," Katharina tutted. "Half of us are flat broke." She pulled a cigarette from her beaded clutch for Christopher to light.

"She's about to say, 'It's all to do with land and blood,'" Thad added in German-accented English. "No need to repeat it for our sake."

Katharina pivoted to me and exhaled a smoky plume. "Thad tells us you're an intellectual."

He must have told them I was a student. I didn't want to embarrass him by telling the truth, but what else could I do? A hot blush rose from my neck. "Mostly, I work at a dress shop. It's not intellectual, or even interesting, I'm sure."

Katharina arched an eyebrow. "But it is interesting, isn't it, Chris? We don't know many women who work."

I didn't know many women who so comfortably spoke their minds.

Thad saved me. "What I said was, Eva is the first woman I've met in Germany who reads books. That makes her more interesting than most of the girls I come across here."

Katharina laughed. "Thad is correct, as always. If you only knew how many of my friends I've tried to pair him with. He quotes Shakespeare or, God forbid, Goethe to test them."

Thad interjected, "'We don't read,' they tell me. We ride.'"

Katharina shook him off. "We're not ashamed of it, but trust me, if you were *just* a shop girl, this one would have passed on you by now."

Whether she meant to demean or not, her words were like helium, inflating my hopes that Thad genuinely cared for me.

"I find it charming that you don't read, Katharina," Christopher chimed. Then to me, he said, "I don't read either. It's why she loves me."

"*Likes* you, Darling. We just like."

"Here comes someone who reads," Thad said.

The AP reporter approached the table. "No Bolshevik rally tonight, Levine?" Christopher asked.

"That was yesterday. Tonight, we take your first born."

"Hush, boys!" Katherina swiped as Christopher helped her out of her chair.

"Will anyone join us for a dance?" Christopher asked, looking at Thad.

I prayed Thad wouldn't ask me. Instead, he said, "Dan, please keep Eva company. I need to excuse myself."

"How could I turn down the company of a beautiful woman?"

I was relieved for Dan to take Christopher's chair. When we were alone, Dan muttered, "I didn't know Nazis were allowed to dance to Negro music."

"Do you think we're all Nazis?" I fired back.

"Katharina may as well be. Her uncle is Franz von Papen. You have him to thank for the current predicament." Thad had withheld that fact, but still, as an orphan, it never had occurred to me to accuse someone for her uncle's sins,

"She doesn't seem like she is. She likes to shock people. I doubt she believes half of what she says. Christopher's American. He seems to care for"—

"I'm guessing you're not from this world, Eva, but there are two explanations for a woman as brassy as Katharina von Steffens. She's either colder than a Siberian toilet seat in winter, or she's unforgivably bored." He downed the rest of his drink. "Maybe it's both."

His back and shoulders sagged from the weight of a long night. That my being out of place was so plain to him made me sag along with him. He didn't notice.

"This is what you'll learn. American diplomats come to Europe for two reasons: to recreate their fathers' world of butlers and summer mansions in countries where the obscenely rich are still respected for doing nothing intelligent or useful; and, to get laid as often as possible without pissing off the girl's Daddy, who back home is always their father's business associate, golf partner or third cousin."

I wanted to scrub the pity from his face. "Do you have two reasons for everything?"

"Occasionally, there are three." Dan laughed under his breath, but the pity got worse. "You'll find this out soon enough, Eva, so I'll tell you, now." He scanned the room, leading my gaze to Christopher, who was flapping his arms like an off-kilter windmill. "These people care about *nothing*."

"Thad does! He works hard. He's smart, and," I stammered, "he wants peace!" I saw too late how childish I seemed.

"I don't know Thad well, but I'm guessing you don't either."

He was right. In the time we'd spent together, Thad had said almost nothing about his past and I'd never asked. I liked him so much I rarely thought to question him. But more, I didn't believe people's pasts should matter, and I was very glad mine didn't matter to him.

"You're bad company, you know?"

"Well, here comes your good company," Dan said as Thad approached.

The music slowed. Thad pulled me up. "Now, we can dance. Hate to abandon you, Dan."

Dan passed me back with an indifferent shrug.

When we were out of ear shot, I said, "I don't like Dan."

"Most people don't," Thad whispered. I put my head against his chest.

When Christopher saw me and Thad dancing so closely, he nudged Katharina. She smiled to see us that way. I wouldn't have expected kindness from Franz von Papen's niece, nor would I have imagined her to be emboldening, but I hoped Thad was thinking of me the way her look suggested he was.

When the music ended and the couples strayed from the dance floor, Thad lifted my chin. "There's one thing Dan's right about, you know. You are beautiful." He kissed me as if I was all there was in the world.

I was happy beyond recognition from the memory of Thad's kiss. *Dideldideldum* played on in my head and a dazzling heat tickled my stomach. I couldn't stop smiling as the last traces of my buzz spun me into sleep.

It wasn't long before heavy footsteps reverberated through my flat. There was a loud thud, the sound of sobs, then more footsteps, quick and irregular. Still in my nightdress, I crept into the hall and leaned over the bannister.

Zara's elderly next-door-neighbor, Frau Rennert, sat slumped against the wall. She looked up at me in shock, her wet face reflecting the light. "My son," she wept. "They took my Robert."

"Who?" I asked, staring down at her knotted gray hair.

"SS," she cried in a high-pitched wheeze. "Blackshirts."

I was confused from sleep, and I couldn't understand. Herr Rennert was nearly blind from Glaucoma. He rarely left the house, except to go to church. Tiny splinters poked into my feet as I ran down the stairs.

Frau Rennert held out her arms to me. There was blood in the cracks of her palms. Its metallic smell filled the air. "They say he's a pacifist. He's on a list. But all he ever did was sign some petitions. He was just a boy. He was against the war."

I knelt in front of her and rested my hands on her knees. "They can't put him in jail for that," I soothed. "They'll talk to him, and then they'll send him home." My coaxing made her angrier.

"What do you know?" she heaved. "You're just a child, yourself. They take anyone they want. They called him a communist, a traitor. It was all on the list. They said he didn't fight."

Her body shuddered and she clenched my wrist. The blood was still sticky on her fingers.

Herr Brandt, another neighbor, poked his head into the hall. "Your constant carping is probably why they took him, you old bag. It's three in the morning. If you don't shut your trap, they'll come for all of us."

"You hush!" I yelled as he slammed his door. "Let's go inside, Frau Rennert. I'll make some tea. We can sit, then figure everything out in the morning." I offered her my hand, but she wouldn't budge.

"They beat him. I tried to stop them, but they pushed me down. There was so much blood on him, but they beat him some more."

Her red lined eyes stared in horror at something only she could see. Fear tightened her voice to a hoarse whisper. "They said it's what they do to mangy, yellow dogs. They put them down."

9

HANS

Magda is a swan. She is regal and graceful, more beautiful than the rest. She's hard not to watch. But if you look too long or step too close, she'll poke out your eyes. Magda's moods the past few weeks aren't because of her miscarriage. They're not from having faced death, or from being separated from her baby, Helge, for so long. Her crying started when the Führer formed his cabinet and Joseph, who had surrendered his life to him, who conquered Red Berlin for the Party, was excluded. Instead, he was given the post of Radio Commissar.

It's a jab to the face when I think of it. It hurts just the same each time. But it only makes things worse for Joseph to see my anger, or Magda's tears, which are an almost audible undercurrent to her soft-soap about how 'Adolph' is saving something even better for him.

It's the night after the *Sportpalast* rally, and I go with Joseph to the 17 room Reichskanzlerplatz apartment Magda rents with the money she got from her divorce from Günther Quandt. She hired one of the top designers in Berlin and spent 50,000 marks to redecorate. The place matches Magda. It's sparing, but elegant, with fine antiques and a grand piano, which she plays beautifully.

At first, Joseph was uncomfortable there, but he's learning to deal well with the servants and the protocols of high society.

To win over the *Junkers* and industrialists, Hitler demands the people closest to him learn their ways. Now, Joseph wears only hand-tailored suits and drops French phrases into conversations. He has also stamped out stories of Magda's past, including her beloved Jewish step-father, her choice to take his name—Friedlander—and her unmentionable, but legendary, romantic shadows.

Once our leaders met the minimum standard of propriety, the walls of the Thyssens, Krupps, and von Dirksen's tumbled down. Joseph and the Führer are as giddy as school girls at how easy it was to climb on top of their wreckage.

As we near his apartment, he has the same look of the conqueror. The rally was tip-top. Hitler is happy, and Joseph is confident the boss still needs him. He's proved he's indispensable. He'll be back in the inner circle before long, and, if all goes according to plan, I'll be with him.

I hope he'll ask me to join the celebratory supper we've been waiting for. Tomorrow, I'll mention it to my office rival, Friedrich Graff. I'll say, in a self-abasing way, 'They only asked me because I worked on the speech.' Then, even though I know he wasn't invited, I'll ask, 'Did you make it to the rally?'

It's petty, but Friedrich makes me do it. Just this morning, as he went off to read the riot act to a pissant station manager in Pankow, he bragged that Joseph nicknamed him 'The Enforcer' because he was the only one in the office with the balls to do what needs to be done.

To gloat about dinner with the boss is amateur, but it's better than knocking the shit out of Friedrich, which is what I've wanted to do for a long time. I'm a head taller than he is. It would be easy to make my enforcement power obvious.

Joseph fumbles for his keys and says, "Magda will have a good dinner prepared tonight, won't she, Hansi?" His dimples cut into his cheek. He's thinking about what comes after the dinner, when Magda, Joseph sometimes says, 'blossoms into enchanting blond sweetness.'

"It's well deserved, Joseph," I say, pushing open the heavy door.

None of the ladies entertain like Magda. It's the cook's night off, and I imagine the smell of stewed rabbit. Hitler loves Magda's cooking. She makes him special vegetarian meals, which he says are far better than anything he gets in the Kaiserhof dining room. I hope she's waiting for us in the black lace dress from Salon Kohnen. She says the Jews have the most elegant shops. She'll hand me a brandy, and when we sit, she'll say something about how well my eyes match the upholstery. "Lorenz blue, I'll call it," she might say, because Lorenz is my last name. I feel traces of Gunther Quandt's world sticking to me, as I'm sure she once did. I'm learning, too.

When we're inside, Joseph's smile fades. The apartment is dark and cold. The hush of women's voices comes from the living room. Joseph says it must be Ello Quandt, Magda's former sister-in-law, crying on Magda's shoulder about her miserable marriage. But when we get closer, it's not Ello's voice we hear.

Joseph's good mood vaporizes. He loses track of his clubfoot. It drags at an angle toward his wife. The only light in the room is from a Tiffany lamp where Magda sits with a stranger. Her back is to us. The stray hair at her nape is knotted in the clasp of her pearls. The stranger holds her hand. She has straight, black hair wrapped in a blood red scarf, and large hoop-shaped earrings. Her eyes are closed, and her lashes make thick U's against her cheekbones. She's one of Magda's gypsies. Astrology is a good sport with Hitler and Göring, so Joseph usually pays it no mind. But after Magda's thinly disguised disappointment in him, I'm afraid he'll think this turn to the stars means she's lost confidence in him. It's going to end badly.

His voice is tight and low. "Get her out!"

Pent up truth flies from Magda's mouth. "Someone needs to tell me what to do now that that dim-witted Emmy Sonneman will take my place as First Lady of the Reich!"

I hate that my swan has turned frantic and ugly and not how she should be.

"Now!" Joseph barks. Every ounce of his tiny body is devoted to controlling his rage.

In the meantime, the gypsy emerges from her trance. At the sight of Joseph, her eyes harden until they look like they might crack. The girl can't control her horror. It's obvious she hadn't known whose house she walked into. Magda reaches for her bangle-decked wrist. Joseph hates gaudy jewelry. *Don't touch!* I want to say, but of course Magda does.

"Please continue," she says. "You've been brilliant."

Joseph takes three slow strides toward Magda. He lowers his oversized head until it's level with the back of her neck. The scene freezes. They look like mannequins behind Wertheimer's plate glass windows. Wisps of Magda's hair float in Joseph's heavy breaths.

I have to fix it. It's what I do. I step toward the girl, feeling cut by the glass that isn't there. "Please," I say, helping her out of her chair. "I'll find you a taxi."

Magda had thought she was one of our führer's chosen. Hitler said as much. He claimed she was the opposite female pole to his one-sided masculine instincts. She was to stand in as the bachelor's first lady. It's the role she's lived for. Everyone talks about it. She's 'Adolph's' other half. The two of them flirt feverishly. It keeps Joseph up at night. 'She's not quite a lady," he says, and it drives him mad.

Now, she's said it to his face, out loud, in front of me, and worse, in front of the gypsy. She all but announced it's her 'Adolph,' not her husband, whom she wants as her leading man.

When Hitler gave the press office to Walther Funk, and the Ministry of Culture to Bernhard Rust, he took a wrecking ball to Magda's hopes and dreams. He turned his back on her devotion. She sees she's been left with a dwarf Radio Commissar, and the dwarf knows it.

The sky has been black for a long time now. The ice cracks under my weight, but the gypsy is light. It makes her unsteady. She's obviously not a real gypsy. A real gypsy can walk on ice. She slips. I reach for her arm to break her fall. She barely looks at me. It's clear she has thoughts about me because I'm in the Party. She thinks I'm like a stormtrooper, beating the shit out of Jews and sleeping with men, not like someone whose first thought is to keep people from falling. But, that's what I do. I help people. I help Joseph, and I will help Magda. I will help her understand that Joseph is so much bigger than what she sees tonight, that he'll be back. We'll all be back. If Magda had seen the rally she wouldn't question it. He possessed the crowd. None of the others can do that, certainly not bourgeois Walther Funk or the backwater schoolteacher, Bernhard Rust. If Hitler hadn't been there, they would have carried Joseph off on their shoulders for what he means to them. She is part of what he means. It's like Hitler says, the Reich needs Joseph and Magda to be together. It needs a loving, German couple, married, with children, to sit for photographs, to set an example. We're not Bolsheviks. A German movement without a family at its beating center can't survive. It can't be loved, and without love, we die.

I look into the rushing headlights to find the gypsy a cab. One signals toward us and I ask her for her address, my breath puffing out in the cold. But when I turn back to her, she's running.

10

EVA

The woman opened the door herself. She asked me to call her Magda. Everything about her was different from the *klub*. Her warmth made the visit seem like a reunion of old friends rather than the commercial transaction it was. She was familiar, not because we knew each other; we clearly did not. It was because she lacked any condescension.

She sat me among her fine things and when she opened her hand, her fingers lifted me into our shared space. Her palm was graceful, though uninteresting, so I chose words that could be splintered, allowing her to take her own meaning.

Her good mood suggested she would guide me well. I told her I saw independence and power. She nodded, so I continued. It was a power that was her own, separate from a husband or father, but she needed to make greater use of it. A light came to her eyes that seemed to remember what she dreamed to be. As the night's black hardened against the windows, cocooning us, her skin melted into my hand. Her comfort drew out my words. I told her she could do great things.

She eagerly added strands. *I was the top of my class in high school. I read constantly. French was my best subject . . . Finishing school was a bore . . .*

She leaned in as she wove herself into my thread, layering her drama with the richest details. *The American President Hoover's nephew asked for my hand. I declined, and he overturned our car. He'd wanted to kill me. I was hospitalized for weeks. Another man, a boy really, shot me when I tried to break things off . . . My ex-husband was a great man, one of the wealthiest in all of Germany, but he wanted a collection piece, a Lalique* Masque de Femme, *something pleasant to look at, not a wife . . . How could I be important to anyone if I wasn't important to him?*

Her cues carried me, and together we stitched our way toward her promise. I told her if she was brave enough to stop waiting for someone else to make her life happen for her, she could be who she wanted to be.

I lost track of time when the warmth around us flared hot. Magda's voice broke off. It built into a rant, and our thread burned away. Confused, I opened my eyes. Joseph Goebbels' bloodless face hovered, inches from mine. It stole the air from the room. My skin pricked with cold terror.

I was so taken by Magda, I hadn't seen who she was. I devoured her praise because I thought she was better than me. She made me think I could be like her, if only my mother hadn't abandoned me on someone else's doorstep.

Each word I'd said, *You can do great things . . . You're very talented;* and her praise, *Fascinating . . . You've been brilliant . . .* swelled in sickening waves in my stomach. My permanent stain had driven me into the hands of demons.

What came next still leaves me ashamed. I can only say that as the rules of civilization fell away, so did mine. I could not understand what was going on around me. I had found myself in Joseph Goebbels' parlor. I'd held his wife's hand.

In that moment, I believed the only one who could save me was the one who knew nothing of me. Thad was kind. He took me to lunch. He didn't care about my pinned-up dresses and scuffed shoes. I knew he didn't love me. It seemed far too much to ask. I would settle for the hope that if I ended up back in the gaze of evil, unaware of who or where I was, if I were denounced, put on a list, or arrested for no reason, he would get me back. That was enough.

When I stood in front of his bathroom mirror, staring at my naked body, deciding whether to make him sleep on the couch for another night, I didn't recognize myself. My moral rules, Frau Pappenheim's rules, were spinning too fast to hold onto. They were so blurred by events, they'd lost their meaning.

Whatever remained of me was clear minded and intentional. I did what Frau Pappenheim raised me never to do. It was the only thing I knew for certain my own mother had done, and it was the thing for which I'd demonized her. With the bathroom light behind me, I stepped naked into the darkness of Thad's room.

"How beautifully unexpected you are, Eva," he whispered, and I gave myself to him. I handed him my fear, and he took it. He took every part of me as if each piece was something he wanted, something that was worthy of his care, his touch, his kiss. When he held all my pieces together, whole in his arms, when his strength entered me and I didn't shatter, I felt unimaginable joy.

11

EVA

"Don't lock it!" I shouted at Ruth, an *Ostjuden* girl who cleaned the shop, hemmed tablecloths, and had a particular talent for clustering tiny beads on gowns. It was past dark, and she jumped at the sound of my voice. When she saw it was me, she stepped outside the lamp's muted glow.

"Sorry," I said. "I have to work." I imagined what she thought of me, an apparent Aryan for whom everything was easy. "Are you alright, Ruth? Is your family alright?" I asked.

"They are good," she said, making herself small.

"It's not right, what's happening," I plead, as if I could somehow atone to her.

She half-bowed. I passed into the shop, and switched on the lights. I studied the space through Thad's eyes: the tin ceiling, scabbed with peeled paint, the fluorescent lights that left a gloomy shine on the industrial green walls, Herr Perlstein's worn down abacus, a stack of receipts gored by a metal spike. I pushed back the heavy gray curtain that guarded our workspace, took out a dress form, and started to sew. I sewed myself into Thad's life, raiding my small savings to afford the expensive fabrics.

Over the next week, I spent nights immune to exhaustion. I embroidered lilacs into organza and crafted spaghetti straps from crêpe de chine. I saw myself taking up the saxophone and drinking cocktails in every color of the rainbow. I was waiting for Thad to make my life happen.

Each night, when I finished, I took every hint of my work home with me, ashamed for Ruth to peer through her darkness and witness my falsehood.

Thad, Katharina, Christopher and I crowded around a table on the roof of the Hotel Eden. Its walls of windows were pushed open, begging for an early spring. The bartender mixed *limoncello* and *prosecco* in champagne flutes, and he knew he had an appreciative audience in our quartet. We felt the effects of his work in short order. Christopher busied himself by sticking Chinese parasols between the teeth of Katharina's combs. "It might rain," he kept saying.

Katharina ignored him, and pointed casually toward the entrance. "There's Alfred Landau. It seems he's left the masses to fend for themselves tonight."

I, on the other hand, couldn't help but be in awe of famous people. Matthias would be mad with jealousy when he heard I'd seen Alfred Landau. My heart beat harder as he approached.

"Katharina." He reached for her hand to kiss. She smiled politely, and introduced me. He brought his palm to his heart and said my name. To hear him say it, to have him look straight at me, made me stutter, "It's an honor, Herr Landau."

Landau turned to Christopher. "Good evening, Mister?" He looked to Katharina for help with Christopher's name. She responded with a disapproving pout.

Christopher rose, taking a small step back to balance himself. "You must remember me, Herr Landau. Your visa application came across my desk a few days ago. I'm trying to remember who on the staff I passed it to." He was glazed over and soft from drinking, but his voice pierced. "It's just there are so damn many of you."

I turned to Landau, hoping he would see in my expression the objection I was too weak to say out loud. He never looked at me. His brown eyes traced each of Christopher's awkward movements as he pawed for his chair and slumped back into it. They followed him as he checked his watch, loosened his tie and scanned the room for the waiter. They analyzed his fingers, which drummed against his armrest, and seemed to laugh just a bit when Christopher took a sip from his already empty glass.

The silence bore into Christopher. "It's nothing personal," he said.

"I didn't take it as such," Landau replied, with a mocking smile. He kissed Katharina's cheeks, nodded to me, and walked away.

I reminded myself to breathe.

"Did you walk too far out on your limb, Darling?" Katharina asked.

Christopher leaned his head against her shoulder, "Why was he so mean, Kat?" She pushed him away.

Thad said, "Irv Thalberg's picked him for MGM. He'll get his visa, no matter what Christopher thinks."

"Yes, he will," Christopher added. "And soon, his tales of death and lesbians will be coming to theaters across America."

Katharina raised her glass. "Thank God for America!"

Christopher clinked his glass against hers. "*L'Chaim.*"

Thad joined the toast. "*L'Chaim,*" he laughed.

I don't know what I'd expected from Thad, but I expected more. Its absence turned my stomach. I'd told myself he was better than Katharina and Christopher because he was with me.

The three of them turned to me with their yellow flutes. I stared at the neon bubbles of his drink, fizzing happily to the surface and popping. I couldn't stand Thad's good mood. "Oh dear," Christopher said. "Thad's taken on with a liberal."

"Not at all," Thad said. "She's just German. Everyone knows Germans have no sense of humor." They watched me, impatient. After a moment, Katharina cooed, "Darling, you're upset." Thad lifted his glass to me again, this time with a nudge in his eyes.

I wanted to be like Landau, to let silence erode their confidence, even for just a few seconds. I wanted them to need my approval, finally.

My satisfaction in all I'd been able to hide from them forced a laugh to tickle my stomach. I raised my flute and said, "I'm joking, too."

The threesome roared. The lemon wedge carrying another foolish umbrella toppled out of Katharina's glass and landed between us. "See Thad," she said. "Germans are funny."

12

HANS

It's a rendering of an idiot, its head a perfect circle, eyes like buttons. Is that a tear it's supposed to be crying? Should I have sympathy for this cartoon? *Klee*, the catalog announces in bold. I turn the page to a spray of black spikes, dismembered insect legs, set on dull white. Kandinsky, I know before I check.

We are shuttering this exhibit. Now, it's mine to justify. *Entartete kunst,* degenerate art, fills my page as if by rubber stamp. Joseph knows I can do better than writing the same, tired lines for the same, tired press releases. These paintings are ugly and useless. They're too easy to be called art. But Klee and Kandinsky aren't in the same league as Germany's moderns like Grosz and Beckmann. I could explain these differences to people, but I'm not allowed. 'Clarity!' Joseph barks. 'The people loathe nuance. We erase doubt.'

Germans are tired of being spat on by the so-called intelligentsia for not finding canvasses of sagging breasts and mops of wiry pubic hair beautiful. They want to spit back. Still, I'm a top aide to Dr. Joseph Goebbels. I want to be more than just their spitter.

My mind wanders to the date I'll have tonight with Dagmar, a new hire in the typing pool. She has a sweet enough face on top of a pin-up girl's body. We've only been out a few times, but I've discovered that, as with the *völk*, she has little taste for nuance, at least when it comes to men.

There's a knock, and my real estate agent is standing in my office. I draw a blank on his name—Schulmann. No, I would remember Schulmann. Schulmann is a Jew. It's Schumann. Definitely Schumann. Schumann could be anything. I stare at his thinning, brown hair that matches the color of his suit. He's as unimpressive as a *hausmaus*; far too nondescript to be a Jew.

"We're scheduled to see the Cohen flat at 6:00. Do you remember? On Tiergartenstrasse? It should move quickly. The seller is eager."

I know this is true because the seller, unlike Schumann, is a Jew. He was in Paris when Hitler came to power. Now, he won't come back. If the right levers are employed, he'll sell well below market value. In addition, Joseph promised that Reemstma, a loyal tobacco company, will happily cover the down payment in exchange for free advertisements in the Nazi newspaper, *Der Angriff*.

When Joseph told me the apartment agent would pay me a visit, there was real pleasure in his eyes. He wanted to reward me for all the nights I slept on the office floor during last year's elections. I was behind the *Go for the Factories* strategy. In July, we won 37.4 percent of the popular vote, and became the largest party in the Reichstag. The stunning victory was what paved our way to the Chancellorship. It changed the course of history.

I was ecstatic that Joseph recognized me this way, but the backdoor machinations still didn't sit well with me. Other people were getting sweetheart deals, too, but I worried. Would the story get into the press? Would I owe something to this man named Cohen? Would he sue me? Could I refund him if he did? Until last month, I barely made enough to buy a few suits.

Stupidly, I looked the gift horse in the mouth. "Are you sure we can do that, Joseph?"

Joseph's expression changed faster than I realized my mistake. "Your body is like the gods of Antiquity, and yet inside, you're soft, eh Hansi?" He goes mad when Germans show weakness. "The Jew is the plastic demon of decomposition. He lives in palaces while the proletarian, the front soldier, lives in holes. We take nothing! We restore everything!" Then, the Conqueror of Red Berlin moved his big head too close to mine and in a soft voice, leveled my punishment. "Besides, it doesn't befit one of my top aides to be living on his mother's couch."

Joseph Goebbels isn't a street fighter. He takes people down with a sniper shot to the heart. "Of course, Joseph," I said, as red blotches sprawled across my neck. "It was foolish of me. Thank you for all you've done." I still cringe when I think of it. I'm always a step behind.

The U-bahn is late and the platform reeks of urine, but I barely notice. My mind is swimming with marble floors and French doors. While the address is on Tiergartenstrasse, my windows overlook the back alley. I don't care. The apartment was so fine, I had to have it. 'Please, call his agent,' I insisted, even before we'd finished the tour. 'I want it now.'

Schumann snapped to attention. "If it's meant to be, it's meant to be."

My excitement carries me past the derelict buildings and boarded up storefronts that line my walk from the station. Finally, I can tell my parents I'm moving out, and up, from our miserable corner of Prenzlauer Berg. Their front room will be theirs again.

It's 8:15 when I get home. There's no smell of grease, no sounds of pots scraping or schnitzel frying. My mother's not home, but I call her name anyway, and wait several beats for a response. This must be one of her nights with Willie, her most recent friend and benefactor. By all accounts, my mother's an exceptional beauty, and despite the scars of poverty and age, she can still land the type of suitor who will pay another man's electric bill.

The front room is dark, and my father's outline sits silent on the edge of the battered divan. My clothes hang on a metal rail to his left, and my shoes are tucked in a neat row beneath him. His breaths are even and long. Though I can't see his eyes, I know he's scanning, watching the autobahn from behind the wheel of his old lorry.

My father lost his job as a long-haul truck driver when I started gymnasium. After months without work, he was hired as a bellboy at the Kaiserhof. He had dominated the highways less than a year before, but at the hotel, the guests blew by him, always with so much importance. He would stand back and let them pass. "They have so much to do," he would say as he puttered around our tiny flat. Imitating his supervisor's incessant wheeze, he pleaded with us to 'Stand back, stand back. Let them pass, let them pass.'

On the anniversary of his hiring, he didn't enter the staff door of the lobby, where he had to wait for all the luggage carts to go through before him. He walked straight into the revolving door, and took it around and around. "So much to do!" he muttered. "Stand back!" He refused to stop until the police dragged him out and threw him into a cell in the Alex. After my mother brought him home, he didn't leave our house again. She took in laundry and lovers to support us, and all he had to say about it was, "Let them pass, let them pass."

I often wish our leader had taken the Kaiserhof as his Berlin headquarters when my father was there. He would have shown my father respect, taught him to hold his head high as a German. Hitler's most frequent dinner companions are his drivers, after all.

But my father's madness came a few years too early, and Hitler, a few years too late. So, when Joseph acts too strong or drives me too hard, I understand why he's racing. He doesn't want to be too late, and I let him pass.

I don't bother to turn on the light. My father prefers the dark. I set my attaché case by the door, hang my coat on the wobbling rack and sit to his right. It's as though we're riding together in the cab of his truck. I try to see what he sees: cows, farms, a church spire poking above the trees. I say to the windshield that isn't there, "The flowers smell good," even though it's winter, and there are no flowers.

He says, "The flowers smell good."

After a moment, I say, "I bought an apartment, Papa. I want you to visit. You'll love it."

Matching the inflection and rhythm of my speech, he repeats, "I bought an apartment, Papa. I want you to visit. You'll love it."

This is not the way I wanted to share my good news. Mimicry is a symptom of my father's catatonia. It only comes out periodically, but it's not unexpected. I return to his truck and imagine horses with their heads bowed, and hay bales rolled into wheels. I make the sky blue. *Real Hitler weather!* To help my father say what he should be saying, I do the only thing I can think to do when he's like this. I say, "Where is it, Son?"

"Where is it, Son?" my father mirrors.

Tiergartenstrasse, is my silent reply. For him, I say aloud, "Tiergartenstrasse? What a fine address."

"Tiergartenstrasse? What a fine address," comes back at me.

Then I add, "One of the finest buildings on the street? You must do very well for yourself." I say 'street' on an up-note and emphasize 'very.' Again, he echoes my words and sentiments just the way I'd wanted.

Internally, I say, 'Joseph Goebbels arranged it for me. I know you've heard of him, Papa. He's always in the newspaper.' Then, I blurt out, "Joseph Goebbels, himself? He arranged an apartment just for you?"

When my father finishes with that, I add, just as it should be said, "How proud you've made me, my son."

Before he can reply, I touch his hand. It is still strong. "I can walk the rest of the way from here, *Vati*."

13

EVA

Zara's dulled knife clicked on the marble slab. I filled metal bins with maraschino cherries and cocktail onions. To be served by men in black tie one night, while tying on an apron and prepping cocktail fruit the next was strange. I reeled to move from Katharina's wry observations to Zara's Berlin accented gossip, from meeting Alfred Landau to Matthias's peep shows. I loved my friends. But it also was tiring, night after night, to discover everything we were not.

Thad had seen the bar, along with my cadre of outsiders. He'd never said anything bad about them. I figured my work at the *klub* made me different, even interesting to him. But there were moments when I feared I was nothing more than a temptation, which when tasted one too many times, would lose its allure.

"How is it that my mother wants me to marry, but then insists I come home on all my nights off?" Zara piped.

"Because she wants everything for you," I said, absentmindedly.

Zara put the knife down. "Then she should be more strategic."

It had never occurred to me that people might want to spend less time with their mothers. Growing up, I wanted so much to spend time with a mother. I pasted myself into the other girls' stories, creating my own memories from theirs. I saw my friend Rachel's mother, with her freckled hands, brushing my hair 100 times before bed, and Shayna's mother rolling dough for *kreplach*.

One night, Helene Rothenberg, one of my closest friends, described how the *Rebbetzin* had invited her and her mother to tea. Helene had described her Galician town, the *Rebbetzin,* and her typhoid stricken mother so many times, I'd reconstructed them in my mind, and placed myself among them. I saw her mother holding my hand and introducing me to the Rabbi's wife. "I remember that!" I burst.

Helene's green eyes flashed as she tried to keep from laughing, but soon her shoulders shook, which made Shayna spit up her water. She whispered a jumble of Yiddish to Helene but the word I heard like a siren was *kurveh*. I didn't need to know the full sentence to understand what she meant. The Rebbetzin would never invite the *kurveh*, the whore, my mother, to tea.

A few days later, the German teacher, Fraulein Zuckerman, approached me. She was upset about Helene, who had cried for her mother after class. Fraulein Zuckerman could never let go of the Ostjuden girls' misery. When Helene so much as stared into space, sorrow raced to our teacher's eyes. Helene could have been thinking of the hole in her sock. She could have been thinking she would rather suck on a cow's hoof than sit through German class, yet every time, the teacher's panicked sympathy flooded the room.

Fraulein Zuckerman said, "Eva, please do Helene's chores this afternoon. She's not up to it today." Her voice had a buttery quality, which always made it seem like she was doing me a favor. I hated that voice.

I knew Helene was scheduled to do pots because she had complained about it all morning. My annoyance must have shown because with an overdose of butter, Fraulein Zuckerman said, "I'm certain you want to help, Eva. Helene's your good friend."

Floating patches of grease pooled against my arms as I scrubbed at the burnt-black bottoms of the pans. My resentment built with every slosh of the rank water.

While I worked, Fraulein Zuckerman stole into the kitchen and took a strawberry ice. We were permitted sweets only on *Shabbos* and special occasions. My shock caused me to splash myself, and the dirty water soaked through my apron. She shrugged her shoulders almost to her ears pushing her cheeks into a helpless smile. "It's her favorite."

By the time I got to do my own job, which was to shelve books and neaten the library, I had to race. My feet ached and I couldn't wait to get to the overstuffed chair behind the W-Z shelf so I could sit for a minute before supper. I had 20 pages left in Jane Eyre, and if I hurried, I could finish it. When I finally reached my seat, Helene was curled up with her own novel. There was a faint pink stain in the notch above her lip.

My anger flared. Not one of my friends or teachers had ever even considered that I mourned, too. They never cared to understand how sad and lonely it was to live without memories.

I turned back to the section of the library with Frau Pappenheim's writings. I'd read them all. Helene, too, sought our spiritual mother's favor, so I knew the power of what I was about to do. I pulled out Frau Pappenheim's, *On the Condition of the Jewish Population of Galicia: Impressions of a Voyage.*

I opened it, and lightly underlined the necessary words in pencil.

The women adorn themselves with garish trinkets, but they do not make themselves beautiful. And to have any aesthetic expectations of living quarters which are so hygienically deficient would seem like mockery . . .

I returned the pencil to the desk and walked out. Helene called my name. She knew I would get in trouble for leaving a book out.

When I didn't come back, she got up to put it away. As I'd intended, the underlining caught her eye. To write in library books was forbidden. I watched her read, and I watched her cry. I hated myself, but I was relieved. Finally, I wasn't the only one wounded by the inescapable fact of her birth.

I never lived down my shame from that day. Shame for what I did to Helene, shame about my mother, shame for impugning Frau Pappenheim, shame for never having known the love that always made Helene cry.

I moved on to cleaning ice buckets and raised my voice as if to be heard over the hollow spray of water against metal, but in fact, I was yelling because I was hurt. "Why don't you just tell her you can't come, if she bothers you so much?"

Zara looked defensive, and then sad. "I'm sorry," she said. "I didn't mean to complain . . ."

"It's nothing!" I barked, slamming the lid back down on her pity.

Thankfully, Matthias breezed in. "I'm writing a short about an American who falls in love with the Geisha he has tattooed on his arm. He strokes her, kisses her, jacks-off to her. He wanders around San Francisco, wearing his soles thin, trying to find her. He finds one woman who is as lithe as his Geisha and another who is as pretty in the face. There is even one whose voice is as songlike as the one in his imagination. But none can rival the complete beauty of his love. In despair, he gets the same Geisha, from the same tattoo artist, inked onto his other arm. When he goes home to indulge his passions, he discovers that when there are two, he has no interest in either of them anymore."

He dropped his hands on the bar. "What do you think?"

I forced myself into his good mood. "How about if he breaks his back as a stevedore to earn passage to Tokyo. By the time he saves enough money, he's stooped and arthritic. There's pain in every step, but he sets out to find the one who is meant for him alone.

"He searches every teahouse in Tokyo until he comes upon her. She moves in perfect silence and pours his tea with a grace he had not imagined in his wildest fantasies. He comes back night after night to watch her, too afraid to speak. Finally, he downs a cup of hot sake and summons the courage. 'My name is Harry,' he says.

"'My name is Suiko,' she says."

"He drops dead from heartbreak, because with a name, she's no longer his."

"Brava!" Matthias reached across the bar and kissed me on both cheeks. "Did Salomé tell you that story?"

"Eva Schmidt's own dark mind came up with it."

"I need to get to know this Eva Schmidt," he laughed. "She's learned the first lesson of German cinema. No joy."

"At least not for the working man," I added.

"Nothing for the working man!"

"You depress me," Zara said. "Both of you. I don't know how you live with yourselves." We watched her dress glitter and swish all the way up to the dance hall. She sometimes resented the way Matthias and I talked. Not meaning to be unkind, she would say to me, "How did you, of all people, become such an intellectual?" Not graduating from university had been a terrible blow for her and she envied my life, which she assumed was without expectations and thus their inevitable disappointments.

When the first customers dragged in, fingering the change in their pockets, still carrying the burdens of work, debt and family in their trudging steps, I realized it was the same time I would have been leaving my apartment to meet Thad, if I'd not had work.

I would have been wearing one of the gowns I'd made and my stomach would have roiled with excitement. As Matthias closed his black curtain to start the peepshow, he said, "You're a good person to share this miserable lot with, Eva Schmidt."

I tilted my head to him to accept the compliment, but I hated that he said it.

14

HANS

Magda is more upset than ever. Joseph compared her unfavorably to his mother. They often fight over the role women should play in the New Germany. It doesn't please Magda to think of herself as on her back or in the kitchen. Joseph's response last night was less than adequate. "Giving birth and rearing children is a life's work, after all. My mother is the woman I have the most respect for. And she is so far from intellect, so close to life."

The lady's pique, and Joseph's renewed confidence that he's back in Hitler's inner circle were enough to make him give her what she wanted, if only to get her to stop her carping. He'll consider Magda's ideas about a new fashion agency for the Reich. She'll take a cure at Bad Reichenhall; and, she can see her gypsy again, who, she claims, is the most clear-sighted she's known.

Because I was at their disastrous last meeting, it falls on me to get the gypsy back. I'm sure Magda's attraction has less to do with the girl, and more to do with needling Joseph. To imagine the gypsy with Magda, the gypsy in his home, will remind him of his shaming at the hands of his wife. The girl is a detested witness, as all witnesses are, and as such, she will burrow into his skin like a tick.

Whatever Magda's reason, I find myself trudging back through neon and whores to the dive they call Karnevalklub. I don't see the gypsy, so I walk up to a sad sack of a man behind the bar. He doesn't hear me so he cups his ear and leans in close. He smells of cheap schnapps and onions. "I need to speak with the gypsy!" I shout.

"Eva," he grumbles. "She's not telling fortunes tonight." He rings a bell in three short bursts and the girl appears. She's petite, with shining black hair, curled under and pinned behind her ears. She's nothing like the ideal woman I write about—a Gretchen with braided blond hair and the hips to bear the desired six children. Still, her eyes force me to stare. They're every kind of blue. I look, and look again, and think something different each time.

She says nothing, but she's nervous. Since our takeover, I've gotten used to this show of respect. I like how my introduction, Hans Lorenz, Senior Counselor to Dr. Joseph Goebbels, affects people. But, in Eva's case, it doesn't make me happy. She steps behind the bar, and the old man squares himself as best he can, given his disfigurement. I try to be polite. I don't like it when people attribute Joseph's bad behavior to me. "It's a pleasure to see you again, Fraulein," I say with a slight bow. "It's Hans. Hans Lorenz."

She nods.

"May we speak privately?" Her inscrutability makes me want her to like me. "To get away from the noise." I mimic the chaos with my hands.

She looks at the bartender, and he nods. "This way." There's an edge in her voice. She's probably five to ten years younger than me, but already she's hard. Most Berlin women are. The so-called freedoms of the Republic have forced them to be.

I follow her to the back. She stares into the grimy crevice where the floor's wax tiles hit the wall.

"Are you actually a Gypsy?" I ask. I don't need to know this. Magda probably would prefer her to be. It would give her another opportunity to flout the rules in front of the other wives. I wish I could dress her down, just once, for the way she thinks she's better than everyone else. Of course, I never do because she is better than everyone else. I'm the one who wants to know about the girl.

"I'm a fortune teller," she says. Her voice is of a German for many generations. It's the answer to my question, but I don't want to stop talking to her.

"But are you a Gypsy?"

"Nobody who tells fortunes in a bar is a Gypsy."

"I have a message from Frau Goebbels." Hints of her horror from the night of the rally show in the part of her lips. "She's asked me to convey her regret," I smile, as though we're sharing an inside joke, "for the circumstances of your last meeting. She would like you to come again. Friday. At five. Please."

The pause is too long. Is it possible she'll say no?

"But I'm not a Gypsy."

"You already said that."

She looks for words in the water-stained walls. "It's just a bar game. I'm sure Frau Goebbels doesn't want me. There are so many people who would be better suited to someone in her position."

Has this non-Gypsy been living under a rock? If Magda Goebbels says this is what she wants, then this is what she wants. The only response is, *I would be honored, Herr Lorenz.*

I can't tell Eva that Magda's request has nothing to do with whether she's actually a real Gypsy. She's landed at the center of an ugly power struggle between Magda and Joseph. Magda made a play for her, and if the girl says no, Magda won't tolerate the embarrassment. Both Eva and I will be in her crosshairs.

She looks over my shoulder for safety. I don't need her to be helpless, I need her to say yes. "Frau Goebbels likes you. She'll want to know why you said no. It's better for everyone if you give it a try."

"It's better," she murmurs. Is it a statement or a question?

"I'll assure Frau Goebbels you'll come."

She nods. Her body blurs as she turns. I can smell spring in her hair. Magda's right. There is something different about her. If I can get her to look at me one more time, I think I may see something beautiful. "Eva!" I shout. She looks over her shoulder. Her eye flickers lavender in the pulsing neon of the dive. "When you're dressed as yourself, you look very nice."

She laughs under her breath. I know women like this. She refuses to believe me, so she won't be disappointed when things go wrong. I wish Joseph were here. Just the tension in her back would tell him what she needs to hear. His words would form mirrors, showing her her stony pride comes from something good inside of her.

So many people say it, it's getting old: if you take my Aryan features and add Joseph's genius, the world will fall in line. My friends say they'd rather be me, with my looks, than Doktor Dwarf, with his brains. I like to hear it, but as Eva walks away from me, I fear my friends are wrong.

The nights are getting warmer. The frost in the air has turned damp. I walk through the Tiergarten's bridle paths to my apartment. A beaded dress, which maps the curves of a young woman's body and skims the thigh too high floats by. A real German girl wearing African looking brass bracelets nests under the arm of a man who has to be a Jew. I picture them gallivanting at Ciro's, or gushing over *lustmord* at Titania Palast. Now their expensive shoes grind the dead leaves into the Tiergarten's paths. This ugly, mud-strewn foliage is a luxury, but these people would never know it. They didn't come up my way, with parks empty of leaves because they'd been scavenged for fuel. They don't care about the Germans who till our soil, drive our trucks and die in our wars. They haven't abased themselves as my mother has, or been driven to madness like my father.

Within five years, I've gone from being a copy editor at *Der Angriff*, living in my mother's flat, to being one of Dr. Goebbels' most trusted advisors, with an apartment on Tiergartenstrasse. I'm living proof of what National Socialism can do for all of Germany.

Joseph says, "The Party is my church. National Socialism is my religion." In that it saved me, it's my religion too. Whether I'm speaking to intellectuals, captains of industry or the lowest paid workers, I ask when subjugation of the self and service to the *völk* were more central and more pervasive than in this German revolution. No one argues. We salute, we sing, we parade, not just because the Führer tells us to, though that's what our enemies choose to believe. We do it because every one of us is strong, and proud, and worthy to be called a German, and because as one, we are better than we are divided. Our faith isn't an abstract idea hatched up by a bourgeois intellectual. Our faith is our union, and we live it every day.

The gypsy doesn't understand this. She doesn't know she's entitled to a better life. I want to persuade her.

I'm lost in the thought when an eerie reddish fringe emerges over the trees. A howling starts. It comes from all sides of the city. Police cars, fire engines and *Reichswehr* trucks roar by in an unending stream. They're heading toward the Reichstag. The smell of burning hits me. Blue uniforms bolt down Charlottenburgstrasse. Their footfalls pound against the pavement in a rhythmic chant. A bright light floods the Tiergarten and its barren trees glow like ghosts. Brownshirts pop out of the dark spaces. "The Communists burned the Reichstag!" their voices shriek. "The Bolshies did it!" Their outrage is gleeful. They're intoxicated by the emergency.

I overheard Göring and Joseph talking in bits and pieces about what seemed to be a far-fetched provocation having to do with the Reichstag. I wanted to ask him about it, but I didn't dare. People have been canned for far less. Besides, the idea was so absurd, I thought I'd misunderstood. What would Joseph say if I asked him now?

As I lie between the soft cotton of my sheets, I smell the smoke of our parliament on my skin. I breathe it in and see the flames. From out of the burning building, the gypsy comes to me. Her hair unwinds down her back. She has never been touched. That I could have her purity, that whiteness, and make it my own, starts my blood flowing. I feel myself enter her. Her face is struck by my force; her hair flares against the sheets. She knows my movements before I take them. It's like she was born for me. I become stronger, so strong I might break her. With a desperate cry she grips me, needing me to give her what she wants, and when I do, she melts, warm and sweet in my arms. My muscles unclench and I shout with all my strength as the pulsing ooze spills over my hand.

15

EVA

Hans Lorenz was so tall, so broad, I couldn't see past him. He was polite, but there was something off about him. He had all the right Aryan features, but there was a grayish cast to his face, as though someone had run an eraser over his sketch, leaving only dulled hints of him behind.

I was stunned he'd come to the bar. I couldn't understand why Frau Goebbels wanted me back. My pleas of incompetence couldn't move him. He said Frau Goebbels would want to know why I said no. He meant she wouldn't accept no. He said it's better for everybody. He meant I had no choice. It seemed he, too, had a stake in this game. If he was afraid, how could I, an ersatz gypsy, an orphan, get in the maw of Joseph Goebbels' wife? Either one of them could get me fired, or put me on a list, just like Frau Rennert's boy. I had no way to get around them. I could only go through them. It was the only way out. As long as my friends never found out, I could pretend it didn't happen. It wouldn't be the first secret I'd kept in my life.

Zara might have understood. Women had to be more tolerant than men to survive. Rudi might have, too. He was an old-style socialist, but he served brownshirts at the bar without comment.

It was Matthias who scared me the most. His judgment would be brutal. It was worse than his anger, because it was so personal, so rejecting. I feared I would lose him because of it, and he was the one person in Berlin I couldn't do without.

Rudi and Zara had families to go home to. Matthias and I had each other. We were the only ones who were alone. It was why I endured his pontifications on the merits of living in a glass house in Berlin-Mitte, or the differences between strolling and walking. Long after Zara and Rudi had tuned him out like a dull radio show, I let him go on. Sometimes, because I knew he needed it, I would concede that he had changed my mind; and sometimes, because he knew I needed it, he would say, "Obviously, you're lying, but that's why I love you the most."

After the Nazi left, I scanned the clusters of customers to be sure Matthias hadn't been watching us. He was nowhere to be found.

I asked Rudi for a break, and pushed my way into the back alley. A heavy mist dampened my cheeks. Against the brick wall, under the yellowish cast of a street lamp, stood a man who looked like Matthias's friend, Johann. They were in the same program and Johann occasionally came to meet Matthias after work. He sometimes drank with us, though he always stayed on the fringe of our group. Matthias had mentioned that Johann's father was an executive at *Deutsche Bank*. I'd thought he was a snob, given the way he smiled at us from a distance, without saying a word.

As my eyes acclimated to the outdoors, I could see the man was, in fact, Johann. His right eye was swollen to near shut. A shine of puss and ointment coated the purplish halo around it. A scab split his lower lip, and his arm was in a sling. There was someone with him, but I only saw his back, which was shrouded in shadow.

The other person's hand reached for Johann's cheek, and with an exquisite mix of care and fear, traced his wounds. He turned his face and slowly kissed the side of Johann's neck. There was no mistaking him.

Johann's elbow, harnessed in his sling, gestured toward me. Matthias turned just enough to see me out of one eye, then collapsed against Johann's chest.

I should have left, but I couldn't move. A sob rose so unexpectedly inside of me, I almost couldn't stop it. "Are you all right?" I asked Johann. He bowed his head, pressing his lips into Matthias's curls.

I turned back into the arcade. Zara and Rudi were talking behind the bar, their faces somber. I heard bits and pieces of what they said. *Raid . . . Göring . . . gay bars . . . Matthias and Johann . . . Johann caught up . . . Eldorado . . . jail . . . Matthias and Johann . . . the police broke the arm; his father did the face.*

Growing up, I'd never heard of a homosexual; though, once I moved, I learned Berlin was famous for them. A few times, I'd peered into Adonis Lounge and Silhouette, but I approached them with the same wonder and confusion I'd had from half the new things I'd discovered in Berlin. I couldn't say what made me so upset until Zara again repeated *Matthias and Johann* in her gentle, unsurprised way. She and Rudi had already known the truth of what I'd seen.

I moved to the end of the bar and glared into its shellacked burl. My rasping breaths embarrassed me. Matthias and I were supposed to be the close ones. Zara was friends with everyone. All the men demanded her attention, but Matthias was the one I thought liked me. We were both well read, we had the same sense of humor, and we were Jewish. He didn't know I was, but I was sure it still bonded us.

I hadn't kept my secrets from him because I didn't trust him. I kept them from him because I knew if he knew what they were, my past would come too close, too often. They would swim in the silence between us, and I couldn't be free from them. On the other hand, his not telling me his secret could only have been personal. Everything I'd assumed about all of us, about this place we shared, was wrong. They shared, I didn't. They understood, I didn't. They didn't need me. I needed them. We were not four. They were three. All I had left to wonder about our four was what I'd done to make them love me less.

Eventually, Matthias approached me. "How's Johann?" my voice cut.

"He'll heal."

"Where is he?"

"He can't go back to his parents, so he'll stay with me until he figures out what to do."

I must have looked surprised because his eyes creased. "Do you have a problem with that?"

"No!"

"Are you not going to like me anymore?" The word 'like' burned me. How could I tell him I thought we loved each other?

"I will always like you, Matthias. I don't think you like me." Rudi and Zara's soft *Matthias and Johann, Matthias and Johann,* still murmured in my ears.

"Why would you say that?"

"Because you didn't tell me about Johann, but you told them. I thought I was," I swallowed the tremble in my voice, "special."

"I told them because they tell me things, too. It came up. It wasn't on purpose."

"But we talk all the time," I snapped.

"We talk about books, about your dates with the American, about whether art is inconsistent with beauty, but you've never told me anything about you."

He was only making things worse. "You must be worried about Johann. We don't have to talk about this."

Zara and Rudi joined us. Zara piped, "All we know is that you're an orphan from somewhere that's not here."

I couldn't stand it. "Frankfurt!" I barked. "I'm from Frankfurt." I hated her at that moment. I hated the way she said 'we,' as if this was something else they'd talked about behind my back. I hated that they couldn't see the difference between my secret and Matthias's. I'd told no one about myself. I'd withheld things that were, not things that are.

"I never talk about those things because they don't matter. They're in the past, separate. This is what I thought mattered!" I shouted, holding my hand out to the bar. "You, and you, and you," I said, pointing at each of them in turn. "Now."

They didn't say anything. I couldn't understand what they didn't understand. "Is my past something I owe you for you to like me? That's not friendship! Friendship lets people be who they say they are!"

Their bodies hovered too close. I hated that I'd been overwhelmed in the place I felt most at home. When none of them offered an *It's not that,* I left. I went to the one person who didn't need to take something from me to like me, and I fell into his arms. He rocked me, and kissed me and asked me no questions.

Rudi was cleaning out ashtrays when I came in the next day. I didn't look at him. "None of this should matter," he said when I turned to hang up my coat. He was careful as he talked. "All this about who and what people are? I'm a cripple? He's a homosexual? She didn't graduate? You're an orphan? It's not important."

"That's my point," I pleaded.

"It's not your point. For you, it matters too much."

"No," I protested. "I'm nothing. I'm the last person to care about that sort of thing."

"You do care, or you wouldn't devote so much effort to not being whatever it is you are." He poured two shots of schnapps and gave me one. I drank it. I knew I'd lost the argument because Rudi, whom I'd never seen touch another person, grabbed my hand. "We've all got too many things wrong with us to be nothing."

"So?" I said to his reflection in the bar's yellowed mirror.

"Forgive us."

Matthias walked in as he said it. "Salomé!" he shouted, and I held out my arms.

16

EVA

Thad was late for dinner. It wasn't the first time, or the second. *Something came up at work*, he would say, as he breezed into the restaurant. *The guys wanted to go out for a drink.* I worried it was a sign of laziness, of how little he had to work to keep me. It nipped at the back of my neck. Rather than sit alone in the restaurant, I walked in his direction, hoping to catch him on the way from the Embassy.

A scrawny brown shirt with a pathetic attempt at a mustache shoved a leaflet in front of me. His face was eager, his movements quick. I tried to dodge him, but he reached across my path. With a forced smile he stuffed the paper into my hand. *HOW TO RECOGNIZE A JEW.*

Everything is bigger on the Jew's face. The bent nose is the most common sign, but it is not all, the article explained. *Protruding lips, fleshy eyelids, and jug-handle ears are all obvious clues. . . . short limbs, bowed legs, flat feet, hair easily mistaken for a Negro's . . . .* Then, a boldfaced warning: ***Not every Jew has all such features, but they all have some. They are bacteria. They want to infect our race. They want your LITTLE COHN.***

Underneath was a drawing of a grinning Jew, with clawed hands, hovering over a *Valkyrie*-esque Aryan. Her eyes were wide in horror. She held her newborn at arm's length, its face a riot of over-sized lips, nose and ears, its hair a mop of tight curls. Beneath it were the words, again, **LITTLE COHN**.

I wanted to cry.

"He's one. She is, too," the brownshirt said, pointing to a couple walking across the street.

"Do you know them?" I asked, as if we were exchanging pleasantries.

"Don't make that ugly face. Look at him. He's smaller than his wife!"

"He's barely smaller than you." It was true.

"Aren't you quarrelsome!" he snapped. "And with no good reason. You're who we're trying to protect."

I ignored him, and walked toward a garbage can to toss the paper. "Give that back! Right now!" he barked. His voice was high-pitched and childish.

I crumpled the leaflet and held it out to him. He reeked of stale coffee. He seemed too young to need that much coffee. A fog settled in my brain. I couldn't figure out why someone younger than me would be yelling at me so viciously.

He grabbed my wrist, his voice tight with anger. "Are you already sleeping with a little, little man?"

"Let go!" I demanded.

He pulled me to his chest and roughly massaged my backside, clawing into my flesh with the points of his bony fingers. He hissed deep in my ear. "I see now. You're not whoring with a Jew, you are one."

Everything turned gray and slow. My mouth fell open, but there was no sound. His words came too fast for me to counter, warping my logic. This swastika man-child had stumbled on the truth.

A strong hand reached under my arm and yanked me backward. "Don't touch her!" Thad shouted, pushing the brownshirt against a lamppost.

The Nazi's face turned scarlet. "She's a Jew!"

I barely heard the exchange. I only could touch where he touched, searching for what gave me away.

Thad held the man by the collar. "No, she's not," he seethed.

A voice battered inside my skull. *I am! I am!* My words came out in a discordant stutter. "I . . . I . . ."

Thad turned to me, and slashed his hand in front of my face. With the same force he'd used with the brownshirt, he said, "She's not."

The Nazi spit on the ground. When Thad made another move for him, he scurried off. Thad watched until he disappeared, and then stared back at me.

Fatigue hurt every part of my body. Being Jewish was the only thing I knew about myself, and it simmered beneath my skin. *I am,* I thought. *It's the only thing I know I am.*

Thad wrapped his arms around me. My body collapsed against him. His heart beat fast and hard in my ear. *I am* sounded in my head with each of his breaths. *I am.* I pulled away and looked straight into his eyes. "I'm not," I swore. "I'm not."

The next day, Herr Perlstein whispered to sympathetic customers. Brownshirts beat his neighbor, a Social Democrat party official, to near death in front of his flat. A shopkeeper tried to help and was beaten, too. Herr Perlstein found a policeman, who looked at him through tired eyes, as though he was reporting a cat stuck in a tree. He ambled to the scene and waited for the stormtroopers to stomp out their savage dance. When he worried the victim might die, he sent them on their way. Of course, Herr Perlstein said, not all officers would have worried.

Paulina, without shame or doubt, asserted to Herr Perlstein that he was wrong. "Stories like these come out all the time in the *Vossische Zeitung* and the *Berliner Tageblatt*. They're owned by Jews, so it serves their agenda."

Herr Perlstein's voice was measured. "I was there, Frau Schneider."

"I don't support violence, Herr Perlstein, believe me, but you didn't see what he did to deserve the beating, did you? You don't know what came before."

Before Hitler, Paulina never would have spoken to him this way. I shook my head.

"What's with you shaking me off? You know how things go!"

Herr Perlstein turned to me with soft eyes. "*Nu?*" he demanded. It knocked the wind out of me. He'd never spoken Yiddish to me before. *Go on,* he'd meant. *It's your turn.*

"What?" I asked, faking confusion.

He clasped his hands behind his back and waited. I turned back to Paulina, and held my hand open in his direction, averting my eyes.

"He said he saw it, Paulina. Isn't that enough?"

When it was time for me to clock out, I found Herr Perlstein behind the metal desk in his office. The glasses through which he had cut me down earlier sat on top of a pile of receipts. Without them, he looked like a different person. He had a flat, brown mole next to his ear, and his eyes were smaller and set wider apart than I'd realized. His face was harshly blank.

Even after the Shabbos incident, I'd always thought he liked me well enough, especially compared to Paulina. He gave me advances on my salary, and he referred me to customers for after-hours work. But if he had any care for me at all, he gave no indication of it at that moment. His quiet ate into me. I was a piece of frayed cloth, and as I scraped the thin threads of my logic together into words, it seemed as though he could see straight through me.

"May I close the door?" I asked. He raised his eyebrows to allow it. I pulled it too hard. A sheet of paper blew onto the floor. I traced its slow fall with my stare. "Forgive me, Herr Perlstein," I said, reaching for it. The blood rushed to my cheeks. "I didn't mean to slam"—

"Is this really why you seek my forgiveness, Fraulein Schmidt?

I followed with a barely audible "Yes," and then, "No." He circled his middle finger on top of an amber paperweight.

"It's just I haven't told anyone in Berlin I'm Jewish. I have no family, no community. I'm not religious. There's been no reason to discuss it."

I didn't know if he understood what I meant or what I wanted from him, but he did nothing to help me muddle through.

"I don't object to being Jewish. It's a fine thing, of course. I know I still am. But now, with everything that's happened . . ."

He drew a line down his desk with his finger until it fell off the edge. "You've made the choice not to tell anyone."

A nauseating warmth rose from my stomach. The speckles in the linoleum tile blurred under my stare. "If you'll allow it," I said. The wall clock beat slow seconds. He cupped the paperweight, running his thumb along its honeyed base. "Will you, Herr Perlstein? Please?"

He cleared his throat and his Russian accented German came out hard. "We shall operate as if I don't know you at all, Fraulein Schmidt."

My mortified thank you hung in the air between us, and I turned my back.

My secret lay on a brown plate on the open windowsill of my apartment. Sleet pinged against the ceramic, and flecked the document with wet dots. I touched a match to the paper's edge. The burn was slow. *NAME: EVA SCHMIDT, PLACE OF BIRTH: FRANK-FURT AM MAIN, MOTHER: UNKNOWN, FATHER: UN-KNOWN* broke into charred flakes. At last, *LEGAL GUARDIAN: BERTHA PAPPENHEIM* turned to soot. I scraped the ashes into the gutter, and watched the ruined evidence of me disintegrate under the pelting ice. I left the window open. I needed to get the smell of burnt out of my hair.

17

EVA

My spiritual mother grew to an impossible size since I'd lit her on fire and dumped her in my gutter. I saw everything through her eyes and levied her judgments. She would have said the crystal chandelier in the music room of the French diplomat's Grunewald mansion was better suited for the lobby of an American cinema. She would have criticized the embroidery on the cocktail napkins for being machine-made, and the gold-tinged landscapes as nostalgic. The chamber music, however, she would have said was divine.

It did her no justice to elevate her in these small ways after I'd damaged her so deeply. But she hadn't prepared me to live in this Germany. She taught us how things should be, not how they were. We'd matriculated upside down. Justice was gone. Truth was erased. Basic language had new meaning. Words like 'instinct,' 'fanatic,' and 'death' were exalted, while 'truth,' 'reason,' and 'intellect' were weak, venal, the odious domain of a subhuman race. Judges now said *Hitler is the law*. Politicians said *Hitler is the truth*. Surely, she could understand in a fact-less world, it only made sense that a Jew could stop being a Jew.

Rapid fire Italian came at me from the left. To my right, the singsong of Dutch fell from the mouths of two of the largest men I'd ever seen. The clash of languages made Thad's colleagues' English harder for me to understand.

Except for Katharina and Christopher, Thad's friends paid little attention to me. Most forgot my name from meeting to meeting. When we were together, they seemed to view me as an attraction, a specimen on which they could test their hypotheses about *'der Vaterland.' Are you one to question authority or to follow it? . . . Is militarism intrinsically virtuous? . . . What do you think of Jews?*

My answers were souvenirs for later use, in letters home or during conversations with colleagues and friends over a drink at the Adlon Bar.

Thad had explained that the embassy staff was split between Germanophiles, like Christopher, and Anglophiles. He hadn't revealed his preferences to me. I guessed he would say he was neither. He was too practical to take sides. That night, I'd stumbled into the latter, and I forced myself to parry with the indignation of a 'true' German. *We're not so unsophisticated, you know! Not all of us are small-minded on the issue of the Jews. . . We* and *Us* spilled from my lips far more easily than I ever would have thought they could.

Thad wove past the Dutch giants to join us. "I assume Charles is trolling Friedrichstrasse?" he asked the Anglophiles.

"Since the sound of the five o'clock bell," one of them replied.

"We'll see him again when he tires of the poor thing," the second added. "Which will be tomorrow morning, between coffee and his first shit."

"Who's the poor thing?" I asked.

Anglophile Two said, "Any shop girl who knows the exchange rate."

"I'm a shop girl."

Anglophile One jumped in with a now familiar refrain. "But you don't seem like"—

"Let's get some air," Thad interrupted. "It's beautiful outside." He pulled me toward the veranda. The moonlight cast a shimmering line across a reflecting pool and the lake below. It was one of the few nights that winter I had been able to see the stars. The blackened forest, which sat minutes from Mitte and all its chaos, filled the air with the scent of pine. My mind looped through the conversation. Each word came back like a slap.

Thad spoke to the moon stripe. "Have you ever been to a place like this?"

It was the first time I'd heard awe in Thad's voice, and it was the wrong time for it. "How could I have? I'm just a shop girl."

"Stop it."

"Stop what?"

"You're not that."

"I am a shop girl."

"You're different. You're smarter than shop girls. You're smarter than most people I know."

Frau Pappenheim had told us we needed to study because if we were smarter than *Them*, *They* still could hate us, but *They* couldn't humiliate us. Again, she was horribly wrong.

"Don't you tire of justifying me?"

He dropped his hands. "I'm complimenting you."

"It's not a compliment to be told you're an exception."

He shook his head slowly and turned back to the water. His voice was cold. "If you stop arguing, I promise I'll never speak well of you again."

I didn't want to stop. I'd supported myself for three years without Thad. I was the best assistant in Herr Perlstein's shop. I had customers at the *klub* who couldn't decide what to eat for dinner without asking me first.

I wanted Thad to assume my abilities, not to be pleasantly surprised when he stumbled across them. I gave him my most impressive justification yet. "Frau Goebbels requested my services."

"For a dress?" he asked.

"She wants Salomé!" I stomped a flamenco beat, then spun away like a dervish. When I stopped, the towering firs spun on. He grabbed my arm and pulled me down the marble steps, out of sight of the people inside.

I abandoned all bravado. "I didn't want to say yes, but I couldn't say no."

"Why would you ever say no?" For the first time, I looked at him as if he were the naïf between us. "Do you plan to kick her out of the *klub*?"

"She asked me to come to her house."

He froze for no more than a second. I pulled my arm out of his grasp. I watched his mind work. "You have to go. There's no other way."

Thad was more attentive than usual in the coming days. He held my hand in public and asked about my customers at the bar. How did I get them to trust me? How much did they reveal? Did I have a lot of repeat customers? He raised my impending meeting with Frau Goebbels in seemingly off-handed ways. Over breakfast at the Esplanade, he spoke softly. "I'm told Dr. Goebbels makes a good impression when it comes to attractive women." I was sure Dr. Goebbels didn't find me attractive, so it was of no comfort. It certainly hadn't warmed him to me at our first meeting. The next day, as Thad waited for the overly solicitous waiter at Schwanneke's to bring him our check, he added, "Frau Goebbels is Hitler's favorite woman," which terrified me. And, as he walked me to the shop on

a particularly cold, early March morning, he said, "Mrs. Sackett-
Speed, the wife of the last American Ambassador, told me Magda
has no female friends."

"So now she's Magda to you?" I asked.

"I was thinking she wants to be Magda to you."

18

HANS

"I like you, Hans," Dagmar says, after she laughs at something I said. We're on the front steps of her building. It's new, but not modern, a cement block whose only effort at charm is a dead sapling surrounded by near-dead pansies. Dagmar is standing under a fluorescent light. It turns her skin sallow but I still see she's blushing. "There," she says, "I said it."

Her statement hangs between us like a heavy bag, waiting to be pounded on. It's mean, but since I picked her up, I haven't stopped thinking about her ears. She's wearing Bakelite earrings shaped like fat buttons. They've stretched her earlobes ludicrously, and her skin is scarlet beneath them. She never once touches them, never mind re-clips them. All I want her to do is acknowledge that the earrings hurt. I want her to slide them off and put them aside the way Joseph's secretary does when she answers the telephone.

Did she wear them because she thought I would like them? I don't. I don't like the color and I don't like fake things. None of this should annoy me, except for the other things I don't like. I don't like that she laughs at almost everything I say. I don't like that she doesn't initiate conversations, except, apparently, when she wants to say she likes me. I don't like that she said she likes me, because I already knew that. And, I don't like that I already knew that because it shows how obvious she is.

I think of Magda. There's nothing obvious about her. Joseph would have tossed her out by now for being a fool. The gypsy isn't obvious either. She would never bare her soul to me like Dagmar did. I don't know Fraulein Schmidt, but that's the point. A gypsy makes her living off of other people's souls, she doesn't offer up her own.

Dagmar pouts, "Maybe I shouldn't have said anything, but you seem shy. My girlfriends said you need a push."

I picture her with the girls in the typing pool eating salad for lunch and whispering about me. *He likes you, he's just shy . . . He's a prude . . . He just needs a push . . .*

Again, she's too obvious. Guilt keeps me from saying what I should: *I don't want to see you anymore.* Instead, I smile, and say, "I like you, too, Dagmar."

She wilts like one of the half-dead pansies.

"Don't you believe me?"

"There's a difference between like and like, is all." She studies her nails. They're painted the same color as her earrings.

"We've been out four times. Is it wrong I don't know what 'like' is yet?

"We've been out four times and you haven't so much as kissed me goodnight."

Would she rather I sleep with her, then kick her to the curb? That's what whores are for. She hasn't thought about that, though. All she's thinking is her chance to nab a high-ranking party official is slipping through her fingers. This girl doesn't like me at all. She doesn't know me. If she did, she would know I'm traditional. When I like a woman, I treat her with respect.

I take Dagmar's face between my hands. Her fleshy cheeks press between my fingers. I plant a hard kiss on her lips. She doesn't kiss back.

"Better?" I ask.

I didn't plan to make Dagmar cry, but I won't drag things out when they're headed for the shitter. Women of the Republic wear their sexuality on their sleeves, or better said, on their lack of sleeves, down their plunging necklines and around their tightly clad asses. Dagmar proved herself to be this type.

It's fashionable in the Party to encourage breeding over marriage, and to despise convention when it comes to fidelity. Joseph assigns numbers to each of his conquests, and his numbers are high. Friedrich Graff claims to be well into the three digits. He tells highly colored stories about what girls will do for a chance at him.

My numbers are low, low enough that I never would share them. Or, if I did, I would lie. I'm lucky because given my apparent desirability to the female sex, people rarely ask me my numbers. They assume I'll outscore them. Joseph's numbers make him very confident about asking. He enjoys how they take people by surprise.

I've always believed the woman I marry should know me first on my wedding night. The marital bed must be sacrosanct. It's the only way to keep faith.

My mother stopped believing in my father. After his breakdown, it was understandable. He wasn't a real man. But she lost her faith well before he turned mad.

I wasn't aware of it until after my father was already gone, and my mother invited Herr Fischer, the first of her friends, into our home for dinner. In front of my sister and me, they juggled suggestion, gesture and silence. I wanted to tell them to go ahead and fuck each other so they could end everyone's misery, but I couldn't grab onto anything concrete in the shadows they threw across the table.

Amid my imaginings of their sex were memories of the ghosts who floated in and out of my childhood. They emerged in corporeal flashes—a leg crossing lamplight or a hand snatching a coat from the rack. There were no faces or names to them, but I'm sure they were there. Their spectral murk devoured my father's brain and drove him to lunacy. Why else would he have so decisively, so permanently, lost faith in our family and our future? Why else would he become unreachable to me, his own son?

19

EVA

"Adolph told Joseph he's indispensable! It's what he's lived to hear!" Frau Goebbels' voice came from behind a partially opened door. She was on the telephone with someone she called Ello. "He's giving him a new Ministry—the Ministry of Information and Public Enlightenment."

I waited on a crushed velvet bench in the foyer, counting the pills on my dress, wishing I'd thought to remove them. After a pause, she said, "Hindenburg will administer the oath . . . Yes . . . Absolutely thrilled."

A maid, close to my age, quickly closed the door. She looked like a child's drawing of a person, a stick figure with over-sized hands and feet. I faked oblivion by studying the cover of a French fashion magazine I'd taken from the marble topped table next to the bench.

"*Herrdoktor* Goebbels doesn't abide snoops," the maid said.

The scold landed on my head like a clump of wet snow. "I wasn't"—

"Eva!" Frau Goebbels' voice cut between us. "I'm so glad you've come." She entered with her baby in her arms. When I stood, the maid snatched the magazine from my seat, holding it between her man-fingers like a dirty rag. "Ursula, we'll be in the parlor. I'll ring you at naptime." Ursula bowed her head, but I caught her dissecting me from the corner of her eye.

"You must meet Helge, Eva," Magda said, jostling the child to attention. The baby sparkled from the fuse of her mother's energy. She nestled against her shoulder, and Magda kissed the top of her head. The instinctive love between them reawakened my sense of being a half-person without a mother of my own. It could have turned to envy, but instead of shutting me out, their faces begged me to join.

As we moved to the parlor, Frau Goebbels saw my admiration and handed me the child. "You're gorgeous with her! Do you have your own?"

Not taking my eyes from Helge, I replied, "No, Frau Goebbels."

"It's Magda. Call me Magda. And you must have younger siblings. It's obvious."

"I'm an orphan, Magda," I said, waiting for her cheerful bubble to jiggle, then pop.

She threw her hands in the air with a dismissive laugh. "None of that matters anymore. Hitler is giving prostitutes mansions in which to run salons, and the Bechsteins, Thyssens and all their titled friends are swarming around. So, pack your shame in a box. You're lovely! You're German! That's good enough!"

Her praise washed through me like a flash of light. I could almost forget who she was.

"Forgive me," she said. "Before we start, I need to pay you." She handed me the biggest check I'd ever received. "It's for the first time, too, with a little interest. I'm embarrassed it's late. I suppose I'm embarrassed about the whole situation last time, if the truth be told."

"Don't worry. I'm sorry, too." For what, I had no idea.

"Joseph isn't like most men. He's come from nothing. He's half-crippled. He's brilliant. More than anything, that's what I fell in love with. He listens, then he takes your thoughts and makes them brilliant, too. If he loves you, he makes them sacred. He makes you better than you ever thought you could be.

"On the other hand," she paused. "As you've seen, he over-thinks. His thoughts feed on themselves, and he whips himself into a fit. He always comes back. You just have to wait for the fever to break."

"I understand," I said, even though I didn't.

"I'm not complaining. Joseph is finally getting the credit he deserves. He's worked so hard. Our lives will be the way they should be." She grew more beautiful as she spoke. She was impossible not to look at.

I didn't know if I was supposed to respond. I couldn't let myself congratulate her.

She became distracted, and I followed her eyes to the street. "Look at them," she said, pointing to a Hasidic family outside. A father carried two patched suitcases and a shoulder bag. The mother pushed a pram jumbled with clothes and housewares. A boy followed her, picking up what fell off the top as she walked: a wooden spoon, a book, and a stray sock. A girl carried a small boy on her back, and a younger girl held an infant in her arms.

Magda groaned under her breath. "It's sad to say, but they would have done better if they went to Paris. People are more open-minded there."

Her sympathy shocked me. I tread carefully. "I work with a refugee." I was too terrified to add the word *Jewish*. "Her life is hard."

"I'm certain of it," Magda replied. "I was a refugee, too, but we were German, so it was easier. I didn't think so at the time, of course. I thought no one ever had suffered as much as we did." She gave a hazy laugh.

"I had no idea," I said.

"Very few people do. It's not the sort of thing one talks about, but you don't mind, do you?"

Was it possible she was asking my permission? "Of course not," I said. I couldn't help being comforted knowing this successful, beautiful woman had struggled in her life, and I was strangely honored she'd chosen to share her story with me.

"We were forced out of Belgium at the start of the war. I was twelve, and a Francophone. I'd known no other home. Of course, that didn't stop my school friends from hurling rocks through our windows.

"The soldiers forced us from our homes and made us sleep outside, under a circus tent, as if we were bearded ladies or exotic animals. Finally, they jammed us into putrid cattle cars and sent us back to Germany. The engineers went as slowly as possible, stopping and starting, just to prolong our hell. You can't imagine how sadistic people can be when given the opportunity.

"In Berlin, we moved to a shelter in a derelict villa at the corner of Tiergarten and Hohenzollernstrasse. I was always dirty, and my clothes grew too small by the day. It was mortifying to be in such a fine neighborhood living the way we did. I remember women carrying five, even six, Tietz and KaDeWe bags, doing everything they could to avoid seeing us. They thought they were generous, letting us pretend we were invisible."

"How kind," I added. I knew too well what she meant. The easiest way for me to stop a conversation was to say I was an orphan. It was prurient for *Them* to comment on or acknowledge my disgrace in any way.

"Once, a young woman, probably no more than 18, walked by with the most beautiful packages I'd ever seen. She had a gold and white striped hat box, and two large gifts wrapped in silver with enormous, glittering bows.

"Her heel hit a crack, and I thought she would fall. I reached for her packages to protect them, to keep them perfect. But she didn't fall. She'd barely tripped. The only damage was from my hands pawing at her things, scraping the sparkles off the bows. She screamed, 'This girl is a thief! Police! This girl is a thief!'

"Proof of my guilt was speckled in silver all over my hands and across the front of my blouse. I thought I'd be arrested. I ran to Anhalter Bahnhof to stow away on a train back to Belgium. I preferred its hatred to Tiergartenstrasse's constant humiliation.

"Of course, there were no trains to enemy territory, so I went into the bathroom, and stood among street urchins, picking at myself until every shiny bit of silver was gone."

My empathy came fast. "But look at you! Everything worked out!"

"Yet the hurt never quite leaves you, does it?"

I could only say yes.

"Eva, I've been wanting to ask you something."

"Of course," I insisted.

"A batty old fortune teller lived in our shelter. She always wore clumpy mascara and had bright pink lipstick stains on her teeth. All the children thought she was a witch. On dares, we would sprint by her room while she leered at us through the crack in her door.

"One afternoon, the witch's voice rasped at me, 'Come in, girly.' I was terrified. Her room had an eerie glow from a lamp she'd draped with a red scarf. I thought I'd choke on the mildew. She pointed for me to sit in a wobbly chair, then she lay a mouse- nibbled animal pelt on my lap. She sat in front of me on a crocheted pouf and ran sandpaper fingers across my palm. She gurgled and rocked as she studied my hand. I was about to scream when her eyes popped open and her clawed fingers came at me in slow, tight jerks, stopping just short of my face. She said, 'One day you will be a queen of life, but the end, when it comes, will be terrible!'"

Magda reached toward me, pleading. "Was the old witch, right?"

In spite of everything I detested about her, I wanted to comfort her as she'd comforted me. I folded her fingers back into her palm. "Your witch was a fraud. The palm reveals nothing about how or when someone will die. She contrived the whole story."

Magda's eyes turned dark. "But I am a queen of life, no?"

"Tell me!" Thad urged, handing me a scotch. He'd been waiting, and I liked it. Often, when he looked at me, I would look away. I knew it made me seem young to him, but that was what he did to me. That night, I stared into his eyes, not once tripping over his gaze.

"It was bizarre. I know how awful she is, but she actually seemed nice, if you can imagine." My enthusiasm revved as my brain flooded with memories.

"Some of them are," he conceded.

"She told me she'd been a refugee. She spoke like she cared about them. Refugees, I mean, even Jewish refugees."

I stopped myself. I didn't want him to think I'd been seduced, so I said, "The rest was more what you'd expect."

Thad slouched. "You can't just leave it at that."

"What else do you want to know?" I gloated.

"Was he there?"

"Goebbels?"

"Yes."

"No."

"Where was he?"

"How would I know?"

"What else did you talk about?"

I didn't want to exaggerate, but I picked my details carefully to construct the most compelling story. "She talked about how much she loves her husband."

"I don't believe even his mother would say that," Thad replied.

I leaned toward him, and as quietly as I could, so that my breath barely reached his ear, I said, "She says he makes her a better person."

Goose bumps raised on his neck as my lips grazed his skin and he pulled back. "Can you imagine what she was like before?"

I summoned my authority as a barroom gypsy. "I doubt he's changed a thing about her. He's changed how other people see her, and therefore, how she sees herself. That's what matters most to her. I expect she's always been the same."

"Which is what?"

"Nothing."

"She's something. She's very attractive. By all accounts, she's quite smart."

Now Frau Pappenheim carped in my ear. I said exactly what she would have said. "She relies on her husband to define her, and that means she's nothing. Her first husband was going to make her a *mondaine,* and when he didn't, she lost interest. Now, it's Dr. Goebbels' turn. She wants to be the Queen of the Reich. 'The Queen of Life,' is what she actually said.

Thad liked it, so I continued. "She's placed herself entirely in his hands."

"Is she happy?" he asked.

"Today she is. Goebbels succeeded, which means she has, too."

"I thought Hitler put Goebbels to pasture."

"No!" I burst. I was astonished to know something he didn't, and I loved correcting him. "He's joining the Cabinet. He's getting a new ministry—Information and Public Enlightenment. I overheard her talking about it on the phone! That's why she was in such a good mood."

The words tumbled out of my mouth before I could stop them and I was left with the feeling of having walked too far out on a ledge. "I shouldn't have said that. It must be a secret. Please, don't repeat it."

He saw my fear and retracted his interest. "Don't worry."

20

HANS

From the *New York Times*, March 23, 1933: *BOYCOTT MOVE SPREADS. Merchants canceling orders for German Goods*; and again, *PROTEST ON HITLER GROWING IN NATION. Christian and Non-Sectarian Groups Voice Indignation Over Anti-Jewish Drive.*

Joseph is certain the Jews we allow to leave Germany are spreading *greuelpropaganda,* atrocity stories, to the foreign press. We've drastically restricted their emigration because of it. Now, the police will vet them before they leave, and if they're allowed to go, we take everything they have. Joseph says, "Generosity does not impress the Jews. One has to show them one is equal to anything!"

At the same time, Hjalmar Schacht, President of the Reichsbank, says the international boycott will sink us. He wants to ease up on the Jews and reign in the stormtroopers. Industry stands behind him.

I find many of the actions against Jews excessive, but if I were to say anything, Joseph would find some synonym for pussy to hang around my neck for the next week. I get a headache thinking about reversing course. Would the Jews get their jobs back? Their homes? My home?

There were a lot of Eastern Jews in Prenzlauer Berg, where I grew up. They were real oddballs, with side curls and loud voices. If they weren't religious, they were Communists. The kids in my school weren't so bad. They were as poor as I was, but the rich Jews took care of them. They didn't worry like I did. They knew they wouldn't starve.

I had a Jewish teacher, Herr Richman, who tutored me after school at no charge. It was after my father's breakdown, and he pitied me. He was what they call a "mensch." I know this because whenever I said something wrong or obnoxious, he only would say, 'I see,' and rest the side of his face in his palm, pulling at the skin under his bulging eye with his pinkie. *The math teacher told me I didn't have to do any homework . . . I see . . . My poem is about having sex with my history teacher, Frau Weber . . . I see . . . I used your copy of The Sorrows of Young Werther to wipe my Papa's . . . I see . . .*

Everything was a lie, except for the bit about wanting to have sex with Frau Weber. Herr Richman could have struck me with his belt for it, but he never got angry because my father was a mad man and my mother was whoring around. He just looked at me with his pitying, taunting eyeball. *Exactly what do you see with your big eye, Herr Richman?* I wanted to shout. *Tell me what I'm doing wrong!*

To distract myself, I think about seeing the gypsy tonight. Magda asked me to get Eva back. I can tell she guessed at my interest, but she said nothing, even after my non-stop blushing at the mention of Eva's name. Leave it to me to fall for a gypsy. There are so many other women I could be thinking about. Just today, Joseph's secretary told me her niece who works in radio wants to go out with me. She's more beautiful than Eva, but there's something boring about her. She makes me feel boring, myself. She's probably another one who's only interested in my position. That Eva has no designs on me is intimidating. Again, Joseph would be clear about this. I'm being a pussy. If a lame dwarf like him can bed movie stars, I can get a non-Gypsy gypsy to sit with me in a bar.

A hollow bang jerks me to attention. Joseph's hand is flat on the brown metal file cabinet next to my door. He's all energy and it's jammed into his tiny frame so tightly he radiates. "The Führer has agreed!" he shouts. "We'll move our own boycott of the Jews up to April first. They've forced our hand. They won't stop until they starve us out. A boycott of Germany's Jews is the duty and the honor of all German Citizens. Write it!"

I'm taking notes so I can quote him in the press release.

My adrenaline crushes my questions. It drives my pen. Germany's aspirations spill onto the page and my hand can't keep up. I have no thoughts, only feelings, and I rise with their surge.

It's too hot in this bar. There are too many people, too close together. Eva is talking to a customer like she cares for him. The man hangs on her words. She says, "Look at your heart line. You're generous, but you act like it's a bad thing. It's not. If you stop doubting yourself, your marriage will last a long time. You'll be happy."

Regardless of whether his marriage will last a long time, it's clear he wants to make love to Eva right now. She has to see it. Why is she smiling?

She looks at her watch. The man gets the hint. He leaves. With his big paunch, he's no competition. Maybe his wife would prefer he focus on his diet instead of his heart line.

"Fraulein Schmidt," I say. I've surprised her again. "Lorenz. Hans, I mean. Hans Lorenz, from the other day."

She looks at me as if I'm a boy hoping for his first kiss, or maybe that's just how I look at myself. At work, I'd barely have the words out before the girl would say yes. I have no such sway with this woman who holds men's hearts in the palm of her hand. "Frau

Goebbels asked for a reading next Saturday." Her kohl-lined eyes widen, without trust. "And, I want to buy you a drink."

She draws out her nod. I get in line behind a couple of brownshirts. They're loud. They embarrass me. She'll think I'm like them.

I put the drink in front of her, but when I sit, I knock the underside of the table. Beer sloughs over the rim and circles into a frothy ring at the base of her glass, then slowly snakes across the table. Eva is getting a rag.

"It was my mistake," I say. "I'll do it." She gives me the rag and I wipe the table until every streak is gone. She thanks me.

Joseph says you have to be who people want you to be. This girl doesn't want to be afraid.

"My specialty is tables," I say.

She laughs now. "You're not bad."

Wheels wobble and squeal as an old Jew rolls a metal bucket over to mop up my spill. His beanie dangles from a pin. His hands are soft. I wonder what office job he lost. He presses down on the wringer, obviously not well enough, because when he pulls out the mop, he drips dirty water on Eva's shoe. Friedrich Graff would make him get down on his knees and wipe her shoe clean. It's probably why his numbers are so high. So many girls in the typing pool, with brains blunted by the incessant clacking of keys, get excited by that. It's clear this girl doesn't want it. I pretend not to notice, as Eva does. Her way is easier. She thanks him. Shmuel is his name. She sips her beer. I'm getting it right.

21

HANS

The dinner party will be the final celebration in the Reichskanzlerplatz apartment. Our führer granted Joseph the right to an old, whitewashed mansion in the secret gardens behind Wilhelmstrasse. It, and the millions necessary for its renovation, will come from the public treasury. Magda will have full reign. Already state gardeners are hacking at the overgrown grass, weeding the ponds and clearing trees to make new paths and flower beds. It's a hidden paradise at the heart of our government. She showed me the plans for an additional floor, a private cinema and heated greenhouses.

Joseph's only objection is that the house is on the newly christened Hermann Göring Strasse. Göring is big and fat, and with all his silk sashes and medals he has designed and awarded to himself, we at the Ministry think he looks like a garishly decked Christmas tree in a Jew's department store. Between that and his morphine-laced monologues, we can't understand why Hitler has made him his number two.

Magda is writing the invitations by hand, which means the evening will be intimate. This is my favorite kind of her parties. "I'd be delighted," I say.

"Invite Eva," she directs.

My words come out in slow motion. "Fraulein Schmidt? I've only seen her once. In that way, I mean—yes. If she'll agree," I stammer, unable to hide the hope in my voice. This gypsy has turned me into Dagmar.

Joseph strides into the room. He pushes my shoulder back. It's an ever-awkward challenge from the little man. "Make her come. You need another tally mark on your sheet soon, Hans. You don't want people to think you're one of Röhm's boys."

I have to offer him something, so I say, "She's a hard nut, Joseph, but I'll crack her."

"That's how we do it, Hansi," he says, squeezing my cheek hard enough to leave a mark.

The lopsided *klub* owner sees me first. He raises one eyebrow, though I don't know what he means by it. Wounded veterans get under my skin. They're an itch I can't scratch. I have a hero's body, but it's untested. I'm not cut out for street brawls. I want to fight a real war, in the uniform of the Fatherland. I ignore the old man and walk straight for Eva. I don't need his permission.

She's collecting coins from the backs of the machine. She's bored and tired. I recognize her slogging movements from watching my mother iron my shirts, set the table, and mop the floor. Eva startles when I say her name. She's embarrassed by her reaction. I start to apologize, and then stop. I have no reason to be ashamed. I'm bringing a coveted invitation. I hand her the card. "Please, be my guest."

She holds it up and turns it around like it fell down from the sky. Her movements are graceful, but her mood is not. She's holding her breath.

"I have to work that night."

"Then I'll speak to your boss," I tell her. It's what Joseph would say.

"No," she insists. "Let me do it. I'll ask him tonight."

"He'll say yes. Tell him the Reichsministerfrau insisted you come." I can't go back to Joseph or Magda with a loss here. They'll lose all respect.

Her eyes dart like trapped flies. Why must she make everything difficult? If we were together, she would be measured by her relationship to me. She would be as good as I am, and the way things are going, I'll be great. All she'd need to do is have children and love them. The Party will give her medals, like a soldier. Gold for eight. Silver for six. But nothing is just 'yes,' or 'no,' with her. It's always "if," "maybe," and "I don't know." I think of what Joseph says of Hitler: *He divides hot from cold. But luke-warmness, he spits out of his mouth.*

22

EVA

Bottles clanked and rattled as the St. Pauli Girl delivery man, Bernhard, dragged his dolly into the bar. We had never said more than a few words to each other. He mostly grunted and nodded, then stretched his back in pained circles while I reviewed and signed the receipt. Each time he tore off my copy, he ripped the receipt at the same spot along the perforation. Then, he'd hold up his hand, stiff as a paw, and grunt an apology.

That day he brought a fat file. After I signed for the beer and he'd done his stretches, he placed a form on the bar. A stray drop of water seeped through it. *Karnevalklub,* he wrote on the top line, with the address. "Who's the manager?"

"Rudolf Thun."

"And Herr Thun's nationality?"

"German. Why do you ask?"

"Is he Aryan?" he sighed.

"Who wants to know?"

"The Party."

"Which party?"

His eyes dulled. "Fraulein, it's a job. They asked me to collect the information along my route, so that's what I'm doing. They have other ways to find out, so you may as well tell me. It's just a list.

"He's Aryan."

"Name the non-Aryans who work in this bar."

"Non-Aryans? I don't know. I'm the only one here. You'll have to come back when Herr Thun arrives." I spoke loudly to warn Matthias to stay in his booth.

The man sagged and pointed his pen over my shoulder.

"Start with him," he said. "He's here."

I swung around to see Matthias stepping out from his black curtain.

"He's German. He's just like the rest of us."

"What's his name?"

"Matthias."

"Matthias what?"

"Matthias, Matthias. I don't know what. I barely know him." My voice was sharp.

"I don't want to note that you refused to answer the question, Fraulein. You've already given me enough trouble." He put his finger next to where I'd signed my name on the receipt, "Eva Schmidt."

Matthias strode over. He snatched the pen out of Bernhard's hand and wrote, MATTHIAS ALTMANN, JEW.

He left the nib on the page. Its ink bled into a circle, blurring the W. I couldn't take my eyes off it. He leaned into the Nazi and without a hint of his lie, said, "I'm the only one."

After the truck rumbled from the alley, I spun around to Matthias. "Why did you do that?"

"What?" he asked.

"Why did you tell him?"

"Because I'm Jewish, Eva."

"How about 'I'm Italian, Greek, a Turk,' anything but what you said. Now you're on a list. What if they make Rudi fire you? You'll end up like my neighbor. They'll come for you in the middle of the night and we'll never see you again."

He looked at me through a fog. "It's not something I've ever thought to lie about."

"This isn't an intellectual exercise, Matthias! Everything's changed. Everyone lies. Now, you'll never be able to deny it!"

"I don't want to deny it, Eva."

The words seared into me. "You don't always have to be the victim, Matthias." I couldn't keep the pain out of my voice, and he batted at it without mercy.

"It beats being one of them, don't you think?"

When I reached my flat, I was too tired to undress. A letter from Frau Pappenheim was heavy in my hand. Normally, I would have rushed to open it, feeling connected to her through even her mundane recitations about the orphanage: *We got a new bench in the courtyard . . . the price of apples . . . .* I cared about every one of her words because she'd chosen them for me.

I ran my finger over its woven edges and faint Gmund watermark. It was the same stationery Frau Pappenheim always used, the same stamp, the same ink. I traced my name, noticing where the pen had scratched along the curve of the *S*, where the ink diluted on the humps of the *m*, then blotted at the t's cross.

The only difference was the person she thought she'd addressed her letter to wasn't me. If she found out all I'd done wrong, she would despise me. I tried to tell myself it wasn't fair. After all, it was her education, the high language, the vocabulary, the characters to analyze and fall in love with, which had created my camouflage. They'd made me a fake gypsy, a pretend West Ender, and a pretend one of *Them*. I didn't know how to be anything more than my words and my characters. I was lost in her mold.

I turned the envelope over to see her address engraved on the flap. *I have to do better*, I said to it. I leaned over the side of the bed to open the bottom drawer of my nightstand. I felt for the knob, and when I pulled on the drawer, the table teetered on its uneven legs, rocking the lamp above me. I shoved the letter inside, and closed the drawer. *For when I'm better.*

23

EVA

The white paper plastered to the door of the shop was the same as I'd seen all over the neighborhood. *Kauft Nicht Bei Juden. Kauft in Deutschen Geschäften.* Do not buy Jewish goods. Buy in German businesses. It had the same tired Teutonic font. Work was slower that day, but it wasn't dead. Herr Perlstein had asked me to watch the register. I opened and closed it in nervous boredom, listening to the coins scrape across the bottom of the drawer. The poke of Ruth's machine punctuated the silence. I ran my hand down the stack of brown packages waiting for pick up. Zeller, Mueller, Hausman, Braun. Would they come?

A brownshirt approached the window. He brought a wet paintbrush to the plate glass and outlined a thick Jewish star. It appeared matte and gray from the inside. Herr Perlstein gave a slow shrug and said, "Given my name's on the sign it seems redundant, don't you think?"

He had spoken little to me since I'd told him of my decision to hide myself. He was polite, but distant, correcting my work with little encouragement and saying hello and goodbye with little warmth. I wanted to commiserate with him, but I knew it would be disingenuous. I clearly hadn't earned the right to speak on the subject, so I just said, "I'll get it off."

Outside, the brownshirt with the paint brush had done quick work. To Wolfe's Apothecary he painted a Star of David, to Kopp's Dry Goods, a swastika, and at the end of the block, to Dr. Kaufmann's Ophthalmology, it was JUDE. An Aryan-looking man with crepe paper skin under his eyes walked out. I tried to catch his eye, to smile or nod, but he fell to the ground. The brownshirt with a paintbrush tripped him, and his bundles scraped across the pavement.

Confused, the man sat back on his heels. I ran to collect his packages. Pistachios had sprayed out from one of the bags. I shoved them back as quickly as I could.

"Traitor!" The brownshirt's voice was shrill. Another of his crew came running. He grabbed the man's shoulders and the painter forced his head back. Slowly, he dumped paint over the man's face. The white rolled off his lips, into his ears and down his neck. The paint bubbled as he fought, but he must have choked on some because it started to spit out in reflexive jerks. They laughed and pushed him down, as if he were a subway turnstile, then continued on their way.

Dr. Kaufmann ran out to help the man. "He was just picking up his glasses," the doctor muttered, more baffled than angry. "People need to see, don't they?"

"Yes, of course," I insisted, but I didn't look at him. I paced the sidewalk, scanning the ground for pistachios, or even just a last bit of shell to thrust back in the bag. "He dropped his nuts," I explained.

The painter walked back to me with his white, dripping brush. "Watch yourself," he said, and painted a cold stripe down the side of my face, cutting my cheek with the brush's jagged metal edge.

There was a time when Berliners would have stared at me with paint on my cheek. Someone even might have offered to help. Now, they looked away. I got into trouble and they didn't want it. Trouble was contagious.

I turned into the closest hotel, hiding my cheek from the desk clerk. I locked myself inside the bathroom. I stared into the mirror. The paint itched where it had dried and started to crackle. When I chipped it away, my cut opened. Seeing the blood made it hurt for the first time. I cleaned everything except a dash of paint on my earlobe, which I left alone, as if to fabricate a trophy for myself out of the old man's courage.

I had another hour until my appointment with Magda. The irony of the First Lady of the Reich breaking the *boykottaktion* by seeing me was lost beneath the cruelty I'd witnessed at the ophthalmologist's office. As I crossed the river, I heard her husband's voice crackling over a loudspeaker from Lustgarden's grand mansion. "We have not hurt one Jewish hair, but if New York and London boycott German goods, we will take off our gloves until German Jewry is annihilated!"

"Hang them!" rose from the crowd.

I averted all eyes. I would do the same with Magda. I would pass through, unnoticed, so it wouldn't occur to her ever to want to see me again. I wouldn't be smart or a shop girl or a gypsy or a Jew. I would be nothing. I would give her nothing. I would slip through her fingers like water before she realized she could drink.

As nothing, as the woman who watched, heard, and did nothing, I went to her house and rang the bell.

"Are you hurt? Who did this to you?" Hans Lorenz led me into the apartment, holding my arm as if I might fall.

"It's just a scratch," I said. I resented his presence. He'd known the time of the meeting, and I couldn't help thinking he came to the apartment just for me.

Magda held Helge in one arm and took my hand with the other. "You'll get an infection. Go ask Ursula for iodine, Hans." She sat me on a blue silk sofa. She put Helge on the floor and sat next to me. The girl fussed, but Magda ignored her.

Hans came back with a wet cloth and a brown bottle. I felt foolish with all the fuss. "You're so kind, but really, it's nothing."

Magda shushed me. Her bracelets clinked as she cleaned the cut and patted it dry. She scraped at the stray paint I'd left on my ear. When she finished, she brought Helge back on her lap and all three of them turned to me. "Tell us everything," Magda said.

I told them about the painter vandalizing the shops. They nodded, concern never once leaving their eyes. Then, I told them what the brownshirts did.

Hans stood up. "What was his name?"

"I have no idea."

"What store?" His size hovered over me, blocking my view. It was hard to think, but I mustered the name of the ophthalmologist.

"Kaufmann," I said. He wrote it down.

"Joseph was explicit," he pleaded to Magda. "Violence was prohibited."

"Röhm's boys are dogs," Magda scoffed. "They only want to fight."

Hans paced. "They say, 'The people crave fear! The people want violence!'" His tone grew sharper and louder with each step.

Magda's anger fanned his. "Papen and his crew tried to get Hindenburg to stop the *boykottaktion*, you know. They wanted him to declare martial law."

"I didn't know," Hans grunted.

"Joseph told me. It wasn't public."

"Those roughnecks would have gotten around it, either way. They're too boneheaded to see that when the world's eyes are on Berlin, when the stock market is at rock bottom, and the Bremen and Europa sail empty, you don't slap a woman in the face with a wet paintbrush."

"Fools!" she snapped

Little Helge reached for me, and I took her from Magda. I kissed her hair. The tops of her cheeks rose in a smile.

Magda took my hand. The care in her touch sent a tingle through my arm. "You were right to tell us, Eva," Magda said. "You should feel at home here." Something broke in me when she said this. I'd intended to disappear before her eyes and in her memory. I vowed never to see her again. Yet, when I gave her nothing but weakness, she still wanted more. In one of the most treacherous houses in all of Berlin, there was a woman who wanted to take care of me.

Hans's face softened with hers. His eyes found mine. He said, "I'm so sorry, Eva."

The truth in his words shocked me. I deflected, "Please, don't worry," but his sincerity had hooked into me, and it didn't let go.

24

EVA

"What did you do to your face?" Thad asked. We were outside a cabaret waiting for Christopher and Katharina.

I repeated my tale of the brownshirt.

"You have to stop having these run-ins," he demanded. It's not a high school debate club. You're not going to win anything. This guy, or the one from the other night, could have"—

"I know!"

"It doesn't seem like you know."

"Why are you blaming me?"

"I'm not blaming you. You have to be careful."

I stared at a klatch of showgirls dressed as langoustines, chatting and smoking in a nearby alley. Their antennae tangled as they whispered, and when they laughed, their shell tails bounced against the trash-strewn pavement.

"Should we go home?" Thad asked.

"I prefer the distraction," I replied, watching the crustaceans' breezy back and forth. I told him what I knew he wanted to hear. "I saw Magda today."

"What happened?"

"She seems so different from Goebbels. She's almost normal. She's lovely with her daughter, and she's very nice to me. I can't explain it. There was also a Goebbels aide— "

"What was his name?"

"Hans Lorenz."

"Does he work for Goebbels or Magda?"

"His card says the Ministry, so I assume Goebbels, but he spends a lot of time with Magda."

"You think, or you know?"

"I think. Why do you care?"

"Of course I care. They're so interesting. Have you met this Hans before?"

"We've talked. He seems," I paused, "interested." I wanted Thad to be jealous, so I pushed. "He invited me to a party at the Goebbels' apartment. He said it would be intimate."

"Wonderful. You said yes, of course."

"What else could I have done?"

"Nothing," he insisted.

"Aren't you supposed to be jealous?"

He was surprised by the question, which hurt me. "I think I can trust you not to throw me overboard for a Goebbels man."

"I would never!"

"Which is why I'm not jealous. Tell me more."

He'd defeated me. He so often did. "I told them about the painter. They were furious. Violence was forbidden. It wasn't in the papers, but Magda said Joseph told her von Papen secretly asked Hindenburg to declare martial law to stop the boycott."

"When was the meeting?"

I sagged. I wished I knew the things he wanted me to know. "I didn't think it was my place to ask."

"Did she say why Papen wanted to stop it?"

"Hans said world opinion, the stock market, German ships sailing close to empty."

"Did he think that or did he know that?"

"I think he knew that. Sorry."

"Don't be. Is there anything else?"

"The rest was Magda and Hans blaming the brownshirts for everything. They hate them, and they hate Röhm.

"Things aren't so black and white for some of them. Frau Goebbels was in love with a Jew, a man named Viktor Arlosoroff."

"That's not possible."

"Now, he calls himself Chaim. He's an Eastern type, an activist. Nothing like German Jews. He emigrated to Palestine, but people say he and Magda almost married."

I didn't know if I was more shocked by the news or by how happy I was to hear it. I was weary from fighting my fondness for Magda, for loathing my instincts about her. Thad proved she really was different. She really was better than the rest.

Thad studied my reaction. He drew me closer to him. His gaze turned mischievous. I wanted to kiss him.

"No one's allowed to talk about it, but everyone does. Arlosoroff's sister was Magda's best friend. They were all in a Zionist youth group together. Magda used to wear a necklace with a Jewish star. Arlosoroff gave it to her. She even changed her name to Friedlander out of devotion to her stepfather, who adopted her and who's also Jewish, by the way. If Gunther Quandt hadn't snatched her up, people say Magda would be growing orange trees in the Promised Land right now. I've heard they were together after Goebbels, but that's just a rumor."

"Does Goebbels know?"

"He has to. Do you remember the headlines? *Nazi Weds Jewess.*"

I loved everything he said. I couldn't keep from smiling.

"I knew you'd like this," he said, as if he was proud, of me or of himself, I wasn't sure. "Nazi leaders don't play by their own rules. They smoke and drink. Their women wear makeup and spend thousands of marks on clothes and jewelry. In Magda's case, they sleep with Jews. Goebbels would do it if he thought he could get something out of it. He has in the past, anyway."

"This has to be another rumor."

"Not at all."

"Do you think or do you know?" I joked.

"Even Hitler has his Jews. He's smitten with Ambassador Cerruti's wife, and she's not just a Jew, she's a Hungarian Jew. Hers is the only dinner invitation he's accepted among the diplomatic corps, and he's done it twice. Not even Mrs. Sackett-Speed had that honor, and she serves lobster with tea. They're all open secrets. As long as you don't talk about them to the wrong people, the SS won't kill you. Luckily, I have diplomatic immunity."

My mind couldn't stay off Magda and her lover. I pictured Chaim/Viktor Arlosoroff to be like the Zionist men on the posters, shirts opened to bronzed chests, sleeves rolled up, unearthing rocks. I laughed, which made him laugh. "See," he said. "The Goebbels' party will be fun. Bring back the gossip, though. Especially anything about the international boycott of Germany."

"Why would they say anything about that to me?"

"They wouldn't, but you can overhear. Anyway, you owe me after what I told you tonight."

"The difference between us being you have diplomatic immunity."

"I keep secrets for a living, Eva."

"Apparently, you don't keep open secrets."

"Open being the operative term."

"Is the Hindenburg meeting I told you about 'open'?"

"No comment." The dancing shellfish went back inside, leaving their cigarette butts to smolder on the pavement.

"Will you tell people at work?"

"Eva, I'm an American." He smiled happily, as if his words should have made me happy, too.

"What's that supposed to mean?"

The marquee's gold light flickered across his face. "We're the good guys, remember?"

A taxi pulled up, spraying rainwater at our feet. Inside, Christopher fumbled for his wallet, and Katharina gathered her wrap. Thad leaned in to hug me, which was unusual, especially in front of his friends. As he held me, he whispered, "I'll never connect anything you tell me back to you—open secret or not—but be sure to keep your meetings with Magda and Hans between us. And, tell them nothing about me. His eyes shifted to the cab. "We don't want it to get back to your friends at the ministry that you're anything more than a fortune teller."

"What else would I be?"

"I'm an Assistant Military Attaché for a foreign power. I like to think our attachment adds complexity to your situation."

A cold rain started to fall. When he stepped back, I didn't let go, as if to keep our attachment, as well as our secrets, more tightly between us.

Katharina went straight for Thad. "Was this your idea?" she protested, pointing to the cabaret. "I'd so much rather go to Giorgio's." She was almost Thad's height and she spoke without deference. I'd never done that. I never thought I could.

"We're not dressed for Giorgio's, Love," Christopher replied.

"Not *love*," she snapped. "We still *like*."

He turned to us and said, "My 'like' is pouting because she couldn't go to her *couturier* today."

"I could go, and I did go. *He* was closed. I thought we'd evolved since the days of the ghettos. It has been 60 years! Shall we send them back? The Party's not thinking about how this boycott punishes Germans. Half the lawyers in Berlin are Jews. Half the doctors"—

"I think that's Hitler's point, Kat," Christopher said.

"Are we never to get sick?"

"Real Aryans don't get sick," Thad joked.

"I'm quite sure there's no such thing as a non-Jewish furrier," she continued, obviously mocking herself. "I'll have to move to Paris! Then what will you do?" she demanded of Christopher.

"Die, my angel, just die." He nuzzled his face into the back of her neck.

"Then, do something! What's the use of having a communist as President of the United States if he does nothing to make them stop!"

"This from a German voter?" Thad replied.

"You'll have to take it seriously when all the Jews in Germany wash up on your beaches."

"Not if Christopher's the gatekeeper," Thad chimed, putting his arm around his friend.

Christopher turned to Katharina and said, "I do my best for you, Darling. There's a sign on my desk: *Radicals, idiots, indigents and high-end retailers need not apply.*"

"Liddy would be proud," Thad said. For my benefit, he added, "Liddy is Christopher's mother. She's made a good life keeping Jews out of things."

"As the old ones sing so the young ones chirp?" I swiped.

"Whether we like it or not, Eva, and I see you don't, if we didn't enforce quotas, we'd be swamped by them. They're a clever race, maybe the most clever. They're also contrarian. They don't absorb well. They don't want to. It's not our fault."

I thought of Frau Pappenheim. She believed being German made her better. She only wanted to be absorbed. We could never forget our heritage, to be certain, but that was between us and God, not us and the state. "The insolent, clever Jew," I said, quoting Dr. Goebbels.

"It's the same everywhere. Where they go, there's no peace. Whether it's Berlin, Budapest or Boston, Jews always have so much more than they're due. Yet, there are endless lines of them waiting to get out or get in, demanding more or less, as long as it's not what is."

"That's harsh," Thad said, giving me a conciliatory look. "If I were their lot, I would want to get out, too."

My chest fluttered. Thad always played the innocent bystander to Christopher's and my spats. For the first time, he was taking my side. I always knew that unlike the First Lady of the Reich, he would never pick oranges in the Promised Land, but I didn't need that. It was good just to feel his compassion.

Christopher slumped. "I don't know if it's your girl or our New York President, but you're going soft, Thad."

"Not soft, rational," Thad replied. He winked at me—also a first.

"It has nothing to do with rational," Christopher scoffed. "It's practical, which, my Teutonic friends, translates to ambitious, if not downright merciless. It serves him well with a few key higher-ups in the office. It will make him a Senator one day."

On the way home, we stopped at a traffic light on Joachimthalerstrasse. An *Ostjuden* woman with her hair wrapped in what was little more than a rag held a net bag open for a hawker. He rummaged through it, imagining the value of her things 'freshened up' and in a store. She, and those like her were sitting ducks, with nothing to offer but junk, a mangled language and prayers to an evidently stone hearted God. The old woman walked away without the bag, but she was as burdened without it as she'd been with it. Her small sale brought no peace.

"Poor thing," I said, and opened my hand to Thad. He didn't take it. Turning from the window, he said, "I know you feel sorry for them. I do, too. Believe me. But it's best to stop feeling. Everything will go so much more smoothly."

The slow rise and fall of Thad's back pushed against mine. His breaths were easy. They carried no weight. I wondered if I'd ever slept like that, holding nothing back, having nothing to prove or cover for. Thad's reprimand replayed in my head. It would have been so much easier to stop feeling. How much happier I would have been living outside the ever-looming shadows of these wailing, waiting people. I didn't know if I could ever escape them. I didn't know if I wanted to. Despite my lies, my past would not go away. It was asymptotic. No matter how much I slashed it, halved it and beat it down, it would never reach zero.

I pressed myself against him, hoping he would turn back to me and pull me closer, like he did outside the cabaret when we'd sheltered our secret between us, and I'd felt its excitement roll in my stomach. But his sleep was too deep, too peaceful. I stayed awake, unable to look at him, unable to reach for him, missing him more painfully with each long breath he took.

25

EVA

I hugged Thad for too long the next morning before he kissed my cheek and closed the door. The sound of its click lit a fuse in me. I needed to make love to him, to feel him inside me so I could have no doubt he was there.

I went back into the apartment. The heavy thwack of typewriter keys sounded from his study. I'd never been inside it, though I'd always been curious.

I peered through the crack in the door. The low light of morning had spread across the floor. Thad was typing at his desk. It was of the same Spartan style as the rest of his furniture, a mismatch for the old Torpedo typewriter, which was tall and black, with gold writing and round white keys.

I pictured his surprise, then the mischievous look that would creep into his eyes when he swept me into his bed. My stomach knotted as I reached for his back. I don't think I'd even touched him when he jumped. He ripped his page out of the machine and crumpled it into a ball. "What are you doing?" he demanded, swiveling his chair to face me. "You're supposed to be gone."

He had a look I hadn't seen before, as if he didn't know what was coming next. "Come out!" he barked, grabbing my upper arm. The hall fell dark as he shut the door against the morning sun.

"I wanted to see you," was all I could manage, but he wasn't paying attention. His face had turned off. The hard press of his thumb on my bicep was the only indication he knew I was there. I searched my mind for what I'd done to cause it. The seconds beat by and his grip grew more painful. After too long, my words slid into place. "Let go! You're hurting me!"

His hand dropped. He blinked in surprise and his face crumbled. "I'm sorry. I'd never hurt you. I didn't mean to. I just–I wasn't expecting anyone. I'm sorry." His stammering took me aback as much as his original anger.

"I wanted to surprise you. It was stupid, but I swear, I didn't see anything," I said, though I'd clearly seen the words *boycott of Jewish businesses, martial law* and *sincere efforts to prevent violence* typed onto the page. There was more, but my error, and his anger, had so shamed me, I'd erased the words from my mind.

He exhaled loudly. "I know you would never pry. I like that about you."

Whether it was a warning or a statement of fact, I didn't know, but he proceeded to do exactly what he needed to do to make the unpleasantness go away. He pulled my hips to his, and pressed himself against me, sending a wave of weakness through me until I could feel nothing but what ached for him.

We faced each other under the covers. Against the white pillow, he looked pure. His skin was without blemishes, his bones strong. I often thought he looked like he'd been made, rather than born. He held out his hand to me. "Am I in love?" he asked, splaying his fingers to exaggerate the bold lines of his palm.

"No," I said.

"Maybe it's not who I am." He stared at the ceiling.

"It's not who you are to love someone?"

"Do you mind?"

"Should I?"

He balled his fist and I got up to go. I couldn't bear to see his face.

There was no bruise, no whorl of blue and brown where he grabbed my arm, but I could still feel it. It was the first time he'd yelled at me, never mind touched me in that way. No one had. Frau Pappenheim never raised her voice, nor did she mete silence as punishment. Rather, she spoke with words so precise, the intensity of her feelings could not be misunderstood. Unlike Thad, however, she never apologized. I heard her yell one time, and it upset me as much as Thad had because prior to that day, as with Thad, I had not known she was capable of losing control. It was not directed at me, and it seemed over the smallest detail, but I never forgot it.

I was watering plants in her office anteroom, and I overheard her talking to the psychiatrist, Dr. Fischmann. He posited that Louisa Warshawsky's hyper-vigilance was due to past trauma and he recommended psychoanalysis.

There was a hard bang on the desk, then the sound of a pen rolling across the wooden desktop and clattering onto the floor. Frau Pappenheim's voice sliced the air, gaining strength with each word. "As long as I live, psychoanalysis will never penetrate my establishments!"

It was hard to name what it was that sent me spinning. Her anger's physical expression, the pounding, the pitched rant, both shocked me, as did its disproportion. That its target was a man and a doctor also unnerved me. But it was the doctor's timid response–*I understand why that might be difficult for you. We'll find another way*–was what made me run from the room, leaving her spider plants dry and wilted, sloshing water out of my can in slippery patches across the floor.

His gentle concession proved what I didn't want to believe. My ever-steady spiritual mother lived with a dark place somewhere inside her that made her capable of rage. I vowed to myself I would never touch it. Not only would the strange word, psychoanalysis, never cross my lips but also, I would not so much as look at Dr. Mannheimer or the hyper-vigilant Louisa Warshawsky again.

I would do the same with Thad. I vowed never to surprise him, never to question his work, and never to return to his home uninvited.

26

EVA

"Did you?" Paulina's voice pierced my memory.

"Did I what?"

"Did you see the dress Frau Goebbels wore to the opera opening?"

"Her name was Friedlander, you know."

Herr Perlstein gave me a sharp look. His stress couldn't be disguised. He never spoke of it, but he measured each piece of fabric exactly, and abandoned nothing to the trash heap, turning scraps into appliqués, buttons and corsages.

"What are you going on about? Who is this Friedlander?" Paulina shot.

"Friedlander is Frau Goebbels. She was raised by a Jewish step-father. She took his name as her own."

"It's made up," she replied.

Herr Perlstein tapped his thimble against the worktable in an agitated pulse.

"The papers said she was a Jew when she got married."

"Look at her, Eva! She's as Aryan as I am. You can be denounced for less!" she snapped.

"Don't kill the messenger, Paulina."

⸱ you're the Jew, Eva, with the way you imagine them
I should check your papers."

"Oh please." I glared at her with well-practiced superiority. Long ago, she'd set me above her. She'd always believed I was, and as long as she did, she would never think I was Jewish.

"Your arrogance is a clue."

With a mix of pride and contempt, Herr Perlstein straightened. "You can trust me, Frau Schneider." He pointed to me. "That woman is not a Jew."

His words were so crisp, they were cruel. He didn't have to play-act. What he said wasn't a lie. It was a disavowal, and he believed every word. He had leveled my half-baked soul to his scrap heap.

When Paulina went to the front to help a customer, he knocked on the table. Not wanting to know what his look would tell me, I shifted my gaze to the mole by his ear. It was red where his glasses rubbed against it. He whispered, "You've made your choice, Fraulein. Don't step in it."

I lied to Zara. I was too mortified to tell her about the Goebbels. Even if I weren't, Thad was clear I shouldn't mix my two worlds. I told her Thad was taking me to a surprise dinner. She made a project out of me, curling my hair and painting my face. When she finished, while I was nobody's Aryan cover girl, I thought she'd done well.

"To say the least, Thad will be happy," Zara said into the mirror.

"He doesn't usually say much more than the least," I replied.

"You're stunning, Eva. If he can't see it, he's a fool."

"He might just be a fool, then."

"He wouldn't be planning surprises for you if he wasn't enamored."

My face fell. Thad would never plan a surprise for me. With him, I was like a little rubber ball bouncing around an empty room. I flew out of control, up, down, left and right, and he, like the walls, had no give.

She pointed at my reflection. "Look what he does to you."

"Stop it."

"You're in love with him."

I felt like crying. "If love is constant, roiling acid in my stomach, maybe."

"Who cares what you call it? Enjoy it."

"He's too far away. All I do is want him, and he's content to keep it that way."

"Do you want to marry him?" Everything she said was wrong. I wanted her to leave.

"I just want to believe there's something between us beyond today." My lameness made me ugly, and I turned from the mirror.

"He barely lets a day go by without being in touch," she urged.

"But I have no idea why."

27

EVA

Hans's eyes never once left me to notice the water stains in the foyer or the web of fractured glass on the front window. If I could give Nazis credit for one thing, it was that they made royals out of the poor, the uneducated and the damned. That's what they claimed, anyway. Hitler was a high school drop-out. He'd been homeless. He made a virtue out of the four staircases I scaled to reach my apartment. There was honor in my view of rusted water tanks and in my courtyard's clothes lines that criss-crossed the sky.

In the car, Hans rested his hand on my knee. I crossed my legs to escape his touch. "I'm sorry," he said. "That was forward."

"It's fine. It's just"—

"Don't apologize. I was raised Catholic. I'm not anymore, but"—he blushed—"I'm traditional. I won't compromise you. It would ruin things, at least the things that are meant to be good. I see other women, but they're not like you. I respect you. I'll do right by you."

My exhale carried such relief, he had to notice. Hans was a gentleman. If he weren't a Nazi, things would have been easy. There were Nazis who regretted the violence, the policies against Jews. They joined the Party to protect their jobs, because they hated communists or they hated France. I had a customer who joined because the Nazis favored divorce and she desperately wanted one. Whatever one thought about this fatuous indifference, there was no doubt about Hans. He was so far beyond a regular party member, so close to the Nazi's black center, he could only be bad. And yet, he was gentle, even kind. I banished the thought. It shamed me.

I won't see him again, I vowed to the ironwork street lamps that lined Charlottenburgstrasse. I counted them down as we approached Reichskanzlerplatz. *4-3-2-1. I'll end it tomorrow. Nothing between us is meant to be good.*

A wide vase of fancifully colored tulips lined the mantel. The arrangement was unassuming, but lovely, just the right touch for the arrival of spring. People milled about, chatting over the gentle strains of a string quartet. I was scared to look too closely at people for fear of whom I would see. I recognized no one except the worst of them all. Goebbels sat on the same blue couch I'd sat on after the *boykottaktion*. He bounced Helge on his knee, and when she reached for his cheek, I thought I saw joy. Happy words floated around them. *What a pretty dress! . . . Helge's a beautiful name for a beautiful girl! . . . She takes after her mother. Am I right, Dr. Goebbels?*

"Luckily for her," Goebbels tossed into the fawning mist. Everyone laughed as if no husband had ever said anything so charming. Frau Pappenheim chided us not to lower our standards of humor or intellect for more powerful people, or for men. Her spiritual daughters were not to strive to be the stupidest person in the room, unless we actually were, and then we were to accept it with grace.

Magda's voice cut through the din. "Give Helge to Ada, Joseph. It's time for bed." She stood in front of the window, the last of the sun a smear behind her.

"Just a few more minutes, Mutti. Please?" the Reichsminister replied, not taking his eyes off the girl.

Magda put her hands on her hips, then held up two fingers. Goebbels buried his face in Helge's belly, making her shriek with joy. "See, Mutti, Helge's not tired," he said to the girl in high-pitched baby talk. "Helge's not tired at all."

Hans and I made our way toward Magda. She said, "Eva, you're the belle of the ball." She hugged me warmly, and handed me a glass of champagne from a tray the maid, Ursula, was passing. I knew it pained her to serve me, so I pretended not to notice her.

I wasn't prepared for what came next, but Magda pulled us through the crowd surrounding her husband and announced, "Darling! Look!"

Goebbels kissed Helge on the forehead, and handed her to the nanny named Ada. His body swooped down then up again in an inverted arc as he rose. My heart jumped, fearing he would fall, and jumped again as I worried he'd heard my quick gasp. He offered me an appraising frown, clearly more interested in my appearance than in any thoughts that lay beneath it. "Fraulein," he said. " It's to your advantage to be out of costume."

My impulse to please caused me to smile. "Herr Reichsminister," I started. "Thank you for"—

With a perfunctory nod, he saved me from saying more, and pulled Hans to his side. He gave him a congratulatory slap on the back. The coarse edges of his voice and the squint of his eye looking back at me confirmed his approval.

Magda squeezed my hand. "Joseph makes a sport of matchmaking his underlings. Typically, he marries them off to his latest flames after he's used the poor girls up. I doubt he'd have a dalliance with you, though. You're too short. And your hair . . ." Her voice faded. "You wouldn't be a victory. You look too much like him."

I swallowed the insult. Her candor was far too bold not to be hiding something. "Joseph lives three times as intensely as normal people. He can hardly be measured by the usual standard of bourgeois morality."

"Right," I said.

Distance shadowed her face. "You're lucky with Hans. His sweetness isn't altogether bad, is it? And the best part is, you and I can spend so much more time together. You're head and shoulders above Eva Braun and Emmy Sonneman. Talk about imbeciles."

"That's kind of you, Magda," I said, but she'd already moved on to the next guest.

I withdrew to the wall, feigning interest in a still life. Hans and Joseph were joined by three others and I could hear Joseph lecturing. "The effects of our boycott are already clearly noticeable. The world is gradually coming to its senses. It will learn to understand that it is not wise to let itself be informed on Germany by the Jewish émigrés."

As easily as that, I had something to bring back to Thad. The disciples' brylcreemed heads flashed in the light. They talked over each other to be heard by the great man. *The Jew-led boycott got the Tsar in the end. The Japanese Emperor will tell you how effective it was . . . Roosevelt is a wild card . . . Rosenberg, you mean . . . Czechs and Poles will use this to provoke war . . . How pathetic!*

A brave voice rose above the rest. "Industry thinks if they're not stopped soon, the Jews' boycott will break us by winter."

A sick chill settled around the circle with the knowledge that the words could not be taken back. They turned to their leader, children whose only remaining question was how much the lashing would hurt.

Joseph's face turned flat. "This is an attitude that predominates in certain ministries and in the Hebrew press. My faith in our führer's handling of the Jews is absolute. We will carry out a campaign of mental conquest in the world as effective as that which we have carried out in Germany, itself." His voice was matter-of-fact, merciful to the apostles as long as they agreed, and they agreed heartily.

A ping-pong of praise ensued. *So wise . . . Wonderful, Herr Doktor . . . It's the only way . . . Heil Hitler.*

As the words fell from their lips, a slow darkness grew on Goebbels' face, the quiet of concern. "The Jew is the eternal destroyer. Don't bring him to my party," he snapped.

There was a burning in the word, *Jew.* He looked straight at me as he said it. *No,* I told myself. Ten minutes earlier he'd complimented me to Hans. He doesn't know. No one has ever known. Not even the mauling Bavarian brownshirt knew. 'He was just trying to insult you,' Thad had said in an attempt to comfort. 'Put your secrets in a box,' Magda would say.

I went to the washroom to calm down. I closed the door, and scribbled what the men said onto a small pad in my purse. I was proud Thad asked for my help. I was scared I was too stressed to remember exactly what they said.

When I finished, I stepped back, and accidentally nudged the door open with my shoulder. I looked back and saw Ursula standing outside with an empty tray. I scrambled to put the pad and pen back in my purse.

"Were you writing something?" she asked.

"Nothing. I dropped my bag."

"'Cuz I thought I saw you listening in there."

Don't step in it! screamed in my head. "I don't know what you're talking about, Ursula, but the way you talk about snooping all the time makes me think you're the one who's listening."

"How you've come up!" she spat. "Don't fool yourself. You're no better than me. You're worse. Mine's honest work."

I brushed by her with as much authority as I could muster, and parked myself near the cellist. The quartet started *Embraceable You,* by George Gershwin. Apparently, I wasn't the only Jew at the party. I breathed and let the bows that played a Jew's music lull me back to sanity. My moods and confidence shifted as fast as lightning in the New Germany. It was impossible to keep up.

Across the room, Magda closed her eyes, enjoying the subversive music. What secrets she held! I imagined her leaning against the shoulder of her Zionist. Was she imagining it, too? She caught me staring and walked toward me. "Gershwin's marvelous. It's a shame the people won't be able to hear him any longer." Louder, she said, "But the Führer has his reasons."

"Gershwin is wonderful." I replied, though I knew next to nothing about him. I needed Magda to stay with me, to hold my hand and tell me how she did it, how she erased herself in the face of all this.

"Dear God," she groaned. "Hans is bringing Count von Helldorf. Don't be deceived by the dopey look, Eva. He's a cur."

The Count looked nothing like a cur. He looked sodden. His eyes sloped downward, in an image of chronic disappointment. "Hebrew music, Magda?"

Magda flicked her hand to dismiss him. "You know Joseph loves Broadway. Allow him a little fun."

Hans introduced me. "Count von Helldorf is a close friend of the Reichsminister. He's invited us to a special gathering at Erik Hanussen's palace. You must know Hanussen, Eva."

I knew precisely who Erik Hanussen was. He was an internationally known mentalist, hypnotist, psychic and fraud who mesmerized crowds in Europe and America. He was an avid Nazi sympathizer, and counted many of the Nazi elite among his most ardent followers.

Hans turned to the Count and said, with some pride, "Eva is a diviner, herself."

"I'm just a fortune teller in a bar, Count von Helldorf."

The Count smiled broadly, but his eyes held their pout. "The whole business is such fun." He extended his hand to me. "Tell me something wonderful about myself."

My breath caught. After my first meeting with Joseph, the idea of disrupting his party with a cold reading paralyzed me.

Magda put her arm around my waist. "Don't you dare, Wolf. She's mine."

"Allow me a little fun, too, Magda. It's only fair."

"Eva has no time for you. She's not a charlatan like your friend Hanussen."

"Why these verbal darts, Magda? You know I'm a fragile soul."

A cackle cut through the conversation. "A fragile soul who commands the brownshirts in Berlin." Joseph stood close behind me. I was sandwiched between him and one of the most brutal men in the city.

"Don't frighten the girl, *Herrdoktor*. She'll think me a beast."

"Your words, Wolf," Magda said.

"What's so beastly about asking a fortune teller for a fortune?"

"Eva's my guest, not a troubadour, and you're not at a picnic at the old Merseburg manor. I'll try not to take offense."

Goebbels stepped in front of me and stared. "Why are you so protective of the girl, Magda? It's true, Fraulein Schmidt is our guest, but if it won't offend you, Fraulein, please, do read the Count's palm. My wife has taken to you. I'm curious to see what she finds so particularly enchanting."

Magda shot him a sharp look. "It's too loud. There are too many people."

"Nonsense! Fraulein Schmidt works in a bar. Allow her to ply her craft."

"This isn't the way it's done."

"She thinks I'll keep you from her, Fraulein, but don't fear. This isn't a test. She's won that argument by now."

Helldorf thrust his hand at me, tired of the back and forth.

I had to be Salomé, to step out of myself. *Watch his body. Hear his tone. Be quicker than him. Don't equivocate. Allow silence. They'll be uncomfortable. They'll want you to succeed.*

The Count's palm lines were faded and short, without intersections. He had no defined fate, community or family lines, and there was evidence of multiple disruptions. The tension rose with the passing seconds. *Surprise them.*

"You have no fortune."

His palm weakened. He didn't like it. "I've always known I have bad luck."

Show no weakness. Adjust. "I didn't say luck, I said fortune, and I didn't say bad fortune, I said no fortune. Nothing crosses. There's no thread, no supporting players, no story that controls you."

This, he liked. "I'm my own man." I spun it out further.

"You say you're fragile, but you're not. There are multiple disruptions. Do you see them?" Everybody leaned forward. "Your life is made up of broken pieces, but you hold what's broken together."

He liked this, too. "It's good, then?"

I gave him a reproving frown. "I tell you what I see. You decide what's good."

"What else?" he asked.

"You're like an octopus. You react to what touches you. You change color, slide through impossibly small spaces. It's how you survive."

A laugh rumbled low in Joseph's belly. "What comes next for our invertebrate friend?"

"If you chase the past you wish you'd had, or the future you think you're due, you'll overstep. It wasn't meant for you."

"Because I have no fortune?" he asked.

"Because hope creates error. Times aren't good for error."

"*Brava*, Fraulein Schmidt. Our hopes are best left to Adolph Hitler!" Goebbels pronounced. He reached for my hand. I don't know how what happened next happened, but it did. His toe touched mine, or mine, his. I wasn't sure. I searched for some muscle memory that would tell me it wasn't my fault. It was just a tap, but he fell straight to the floor, like a sail dropping slack down a mast. His face jerked in pain, then his neck snapped forward. When he looked up, his eyes burned with disgust. But, I saw them too late. I'd already dropped to my knees to help him. I thought anyone would do the same. Only Magda did. She pushed me back and reached for him, trying to help him up. Her touch took his eyes off me.

He clutched her by the neck and pulled her onto the floor. His bulging veins made his hand wretched against her skin. "Yes, that would have suited you, standing there like my savior," he seethed. A laugh much bigger than should have come from his meager frame barked at the now despised witnesses. When it stopped, the only sound left was the creak of the floorboards as he leaned his weight on Magda to push himself to standing.

I reached for her, but she pulled away. The air between us stilled. After a beat, she rose, smiled at her guests, and, as if she were a wax cast of herself in the old *panoptikum*, she held out her hand to her audience, announcing, "Dinner is served."

28

EVA

It was in her hands, how she'd flexed them as she rose, careful not to touch her dress. It was in her shoulder, as she rolled it back to adjust her sleeve. It was the single, deep breath that washed over her, bringing each part of her back to life. I saw it so clearly, it had to be true. This powerful woman lived in disguise, keeping her past, her truth, in a box that was only for her. We were the same. We were hiders, and we were doing our grossly insufficient best to survive.

I wanted to test the connection to be sure it was real. I wanted to thank her for saving me, for showing me one could survive trapped in an unwanted life. I'd never been to her house without an appointment, but she'd told me I belonged there, with her and Helge, as if she believed in our connection, too.

The memory of these words was enough to lift my hand to her doorbell. My excuse was a delivery in the neighborhood. Magda accepted it without question. "Sit with me," she said. There should have been an awkward moment, given what I'd seen of her marriage. Her face lacked any hint of unease. "Did you enjoy the party?" she asked.

"It was beautiful," I said, not sure what else I could say.

"And it was, but that's not what I meant," she replied. She wore a black pearl choker that glimmered when she moved. "Did you enjoy Hans?"

"We've only seen each other a few times. He's very nice, but I don't think"—

I stopped. I didn't know if I was supposed to tell the truth. She leaned toward me, nodding.

"I don't think we're suited."

She squinted, pondering my words.

"Romantically, I mean."

She sighed. "You don't like him. There's nothing you can do about that."

My shoulders fell in relief. "We're too different."

"It's sad for Hans," she continued. "He's obviously smitten." She poured tea into Imari teacups. They had an orange and blue cherry blossom pattern that nearly matched the set Frau Pappenheim used to use. "Is there someone else?" Her tone was amenable to the idea, but I held back.

"You're an attractive, intelligent woman, Eva," she said, handing me my cup and saucer. "I would be surprised if there weren't."

"In a way," I said.

"Do you love him?"

"I don't know," I sighed. How young I must have seemed.

"You're lying." She took my hand. "One moves on from love, you know. It is what it is, when it is, and then"— Her voice wandered out the open window. I imagined it carried her across the sea to Victor/Chaim Arlosoroff. I had romanticized him to the point I couldn't accept anything other than her loving him. I said nothing. She would have to speak of it first.

"Then what?" I asked.

"Then, there's next time."

"You've loved someone before," I said.

She smiled. "It was what it was when it was."

"What was it?" I held out my hand for hers, to give her a reading. She opened her palm, and I ran my fingers over its mounds.

"It was maddening."

"He didn't love you?"

"He couldn't."

"Why not?"

"Too many people loved him. He was too sure of himself and his path. He was too strong."

What she meant was painfully obvious as I thought of Thad. "He didn't need you. You could be towed along the tracks, but you couldn't change the course of the train."

She liked the analogy. "I was his favorite car."

"In this way, he diminished you."

"In every way."

"Do you still love him?"

"Do I?"

Thad traced a line between my breasts. "Why didn't you invite me to the reception tonight?" I asked. His finger paused for only a second.

"Because I thought you had work."

"I told you I wasn't working."

His eyes followed the track of his finger up and down my chest. "I guess I forgot. You didn't miss anything. It was for the new Japanese Ambassador, Nagai. He comes down hard on the Brown side. It was non-stop Rising Sun and Teutons—not your crowd."

"Was Katharina there?"

"Only for a few minutes," he said. Of course, I thought. Katharina was always there. But Christopher loved Katharina. Thad laid his head on my pillow, and whispered in my ear. "Who cares about an embassy reception when you've said nothing about the Goebbels' party?"

I dropped my complaint. "It was terrifying," I said. I told him first about when Joseph hurt Magda.

"Are you surprised?"

"Who would do that, never mind in a room full of people?"

"I didn't realize the faith you'd placed in the leadership of the Third Reich." He played it off as a joke, but he didn't smile.

"She's so much better than he is. President Hoover's nephew proposed to her. Did you know that? When she said no, he turned over his car and nearly killed her."

"You've fallen under her spell."

I was tired of the way he could set me up, then tear me down. "Joseph Goebbels nearly strangled his wife at a party in his own home—her home, actually. You don't need to be mesmerized to see he's the lucky one in their marriage." Thad didn't respond. "Are you listening?" I demanded.

His face was neutral, his breathing steady. He wasn't ignoring me as much as he was thinking of something else. It was the same as the morning we fought, when he grabbed my arm. He disappeared.

I counted silently, and at six, he came back, just as he was before. "It seems you're the one who's mesmerized," I joked.

"It's a rare man who credits luck in his relations with women," he said.

"And you?" I pouted.

"What about the international boycott."

"I'm sure you can guess. The Jews are the eternal destroyers. They rule the world: they brought down the Tsar, they control President Roosevelt, they'll draw the pathetic Czechs and Poles into war with Germany. It was hard to take what they said seriously with all the groveling and head-bobbing."

"They believe their own propaganda."

"One thing stood out." I paused, waiting for him to ask me for it, but he only circled his finger to get me to move on. "Out of nowhere, a man announced that industry believes the boycott will break them by winter."

Thad perked up, giving me a quick thrill. "What did Goebbels say?"

"The silence was brutal, but Goebbels recovered. He said something about how he has total faith in Hitler to handle the Jews. They all bowed and scraped, and it was over."

"*Heil Hitler, Heil Hitler, Heil Hitler*?" Thad asked.

"You left out a *Heil Hitler* but, yes."

"Who said they would break?"

"I've never seen him before."

"What did he look like?"

"Glasses, straight brown hair, lots of brylcreem, double breasted suit. They all wear double breasted suits."

"How old?"

"Early thirties, maybe."

"And you didn't catch a name?"

"No."

"Did you ask anyone?"

"Of course, not! I was Hans' appendage. I was invisible!"

He proceeded to do what he always did when we talked about the Goebbels. He peppered me with questions I had few answers to. He was like a movie director, pressing play, stop and rewind, over and over again until he saw the film at every angle and made his choices. *Which industries was he talking about? What did he mean* by *winter?' November? December? What was Goebbels' tone? Expression?* He cut and spliced my stories into his own, leaving 95 percent of what I said in a pile of trash on the floor.

At the end of his interrogation, I was tired, but he was pleased. He rolled on top of me, spreading my legs wide with his knees. "You see, Eva. I am lucky to have you."

29

HANS

I have a blind date tonight, but a date nonetheless. After assuring Eva of my intentions, I need the outlet. The new girl is Viktoria Morelli. She works in the print office. Friedrich Graff gave me all sorts of soft soap on her—not a good sign. A man shouldn't have to be told what to look for in a woman.

We meet in the Ministry lobby, which is under renovation. It's a mess. The hammering is non-stop. The floor is coated in dust and crumbled plaster. Caged bulbs cast murky light, but I can see Viktoria is just as she said she was over the phone, 'a less pretty version of Louise Brooks.'

She has a short, dark bob and bangs. Her eyebrows rise in an off-center point, making her already generous eyes even more so. She's pretty enough to stir interest, but not pretty enough to be intimidating. With more makeup, the Louise Brooks comparison would be closer to the truth. Still, it was a funny thing to say. Perhaps she's funny. Friedrich wouldn't have cared about that.

A street vendor loads cages of brightly colored birds onto the back of a truck on the corner of Tauentzienstrasse and Kurfurstendamm. They have a great deal to say about it. Viktoria covers her ears. The low sun has wrapped the spire of Memorial Church in yellow. "It's beautiful," I say.

"I don't like dark churches," she replies.

"All churches are dark."

"I don't like churches, then." We start to walk. "What don't you like, Hans?"

I look in the storefronts. "I don't like bald mannequins."

She studies the mannequins. The ceiling light makes their skulls glow like space aliens.

"I like them," she says. "They don't look like anyone, so no one can say the clothes were made for someone else."

"That's too many indefinite pronouns in one sentence," I say.

"So that's another thing you don't like."

"I don't like bad grammar. Now, you go."

She looks at a trio of plants hanging from a wire in a café window. She draws her finger along the plate glass, leaving a long smudge. "I don't like house plants."

"Have they ever done anything to you?"

"They died on me, is what they did. Have bald mannequins ever done anything to you?" I see her smile as she turns away. She steps ahead of me, and points to a cigarette butt, which is flattened into the sidewalk.

"I don't like litter," she says, five steps ahead.

"I don't like litter, either, and I don't like smoking."

She turns around. Walking backwards, she pulls a cigarette out of her purse, lights it, and takes a long draw. Now, she looks exactly like Louise Brooks, with her amused stare that cares nothing for what I think. I brush the smoke from my face, and smile. "I'm sure you already know this, but you will be a terrible wife."

Viktoria leans naked against her bedroom wall, her hair tufted in fine knots. Morning light falls through the slats of her metal blinds.

She smokes. I reach for her breast. It fills my hand. Her eyes shift to me, like my fingers are ants at a picnic. I put her breast in my mouth. She stubs out her cigarette on a book.

"Do you want me to stop?" I ask.

"Please."

I roll onto my back. "Shall I call you again?"

With no concern for her bareness, she gets out of bed and surveys me from head to foot. She's checking mental boxes. "For now," she says. "Why not?"

30

EVA

After we made love, Thad told me he had to leave on a three-day inspection trip to the North. "Why didn't you tell me before?" I asked.

"We had more important things to talk about."

"But, we're supposed to go to Katharina's tea this afternoon!"

"Go without me. Christopher and Katharina don't bite."

"Sometimes they do," I moaned.

"Go," he said. "It will be rude if you don't."

The tea was in the Adlon lobby. Katharina used to go with her grandmother and she was nostalgic. Christopher ordered a magnum of *Deutscher Sekt* and an étagère of *petit fours* and tartlets. The sweets weren't enough to absorb the drink, and we sank irretrievably into the soft chairs, intoxicated and loud amidst the din of jazz piano and clinking china. "*Oma* would be proud," Katharina pronounced as Christopher paid the eye-popping bill.

We raised our empty glasses and he toasted, "To *Oma*!"

"To traditions!" I added.

"To good friends," Katharina said, tilting her glass toward me. I wished Thad knew how well I was getting on without him. I hoped they would tell him.

"I'm not ready to leave," Katharina averred.

I, too, was dizzied, and thought it better to stay put.

"Fine by me," Christopher replied, "but I'll take a turn in the cigar lounge."

"It seems we've been dismissed," Katharina griped.

"Time for some girl talk, girls!" Christopher crowed.

"How do I stand you, truly?"

"Because somewhere in your withered, Prussian heart you love me, Darling, and you can't let me go."

"Go to your men. We don't want you," she said, holding up the flat of her hand.

When he neared the cigar lounge, he turned back to me, holding his finger and thumb a centimeter apart. With his typical good cheer, he mouthed, "I'm this close."

Warmth flushed Katharina's cheeks, but she quickly recovered. "Let's make him pay." She signaled for the waiter. "Another bottle, please, on Mr. Winslow's account."

My mind searched for conversation topics, and as quickly, dismissed them as dull. I knew better than to blindly fill the silence. Finally, she said, "How very different these Americans are from us, don't you think?"

Her use of 'we' and 'us' buoyed me. "I think you're all different from me, German or American."

Her eyes teased. "Come, now, Eva, you know that's not true. There's something about you that fits right in. Christopher and I imagine you're the love child of a baron and a lady's maid, or perhaps a professor and his student." She paused. "What do you think? Who was your mother?"

Her amusement was a poor match for my mortification. To punish her, I replied, "I suspect she was a whore, Katharina."

A delighted laugh filled the space. She clapped her hands. "You're so marvelously fresh. I can see why Thad likes you so much. I was wrong. You're very American."

"How do you mean?"

"You don't fit your mold. You live outside your lot. So does Thad."

"Thad?" I pushed.

"You must know he's not the least bit rich. His family was quite well off, but—"

"The economy is terrible." I rushed to finish her sentence, hoping to hide my surprise.

"Oh, no. That's not it. His father, Edward, is it?" She waited for my confirmation, but I could offer none. Since I'd known her, I'd never felt so inadequate. I never knew what it was I was supposed to know. She brushed off the lapse and announced, "For the purposes of the story, we'll call him Edward. I like that name.

"Edward fell wildly in love with an off-the-boat Irish Catholic. Her name, I definitely remember. It was Colleen. She'd been working in the kitchen of his parents' Philadelphia townhouse. Christopher met her. He said she looked like Clara Bow, but when you added sound to her film, the whole thing collapsed beyond repair.

"Needless to say, Edward didn't see it the same way, and when he announced his intention to marry her, his parents disowned him. He went ahead with it in spite of them, or, more likely, to spite them. The young couple moved to a tired little spot called Williamsburg. Or Williamsport? It's not important to the story. Please stop me if you know all this. I hate to be a bore."

"It's not at all boring," I said, too eagerly.

"He opened a storefront law practice. As is so often true for romantics, the business side never came through. There was never enough. Thad was their firstborn, and a few years later came another boy, who was mongoloid, which didn't help their situation. His name? I have no idea. It wasn't long before Edward's practice was in trouble, and the family faced real hardship.

"Edward didn't take to the come down. He gambled to rebuild his fortune, and as you would expect, his debts amassed and the collectors came knocking."

Not that it would have mattered, but this was not at all what Thad told me about his family. He said he had older brothers. He said they'd taken over his family business, that he could have been the general counsel.

"When Thad was 12 or 13, Edward left supper before the meal was finished, presumably to gamble. Colleen was a hothead, and she chased after him, demanding he return to the table. Edward shouted that none of it would have happened if he hadn't settled for Irish trash. She threw a vase that barely missed his face. He pushed her against the wall, calling her every hateful epithet there is for her kind.

"Being simple as he was, Thad's brother wanted to make everything better. He ran to Edward and hugged him around the waist.

"Apparently, mongoloids can be abnormally strong and the boy was, especially when he was upset. He must have hurt Edward because Edward snapped. He attacked his son. Thad and Colleen tried to stop him, but he'd gone mad. When he was done, the boy was dead."

Cold horror left me mute.

Katharina pressed on. "Colleen told the police officer that when she'd asked the boy to bathe, he worked himself into a fit. She said he'd beat his head against the bathtub multiple times, then threw himself down the stairs.

"Her weeping and self-flagellation led the officer to offer his condolences, tip his hat, and wipe his hands of the whole affair.

"Without a word to his wife or to Thad, and with his dead son's body laid out in the hallway, Edward walked the officer out of the house, and never came back.

"Desperate, Colleen contacted Edward's spinster aunt, who took pity on them. She sent a monthly check for the rent, and Colleen got a job ironing at a Chinese laundry. When Thad was 14, the aunt paid for him to go to boarding school in New England. Then on to Princeton.

"When the aunt died, she left Thad some money, but it seems the Suffragettes and the Negroes got the lion's share."

"Did he tell you all this?"

"Good God, no! His aunt told every detail to Christopher's parents at their boarding school commencement dinner. All the while, poor Colleen sat at her side, hearing every word. Those are American manners for you.

"Please, don't tell him I told you. I shouldn't have said anything, though secrets do flow more freely with the bubbly. Christopher will have my head, but that's what he gets for leaving us alone together. You see, Thad's been able to shed so much of it."

"He doesn't need to shed anything," I insisted. My heart broke for him. I wanted him to come home so I could tell him the story made me want him more.

"Don't take it the wrong way. We admire him. And you. In many ways, it's better to be in your shoes, freed from society's restrictions. I just don't have the courage to break away. Society does have its allure, after all." She opened her hand to the marble arches, and the grand piano.

"I like Thad. I don't care what his world is." In his whirl of half-truths, I felt more whole than I ever had when I was with him. I'd manufactured so many reasons Thad was sticking with me, from sex to my connection to Magda, but Katharina's story let me imagine he genuinely wanted me, that one day, he might even find a way to love me. I offered him space without judgment. I required no effort and inflicted no inferiority. I could support him because I was like him. And, as someone carrying bruising secrets, he was like me.

People say that when in love, you love someone, even for his faults. At that moment, I knew it was true. I loved that Thad lied.

"It's of little consequence for him here. He's paid in dollars. His superiors adore him. He has just the right touch, all the right airs. Christopher says he'll be a Senator from Pennsylvania one day, and don't think the Irish bit won't help."

Outside, the sky was closing in with the dark-fringed blue of twilight, but Katharina's face shone with a certainty I never could imagine possessing. "He's one marriage away from erasing the whole thing. Christopher's cousin in Pittsburgh is willing to step in when she finishes college. The match is all but done."

31

EVA

I stood in front of the yellowed bathroom mirror and drew dark lines under Salomé's eyes. I let my hair out of its bun and brushed it 100 times. Then I took my brightest scarf and tied it around my head until it hurt. My disguise couldn't hide the truth reflected back at me. I was raised in a junk shop. People didn't keep junk. They dumped it. That was why there were junk shops.

I breathed the *klub's* smoke-deadened air, and steeled myself to the cantankerous assault of the arcade's blips and wails. My loud was the loud of carnival games and canned music. Thad's loud was 20-piece bands and detached wit.

I went from machine to machine to empty the change. The *pfennigs* were sticky with beer and grease. The floor was covered in dirty swill. Katharina's jasmine scent would have no chance against the clammy stench of stale alcohol on metal.

The finite in my relationship with Thad was in his voice and on his face. I'd read it in his palm. I'd felt it every time he came late for a date. He didn't pretend it to be any other way, and I'd accepted it. I accepted it because I hoped one day he might grow to love me. But, the hope was only a distraction. The truth was I needed him, and I would have taken him any way I could get him.

We had planned to meet at Café Pfau when Thad returned from Kiel, but, with its hand painted plates, rush seats and flickering tea lights, it was the wrong place to battle over his secret engagement.

I had thought all day about what I would say, never coming up with a satisfactory answer. I was disadvantaged, being so inexperienced in love.

When he turned the corner, he looked so happy to see me, I was almost tricked into forgetting my anger. "Let's go home instead," he said, and took my hand.

We'd walked less than a block when an outsized raindrop landed on my cheek. He stopped to wipe it.

"Are you engaged?" I asked.

The punch didn't land. "What makes you ask that?"

"Katharina told me you had a wife picked out."

"Is having a wife picked out the same as being engaged?"

"So, you are."

"I do."

"Do what?"

"Have a wife picked out."

"You do?"

"It's you who claims to know."

The rain left fat marks across the sidewalk and the temperature was falling fast. "Don't pretend you have nothing to account for."

"I'm not pretending. This is a mad conversation."

"Tell me the truth, then."

He sighed. "There is a girl."

"In Pittsburgh," I added.

"She's charming, pretty and appropriate in all the right ways."

Each compliment pounded me deeper into the earth. "Then, what are you doing with me?"

"I like you."

"You're betraying her."

"I've met her three times. We have no obligation or commitment."

"That's what you don't have. What do you have?"

He frowned, leaning back on his heels. "An unspoken understanding that we would be good for each other."

"Do you call that love?"

"I call it mutual respect."

"Katharina says it's all but done."

"Christopher wants it done. He thinks she'll make an excellent Senator's wife, and he wants me to be a Senator."

"What do you want?"

"I want to go to the apartment, have a drink and then, if you'll allow it, make love to you. But, it seems our plans for the evening don't match."

"Because you're withholding information!"

"There's no information! You're asking me about something that doesn't exist."

"Why would Katharina say what she said, then?"

"Because Katharina speaks with impunity! She says whatever she wants, whenever she wants, then five minutes later, she forgets she's even thought it."

"Do you want to marry this woman?"

"Maybe someday, but maybe someday I'll marry that old lady in the green trench coat," he said, pointing to a jowly woman, who had planted herself under an awning to wait out the rain.

"The notable difference being she hasn't been picked out for you."

"I'm telling you, I don't know what will happen with Betsy. I've promised her nothing. I owe her nothing. It's the most honest answer I have."

I'd worn him down, and he me. There was no place left to go. I don't know why I expected more. "I suppose a German shop girl would be a terrible Senator's wife."

"You mean an orphaned German shop girl who works as a gypsy at a dive bar?"

"You forgive nothing."

"I like you, Eva. I like you a lot. I missed you when I was away and I was thinking about you the entire ride back. You're not Betsy, and I don't want you to be Betsy. I just want to be with you. Isn't that enough?"

"Do we have mutual respect?"

"Am I standing in the rain having this conversation with you after having spent all day on a train from Kiel?" He pushed a lock of drenched hair behind my ear, and pulled me to him. I rested my forehead against his chest, staring at the puddle forming around our shoes.

"I need to know something," I said, without looking up.

"What is it?"

"Do you love your mother?"

The spray of wheels on water sounded next to us. His body stiffened, then his chest fell. I feared he would run away.

"I love her very much."

"Do you keep in touch with her?"

"I write when I can." There was guilt in his voice. I was hurting him, but I needed to know if he was his father's son.

"Are you proud of her?"

He looked away, then at the ground. There was a newspaper trapped in the storm drain, bleeding ink. He was still as he thought, absent again. His story lived in his silences. If he were to open his mouth to speak, his shadows would fall out. If there was one thing I'd learned about Thad, he allowed himself no darkness.

"I'm sorry," I said. "You don't need to answer."

He stared into his hands, turning them up and down. "She had burns. All the time. All over her hands, from ironing."

Holding his palms open between us, he looked at me. "My mother is brave. It was all my father left her with. My brother Henry was good. It was why my father hated him. My mother lost everything. Henry was murdered. I," he paused, "went off to prep school to live the life my father believed he was due. Of the three of us, you can guess who I'm not proud of."

32

EVA

A muted *Für Elise* came from inside Magda's apartment. When no one answered the bell, I pushed at the door. It fell open to the rise and fall of piano music interspersed with Helge's cries. "Magda?" I called, but she didn't respond. I found her in the parlor, stiff-backed and pale, playing the song from memory. Helge rolled from side to side at her feet. As the baby's sobs grew louder, the notes rose with them. "Is everything all right?" Magda rocked with the music, her eyes unblinking. "Should I hold her?" Magda still said nothing. I shouted, "I'll come back another time."

Magda tilted her head to one side, and smiled at the keys. I turned for the door. Her deadened voice followed me. "I sacked Ada, the night nurse, and the wretch made such a fuss, she spun the baby into a tantrum. Will you take her?"

The girl's face was red and swollen from crying. I lifted her, and her little chest jerked in spent heaves.

Still talking to the piano, Magda said, "It's Ursula's day off, and Joseph is on his way. The Führer expects us for dinner at the Kaiserhof." Her words were wisps, coming out one at a time. "I don't see how I'll be able to go."

Helge resumed her protest. She was startlingly loud. I had to hold her with both arms to keep her from writhing to the floor.

Magda faced me. "Make her stop before Joseph gets home. He won't stand for it, and my headache is murder."

She brought her hands to her temples and rushed to her bedroom. My head was pulsing too. I brought the girl into the nursery. It was a princess's room, with satin pillows and raw silk drapes. There was a shelf full of Kestner dolls and sterling frames with photos of Helge, Joseph and Magda, Helge and Magda's son Harold from Gunther Quandt, and larger than the rest, Helge in her 'Onkel Adolph's' arms. I hushed frantically in the girl's ear, but she wanted none of me. I handed her one of the porcelain-faced dolls. She knocked it to the ground. I swayed and bounced her. I was close to crying, myself.

At last, I pulled the chain on her mobile. It was a pink and white circus tent. Embroidered elephants and bears circled to Brahms' lullaby.

I hummed along with it, swaying her until the crying devolved into a shaky hum. I turned off the light and stroked her hair. Her body, bit by bit, relaxed. I dropped into a rocking chair and continued the song long after the mobile had unwound. I didn't stop until her breaths grew long, and she was nothing but heat.

Each one of the girl's breaths fanned a longing in me until the warmth we shared was tinged with the darkness of all I'd missed as a child. I imagined it to be like a mother's vertigo, where love, and the fear of its loss, could tear you apart. I gripped Helge more tightly, needing her assurance that even I, whose own mother had stepped back from the maelstrom, might one day know this kind of destruction.

"Krupp, IG Farben, and United Steelworks," Joseph's voice cut through the wall of the nursery. "Von Boehlen, Bosch, Schnitzler, the typical plutocrats." He paused, then started again. His voice was muffled. It finally rose in anger. "We got three million out of them, but we gave unprecedented rearmament..." I couldn't make out the rest of what he was saying. "U-boats," popped up, then, "Admiral Raeder," and "Kiel."

Thad had just returned from Kiel. His terse *who? what? and whys?* whirred in my head, but I couldn't hear more. I had to get closer, so I carried the sleeping Helge into the hall.

The door to the adjoining room was ajar. I edged closer. I saw the back of Goebbels' head and the curve of the phone horn. "They've turned their backs!" he barked. "We didn't sacrifice your men to the Red murder columns to line industrialists' pockets."

After several seconds, he shouted, "What else do we have to give!"

The girl wailed. I froze. The phone crashed on the cradle, and Joseph's head spun around. His bulbous eyes came at me through the crack in the door.

"What are you doing, Fraulein?" He yanked the door wide.

My voice shook as I dug for an excuse. "Helge fell asleep in my lap. I came to see if Frau Goebbels wanted me to put her to bed."

"Did Frau Goebbels ask you to do that?"

There was no ground beneath me. The girl's cries fractured my thoughts. If she wasn't so loud, I might have thought, but she was. I lied before I could think. 'Yes' barely came out.

"The child is crying, Fraulein. I can't hear you."

I shouted, "Yes."

"Yes, Frau Goebbels asked you that?"

"Yes!" I shouted, again. Magda's heels tapped toward us.

"Frau Goebbels doesn't ask people to find her. If she wants you, she rings for you. Did Frau Goebbels ring for you, Fraulein?"

"No," I answered, then, louder, I repeated, "No, she didn't ring for me."

Clipping on large gold earrings, Magda said, "*Engelchen*, Eva's not a maid. She was doing me a favor. Why would she ever wait for a ring?"

The girl quieted with the sound of her mother's voice, and Magda took her.

With none of the coldness leaving his voice, he said, "Fraulein Schmidt was outside my study. She insisted you'd asked her to find you before she put the child to bed."

Joseph's doubt bore into me. Magda looked me up and down. The silence ached. It took too long. Joseph noticed. Sour bile stung the corners of my jaw.

Magda came back to life. "Darling, you've had such a long day, and still you're worried about me. The truth is, Helge's been wound up since I sacked Ada. Eva finally calmed her. I wanted to check on her before we left. Eva was doing just what I asked."

My breaths eased, and I collected my thoughts. "Shall I put Helge to bed, now?"

Magda handed Helge back to me. "Please do, Eva."

Joseph brought his hand to his chest, and bowed slightly. "I've been foolish, Fraulein Schmidt. Allow me to put the child to bed."

His hands grazed mine when he took her, leaving a chill where he'd touched. He kissed her, and she nestled against him. He kissed her again. "*Vati* loves his little Helge. *Vati's* sorry his baby had a hard day. *Vati's* so sorry," he repeated, and opened the door to the nursery. A funnel of light spilled across the nursery floor and cocooned the rocking chair I shouldn't have left. He placed her gently into her crib, keeping his hand on her back as she adjusted. Magda closed the door behind them, and started back to her bedroom.

"I'm sorry Magda," I said. "I thought I should find you. I didn't know what to do about bedtime. Helge was upset and Dr. Goebbels was so angry at me, but I didn't know why. I was confused. I said something stupid."

Magda raised an eyebrow. "That must be it," she said. It was a brush off. She looked at her watch. "Ada's left us in a terrible spot. If you can stay until we get back, it will be so helpful."

"Of course," I whispered.

She squeezed my wrist. "With you, it's as if I were staying with her." Her fingers dragged off my arm as she turned back to her room.

Joseph made a show of silently closing the door, and then turned to me with a conspiratorial smile. In a hushed voice, he said, "Leaving undetected is the hardest part." He cocked an ear toward Helge's door. I could see him mentally counting down the seconds. After 30, he stood straight.

With his hand held out, he guided me farther down the hall. He didn't touch me, but I felt his push. When we were a safe distance from the nursery, he shook my hand. Without letting go, he spoke. "Magda was right to let Ada go. She violated our trust."

My hand started to sweat in his. "I'm sorry," I said, wanting to pull away, but he held it tighter.

"When you let a woman into your home, when you entrust her with your child, you bring her into your family."

The mound under his forefinger pressed into my thumb. "We need complete faith in those who work for us. Any untruth by them to us, any representations about us to others, any storytelling at all, is a betrayal. Ada will hear from me, as she has heard from Magda. She'll learn from her mistake."

A thin layer of sweat spread to my scalp, and under my arms. His cologne caught in my throat. In my fight not to cough, hot redness covered my face. He saw it, but he didn't let go of my hand.

"I say this so you'll understand. Magda, in almost every case, employs impeccable judgment in selecting her staff. I'm quite certain this unpleasantness with Ada won't recur." He stared into my eyes for a long beat, then, with a lipless smile, he dropped my hand. "You've done us a good turn, tonight, Fraulein Schmidt. My wife has decided on you. She does seem to love you."

33

EVA

A blue and gold box of Lindt chocolates arrived at Herr Perl-stein's from the Kaiserhof gift shop. The card was handwritten.

Magda and I are grateful for your help last night. We couldn't have done it without you. Enjoy!

Yrs.
Joseph

I desperately tried to remember whether I'd told Hans or Magda the name of the shop. If I didn't, Joseph would have had to find it on his own. Were the chocolates a warning? Was he telling me I couldn't escape him? I crumpled the card and shoved it in my apron pocket. I still felt his sweat on my hand. I saw his mouth saying, 'She will learn from her mistake.' Its long, weak line was branded in my memory, waiting for any false step.

Paulina clapped her hands. "They must be from the American. Who else would buy imported chocolates?"

"Take them," I said, shoving them at her. "I don't want them."

Her glee turned to suspicion. "Why do you think I want them, then?" She thrust her chin at Ruth. "Give them to the girl." Paulina held the box out. "These are Swiss chocolates, Ruth. Very fine. They cost more than you make in a week. Would you like them?"

Ruth hunched so only her eyes peeked over her machine. "*Tref*," she said.

"You're in Germany, now. Speak our language."

"Not Kosher." Ruth stuttered, her face blotching red.

"Isn't that grand! She's too good for them." Paulina's face tightened into a sour pucker. She gave me back the box, but didn't take her eyes from it.

I untied the gold ribbon.

"I suppose, if it's all the same," she started.

I slid my finger beneath each piece of tape and carefully unwrapped the paper.

"A few wouldn't . . ."

I opened the lid.

"A few couldn't . . ."

Fixing my eyes on hers, I tilted the box until every last chocolate thudded into the trash.

"Magda saved you. Why?" Thad asked. A Moorish lantern cut shadows against the restaurant wall behind him. We sat at a brass tray table loaded with grape leaves, haloumi, kebabs and steaming flatbread.

"I have no idea."

"You need to know. She wants something from you. What is it?"

"Goebbels said she's decided on me. There's not always a reason." I smiled. Thad didn't.

"You can't count on that. You got lucky. Never lie. I don't know why you did."

"I panicked!"

"You shouldn't have. Women walk with babies all the time. Make him think he's paranoid for asking you. He already knows that about himself. Strike your chord. Be the gypsy. You're strongest when you're her. Only lie if there's no other way out."

"The gypsy's a lie, Thad! Goebbels can crush her. Then she'll be gone, and there'll just be me."

"I don't believe that." Thad took a sip of Raki.

"He hates me."

"Goebbels doesn't hate people. People are only good for him or bad for him. He doesn't know about you, yet."

"I know he thinks I'm bad for him."

Thad speared his kebab with his fork and dipped it in yogurt. "If he does, it's because you have power over people."

"That's absurd." The conversation, along with the piles of food, made me nauseous.

"Tell me you know this! You trade in self-fulfilling prophecies. You see how things should be for people, you persuade them, and then you push them to where you've said they should be. Goebbels thinks only he should be able to do that."

He stopped talking when a waitress brought us tea. He took his with sugar, and without asking, he put a spoonful in mine.

I pushed it away. "I'll quit. I won't go back there."

"I don't think Magda will let you go. Besides, you seem to like her."

"Don't say that!" He'd struck his chord.

"There's no shame in it."

"For you, maybe." A dollop of his yogurt landed in anchovy oil.

"I don't understand," he said.

"I don't want her to like me, and I don't want to like her! I don't want you to want me to like her! It would be a lie! You said not to lie!"

But it wasn't a lie. I had decided on her, too, and Thad told me that made me strong, and powerful.

34

HANS

"There's a stupendous piece of ass everywhere you look." Helldorf points to a six-foot blond who waits, rapt, for Erik Hanussen to start his show. "Her, too," he says of a Garbo doppelganger who's trailing her fingers through a fountain. Eva's not listening. She's looking at anyone but Helldorf. I'm sure Magda got in her ear about him. Eva refused to come until I showed her his handwritten note with the SA insignia. *I insist you bring your diviner. I'm not through with her yet. Your names are on the list.*

"Women love magicians," Helldorf says. A uniform helps, a nice car, but there's little women won't do for magic."

Lizards and snakes crawl in multi-colored paint across the floor. Slanty-eyed Buddhas hover in corners, and the walls are tiled with lions, scorpions, and rams. Every type of person is at this party. There are models and mobsters, Nazis and Social Democrats. The magnificent German mistress of the Egyptian envoy, Hassan Nachat Pasha, is here, though the Ambassador is not. Only the wildest among the diplomatic corps would show their faces at the Palace of the Occult. When Eva and I walked in, I swear I even heard a couple whispering to each other in Yiddish, as if it were a love language. Some of my schoolmates spoke Yiddish. There's nothing romantic about it. Although, there are a few words better said in Yiddish than in any other language.

"Maria Paudler's over by the bull," the Count continued. "She's one of our brightest stars and this *Yid* got her to faint, just by touching her face."

"It's true? Hanussen's a *Yid*?" I grabbed Eva's arm to draw her into our conversation.

"He desperately tried to hide it." In a squeamish falsetto, Helldorf aped, "Please, Count, it's Communist propaganda. I've given my life to the Führer. Why do you think they've got it in for me?"

"What will you do to him?" I ask.

"For now, I'll take his money, as well as the earthy blond with the big lips he promised to send my way tonight."

"Who's he?" Eva asks.

"Hanussen," I tell her. I can't get over it. This man floats the SA, advises the Führer, and publishes a Nazi newspaper.

"What did he do?"

"He's a Jew!" I announce.

Eva draws back, shocked.

"It should disturb you, Fraulein," Helldorf interjected. "His lies are mind bending. Could there be anything more despicable or more pathetic than a Jew who spends all his time and money kissing my ass."

"*Chutzpah,*" I blurt. It's a mistake to speak their language in front of Helldorf. There are few in the Party who outdo him when it comes to Jew-hate, but I've had *schmuck, schnoz, and schlong* pattering around my head since I overheard the Jewish couple. "I think that's what they call it. *Chutzpah.* They're proud of it."

"No one should be surprised. Most magicians are Jews. Deception is their natural state. Houdini was the master."

"Houdini never lied." Eva's voice is curt, almost rude. Has she forgotten who Helldorf is? "Everything Houdini did was explained by science, sleight of hand. He despised clairvoyants. He said they were thieves."

I have to stop her. "Your theory is proven correct, Count. Eva, too, has an out-sized fondness for a magician. Lucky for me, hers is dead."

"He was an escape artist," Eva says.

Now she's correcting me. There's something wrong with her tonight.

Helldorf takes over. "Forgive me for being imprecise, Fraulein Schmidt. I see I've touched a nerve. Though, I am curious how you would distinguish your work from that of the thief, Hanussen."

"I don't lie!"

She's too strong with this.

"I give people my best guess. There are no guarantees."

"No guarantees. That's exactly what Hanussen says. I'm disappointed. I liked the fortune you gave me. Now you're telling me to take it with a grain of salt?"

"It's your choice, Count Helldorf." Her jaw clenches. She straightens. She's becoming the gypsy, without fear. I'm afraid for her.

"What is it you think you do for people?" the Count asks. He's changed, too. He's the interrogator. Does she see it?

"I give my customers advice without judgment. I take their side."

"Is that what Frau Goebbels wants from you? The honor of your sympathy?"

Helldorf thinks he's got her. I glare at Eva to end it. She gives me a quick look. She must see she's in over her head, but she takes a breath and musters even more confidence.

"Empathy is the goal for all my customers, Count Helldorf. Even you."

I can't believe this. She doesn't know his game.

"So, you're a psychologist. You're Dr. Freud."

She fakes a pout. "You've hurt my feelings again. Psychology? That profession actually is controlled by Jews."

"So, I don't have to be concerned about your origins, Fraulein Schmidt?"

She holds out her palm so her fingers almost touch his chest. Her eyes are electric. "What do you think?"

35

EVA

"You've talked me into knots, Fraulein," Helldorf said. His breath smelled inky from drinking. "I have no reason to believe anything you say, yet I believe everything that falls from your lips." He ran the back of his hand down my cheek. His signet ring slipped like ice across my skin.

I believe you, he'd said, *but I don't have to,* he meant. I'd been strong. I never lied. It took everything I had, and it did nothing to silence my fear. I pictured Helldorf's thoughts. *You thought the idea of a Jew giving comfort to the most powerful among us was too grotesque for even a Nazi to imagine. There is nothing a Nazi can't imagine.*

"She has that power," Hans added, nervously tapping his thigh. I didn't look at him.

The Count pointed to a trio of brownshirts. "Watch her or you'll lose her to one of these roughnecks. She's much too good for them."

"Perhaps I should learn magic," Hans said.

"It couldn't hurt." Helldorf bowed, and left us.

When he was gone, Hans turned on me. "If you were a man, you'd be dead by now."

Hanussen entered from a draped archway. He homed in on the Count. The two shook hands. Hanussen had to stand on his toes to whisper to Helldorf. Helldorf threw his head back in a loud laugh. Hanussen reached into his breast pocket for an envelope. The Count slid it into his own. He placed his arm around the little man, and they talked more. It was Hanussen who finally begged off.

Hans watched them, too. "To state what is obvious," he said. "Whom the Count is pleased with today, and whom the Count is pleased with tomorrow, is entirely incidental."

"I understand." I had no more energy for Hans. Helldorf had come too close to breaking me.

"You don't act like you understand."

"He called me a fraud!"

"You brought that up. He was making small talk about magicians."

"Are you angry, worried, or just jealous? I can't figure"—

"Stop!" he demanded.

"Stop what?"

"Stop figuring out. Stop thinking. I'm tired of your mask. You should be yourself when you're with me."

The urge to scream banged at my temples. *Who is that? Who could that possibly be?*

I wanted to be in the orphanage again. I wanted my spiritual mother. I wanted to see her, and to talk to her about Goethe and God. Just to hear her voice would be enough. Her absence followed me home in the car. It sat with me through Hans' silence. It carried me up my four flights, past the broken spindles, and over the paint splattered steps. It drew my hand to my nightstand, and I dug out the envelope I'd buried unopened weeks before, waiting for a better day.

March 5, 1933

Dear Eva,

I wrote this prayer last year as the anti-Semitism built: Thunderous rage fills me! I will preserve it, it shall burn in me—as long as what rightfully arouses it exists. I will not become lenient. I hope that I may retain the strength to cry out in passionate anger, again and again, to condemn every injustice!

Eva, pray to stay on the right path, to be strong and clear-eyed in the face of evil.

As Always,
Frau Pappenheim

Her pride was a blunt object, beating me over the head. I read the letter again and again, searching for a place into which I could fit. I scrounged for a hint of something that was meant for me, not for the person I should have been, not for the person I'd left so far behind. There was nothing. I took out a sheet of paper and scrawled her a note. *I miss you. I'm doing my best. It's not close to enough.*

36

EVA

The fan blades cast sweeping shadows across the *klub* floor. Matthias and Zara sat, shrouded by the dim light. Matthias gazed at two cardboard suitcases by his feet. Zara seemed to be pleading for something, but her words bounced off him. They were like magazine photos slapped together in a montage.

My heart sank. "Where are you going, Matthias?"

He blinked. His voice was dull, rhythmic. "I lost my scholarship. I was evicted from my flat. Johann moved to Hamburg to live with his sister. I have no place to go." He turned to Zara, his expression unchanged. "Am I forgetting anything?"

Only his coldness registered with me. "But, you're so close to finishing!" I said. Jewish people were losing academic positions everywhere, as were professionals, and any kind of civil servant. It was national policy. But it seemed too big to be true. "Get your advisor to help you," I insisted. "Or, that Professor who likes you, Professor Segel."

His dazed complacence unraveled. "He's been fired, Eva!"

"I'm sorry. I'm just shocked"—

"How many shocks do you need before you stop being shocked? It's the law! What don't you understand?"

hing! I don't understand everything!" Matthias always
...st answer to any problem. I needed him to have an answer
to this.

He withdrew into his bubble.

"He needs a place to stay," Zara said.

"Stay at my place," I insisted. "I sleep at Thad's apartment often
enough." I wished I had thought of it from the beginning, and I was
relieved to have something to offer.

Matthias shook his head. "What happens when you're not at
Thad's?"

I wasn't going to let him back out. "You can sleep on the floor.
It's better than on a bench in the Tiergarten."

"And Frau Koch?" Zara asked. Our landlady presided over her
unwed tenants like an abbess. She would never allow it.

"We'll tell her you're not really a man. In that way, I mean."

"She won't approve of that either," Zara chided.

"Stop saying no and think of something better!" I snapped. I was
proud to be clear-eyed for once, as Frau Pappenheim had demanded.

Matthias's leg jiggled up and down.

Zara thought for a minute. "She lets my brother stay with me
when he comes from Leipzig. We can say Matthias is your brother."

A spark of possibility flashed across his face.

"No!" I stammered, before she finished the sentence.

"Why not?" Zara pushed.

"Because, it's an obvious lie."

"How would Frau Bloch know that? No one knows a thing
about you."

"Stop going back to that! She knows I'm an orphan."

"Then say he's your cousin, or your father, for all Matthias cares.
Say he traced you through your orphanage. Say it's a miracle." Her
rhinestone barrette cast a shimmering glow on my arm.

"Why don't you say he's your brother?" I demanded.

Matthias's jaw clenched. He'd started to read beneath my lines.

"Because Frau Bloch knows my family. Besides, Matthias and I look nothing alike. But you"—

"Stop, Zara," Matthias interjected.

I was digging my own grave and I didn't know how to stop. "I'm going to sneak him in," I said, ignoring Matthias. "That's how I want to do it."

"You're both daft," Zara started.

"Zara, leave it," Matthias snapped.

"But why?" she begged.

He turned to me, giving me one more chance to alter my course, but I saw in his eyes what he already knew. With the same resignation he had when he told us he'd lost everything that mattered to him, he said, "She doesn't want people to think she's Jewish."

At last call, the tail of Matthias's film slapped against the projector. When he didn't come out, I pulled back the curtain. He was watching the metal reel circle around and around.

I held up my keys. "Come. At least for tonight. It's so late, and if you leave early, she'll never know."

He turned off the projector and everything went black. "I don't think so."

"I'm sorry, Matthias," was all I could say.

"I don't blame you," he said into the darkness. "You don't have to be different from the rest."

We were close enough to hug. "I'm going to stay in the basement," he told me. "Rudi's bringing blankets. Shmuel's already down there. We'll make a *shtetl*."

"Please, I want you to stay with me."

The overhead fluorescents sizzled and cracked, then flickered on blindingly bright. "But I don't want to stay with you."

37

EVA

"I have an early train tomorrow," Thad said when he opened the door.

"To where?"

"Vienna. For three days. It came up at the last minute, or I'd have told you."

I'd been on the edge of tears since I left work, and I feared this news would push me over. I couldn't bear for him to see it, so I studied his bookcase.

"Sit," he said, moving his cleaning off the couch. "I'll get you a drink." I watched him pour, and forced myself to cheer up.

"The head of my orphanage says beauty is as vital for the Viennese as air and water are for the rest of us."

"Maybe for some of them." He handed me my drink, then disappeared into his bedroom without a word. I had the feeling he was already gone.

"Take me with you! Ugly is what's vital here."

"That would be nice." His words dissipated as they reached me.

"Matthias lost his scholarship. He lost his lease."

"It's hardly surprising." Thad's belt buckle clanked to the floor.

"That's why I want to go with you!"

"You can't. It's for work."

I let the ice in my drink numb my lips. "You should be more like Christopher."

"Lazy and anti-Semitic?"

"Work never gets in the way of doing what he wants."

"Christopher doesn't care if he gets fired."

"Still."

"Do you want to be like Katharina? Spending afternoons in fittings and dressing for dinner? I assure you, very few women can pull it off with any success."

"You think I can't?"

"I'm saying Katharina's unusual because she's still interesting despite living an entirely uninteresting life."

"My life could hardly be called interesting."

"You're a fortune teller to the First Lady of the Reich. That's interesting by any standard."

The last time I'd seen Magda, we set up regular appointments. "I'm going to see her Mondays at 3:00."

He stood straighter. "See? Katharina would never do that."

"You mean, Katharina doesn't require a time slot to see people."

"If you were like Katharina, Magda wouldn't want you to come in the first place."

"Why not?"

"You would threaten the order of things. Magda needs to be the Queen Bee."

"So, I'm a drone?"

"You do little to challenge her."

"She pays me. I have a job. It's to listen to her. It's hardly appropriate to upset her."

"Why are we fighting about this?" he muttered.

"Because you act like I'm her maid."

"If you don't want to feel like a maid, do what Katharina would do."

"Put a von in front of my name?"

"Is it possible you've not already considered this? Use Magda. Use her underling. Get something out of them for yourself."

"How on earth would I do that?"

He kissed me on the head. "You're the one who sees the future. Make it less ugly."

Shmuel swiveled his mop in mesmerizing eights. He didn't look up when I entered. His yarmulke dangled from a bobby pin. I asked for Matthias and he grunted toward the basement. I couldn't help being hurt by his coldness. I'd always been nice to him.

The basement was dark and I had to feel my way through a maze of empty kegs and boxes to reach the line of light beneath the door to where Matthias was holed up.

I knocked, but got no response. "Matthias!" I shouted. "Please let me in." I was sad, and afraid to see him, but I wanted to get it over with. When he still didn't answer, I opened the door.

There were two piles of blankets, which must have served as Matthias and Shmuel's beds. Behind each were their worldly possessions: clothes, a few photos, dopp kits. Shmuel's side had leather bound books with gold letter-pressed titles, *Torah*, *Talmud*, *Mishnah*.

Matthias's side had a typewriter and a black movie poster with a menacing white hand. *M* was painted across it in blood. *M* was the first movie he worked on for Fritz Lang, and the man himself had signed the poster.

Matthias sat cross-legged at a card table, scribbling in a notebook. He was entirely unaware of my presence. A plate of half-eaten eggs and a drip stained coffee cup were pushed to the side. He was wearing the same clothes he'd worn the day before. His shirt was untucked and unbuttoned. He hadn't shaved.

"Matthias!" I called.

He looked up, blinked twice, and brushed his hair off his forehead, leaving an ink smudge over his eyebrow. "It's you," he said.

"How are you?"

When he rose, his raw energy sprang at me. "I'm great. I'm stupendous." His hands were shaking from too much caffeine. "I've figured everything out!"

"What, Matthias?" I urged, wanting a reason to be hopeful.

"It's all in here." His eyes blazed as he shoved the pad into my hands. There were pages of blue notes, black Xs and red arrows. It made no sense. I didn't know what to say. "Don't you see?" he asked. His sincerity took me aback.

"See what?"

"How German universities, which are full of highly intelligent and rational people, willingly embrace the distinctly unintelligent and irrational axiom that"—

Matthias grabbed his notebook from me and scrawled in letters too big for for the lines: MASS THEFT = JUSTICE

I was scared to say the wrong thing, so I just asked, "How do they do that?"

Exasperated by my slowness, he said, "Universities are not rational, they rationalize. That's what's here. It's a mathematical proof of the irrational."

"Of course," I said too eagerly, as if that could release me from his mental flight.

"The Nazi professors, deans, student groups, whoever else, can't start out advocating mass theft. Too many students would reject them out of hand, find them cruel. So, they break it down into successive steps, taught over time. Matthias points to his notes, and reads:

1. Germans = good/decent people. Good/decent people deserve good decent life, i.e. flats, scholarships

2. When good people don't get what they deserve, they're denied Those denied = victims.

3. Zero Sum Game: To have less than deserved requires someone else to have more than deserved. (By def. we live in a world w/finite resources.)

4. Jews = less than 1% of German population, but = 30% of lawyers, 16% of doctors, etc. Jews deny aryans → Jews owe aryans.

5. In state of laws, debts not willingly repaid are recoverable by the force of those laws.

6. Fairness dictates state MUST take Jewish property/positions & give to aryans.

Matthias coughed from all his talking, and drank the cold coffee until he stopped. He was coming to his conclusion and I was more than grateful. He said, "The University has done its job. Its patience has been rewarded. A highly rational professor doesn't have to say anything more than, 'what does one plus two plus three plus four, plus five, plus six equal?'"

I said nothing; he sagged.

"JUSTICE, Eva! They think it equals justice." He slapped the notebook back on the table, and with a red pen wrote, QED.

His intensity pushed me to retreat. "That makes sense, I mean, I . . . it's interesting. Definitely."

The energy in his eyes softened into sadness. I couldn't bear for him to be disappointed in me again, so I said, "Of course, you're right. I see."

I pushed through the dark piles, rattling the boxes of empty bottles with my stumbling. I ran up the stairs, praying I wouldn't run into Shmuel, with his aloof contempt. I hid in the office for the 45 minutes it took for Rudi to arrive so I would not have to be alone with these two broken men.

Matthias had cast me as one of Frau Pappenheim's *Them*. He'd erased me. I was part of his Greek Chorus, indistinguishable from the darkened mass watching his tragedy unfold. Herr Perlstein, Matthias, Shmuel and even Ruth, saw me that way. With the flood of their disappointment pouring in, I had no more thumbs to jam into the dikes.

I wanted to go back to when Zara dreamed of a boyfriend, Matthias dreamed of making movies with Fritz Lang, and I dreamed that friendship was enough to make a home.

I had to act. Thad had planted the seed. My Nazi acquaintances would be my life raft. They would make my little corner of Germany beautiful again. They would give Matthias his scholarship back. He and Shmuel and everyone else would see that I was better than they thought, that my friendship was worth something. Life at the *klub* would go back to normal, and we could all rest on top of the water, with the sun on our faces, even if just for a moment.

Hans had said he would come by, and I'd agreed because I was going to tell him I didn't like the way he treated me with Helldorf, that I didn't want to see him again. But for Matthias, for all of us, I changed my mind. I stole into the bathroom and took off my jewelry, reclipped my barrettes and pinched my cheeks to redden them. I checked myself in the flecked mirror, and waited.

38

HANS

"What is it?" I ask Eva.

She shakes her head.

"Tell me," I plead. She has the lost look of a girl without a mother. Most people wouldn't notice, but I'm a boy without a father.

"It's Matthias."

Icy water splashes in my face. "Did he hurt you?"

"God, no. He's one of my best friends."

The cold becomes an itch. "What is it, then?"

"He lost his scholarship. He's so close to finishing, and he was expelled. It's not fair."

This notion of fairness is frustrating. There are winners and losers in any system. In the Republic, the Jews were winners and the Germans were losers. Now it's our turn to win. But people only see the negative. Eva's a daughter of Weimar, and in so many ways, this is still Weimar's Berlin. If you aren't pessimistic, if you don't find fault in everything, you're stupid. In Berlin, if your life isn't miserable, you must be doing something wrong.

I point to the smut peddler's black curtain. "Did he put you up to this?"

"He never would do that! You asked why I'm upset. I told you. I thought you wanted me to be open with you. You said you wanted me to be myself. I want to help him. I don't know how."

Something changes in her face. She has an idea. It attaches to me. I can say the words before she says them.

"If it's not too much, could you help?" Her bottom lip softens. It is the slightest bit wet. She finally understands what it means to know me. I should tell her how things should be, that Germans should prosper in their own country. I should tell her that I could spend my entire day making exceptions for this Jew or that Jew, and sometimes I do. I hear stories that are so awful, they make me want to call the whole thing off. But I won't. *That* would be unfair. Of course, I don't say that. I like that she thinks I'm powerful. I like that she thinks I'm kind, and I love that this beautiful creature looks at me like she needs me very badly.

"Perhaps," I say slowly. Her shoulders rise, her mouth opens more, she holds her breath. "I may be able to find a solution."

Her relief melts me. I turn her chin to face me. "On one condition," I say.

She's nervous. She thinks she's going to have to pay me back, but that's not it at all. I'm going to give her something else. I kiss her, so gently, on the lips.

A faint smile. A slightly audible thank you. It's all I need.

39

EVA

Matthias drew invisible circles around himself that warned not to trespass. Even when he was behind me, I could feel him watching, and when I looked at him, his eyes clung to mine, as though they were all that were left of him. He'd seen a man with a swastika kiss me, and he cut me off.

A quiet moment left us no excuse not to speak. "What is it?" I asked, moving to Rudi, who stared over his glasses at the cash register, as if suddenly the numbers and buttons demanded his entire focus. Matthias's stare didn't break. "You scare me sometimes, Matthias."

"I don't scare you. I make you uncomfortable."

"Have it as you like, but I wish you'd stop."

"The difference is important. I would never hurt you. I wouldn't hurt anyone, so it can't be that I scare you. It's your friend with the swastika who should *scare* you."

"He's not my friend! And honestly, he wouldn't hurt me either," I said. "He probably wouldn't hurt a fly."

"I expect he wouldn't hurt you or a fly, Eva, but he would hurt me. That's the problem. We both know that doesn't scare you, and *that*," he paused, "is why I make you uncomfortable."

"No, Matthias! You make me uncomfortable, you *hurt* me, because I care so much about you, but you're so angry, I don't know where it stops."

"It doesn't stop with you kissing a Nazi, if that's what you want me to say."

My restraint turned to rubble. "And, it doesn't stop for the second it would take you to see *he* kissed me, and *I* walked away from him. It doesn't stop for you to consider that I never would have that kind of relationship with him, and it doesn't stop even though you know I'm on your side."

"Not kissing back isn't the same as being on my side."

A flare went off in me. "I did it for you, Matthias! I did it because he said he would help you get your scholarship back!"

Matthias's anger blunted into shock.

"What now?" I demanded.

His hands shook as he pulled his hair back from his face. Each word required its own exhale. Each landed a separate blow. "You—Actually—Thought—I—Would—Take—It—Back."

"Forgive me for trying to make things right, Matthias! Forgive me for wanting you back!" I shouted.

His incredulity erupted in ashy spew at my feet. "How pathetically you're grasping at straws. How desperately you want to do your bit. You didn't do this for me. You just want to stop feeling guilty."

"You have no idea what you're talking about, Matthias." I couldn't compete with his anger. I turned to Rudi. He held up his hands.

Matthias's sunken chest, his hunger, was the last thing I saw of him when I turned away.

I went to Thad's apartment. He was still in Vienna, but I didn't care. I loved the first moment I walked through his door. I loved his clean order, and that there was nothing extra. I loved the smell, which could only belong to a man. I loved that it was high up, and that I could breathe there.

Matthias made me feel so foolish. Maybe I didn't think things through, but how could he say I did it for myself? I did it for all of us, for the family we'd been. It was easy for him to use his wide-angle lens on life. He stood on the shoulders of others. He had a family to catch him when he fell, a community, a university to give him new perspectives.

I was taught strict rules to keep from offending people by my existence. I was taught to slide into my narrow space and conform to its edges. How could he blame me for needing our little life more than he did? How could he blame me for not being able to see past it?

If he didn't want the scholarship, he wouldn't get it. I would tell Hans no further effort was needed on his behalf. We would proceed any way he chose. I would expect nothing from him. The way we'd been before, the home we'd built together, was gone. There was no hope left in it.

I took off my clothes and climbed between Thad's cold, freshly ironed sheets. I cradled his pillow between my arms and for the first time in three years, I prayed: *May it be your will, Adonai, My God, and the God of my ancestors to lie me down in peace, and then rise me up in peace. Let no disturbing thoughts upset me, no evil dreams nor troubling fantasies. May my bed be complete and whole in your sight . . .*

40

HANS

She hadn't bothered to speak to me directly. She left a note at the receptionist's desk, and it was placed in my downstairs mailbox. Apparently, re: the matter of Matthias Altmann, there's nothing to be done. The smut peddler likes his life at the bar. He needs the money, wants the free beer. I'm to forget her request, though she's grateful for my offer to help.

The problem is, my secretary didn't bring me my messages until after lunch, after I had called in two favors at the University. I asked my contacts to give Herr Altmann a veteran's waiver, saying he fought for the Fatherland in 1918, at the age of thirteen, when all was lost. It wasn't recorded because of his age, the chaos surrounding the defeat, etcetera, but I knew his commander, and I could attest to the story. Anyone who checked would see it was a lie. His age wouldn't line up, to start. But no one will check because merit has nothing to do with this. It was a favor done for me so I could do one for Eva.

That's what pisses me off. I'm tired of her judging and questioning each little thing. Her guilt over Matthias Altmann is selfish, not moral. She wants all the good we bring without the compromises. She needs to think she's better than us.

212 / Jill Morningstar

Why can't I be done with her! My life would be so much easier without her constant torment. I brought a waitress home from the Augustiner Brauhaus last week. There was nothing tormenting about her. She was all in. But, of course, Eva's the one I can't resist. With her, I'm smart and strong, and better than I am.

The phone rings. I bark *Lorenz* into the receiver, wondering who could be bothering me at this hour. Joseph is at a film premiere. I couldn't go because, having spent so much of my day doing Eva's bidding, I got little actual work done.

Magda's voice demands, "Where is he?"

"At the premiere," I say.

"I'm at the premiere and I assure you, he is not."

"Then he's running late. He had pre-theater dinner with von Ribbentrop."

"No, Hans. He was here. Now he's gone."

We've been through this before. She knows I know Joseph ran off to sleep with the starlet. She's weighing whether to blame me for lying to her, because doing so would expose her hurt.

"Pick me up." The phone bangs hard in my ear.

The wind lashes Magda's gown against her ankles. Wisps of hair wing across her face. Joseph's car is gone. She doesn't look at me when I pull up. She's picturing Joseph doing what he's doing. The worried film director helps her into the front seat. "Do feel better, Madam," he says.

After he closes the door, she barks, "Take me home." She stares at the dashboard as if she'll smash it.

I've learned not to speak at times like these, and I merge into the traffic. I only see the trail of tail lights in front of me. Her tension wrings the air from the car.

"Stop here," she says. It's a block before the entrance to her building. She can't think I'll drop her short of her door. Her head tilts to the side and she studies my face. I stare straight ahead, unsure what to do.

From the corner of my eye, I see a smile. I feel the cool enamel of her nail polish tracing my jawbone. It curves around the back of my ear and rakes through my hair. My body is stone. She rests one finger on my lips, then slowly draws it under my chin. It presses against my throat. I can't unclench myself. If anyone witnesses this, I'm dead. Her face is so close to mine, it hurts to look at her. She can't be doing what I think she's doing. Her breath tickles my lips.

"It's true what people say, Hans," she whispers, sending a chill up my neck. "You are too sweet to love."

41

HANS

It's a Yiddish word, but it fits in my case. *Schnook*. I'm a *schnook*, a dupe. I let people stomp all over me. I learned it from the *Yids* in my school. With Magda's Jewish background, it's probably what she was thinking when I sat in my car like a *putz* while she humiliated me to my face. There's another one. *Putz.* I'm a *putz,* a fool. "Too sweet to love," is how she put it with her breath on my lips. "Too sweet to love," I say, picking up the Waterford decanter from my mantel. "Too sweet to love," I repeat as I take one of the matching snifters from a silver tray and pour a double shot of brandy. The tray is tarnished. Did my maid do slip-shod work because she knows I am a *schnook* and a *putz* and I don't have the balls to tell her to do it again?

I need to know who planted the idea of my weakness into Magda's head. It couldn't have been the girls in the typing pool. They would never call me sweet after what happened with Dagmar. Nor could it have been the women who fawn all over Friedrich Graff. I'm certain I'm too sweet for them, but Magda wouldn't have talked to them, or to the girls from the typing pool or to Viktoria Morelli or to the waitress from Augustiner Brauhaus, for that matter. There's only one woman I know to whom Magda gives the time of day, and I have a simmering pit in my stomach when I think it was her.

I had thought Eva was different. But apparently, even the nicest girls don't want to have anything to do with the nicest boys. No one falls for a *schnook*. I know this, but I let her trample all over me to help Matthias Altmann. *Too sweet!* It's my curse.

I sit on the divan. It and an end table are the only furniture in the room. The emptiness depresses me. The sofa is too far from the fire, and now I'm cold. When I move it closer, a painful twinge shoots up my back and I drop it, driving a divot into the wood floor. It wouldn't have happened if my rug wasn't on back-order. Everything is shit.

I move the end table forward, but I forget to remove the papers. The contents of my office inbox fall every which way.

"Fuck!" I shout, and hurl my empty glass against the couch. The glass doesn't break. I pick it up and whip it to the ground. Shards of wet crystal skate across the floor. "Fuck!" I shout again, because the snifter was part of a set. I down another brandy, and when it's gone, I throw that glass at the wall. I drink one more. It's heat tempers me. My jaw relaxes first, then my neck, shoulders and back. I get on my knees to gather the loose papers. There are memos, a stack of articles I was too bored to read at work, and a flier for a Swabian restaurant near the ministry—'The best *spätzle* in Berlin!'

Under the divan, askew among crystal chunks, is an envelope with Eva's handwriting. A nervous flutter tickles my stomach. I take it into the hall to get away from the mess. The card is robin's egg blue with white trim.

Dear Hans,

Thank you for helping Matthias. So many others would not have gone out of their way for him. That is what is kind about you. I'm sorry for the wild goose chase. Despite how things ended, I'm grateful for your generosity.

Respectfully,
Eva

I etch *kind*, *grateful,* and *respectfully* into my brain. My thoughts slide into their proper place, and everything is clear again. Eva is different. She doesn't love me, but she's not cruel like Magda, or a climber like the ones who go with Friedrich. She's better than them. With her, I'm not a *schnook* or a *putz,* and she knows it.

42

EVA

The morning after Thad got back, he walked ahead to hail a taxi to take me to work. The wind blew my scarf into my face. I reassembled, and heard someone say, "Fraulein Schmidt." It was Ursula. She was cradling a dress box. Salons always opened early for Magda.

Thad didn't see her and shouted, "I might be able to see you when you get off work tonight. I'll leave a message at the bar." His American accent sounded more extreme with each word.

"Is that man talking to you?" Ursula asked.

"I thought he was talking to you, Ursula."

"But you walked out with him."

"I've never seen him," I protested. "*Mein Herr*!" I shouted. "Are you speaking to us?"

He looked back as a taxi pulled up. Gripping the door handle with one hand and without missing a step, he said, "My apologies, Madam, I mistook you for my wife."

When the taxi pulled away, Ursula's eyes grew mockingly wide. "This sure is a big coincidence with you working in a bar, and all."

"What's your point, Ursula?"

She gave an exaggerated shrug. "I just never heard of a Ku'damm husband with a wife who works in a bar. You think I'm stupid compared to you, but even I know it's awful strange at 7:30 in the morning, to see you running out of the very same building, with the very same foreign-talking Ku'damm husband whose wife does your very same job."

"I delivered a suit before work, Ursula." I pointed to her box from Salon Grete. "We're alike that way, delivering other people's clothes."

Ursula rocked the dress box like a baby. "Still, it makes for a good story, this big coincidence, don't you think?"

"What do you say, Eva? You're the professional." Magda turned side to side in front of her dressing room mirror. The dress was a floor-length, black, silk halter.

"It's elegant, Magda. It fits you beautifully." I straightened the hem, then angled a mirror behind her so she could see the back. I searched every part of her for evidence she knew about my 'big coincidence.'

"Hand me that," she said, pointing to a silver fox stole. "Does it work?" she asked after she tried it on.

"It's perfect," I said, because it was.

When she stepped back from the mirror, her heel caught in the corner of the dress box. "Ursula!" she snapped, kicking the box away. Ursula rushed in from the bedroom. "Do something with the trash, please." Ursula snatched the box, and chased after stray sheets of tissue paper as she left.

"Grete's a miracle worker," Magda said. "I was fitted yesterday. The Jews do have the best salons."

"I work for a Jew," I said, and held my breath.

"You must be good, then!"

"Herr Perlstein taught me well. The customers love him."

"I've always said, if the Jews leave Berlin, all its elegance will leave with them."

I jumped on her words. "Herr Perlstein won't leave Berlin. I could show you his—"

She stopped me. "Eva, you do have some explaining to do." Everything slowed. "Ursula told me she ran into you on the Ku'damm suspiciously early this morning. She said you were with a man! Is he the one we've discussed?"

Ursula poked her head across the threshold. "He was a foreigner, too! I could tell by the way he talked."

Magda's back shot up, and my stomach plunged. "Is this true, Eva?"

"He was nothing of the kind!" Blood burned in my face. What I'd said made no sense. "I'm sorry. You both were speaking at once. I couldn't follow.

I told you, Ursula, I didn't know that man. I don't understand why you're insisting on it. I was delivering a suit to a customer who's leaving on a trip today. And no, Magda," I sighed, forcing my tension out. "Unfortunately, I'm not seeing the man we discussed, and he's not a foreigner.

Four lies. It was ridiculous for Thad to tell me never to lie when my whole life was a lie.

Magda turned on the maid. "We don't abide malicious tongues, Ursula."

Ursula looked down. "Pardon, Madam. I must have misunderstood."

"Now, please, set up tea and biscuits in the parlor. How about chamomile today, Eva?"

"Whatever's easy, Ursula," I said with a casual smile, but there was pleading in my voice.

When she was gone, Magda said, "You do love this man, whomever he is, don't you?"

"Yes, Magda." No more lies.

She gave me a gentle nod, and stood up. "Don't pay Ursula any mind. She's not very bright. Joseph likes her, but only because she's protective of him."

I couldn't hide my terror. "Will she tell him I was with a foreigner?"

"You said you weren't."

"She still told you."

"Ursula knows Joseph doesn't tolerate lies."

I thought back to the sacked night nurse. *Ada will hear from me,* Joseph had said. "But what if he believes her?"

"Should he?"

"Of course not!"

"Then I'll be clear. I like you, Eva. I like you better than I like Ursula. Joseph likes Ursula. He likes me better than he likes Ursula. Ursula," she paused, "has no place to go with this. Now, unzip me, will you?"

I unhooked the clasp and pulled down the zipper. She looked at my reflection. "It's strange," she said. "You remind me of someone I used to know."

"I hope someone good."

She smirked. "I knew her in high school. We both needed to prove ourselves. We worked harder than everyone else. You have the same compulsion, the same need to please."

A tingling started in the side of my face. I didn't like her studying me, taking me apart, as if she were able to see in the mirror what I saw in myself.

"We were best friends." The words landed in sick thuds. Thad told me about Magda's best friend. She was Arlosoroff's sister. She was Jewish. There was a vexing flutter in my ears.

"She always liked to debate, but she rarely revealed her own opinions. She just asked questions, getting me to circle around to her point of view."

"Should I help Ursula with the tea?" I pleaded.

"She's gone from Germany, now. It never was her home. Not in her heart."

Magda let the dress fall. She stood in just a bra, with her hands on her hips. I looked away. "Look at me, Eva."

I raised my head, but I was falling.

"It's uncanny. You are so much like her."

From somewhere else, Salomé's voice came back. "Is she a gypsy?"

A humored smile parted Magda's lips. "No," she drawled. "Not in the least."

I was brittle, even as Zara whispered into my ear. Berlin University had written. Scholarship funds had been made available. They were looking for women to teach girls. "I know it's wrong, but I can't be a dime-a-dance girl the rest of my life."

An anxious voice droned in my skull. *Magda knows.*

"My father still has no job. If I don't take it, someone else will."
She can't know. She kissed me before I left.

"Matthias and I aren't even in the same department. Whether I take it or not makes no difference to him, but you know he'll blame me."

Magda said, 'I look forward to next time.'

"He may be right, but this could be better for him, too."

'Thank you,' she'd said. Twice.

"I'll be working less and Rudi can pay him more. He wants to be a movie director, not a lawyer."

She doesn't know.

"In a way, it's better for both of us, but he'll still hate me for it."

I have to be so much more careful.

Rudi looked up from a stack of receipts. "Matthias is gone. He left this morning."

"For where?" Zara asked.

"Laupheim," Rudi said. "He left this morning."

I wasn't ready for this. "But things are so much worse outside Berlin."

"He wanted to be with his family," Rudi said.

"We're his family!" I snapped.

His eyes magnified to fill the lenses of his glasses. "It's not about us," he scolded. "They need him."

I stared into the black curtain, searching for the Matthias of old, but I could see him only as he was during the past weeks, with his unkempt hair and unsettled anger. He wore his trauma like a war wound, a permanent scar. We could never forget it.

I turned to Zara. Her face mirrored my own mortified relief that we would no longer have to see his wounds, that the dogging guilt he'd held over us might finally vaporize, and that the space could be ours again.

43

EVA

"Take off the apron! We're going to Luna Park!" Thad announced. After a morning enduring the sewing machines'
portentous silence, his presence was a light switch turning me back
on. His flash made everything bright. "Some of the guys are golfing
at Baron von Dietrich's estate, but I stayed back."

"I can't imagine you'd rather go to an amusement park than
golf with your friends." I was glad he'd chosen me over them, and I
wanted him to admit it.

"The Baron complains I don't elevate his game." When he
pushed open the door we were met with a rush of warm air. It
brought me back to the Berlin I'd taken as my own. The café patios
were open and people lingered casually at lunch. An older man
nodded at me when I passed. Another left a generous tip. There
was the mother who dabbed at chocolate on her son's face, and the
pretty girl who couldn't resist squinting into the sun. These people
looked and acted the same as they did last spring. They surely could
remember what things used to be like, what was required of us as
good Germans. They would return to Herr Perlstein's shop. They
would give Matthias his scholarship back, or at least they would
think he should have it back. These light and lovely people could

see that mass theft has nothing to do with justice, and things would go back to normal again, as surely as winter became spring.

A clean-shaven brownshirt, younger than me, approached the patio with a stack of flyers. "Rally tomorrow! Rally for the Führer!" The kind mother and her chocolate-covered son rose, raising their arms in salute.

At Luna Park, Thad took me to the Bavarian Beer Village. He ordered *schweinebraten*, pork roast, for both of us, and I interrupted to ask for *sauerbraten*. I didn't keep kosher. I mixed milk and meat and ate from unclean plates, but pork instilled in me in fear of God.

The waiter, dressed in lederhosen, insisted the pork was the specialty of the house. "I had it yesterday," I said quickly. I didn't need to make excuses with Thad. He didn't track my preferences from meal to meal. My statement was directed at the waiter, and at the always lurking brownshirts with their groping hands and buckets of paint.

Without comment, he filled our steins with beer flowing from the mouth of a gnome statue.

"Look at that," Thad said. He reached for a grease stained copy of *Der Angriff*, which had been left at the next table, and read aloud.

The body of a Jew was found in an evergreen grove on the road from Bayreuth to Neuhof. He had been shot to death. His face was unrecognizable. At the morgue he was identified as Hermann Steinschneider, who under the name Erik Hanussen, had a certain vogue in Berlin as a clairvoyant.

A sharp pain yanked in my chest. "Why would someone kill him?"

"I suggest you ask your friends at the Ministry. They'll have a pretty good idea what happened to him. Why? Do you care for him?"

"I just saw him! He does what I do!"

Thad jiggled his leg under the table. "That Hanussen was a fortune teller wasn't his problem, Eva. He was a Jew. He lied about it. What did he think they would do?"

My mind raced as we walked down the terraces to the Halensee. *He was a Jew. He lied about it. What did he think they would do?* grated in my head. We passed the tart chute, named for the girls who would slide down it into their lovers' arms.

"Too bad it's closed," Thad said. "I would catch you."

"I'm not a tart," I said. *His face was unrecognizable,* came back. I pictured it.

"You've worked yourself into a foul mood."

A hunchback called to us from the *volkerschau,* the human zoo. He was selling postcards of war-painted American Indians and Pygmies wearing powdered wigs. A fat-faced Samoan taunted me from the rack. He became Hanussen staring up at Helldorf, his smile reducing his eyes to slits.

"No shows anymore," the vendor said. "Per order of the Propaganda Ministry. They don't want to create sympathy for the lesser races. I expect they fear we'll love the natural peoples as we do our pets."

Thad chuckled. "Are you going out of business?"

"The zoo's adapting. We have a new exhibit. It's welcomed by the Party, *Zwerge und Tiere,* Dwarves and Beasts. It will have no anthropological merit," he grumbled. "There's no learning in it."

My brain was swimming in Bavarian beer and panic. Of all people, Hanussen should have been able to find a way out. Had he tried? I was raw. "Who needs Samoans when we have a great show of our own with the Jews."

The hunchback's red eyes swiveled up at me. "Jews are the opposite," he barked. "There's nothing natural about the Jews."

"They live and breathe among us."

"Dr. Goebbels is correct. They're insolent and clever. There's nothing loving about them."

"They refuse to be our pets?"

Thad interrupted by buying the American Indian postcard. "For my office," he said, and dragged me away.

When we were out of earshot, he hissed, "Why can't you keep your wits about you?"

"Because I can't stand it."

"You need to learn to stand it or you won't survive. If that man knew your name, he could denounce you. I've seen what they do to people who are denounced, even American citizens. Yesterday, Christopher visited a guy from South Carolina in the hospital. He was flayed so badly you could see his back muscles under his skin. He could die because he refused to salute a bunch of brownshirts."

"I hate that old man. I want him to know I'm not like him."

"You have to know when to walk away from people like that. You knew what he was like."

I was about to protest, but he silenced me with a glare. "We were having fun. Can't we continue?"

He looked like he was ready to walk away from me. "You're right," I said, and took his hand. "I'm drunk. I'm sorry."

"Good!" he proclaimed. "Because this is serious fun." He pulled me onto the Devil's Wheel.

A group of brownshirts collected to his right. Thad watched me watch them. I grabbed his hands and squeezed them hard, suppressing my not fun feelings.

An alarm shrieked. The floor shook. My legs tensed as we started to spin. The ride's whipping speed brought tears to my eyes, fracturing Thad's image into an ugly blur. He was laughing at me. A scream scraped at my throat. I clung to Thad's hands until he let go. An exploding black, seared by fluorescent dots, blinded me and I went limp.

Somehow, I didn't hit the ground. The ride stopped. A merciful soul held me in his lap. "That was rough," he said.

The room kept spinning. Thad laughed as he staggered toward us. I was furious, and I turned to my rescuer. I saw brown fabric, a shirt buttoned all the way to his throat. I turned cold.

"Can you stand?" he asked in a pleasant voice. His face was inches above mine. He had a port wine stain at the base of his jaw that crept down his neck in a slow leak. His hand lay where the Bavarian brownshirt groped me. Would he discover me, too? I pushed against him to stand.

"Good catch," Thad said, pulling the brownshirt to his feet. "It's her first time on the ride." The brownshirt laughed. As I walked away, it felt like I was going down a moving staircase. When the sunlight smashed into me, I leaned over a railing and heaved into a bed of mulch.

Thad came up behind me. "Internal Memorandum, Attention: Thad Cartwright," he proclaimed. "Devil's Wheel before beer garden next time."

"Does she need water?" the stormtrooper asked.

"I'm fine!" I snapped.

"That would help," Thad replied.

I wretched again, splattering beer and *sauerbraten* across the woodchips. The brownshirt handed Thad a paper cup. "Take a sip," Thad said.

I ignored him.

He sent the SA man away with another thank you, and walked me behind a machinery shed.

"What are you doing?" he barked.

"Do you think this is a game?" My eyes stung with rage.

"It was an accident!"

"It was a test! You did it on purpose. You were cheering us like we were Pygmies in the *volkerschau*. Did you want to see how well I would walk away? Or, was it just to see how fun I could be?"

"That's ludicrous! As is treating a man with a truncheon like he's the enemy when all he did was help you!"

"He is the enemy!"

"You spend half your time with the worst of them. I wouldn't think you'd mind."

I felt a tremor first in my palm. It rolled up my arm. I wanted to hit him. "You're the one who says I can't say no. You're the one who drills me for every last detail about them! You can't do that one minute, then treat me like I'm one of them the next."

"I'm asking you to be more careful. What else should I do?"

"Stop trying to make me more: more brave, more strong, more fun, more like Katharina, more of anything different than what I am! I want you to want me!"

A line of sweat slid down his neck. "This isn't personal. I'm trying to protect you. That's what you should take personally."

"There it is! 'You should! You need!'" My rage only pushed him farther away. It was like he'd turned my volume to zero. "Nothing is personal to you. At best, we're data points for your memo's to Washington. At worst, we're all just amusements to spice up your banter at the Adlon bar. I can hear you and Christopher now. *What do you get when you cross a savage Hun together with an insolent, cle—*

I stopped breathing. I stopped hearing. I hadn't said it. I'd said nothing. I forced out every word that came to mind when I imagined myself in Thad's eyes. "Orphan! Shop girl! Gypsy! Gold digger! What else, Thad? What else do you see when you look at me?"

He was looking, but he wasn't seeing. He never had. My anger couldn't touch him. He was just exhausted by the non-tart with whom he wanted to have fun, but would never marry. And for that, I'd come so close to revealing myself.

Thad had taken everything from me. He'd divorced me from any moral integrity I had left from my spiritual mother. He'd extracted me from my friends at the bar. He'd driven me to the Nazis. Then, after he whipped me around and shook me upside down so the only thing I had left to keep from him was my greatest weakness, he still couldn't stop trying to improve me, as if I'd given him nothing at all.

"I'm done with this," I said, and ran all the way back to Scheunenviertel.

44

EVA

A day went by. There was no word from Thad. I punished my-self by walking in front of the Embassy, past the wrought iron gates, past the Jews lined up in front of the consular offices at the Esplanade, desperate for visas. I pictured Christopher inside, judging women's jewelry and furs to see if they were real, assessing the quality of leather that wrapped men's briefcases, trying to determine if this lawyer or that professor was *Likely to Become a Public Charge*, a parasite in the land where Thad always joked the early bird catches the worm and good things come to those who wait.

I peeked into the cafés we used to frequent, hoping he would see me, but he never emerged from the cliques of happy, busy people. Nor did he come to the *klub* or to the shop. He owed me no obligation or commitment.

That night, I dressed up and walked into the Adlon bar, as if I had any business or any money to spend there. I downed a shot of their cheapest schnapps and sat for the rest of the evening, smelling whisky, expensive tobacco and fresh cut flowers, an olfactory map to a world I'd studied to within an inch of its life, but no longer recognized me.

On the second day, I walked down Unter den Linden in my shop clothes. I looked like someone's maid. I was no longer an exception. I'd returned to my proper place.

A woman's voice sounded behind me. "I consider it my duty to look as attractive as I can. I will try through my own example to make German women into true representatives of their race. Germany should not have to look to Paris for good taste." It was Magda. I was mortified as much by how I looked as by what she'd said. I made for the corner, but it was too late. She called my name.

She was with a female reporter and she played the role of starlet beautifully. "Eva," she gushed, kissing me on both cheeks, "I've been so busy with the renovation, I haven't had a chance to breathe, never mind to see friends." She threw up her hands. "And look at me now, already having to run. We're talking about a fashion agency for the Reich.

"But, please do come by. Don't wait for Monday." She said 'do' and 'don't' with too much emphasis, more to the reporter than to me. I should have expected it. The exchange was for the writer to capture the *Reichsministerfrau's* authentic interaction with the working class.

When I stepped away, Magda came closer, blocking the journalist from view. It was as though a shade rolled up between us and the sun came through and warmed my face. "Come this afternoon," she said gently. "4:00 is good. I'll be at the apartment. I can see you're not well." She squeezed my forearm, and as fast she came, she was gone.

How strange that Thad had vanished the instant I'd run off, leaving me in the cinders. But the First Lady of the Reich, the woman Thad had wanted so much to know, was still here, and she had called my name.

"You judge my marriage," Magda said that afternoon.

"I would never do that," I insisted.

"My parents judge me for it. My former husband and many of my old friends do, too."

"But I don't."

"Why not?"

"It's bad for business."

"That, I can believe." She massaged the side of her neck, and said, "I'm going to tell you something even my former husband doesn't know. You can't share it. Not with a soul, do you hear me?

"Of course, Magda." I liked to hold her secrets.

"I was illegitimate at birth, too, Eva. I didn't find out until after Joseph and I were engaged. My father eventually married my mother, but they divorced soon after. They hid my taint from everyone. You know how damaging it can be."

It was as if she stripped a layer of darkness from me. Again, one of my worst things was part of her. She seemed to know exactly what I needed to hear, and she offered it selflessly.

"But Joseph accepted you!" I said, finally glimpsing why she must have loved him.

"Relationships redeem us, Eva. Joseph's strength made me stronger. My blond made him more beautiful; my height made him taller. My social grace, as he calls it, made him more gracious. His love lit up with how I bettered him.

"When I told him about my family, what made me better evaporated. His love went dark. It might have still been there, but if he couldn't see it, he didn't know if it was worth it."

"I'm so sorry." I felt her humiliation as an ache in my stomach.

"He couldn't pretend past the disgrace. I couldn't fix it, but I also couldn't let this one bad thing define me."

"What did you do?"

"I fought him, the way I always do."

"You had to!"

She smiled with appreciation. "Joseph said we had to take it to the Boss. He didn't want to bring shame to him or to the party. I knew he would cancel the wedding if Hitler objected.

"I've never thought of myself as weak. To beg at the Führer's feet was unbearable. He's always had an exalted image of me.

"When we arrived at his suite, he sat next to the fireplace. One of his drivers was on the opposite sofa. The driver didn't get up, so Joseph and I were forced to sit on a small bench in the back of the room, beyond the fire's heat. Joseph's blame pressed in on me. While he and the Führer exchanged inane pleasantries, the driver poked at the blackened logs until they broke into chunks, sending sparks up the chimney. He had no regard for the noise, no regard for the mess, and no regard for the smoke stinking up the room. I had to stop myself from throwing up all over the rug.

"When he finished, he stared at me, blank as a board. I'd been married to one of the wealthiest men in all of Germany, and this dolt, this former stone mason and ex-con was poised to witness my humiliation. I was already beneath him. No one would see past this stupid thing, not Hitler, not Joseph."

"But here you are."

Her face brightened. "I confessed, and Hitler brushed it off. Just like that." She aped his motion. "He said he loves all German children, regardless of provenance, and, as if amused by his power to forgive, he laughed, so we laughed, too. Even the driver laughed, then he got out of his seat and held the door for us to go.

"You see, Eva, Hitler erased my shame, but he shouldn't have needed to. Shame wastes us."

"It's always there for me."

"Say no to it. Take your freedom. You don't need someone else to approve it for you." As I digested her words, she saw my amazement. She cupped her hand over mine. "I just thought you'd want to know."

45

EVA

A camel's hair coat lit up in the neon flash. Thad's cheek beat black then red then black again in the rhythmic light. "Come talk to me," he said.

"I'm working."

"Take a break."

"I've taken a break."

"Just a cup of coffee. It'll be ten minutes." He held out his hand for me to pass, and followed me to a near-empty Chinese restaurant across the street.

Thad asked a half-bald Chinaman for a table in the shadow of a lacquered screen. I knew what the Chinaman thought, a well-dressed man with a made up, younger woman asking to sit in a darkened corner, but he did Thad's bidding. He summoned a girl to the table. Avoiding eye contact, she wiped a grayed rag over drabs of thick, brown sauce. Thad ordered tea and a plate of dumplings.

"Obviously, you're angry," he said. "But it has nothing to do with whatever you imagined happened at Luna Park."

"What's it about, then?" I wanted a reason to tear him apart.

"I think in terms of how things are. Things are good. You measure things by the likelihood they'll become what you want them to be in the future. I can't make that kind of choice. I have no idea where I'll be a year from now. I could be here, I could be in Tokyo. There's nothing I can do about it. I'm not in a position to commit to anyone."

It was as though he'd read about us in a War College report, and was retelling proven facts, all of which were geared toward making me look pathetic. I hadn't pressured him. It was the facts of my existence that did. I was poorer and weaker. I needed him more than he needed me. I could never escape it.

"Name one time I've made demands on your future."

"You do when you can't see past what's missing to what's actually there."

"You're a true American optimist," I swiped.

"And you're maddeningly negative. You're that way about yourself, too. You only think about what you're not." Counting my sins on his fingers, he enumerated, "You're not Betsy. You're not Katharina. You're not a tart. You're not someone's daughter"—

"Stop!" I banged my hand on the table, sloshing water from my glass. "That has nothing to do with it!"

He talked over my anger. "You're intelligent, talented, beautiful, and entirely unusual. But that's not good enough for you. There are plenty of Betsys right here in Berlin. I chose you."

He stroked the underside of my forearm with his thumb. The votive candle flickered with his movement, making shadows across my arm. I pulled it back. "Tell the truth, Thad. Would you be here if I wasn't close to Magda?"

He half-smiled when I said 'close.' I knew he thought Magda saw me as a servant, and it drove me mad. I feared his disdain too much to tell him that just that day, Magda had held my arm and told me her biggest secret. How could I retell the warmth in her voice and in her touch? He would never believe it.

"You hadn't met Magda when I started seeing you," he snapped.

"But you stayed for her. You wanted me to spy."

"You're not a spy, Eva. You're just well-positioned."

"And if I stop seeing Magda and Hans? If I lose my position, what then?"

Thad tapped a code on the table with his middle finger. Short, short, long. Short, short. "Then you'll be making a mistake. Everything's going so well."

"For whom, Thad?"

His face grayed. "For everyone, Eva."

"For you. It's only better for you. You're terrified I'll choose you over them, and they're the one thing I have that you need."

"I don't need anything from you. I have far better ways to get information. I also don't see why you think you have to choose one or the other when you don't."

"Because I was never enough for you without them. More precisely, I was never enough for whom you think you can be some day." It was the cruelest thing I could think to say, but he was unfazed.

"This is you talking about yourself. I'm through explaining myself. I can't force you to trust me."

I wanted to see beneath his words. "Tell me you'll never ask about Magda again. Tell me to stop seeing Hans," I demanded.

"Don't play games. You always say how much you hate Nazis. You have the chance to do something real against them, but you won't take it. I thought you were better than the German liberals who pack up their morality and move to Paris. I thought you wanted more in life than what you could eke out of it for yourself."

"I thought I was only well-positioned."

"If you're more intentional, who knows what you can be."

I shook my head. "You're the one who said to walk away."

"I said you need to know when to walk away."

I was spiraling. "This isn't about Germany. That's what you want it to be about. It's about just us."

The corner of his jaw pushed out and he glared. "I hope you know there's no 'just us' left for you anymore."

He dropped too much money on the table and walked out. I wrapped my hand around my cold teacup and dripped the dingy brown liquid into a pool around the coins. Without Thad's protection, the Chinaman was more open with his judgment. He shifted his gaze from me to the girl, with a look that suggested she was his by blood. Then he turned back to me with more contempt. "You done, lady?"

I plastered on a pleasant face to establish it was I who did the jilting. After all, what's more pathetic than a whore who lets her hopes run high? I mopped up my mess with a napkin and returned to work.

46

EVA

Hans took a table in the middle of the Excelsior bar. He accepted his colleagues' congratulations with well-practiced modesty. Beneath his cool, he was giddy. "Forty-thousand students and teachers, the Reich's brightest lights, all here because of our work," he explained. He took credit for everything at the demonstration: the raging bonfire, the attractiveness of the boys, and even the summer-like weather.

He'd written Goebbels' speech, which he repeated from memory: *The era of exaggerated Jewish intellectualism is now at an end . . . the future German man will not just be a man of books, but also a man of character!*

A reporter approached the table. "Edgar Mowrer, *Chicago Daily News*," he said, and offered Hans his hand. Hans declined to shake it.

"Was the burning a success, Herr Lorenz?" he asked. "Has the Fatherland's last independent thought vanished into the night?"

It was like flying to hear someone say these words in the open, without fear. The man was magnetic. I wanted to be like him. I wondered if Thad was right when he said I could be.

"We're not stupid, Mr. Mowrer. We know ideas don't burn. We torch the people's devotion to these ideas. As the strongest of men, we declare them lighter, and less consequential than air."

The reporter glanced at me, sparing no judgment, and my confidence crumbled.

"Is this the start of your Second Wave?" he pressed Hans.

"I don't know what you're talking about," Hans shot back.

"Reliable sources tell me Röhm and his SA boys are preparing to fight. What is it Dr. Goebbels says?" He turned his pad over and quoted, 'They're up to two million, and they've lost the fear of death.'"

"We won't give in to people who heil to extract favorable policies, then steal from the workers in our name."

"To whom are you referring, Herr Lorenz?"

Hans jabbed his finger on top of the table. "That's enough, Mr. Mowrer."

I'd never heard Hans speak so rudely before. Mowrer was pleased to have provoked it. When he left, I tried to catch his eye, to somehow win his approval, but he ignored me. Hans said, "He never should have spoken that way in front of you, Eva. It was an insult."

"I wasn't insulted."

"He insulted me in front of you, which means he insulted you, too." His sense of possession slid under my skin. I wanted to fight back, not for Thad, for me, to see if I could be like Mowrer, to see if I could make Hans fail.

"What does it mean when you say Second Wave?" I asked.

"It means to remove from power anyone who would fight for their narrow, financial interests, rather than for the good of the people."

"You sound like you're giving a campaign speech. Who do you mean? Will there be violence?"—

Hans squinted, as if I was a harsh light. I'd overstepped already. Hans snapped, "Mowrer refuses to accept that we have an entirely lawful revolution. If he prints his lies, we won't be able to guarantee his safety. His days in Germany are numbered."

"You threatened him for asking questions?"

"Not for asking questions. I take questions all day long. He's putting his nose where it doesn't belong, then lying about it in the press. It's not a threat. It's a warning. We're saving his life."

His heat assaulted me. Was he warning me too? My body itched as he sat silent. His face grayed. His gaze fixed on the bar. "Do you know that man?" he asked. "He's staring at you."

I froze. It was Thad. He leaned against the bar. His white collar glowed in the light. My voice rasped. "I've never seen him before." I was suspended over the scene, looking down at the two of them, numb.

"Not even in passing?"

"Why are you attacking me with this?"

"Why are you upset?"

"Because you don't believe me."

He backed off. "I should be happy when other men think you're attractive. Although," he paused, "not that one." I wiped my sweating hands against my skirt. "He's not German. I can see it clearly. He looks British, maybe American."

I fixed on each one of Thad's movements. If he said my name, or even approached me, he would prove me a liar. Yet, Thad showed as much concern for my peril as he did for each sip and swirl of his drink.

"You're looking at him, Eva. Do you think he's good looking?"

"Not at all."

"It's fine for you to admire him. You are a normal female, aren't you?"

"I'm looking at him because I disagree with you. He seems German to me."

"I'm well trained in this. It's not just how a person looks, it's how he carries himself. At the same time this man wears a dinner jacket, he slouches against the bar like a cut-rate cowboy. Only an American would stand like that. Should I ask him?"

"That would be rude."

"What's wrong with asking someone where they're from?"

"It's a question I would expect from an American, actually."

"You can be cruel, Eva. I don't like it."

"Forget that man. Tell me more about the event," I pleaded. "Tell me how things will get better."

Hans watched Thad toss bills onto the bar. He stared as Thad walked toward our table, his face a cool pool of indifference. How well I knew that face. *Walk away, walk away,* I repeated in my head, but Thad controlled the moment.

Hans sat up straight. His swastika lapel pin sparkled in the candlelight. When Thad was so close I could smell him, Hans held out his hand. Thad took it, as if surprised. My pulse thrummed in my temples.

"Hans Lorenz," Hans said. "Ministry of Information and Public Enlightenment." He handed his card to Thad. To see them touch turned my stomach.

Thad scanned it. "Thad Cartwright," he said, giving his card to Hans.

"My guest owes me a drink. I'd guessed you were an American, but an Assistant Military Attaché at the Embassy of the United States of America is an unexpected pleasure. Eva, we must be careful about what we say in front of this man. He's a spy."

"Only as a hobby, Herr Lorenz. My position is open, and far less interesting than you've implied."

"Excuse me, Colonel Cartwright. I've been rude. Meet Fraulein Schmidt."

Two words, 'We've met,' were all Thad needed to put an end to me.

"It's a pleasure, Fraulein Schultz, is it?"

I couldn't catch up. The silence raged until Hans interjected, "Schmidt, I said. Fraulein Schmidt." He enunciated the T obnoxiously.

"Forgive me, Fraulein Schmidt," Thad replied. "I have to head out, but enjoy the rest of your evening." His eyes dug deep inside me, bringing my nerve endings alive. He nodded goodbye. Hans did the same. As calmly as he'd come, he wove through the crowd and out the door, leaving me gasping for air in the bar's blue hum.

47

EVA

My anger poisoned each stitch I sewed into a summer shift. Thad made it so I couldn't go back to him, even if I wanted to. There were no more innocent explanations for us. He'd answered my question. Without 'my' Nazis, he didn't want me. He shouldn't have wanted me anyway. Despite my best efforts, I'd stolen nothing from Hans. I was stupid to think I could match the reporter's efforts, that I could do what Edgar Mowrer could not. So was Thad.

A tension headache burrowed into the base of my skull as Paulina chattered on about how she and her husband Werner were going to take advantage of the new opportunities. They would open their own shop. She picked up a tangle of thread that had fallen at Ruth's feet. "None of this!" she announced. "And none of this!" she said again, pulling at the drab gray sheet that separated the storefront from the workroom. "It will be spic and span, tip-top." I hated her stupid sayings.

When Herr Perlstein entered, she said, "Frau Goebbels herself will want me to make all her dresses." My silence in response layered on one more failure. He ignored us and motioned for Ruth to come to the front.

Paulina rushed to my side. "She's the first to go."

Of course, she was right because Aryans were protected from job loss. I walked to a dress form close to the front and pretended to pin the hem on a linen skirt. Herr Perlstein was speaking Yiddish, so I didn't understand all of what he said, but the gist was clear. He was warning her. If things didn't get better, he would have to let her go. He didn't want to. He had no choice.

As a religious girl, he was forbidden to touch her. He maintained his formal stance with his shoulders back and his hands held behind him. She couldn't see the back of him, so she couldn't see what I saw. His regret was plain in the way he gripped and re-gripped his fingers, in the way the back of his neck burned red at the hairline. She also couldn't know what I knew—that he cared for her deeply—because she had never seen the way his eyes went blank when he abandoned all attachment.

I wanted to let her know all this, but I couldn't reveal that I understood the Yiddish he spoke. She was like I was three years before, innocent and daunted. But I was certain she would never turn into what I'd become, and her gaze left me ashamed.

Herr Perlstein's door was open. I approached cautiously. He blinked his small, wide set eyes and stared with the flat face he reserved for me alone.

"Please," I said. "Give her some of my hours."

He nodded slightly, then returned to his ledgers. "Thank you," he said when I turned my back.

Ruth's long skirt dusted the floor as she pushed the trundle of her machine with her foot. She never took her eyes from her work except to look at the clock.

"How many are in your family, Ruth?" I asked. We were the only two left in the shop.

She seemed afraid, as if I were a Nazi making lists. Finally, she said, "Eight."

"Are you the oldest?"

"Yes."

"Will you celebrate tonight?" I asked.

"*Shabbos?*" Her eyes widened.

"Will you keep it?" I followed, using a term she might have used. I was tempting myself with this walk back into my old world. I'd loved *Shabbos,* and I wanted the feeling back. I was proud to wear my dress clothes, and to eat the extra courses, served one after the other. I loved the songs and the time we were granted to linger at the table without a bell calling us to study or do our chores. Most, I loved Frau Pappenheim's slower, softer self. She did nothing to direct us; but rather, took in our words, shared her ideas, and assured us of her love.

Ruth was confused, so I explained. "My best friend is Jewish, but we've grown apart. I want to be friends with him again." To say it almost made me cry.

She nodded. "I will keep it." Of course, I'd known her answer already. To observe *Shabbos* was what defined a religious Jew.

"My friend would tell you, *Gut Shabbos.* Did I say it right?"

"Yes. It's very nice."

"So now, I will say it to you. *Gut Shabbos*, Ruth."

She smiled broadly. "*Gut Shabbos,* Eva."

At closing, Ruth said, "You have good weekend, yes?" I said, "yes," but I wasn't ready to let her go. I didn't know if it was envy or Matthias that made me follow her, but I couldn't stop myself.

She walked quickly, looking neither right, nor left, until she got to Hamburgerstrasse. Her chin rose first, then her shoulders dropped. She tightened the bow on her pinafore and slowed her stride. For the first time I saw something graceful in her. She seemed older. She took me down a side street, and called out to someone as she entered a shop. In Yiddish, her voice flowed. A minute later she came out with a net bag filled with *challah*. When I reached the bakery, the smell of bread pulled me in. Metal trays piled with braided loaves lay behind a glass barrier. Their eggy glaze shone under the fluorescents. The smell brought me back to the orphanage when we ripped off steamy chunks of the braid and took our first bite.

The baker walked to the front, sweating from the ovens. His forearms were as thick as the loaves. I don't know what I thought he would say to me, but I dreaded his mistrust. "Name?" he asked, as he reached for a beat-up clipboard.

I was so pleased he thought I might have ordered, my whole face lit up. "I didn't order in advance."

"*Shayna*, pretty girl," he said. "You have to order by Thursday for Friday. Everything's taken. Try again next week. I'm happy to bake bread for you."

I would have paid almost anything for a piece of that bread, but his Yiddish words, meant for me, seeped into my chest with a slow warmth. "*Nexte Vokh*. Next week," bubbled from inside of me, and it was good enough.

The yeast smell clung to my clothes and hair as I left the bakery. I could have stood there, watching the people go in and out, thinking back to my childhood. I could have cried for the things I'd left behind, but if I did, the remnants would have stuck to me like the smell of bread, and I would not have been able to shake them off.

48

HANS

"Frau Goebbels is here to see you, Herr Lorenz," my secretary Anneliese says. Bile explodes in my gut. Magda never comes to my office. I shove my clutter into my desk and button my suit jacket. I haven't seen her since she touched my face and leveled her peculiar sort of insult. Anneliese steps into pause. "Of course, Herr Lorenz, I'll send her right in."

I rush to the door to open it but Magda is half way through by the time I get there. Anneliese is behind her, looking at me oddly, as if that's helpful. "Frau Goebbels," I say. There is an off-shine to her skin.

"Hans." She offers me her cheek, then sits in front of my desk. I'm not sure if I should sit behind the desk when the Reichsministerfrau is in the room, so I grab a stool and pull it next to the sofa. The stool leaves me with nothing to do with my hands and I rest them in my lap like a child. She stares at the standard behind my empty desk. It was sanctified by contact with the *blutfahne*, the blood standard of the Reich, the flag drenched by the martyrs' blood during the 1923 Beer Hall *Putsch*. The Führer presented it to me after we won the Reichstag last year. If I were sitting in my usual seat, I would be framed by it. What kind of idiot sits on a stool? A *putz* and a *schnook*, that's who.

Anneliese brings tea. When she's gone, I ask, "What is it, Magda?"

"I've been contacted," she says, looking at my empty chair.

"By?"

Now she smiles, so I smile, too.

She puts a spoonful of sugar in her tea. "By someone I used to know."

Her coyness comes close to flirtation. She's doing it again. "And?" I say, unable to hide my impatience.

Her spoon scrapes the porcelain of her cup. She watches the sugar dissolve, then adds more. The scrape resumes, slow and taunting. "He's a Jew."

How well she plays me! She knows I can't resist helping her, or any woman for that matter. I wouldn't have thought she would concern herself with this Jew or that Jew. It must be more serious than somebody losing a silly scholarship.

I move to my desk to write down the man's name, arrest date and detention site, if known. I'll put in a call, make sure the poor soul is still alive, and advise the SS, the *Sicherheitsdients*, SD, the *Staatspolizei* or whoever is holding him that the Ministry expects to be apprised of his progress toward release. I will then report this progress to Magda in exchange for a pat on the head and the warm feeling it brings, in spite of myself.

"What's his name?"

"Viktor Arlosoroff. He goes by Chaim now."

She's taken a bat to my face and her nonchalance can't conceal her pleasure at having floored me. "He's the Foreign Minister of the Zionist Organization. He's in Germany from Palestine and will request a meeting with the Reichsminister about the Jewish question. His proposal makes a tremendous amount of sense. Be absolutely sure his request gets to Joseph."

I open my mouth to speak but her smirk cuts me down. "Don't pout, Hansi. Do your job."

She's left me in a basement with rising water and locked the door behind her. It's already past my ankles, but it may as well be at my neck because I'm paralyzed. She is smart enough to be kind, but her kindness goes away as fast as it comes. Today, she's been reduced to a venal nub. I won't be fooled to think she came to me because she trusts me. She turns to those she can use. We are her sweet ones.

She should have let the request go through the proper channels. Does she think I don't know the rumors? Just to say the name Arlosoroff in Joseph's presence is enough to land me back on my mother's couch, but to explain that Magda intervened on his behalf? I can't think what he'll do.

I experienced his torment over Magda's past for the first time last summer. They'd been to the North Sea and he came back brooding. Apparently, she talked to him about her past dalliances and he was deeply disturbed. There was no jealous rant, no petulant rage. I sensed from him something I'd thought was impossible. He was afraid. He said, "In Magda's earlier life, she was very irresponsible and thoughtless. And now we both shall have to pay for this. Our fate hangs on a slender thread. God grant that we are both not destroyed by her undoing."

Of course, he never mentioned the Jew. He didn't need to. Only one transgression could be so poisonous as to have provoked Joseph's extreme reaction. The only other time he has ever spoken of it to me, he moaned in stunned dismay, "She hasn't yet broken with her past." Was it possible, even after she'd been with Joseph, that the unspeakable continued?

I vowed to him that whatever happened would never be discovered and I kept my vow. Any hint of criticism of Magda by the press has been met with an SS horse whip. I've made her untouchable. Now, she's asking me to raise the issue, myself. I want to send the SS after her.

No matter how that woman tries to win me back, no matter how beautiful she makes herself, or how charmingly she flatters me, I will never forgive her for this. I dig the end of a paperclip into my palm.

Everyone in the office is driving me crazy. I don't like most of my colleagues to begin with, but after Magda's visit, I fucking hate them. Their grammatical errors, their messy desks, their loud chewing, all get under my skin like a rash I'm not allowed to scratch. I have to get out of here. I escape to Viktoria Morelli. She gives me what I came for, but her non-stop sarcasm and indifference makes me feel almost as low as Magda did. Eva's the only one I can tolerate, right now.

I ring Eva's bell too many times than is polite. The proprietress comes out in a quilted housecoat buttoned to the neck. She's unusually small, in the shape of a trash can. I explain my business, but her unusually small eyes show no mercy. "Fraulein Schmidt isn't home."

"I'll wait."

"You're not permitted," snap her unusually small teeth.

"I'll wait outside," I say.

"This is an honorable house."

"I'm certain she'll want to see me," I say, but I'm not certain at all. She doesn't budge. "I'll let her decide that, young man."

I should be grateful to her for her protection. "Tell Fraulein Schmidt I was here."

"Very well," she says, crossing her arms under her breasts, which are not small at all.

The alley reeks of trash. A vagrant picks through a barrel, then knocks it onto the street. The clatter of metal explodes in the empty space. He staggers a few steps. His feet are wrapped in rags. He collapses under his own weight, muttering about Jesus, Mary and Joseph. A river of urine slides toward me. His Gods have done nothing for him.

It's not safe in this alley and I should wait for Eva to come home. She won't like it, though. She'd remind me for the fiftieth time that we're not dating. Something scratches next to me and a rat bolts from a nearby downspout. My heart pounds from the fright. The vermin's hairless tail is erect, telling me to fuck off. Like the unusually small landlady, this hideous creature wants to keep me from Eva. I need to get out of this alley.

I pass the drunkard and hover above his stench. I should help him. I kick him to rouse him, but his body is limp. I kick him again. This time, my ankle buckles against his dead weight. The pain makes me kick harder. All I want to do is give him money, but he won't listen. "I'm trying to help you! Take my money!" I shout as I kick. "Why are you like this, you fucking slob?!" I stomp on his hand. His left eye pops open. It looks at me in shock, then fear. His tired mewling begs me to stop.

I could end his pitiful existence right now, but I kneel next to him instead. "Look at me," I softly encourage. He turns his red, dirt-smudged face toward mine. The smell of urine and rot clogs my throat. I shove a few loose marks at his face and watch them fall to the ground. "You're a disgrace," I say, as cold sweat sprouts behind my ears.

Eva lays a cloth over her table. "How much?" I ask.

"It'll cost you," she smirks. I'm too tired for sarcasm.

"Why do you hide in that costume when you look so much more beautiful as yourself?"

"People speak more freely to a disguise than to someone they might run into in the grocery line."

"Not when they trust each other," I urge, and give her my hand. "Please, I need your advice."

Her face opens slightly, and my body relaxes. Finally, someone wants to help me. No one does that. She takes my hand. Even her fingertips are soft. I think of the whores I've banged to get my numbers up. I picture their cragged nails, dirty hair and chapped lips that scrape coldly at the side of my neck, avoiding my mouth, my eyes. I imagine Viktoria, with her hard, athletic figure, having her way with me. I can't imagine another woman's body could be as gentle as Eva's.

"What's wrong?" she asks.

Everything, I think, but I say, "What should someone do if he knows something about a friend's wife that will make his friend extremely angry, both at his wife and at the man who delivers the information."

"I wouldn't speak of it."

"But what if the friend will find out, and could find out the man knew, and didn't tell him?"

"And this man is you?"

"And what if the wife is also a friend?"

Her mind is working.

"Has the wife betrayed her husband?"

"Before they were married. Before people understood how damaging that sort of relationship is. But I'm worried she's rekindled the flame. And the man she did it with? There's nothing I can say about it other than if it's true, only disaster can come of it. For her and her husband." And for me, I think, but I don't say it. Still, I need Eva to know how important this is, and I can't stop myself from saying, "Maybe even for the Reich."

This shocks her. It's a sign she's faithful, herself. "I'm sorry to bother you with this." It's a lie. I don't want her to think I find such behavior in women scintillating, or in any way normal, but I'm very glad I came to her tonight.

"Could this friend make things difficult for you at work if he were angry?" she asks.

"More than anyone else." I catch her eye. She knows who we're talking about.

"If you don't know the nature of the wife's relationship with her past lover, why lead your friend to believe she's betrayed him? If you care about the wife and the husband, you have to be sure you're right before you unleash consequences you can't control."

I know she's right. "I'm only sure she talked to her ex . . ." I can't use the word she used to describe him. "Acquaintance," I say. "I don't know if there was anything salacious. I don't want to know."

She reaches for my hand, and says with an authority I want to obey, "Then don't. Don't believe a word of it."

"But the wife still wants the husband to know she's seen him. She wants her husband to help this man. She says he can help the Reich."

"Then tell him only what the wife wants him to know. But do it with kindness, so her husband knows you're his friend, first."

She says what I already know. "We agree." Our silence is long and comfortable. I wish it was like this all the time but there are too many of her—the gypsy, the sweet shop girl, Magda's confidante. *Just give me one of them!* I want to say. I'll get to know her. I'll care for her. I'll love her.

"What else do you see," I ask.

She looks into my hand again and runs her finger across its lines. Her touch sends a spark through me. "I see a kind man in an unkind world. It takes strength to be this way, to stand up to those around you. Don't leave your kindness behind because the world is changing and powerful people want you to change with it."

This is not at all what I was asking and it's not at all what I want to hear. She's slipped away. "But what would your love-o-meter say to me?"

She lets go of my hand. "It would say that love comes too easily to you."

Her lips circle as she says, "you," and I'm kissing them.

49

EVA

I itched to wipe his taste from my lips. "I'm sorry," I said. "I've just finished with someone. I can't be with anyone else right now."

"Did he treat you badly?" he asked. His intensity hovered, sealed in by the bar's haze. It was as though he cherished my weakness. "It was no one's fault. We both wanted the separation. But, I'm not ready for something new."

"I see." He seemed humored, as if I'd misread his intentions. "We've discussed this, Eva. Even if you want more, I'll never ask you for it." A blush crept up his cheeks. "I like being with you. We're getting to know each other to see if one day we can trust each other."

"You kissed me."

"I'll take it back, then." He held my hand loosely between his fingers, then dropped it.

"What's your faith, Eva?"

The question jolted me. *He doesn't know. No one knows.*

"Not like yours, Hans."

"I don't mind, although I do wish you understood us better. But I'm not asking that. Tell me what you believe. Having faith in something is important." His face was still, inviting. "Answer me, Eva."

"I guess it's in the goodness between people."

He frowned as he thought. "You mean trust."

"That's another way to say it."

"Do you trust me?"

"Can I?"

"How could you ask that?"

I shrugged. "If all your faith is in Hitler, you must think what he thinks. For me to fully trust you, I would have to have all my faith in him, too, because I can only know you through him."

"You're drawing a caricature."

"Tell me how you're different, then."

"Because I know who you are, and what you think about us, and I still trust you."

I wondered if Magda knew how close to the surface her secrets were, and how close Hans was to sharing them. It had been too easy to get him to tell her story. Hans was afraid of what Joseph would do to him because of Arlosoroff, but I feared what Joseph would do to Magda. Part of me wanted to warn her right then, but I adored that she did things to make Joseph angry. The Magda I knew would take the side of Chaim/Viktor Arlosoroff. The Magda I knew loved Chaim/Viktor Arlosoroff. I believed in the Magda I knew. I didn't want her to stop doing such wonderful things.

Come by tomorrow. –M, was all the note said, then, an address on Hermann-Göring-Strasse. The note made me light as I climbed the steps to my room. I hoped its timing and my conversation with Hans weren't coincidental. I hoped she wanted to tell me her side of the story. Unlike Hans, I wouldn't share it with anyone. Her love was nobody's business. Without Thad and Matthias, I needed

Magda more than before. Even though I tried not to, a growing part of me forgave her for her marriage, as I'd hoped to forgive myself for my own mistakes. We both lived on top of our own mountains without enough oxygen to do more than the least.

Only people like Thad, who didn't understand fear, or Matthias and Herr Perlstein, who had nothing to lose, expected heroics. Didn't they know you need a place to belong, a home, before you can defend it? I couldn't ask more from Magda than I did from myself.

After work at the shop the next day, I went to the new residence. The outside wasn't much different from the surrounding government buildings, but I knew Magda would bring it alive. I pictured Helge's room with a canopy bed. Magda would have an oval boudoir, with moldings and frosted crystal perfume bottles. I refused to picture Joseph, her jailer, anywhere in the house.

Magda let me in. She took me past ceremonial rooms where builders patched ceilings, and painted moldings and chair rails. She opened the door to a smaller room. There was an illuminated fish tank and bookshelves. French doors opened to the gardens, which were in full bloom.

"The house is obviously uninhabitable, but I've already finished this room for myself. It will be my sanctuary," Magda said, sitting on an overstuffed couch. "Only I can come in here."

In fact, the room belied the existence of humanity. The paintings were landscapes. There were no clocks, no pens, no typewriter. There wasn't a portrait or a photograph of another person to be seen, not even Helge. My eyes fell on a pile of books, the top of which was the *Dhammapada*. I gathered it was Buddhist, based on its cover drawing of an oriental statue with its hands pressed together.

"I would want such a peaceful space for myself, if I were you," I said, tying another thread around our bond.

"I like you so, Eva. There's something about you that reminds me of me. I trust you. That's why I want you here—so we can share things we wouldn't share elsewhere."

"You can tell me anything, always," I said.

She hesitated for a moment. "Of course, whatever I say here, can never be repeated."

"I understand," I said, talking over her words.

Her head tilted to the side, dismissing my certainty. "I don't mean just that you should hold my secrets, which any friend would do."

I nodded with canine loyalty.

Her voice was precise. "I mean, what I say here ceases to be true beyond that door. It holds no bearing outside my sanctuary. Its meaning dissolves into nothing."

She reached for the *Dhammapada* with her left hand and drew her right pointer finger in a slow arc toward the door. She was two-dimensional, a Gothic Madonna painted on wood. "If, for example, you were out there and you were to suggest I possess this book," she paused, "you would be lying."

I wasn't sure I understood, but she was so sure of herself, I said yes.

"I don't say it as a threat, Eva. I'm explaining what happens. The conversation we're having now is the only thing you will hear in this room that you can take with you when you leave."

I held out my hand for her palm, but she turned toward the French doors. A robin landed on the lip of a granite urn, and when it flew away again, she spoke, never taking her eyes from the glass panes that protected her from her life.

"I heard his voice," she said. "My old friend. On the phone. To hear it was all I needed to feel all of him again. His voice holds you, Eva. I felt it in the backs of my arms, pulling me in. It's the voice of a glacier lake, still and dark, unafraid of the sky and mountains that surround it."

"How did you feel?"

"You know how I felt," she snapped, then paused. "Regret," she finally said.

"About what?"

Distress spilled over her face. "That he was the giant in my life . . . That I've made a"—

"Mistake," I said for her. It was an error. I should have let her say it.

"What good will it do to dwell on it?" she asked. I could feel her outside world creeping in. I needed to keep it at bay.

"You can't make that choice. He's with you."

"My mother always said he drove me to distraction because he was always present, even when he wasn't."

"But it's more than that. It's as if he generates your thoughts. You use his mind to view the world."

"It made me hate him as much as I loved him."

"Why did he contact you?"

"He wanted Joseph's help. It had absolutely nothing to do with me. It had to do with his cause. Just like before. It was never about me."

"You love him, still."

She stared at the slug fish mauling the side of the tank.

"Nowhere but in this room."

50

HANS

Joseph's manicurist brushes by me with her round leather case. She has the see nothing-hear nothing look so many service people get around Joseph. He's leaning into his sunlamp's metal disk, his eyes protected by opaque glasses. He doesn't acknowledge me.

"I've spoken with my friend on Hjalmar Schacht's staff at the Reichsbank. He's trustworthy—a party member from the old days. Schacht's American trip is a disaster. Hundreds of thousands are marching against us in their cities. Schacht says all he hears about is 'Jews, Jews, Jews and the Jewish question.' He threatened nonpayment of debts if the international boycott continues. Secretary Hull blew his stack, and Schacht took it back, but the truth is, my friend says we'll run out of foreign currency in a few weeks. We won't be able to pay, even if we want to."

I get nervous as I get deeper into the issue of the Jews. I have to continue. I'm only reporting information. There's nothing of me in this. "My friend says there's an idea floating that should help. He says Jews from Palestine want to use émigrés' assets, if we unfreeze them, to buy German goods to aid in the development of Palestine. They would purchase our goods in sterling. The Jews would get their merchandise. We would get their foreign currency. And we would get rid of our Jews.

"Schacht is for this?"

"Schacht thinks the symbolism of the Jews breaking their own boycott is our best way to kill it, altogether. He's convinced if the international boycott becomes more widely organized, or worse, officially sanctioned, it's the end of the Reich."

Joseph digs his manicured nails into his knees. He grunts into the lamp, his chin protruding into the glow. Even with this dismal news, he won't allow an uneven tan.

"People want you behind the deal," I add, trying to build him up.

His black glasses make him impossible to read. I have to go on. "There's something else." I relax my voice so my words carry no suggestion beyond the stated facts. "A man by the name of Chaim Arlosoroff, who claims to be the Zionist's foreign representative, has requested a meeting with you to address this matter." I brace for a tsunami, but Joseph's pose is iron. "And Magda asked you to accept."

Joseph's skin reddens in the lamplight. A vein connecting his hairline to his left eyebrow hardens into a cable. Smaller veins pop up around it. Nothing else about him moves until sweat traces a thick line in front of his ear and drips onto his shirt.

The next day, Joseph sits in my office, inspecting his shoeshine. He's said nothing about the Arlosoroff situation. I expected this. He doesn't run solutions by the messenger. Joseph kills the messenger.

He mentions offhandedly that he doesn't like MGM, Paramount, Universal and Warner Brothers playing in the Reich. After the *boykottaktion* and the book burning, it makes us look incompetent and half-hearted to show Jewish movies. Of course, he says, we can't take people's movies away until there are enough German films to replace them. He tells me to get on Babelsberg to speed up production and he mentions the name of an actress he wants to sleep with as someone who must get a starring role in something soon.

I consent whole-heartedly. He could tell me I was a pig, and I would dive naked into slop for him today.

"Also, get me a meeting with Theo Korth and Heinz Grönda."

Their names are familiar because Consul Wolff sent a communiqué from Palestine reporting the two had left without completing their mission. Joseph had dispatched them to retrieve German gold from the Jenin Valley. They were supposed to extract it without surrendering any to the British.

"I want it today."

I nod four times. Joseph senses my need to please. I've set myself up. He slaps his palm on his armrest as he rises. When he reaches the door, he grips the jamb and lets his head fall forward. "Now, tell me, Hansi. How's your gypsy?"

He has the hint of a sneer. As I've humiliated him about his wife, he will humiliate me about Eva. "She's well."

He raises his eyebrows in exaggerated surprise. "Have things gone south?"

I have no choice but to step lightly. I don't know what Eva told Magda or what Magda told Joseph about us or about Eva's late, great mystery man. "Not at all, Joseph. She's just out of a relationship, so we're taking it slow. But we're seeing each other. Definitely." My dancing is awkward and out of sync with the adrenaline shooting through me.

His laugh rumbles from his stomach. "The girl's too quick for you. Do we have to import you an ox from the frontier with as much intelligence in her head as she has in her balloon boobs? Some all-ass Gretchen with river barges for feet?"

My skin burns hot.

"What do you say, Hansi?" he begs. "I'll order you a Gretchen to blow your cock. My treat."

My voice comes out too quiet. "I want Eva, Joseph."

He drags toward me, leading with his face. He has a carnivorous smile that comes too close and he imitates my voice in falsetto. "You want Eva, Hansi?"

"Yes," I say louder.

His laughs come out a syllable at a time, jerking his body. He pats my cheek like I'm a child, and barks, "That's my boy."

Joseph's bullying whittles me down to where I'm smaller than he is. It's Magda's fault. I wouldn't be surprised if she were turning Eva against me, just to keep her hand in the Ministry's pot. She deserves some pity. Joseph plays the field without shame. His latest is Hela Strehl, a beautiful, bright fashion editor at *Scherl Verlag*—no ox-like Gretchen, to be sure. Still, something in him needs Magda to be his wife. He says she's his queen, his mother and his lover, rolled up in one. She's indispensable. It's why he fights with her, why she gets under his skin like no one else. Magda knows she has this power, and when she exerts it, his pain lands like a pile of shit all over me and anyone else who gets in the way.

I want to see Eva. We have to move things along. Trude Becher tells me Magda is meeting her at 3:00 at the new residence. I'll meet her there, by coincidence, of course, and maybe the rest of the day won't be such crap.

I dial up Korth first. It's odd that Joseph would have anything to do with foreign agents, but I do as I'm told. "Did you succeed?" I ask.

"Everything's in place, per the Reichsminister's instructions," Korth replies.

264 / Jill Morningstar

This is odd. Either he has the gold or he doesn't. With our currency so weak, every little bit helps, and gold helps a lot. "The Reichsminister wants to meet today."

"I'll be there," Korth responds. His voice sounds like the desert from where he's come, tough and dried out by the sun. Part of me envies his life as an operative. But with the constant travel, with all the secrecy, there's no hope for a good family life. I want to tell my wife everything. I want her to listen. Lies destroyed my parents' marriage. I won't repeat their mistakes.

"Eva," I shout, faking surprise. "What brings you to this part of town?"

"I met with Frau Goebbels," she says. She's in a good mood.

"Did you do a reading?"

She smiles but says nothing. I won't push her, although I'd give almost anything to know what Magda says to her. "I'm glad to see the two of you getting on."

"I like Frau Goebbels very much. She treats me like a friend, even though she doesn't have to." Her voice almost flies. I know how easily it happens. If she wants to, Magda can give you wings. But Eva's innocence amazes me. For all she sees in the future, she doesn't understand her most important client particularly well.

"She's admirable," I say, hoping Eva will see it's different to like than to admire.

"She's a good person."

"She knows what it is to be good. She does good things."

"And she's brave."

"Bold," I reply. Eva isn't hearing my words as distinctions. They're added praise. She sees what she wants to see in Magda. It's a child's view of parents. They can do no wrong. Until they do.

Eva never had parents. She thinks if she did, her holes would be filled and her pieces would be put back together. She doesn't know that the people you adore more than life can hold your perfect love in their hands, can feel every ounce of it, and drop it in the dirt.

I point to a bench. "Do you have time?"

She shrugs, and we sit.

"I have parents, Eva. I know you don't. It's not right to compare, but in some ways, I understand you. My father lost his mind when I was young. Sometimes he doesn't recognize me. He doesn't know what I do. He doesn't know himself. It's good he's alive, but he's also not alive. He's not my father anymore."

I've told a few women about my family. Invariably, in the most gentle way, they float and curl like smoke, ridding themselves of all that was good between us until it vaporizes, and they're gone.

Eva's eyes don't grow wide. She doesn't search the distance for something familiar to take her away. She's still with me.

"I don't mean to make you sorry or sad. I just want you to know there have been times when I've thought I could replace him." I point back to the residence. "Perhaps you've noticed." I laugh. After today, it feels good. She laughs, too, kindly, because she understands me.

"Maybe you've thought you could replace your mother." I put my hand on her knee. She doesn't move it away. "It doesn't work. It will never work."

51

EVA

Hans was wrong. I hadn't looked for replacements. I looked for my mother. When young, pretty volunteers came to the orphanage with bags of second-hand books and toys, I studied each one, waiting for someone's eyes to bounce off the other girls and land on me. It's what my eyes did. They stumbled from one would-be mother to the next. I attributed the mole on the curve of my jaw to Frau Nathanson, the red in my lips to Frau Kruger, and my blue eyes, which everyone always complimented, to Fraulein Rabb. They were just hopes. They faded to nothing when neither Frau Nathanson, nor Frau Kruger, nor Fraulein Rabb, nor anyone else ever greeted me with the relieved exhale of discovering something they'd long ago lost.

After months of this futile mapping, my eyes fell on Frau Pappenheim. Fragments of memories wrote themselves into a fairy tale. Frau Pappenheim and I were both small. We had dark brown hair and blue eyes. But the true reason I believed in our connection lay in what most people couldn't see. Like me, she was always alone. Even when people surrounded her, even as they obeyed and adored her, she stood apart. She lived on the edge of feeling, never quite belonging.

I loved this in her, and my love proved my case. Frau Pappenheim, whom I admired more than anyone else, was not my spiritual mother. She was my actual mother.

When I was born, Frau Pappenheim wasn't married, so she couldn't raise me as her daughter. At the same time, she couldn't bear to give me up, so she kept me as her orphan, one among many, all the while holding a special place for me in her heart.

I worked hard to be worthy of that place. I asked for chores near her office. I did extra credit problems, and edited and re-edited my assignments so the teachers would show them to her as examples of their students' best work. At assemblies, she called my name, the name she gave me, the name that honored her own mother and no one else's. *For receiving 100% in mathematics, for explicating this poem or analyzing that scene, we honor Eva Schmidt.*

There was love in those words. The other girls heard it, too, because beneath their polite claps, they laughed. They called me her *hündchen*, her puppy dog. Even they thought I belonged to her.

After one assembly, I approached her. "Thank you for your kind words," I said, because that was how she would have said it. When I turned to go, she ran her hand down my braid. Its gentle pull tickled my scalp, sending a rush of gratitude through me. I flung my arms around her waist, and pressed my cheek into the softness of her chest. Her heartbeat matched my own.

"There, there," she said.

I squeezed harder. "Finally, we're together."

"So it appears," Frau Pappenheim replied, her voice sharp. "Run along, Eva." She peeled my arms from her waist, straightened her skirt, and returned to her office.

Esti Altermann came up behind me. She was a few years older than me, and had seen the whole thing. "You are her puppy, aren't you?"

"I'm not her puppy, I'm her daughter!" I shouted.

Esti laughed. "That old bag hasn't been touched by a man since her doctor delivered her."

"How do you know?" I demanded. My panicked breaths rasped in my throat.

She softened. "She's much too old to be your mother. It's impossible."

I was too broken to move. Shame over my pathetic, stupid hope flamed across my cheeks. Esti was right. Of course, she was right. "I know that!" was all I could say. Then I begged, "Please, don't tell anyone about this."

She wiped my tears with the cuff of her blouse. "I promise I won't tell anyone if you promise you won't be sad. You have no one to miss. How can you be sad?"

That day, I learned the last, new thing I would ever know about my mother. She was never coming back. She knew precisely where to find me. She probably could have picked me up on the way to the library, or to get bread for dinner. She didn't choose to. She was content to leave me with no one to miss.

My only remaining question was whether she'd held me before passing me off to the Bavarian maid. Had she, even for a minute, let me rest against her body so I could make her warm?

I had no expectation that Magda would become my mother. I just needed her to open that place in me that never had been touched. I needed her to carry a trace of my warmth.

52

HANS

The Kaiserhof has the most elegant dining room in Berlin, with two-story Palladian windows and moldings even the most pompous Frenchmen stop to admire. Hundreds of chandelier bulbs dazzle the room with light. The maître d' greets me as Herr Lorenz and shakes my hand. I reply by insisting he use my first name. I learn everyone's first name. I've memorized the names of Joseph's maids and secretaries, and all the guards and janitors at the Ministry. After all, the Führer spends most of his time with his drivers. They don't sit outside in the cold, waiting for him to finish his meal. They sit at his table. The people who serve us are shown respect. In the best case, the old guard and intellectuals are blind to their servants. More likely, they treat them like dogs. But we salute ours. *Heil Hitler* makes us equal.

With one turn of my head, I see Joachim von Ribbentrop at one table and Rudolf Hess at another. Will they remember my name?

To my other side is Dieter Müller, my friend who works for Schacht at the Reichsbank. With his neatly combed hair and well fitting, double-breasted suit, he looks like Gary Cooper. He comes to say hello. When I introduce him to Eva, he kisses her hand—very gracious. I'm glad she can see there are party members who are also gentlemen.

Dieter turns to me. "Hans, I need to speak with you. Please excuse us, Fraulein Schmidt?"

Eva nods. I place my napkin on top of the table. The waiter rushes over to refold it. He eyes Eva. She looks like a Kestner doll. Her skin is fine and her hair is dark silk. Her eyes are bright, like they've popped open for the first time and the world is better than she ever thought before.

I follow Dieter past a dark wood bank of telephone booths to a quiet corner. He comes straight out with it. "At the end of the American trip, Schacht received reliable intelligence that the French want full implementation of Versailles." The word is a punch to the throat, but he continues. "The Jews are a red herring. They intend to partition Germany."

"That would be war!"

"A war we can't win. General Blomberg has no doubt." His eyes become slits as he lights his cigarette.

"Is the intelligence reliable?"

"It's from a higher-up in the American foreign policy establishment. Schacht believes it enough to insist on a meeting with the Führer as soon as he gets back."

Just the rumor makes me want to fight the French. Of all the countries in the world that stuck 1918 in our face, none was worse than France. I have boyish fantasies of leading a battalion of our best men into Alsace to plant the swastika atop the Strasbourg Cathedral. "We'll have to speed up re-armament," I insist.

"With what currency? To fight is suicide."

The old depression quickly clouds my vision. After all our work, we're still so far behind.

Dieter's voice is unwavering. "The Palestine deal is our best way out. Make sure Doktor Goebbels understands."

I have learned never to speak for Joseph, or to presume anything about him to anyone else. "I'll tell him what you've told me."

"Is everything all right?" Eva asks.

I can't tell her what I want to shout to the entire dining room. The French are trying to chop us up and cut off our pricks. Anger pulses in the back of my eye. I reply with Hitler's words, *Injustice fuels our strength.*

"What happened, Hans?"

I glance around to be sure no one is listening, then I lean toward her. She's hard to predict, but I do trust her. She's the only person I know who truly has no agenda of her own. Still, I must be careful. If this were to get out, people would panic.

"It's a diplomatic issue, but it can be fixed."

"You trust your leaders." She's teasing me. She'll say I'm giving a campaign speech.

"It's not that"—

"Is the Ministry involved?"

"Joseph has the Führer's ear, so no matter what the issue is, people want our help."

"What's the issue? If you can tell me, that is." The line of her lipstick is perfect. Her mouth is weakening me. I want to explain everything to her. I need to let some of the air out.

"The Jews and labor unions are riling things up internationally. Their boycott is doing massive damage. The Western media has brainwashed their governments. But you shouldn't worry about this."

"I am worried, though," she says. "And your worry makes me more worried. Is there anything to do?"

She needs to stop this negative talk. Her faith in the Party is too weak to begin with. I lower my voice, inviting her to come close. Her scent calms me.

"There's a plan to hoist the Jews by their own petard."

"What do you mean?"

I can feel her voice down the side of my neck. No one's paying attention to us, so I whisper, "I mean, the Jew will be the one to get us out of the mess he's created."

"But how?" Her eyes shine like blue bulbs. The smooth softness of her breasts peeks up as she leans against the table. Back to her face, I instruct my eyes.

"The so-called Zionists want Germany's Jews to move to Palestine. It's complicated, but at the most basic level, if we let them leave, and put their blocked assets into a special British bank, the bank will use those assets to buy German goods, which will then be used to help resettle the Jews in Palestine. We get their sterling, but even better, the first tractor they buy will blow their boycott against us to pieces."

She draws a short breath and her lips part. "I don't understand."

I want her to understand. I want her to shoulder some of my weight. "The Jew's boycott will bury us if the West pursues it. Not just our economy, but our ability to defend ourselves against our worst enemies. If the Jews break their own boycott, the West can't use them as an excuse to destroy us." I find myself smiling because in explaining the plan, I realize its genius.

Eva's not smiling.

"Now, it's your turn. I've told you a secret. You tell me one. Anything you want!"

"But, what if they don't want to go?"

"Who?"

"The Jews. And if they do, won't it also hurt our economy? They have jobs. They pay taxes."

As always, she's right and wrong. This is why women and government don't mix. Women can't sort things. They get caught up in details, then use them to poke holes in every plan. When they've finally sent the balloon crashing down to earth, they cry.

Her mouth opens to speak, but over her shoulder, I see Hess. He's walking straight for me.

"Hans!" he says. He remembered my name! His voice lifts me from my chair and he shakes my hand. Our leaders know what they're doing. They'll take care of us.

53

EVA

Hans insisted on bringing me home. He engaged a driver from the Ministry motor pool. We sat in the back of the Mercedes. The leather seat creaked each time I shifted away from him. I could only see Frau Pappenheim and her friends moving to the desert, their antiques liquidated and reborn as cranes and cement mixers.

Hans stared happily out the window, watching the monuments whir by. "It's strange," he said, "to be chauffeured from the Hotel Kaiserhof to Scheunenviertel." He dropped his hand onto my knee, then pulled it away, apologizing.

When we arrived home, I jumped out before the driver had turned off the ignition. Hans chased after me. We stood together on the steps. I don't know how I thought it could have been otherwise. He took my key and opened the door.

"You make bad things good, Eva."

"You're very kind, Hans, really"—

"I hope so."

"You remember what we talked about."

"I remember exactly. I said I respect you. I said I'll be patient, and I'll do nothing to compromise you. I didn't say I would go away." His shoulders sagged and he turned to the car.

"Thank you," I called after him.

Frau Pappenheim's handwriting peered out of my box. I wished it had an answer to what I'd just stumbled into, but the bravado of her recent letters was nowhere to be found.

13 May, 1933

Dear Eva,

> *I can not stop smelling the burnt. I wonder whose words I breathe from this soot-choked air. Professor Katzenstein was arrested the same night as the book burning, as was Professor Learsy. They haven't returned.*
> *Nazis can no longer fail any class, by edict of the Education Ministry. And then, the grotesque Statement of the German Student Body: "When a Jew writes in German, he lies."*
> *If there is one thing of which Jews are guilty, it is of having too much faith in our countrymen, who only can believe we hate them.*
> *We have only each other now.*

As Always,
Frau Pappenheim

I'd thought despair was impossible for the strongest woman I knew. I clutched the paper to my chest, and noticed more writing on the back. There was no greeting, just the date.

14 May

> *Helene Rothenberg's husband, a father of three, disappeared three weeks ago. He was sent back to her in an urn*

*today, Mother's Day. The Gestapo demanded payment for the
package. They return bodies Care of Delivery.*

*The West is our best hope. They must intervene. Our central
organizations say no, but Göring has a gun to their heads.*

*The rest of us must breathe life into our community.
Zionists, Communists, Orthodox, Atheists must come together
in strength. All is forgiven.*

*I'm helping Martin Buber build Jewish Schools. Education
is my only weapon.*

Be careful, Eva, but be strong. Find your weapon! Breathe life!

I should have beaten myself up for leaving Helene and our
spiritual home. I should have cried for the dark hole that replaced
my faith. I should have seen what I'd become through my spiritual
mother's eyes, and I should have despised myself.

But I didn't cry. I didn't hate myself. For the first time since I left
Frau Pappenheim, I could do exactly what she wanted. Hans had
handed me my weapon, and I would use it.

54

EVA

I banged on Thad's door. It was midnight, and he easily could have been out, but I couldn't wait. When he didn't answer, I banged harder. Finally, there was a rumbling. He stood in front of me in his bathrobe, confused. He shouldn't have been. I was doing to him what he told me to do with Magda and Hans. I was getting something out of him for myself.

"I need to talk to you."

He shook off his fog. "How about a drink?"

I went to pour it myself. The low ball scritched against the glass shelf. Thad took the glass. "Ice?"

"Just pour." I sat on the edge of the couch. He put the drink in my hand and stepped back. "Come closer," I said.

He pulled up the sharkskin ottoman and sat in front of me, his face calm. I explained about Dieter, and the negotiations with the Zionists. I told him Schacht believed the international boycott would bring down the Reich.

"And the negotiations would bring down the boycott," Thad said quietly.

"That's why I'm telling you."

"Who's negotiating for the Jews?"

"Zionists."

"From Germany?"

"Hans just said Zionists."

Thad didn't respond. I didn't know what I'd expected from him but it wasn't silence. "Well?" I prodded.

"It's the Nazi's perfect solution. They get their foreign currency, and get rid of their Jews, guilt-free."

"I was able to infer that. Tell me it will help. It's the only reason I'm here."

He smirked at the qualification. "And I was able to infer that from our conversation at the Chinese restaurant, Eva."

"So, tell me."

He sighed. "This deal, their economic forecasts, the effects of the boycott, everything Hans said, it's actually quite interesting." His enthusiasm grew as he spoke. I felt hints of the old excitement, until my memory of the Excelsior flooded back. I saw his slow walk to the table. I heard his cool voice. *Forgive me, Fraulein Schmidt,* he'd said, as he released my hand and watched me fall.

"Why did you do what you did at the Excelsior?" I asked. I couldn't let it go.

"I didn't mean for it to happen that way. You both saw me. I wouldn't have said anything if Hans hadn't stopped me. I walked by you to ignore you. I wanted you to know I would never betray you to him, or anyone."

"That's charitable," I snapped.

"Stop fighting, Eva. I'm glad you came." He had a seriousness I didn't recognize. I willed myself not to interrupt his pause.

"You need to understand something if you sincerely want to do something here. Whatever it is that makes you think I, or anyone else, sees you as lesser, whatever anger you have at me or your mother or the world for what it has inflicted on you has to go away now. You can have only one fight."

He dropped a copy of the *Herald Tribune* on the couch. The headline read: *Jews Banned from Buying Food, Medicine in Towns Across Germany.* "This is your only enemy. Do you understand?"

"Yes," I said. "Obviously, I do."

"It's not at all obvious. You have to promise me you're deciding this for yourself, not for me or for us. I'll do everything I can to protect you, but things can go wrong, and when they do, you're the one who will suffer.

"Hans shouldn't have told you what he did tonight. His wall is down. He's going to tell you things that are dangerous for you to know. You'll be at risk. You may already be. You can still get out of it if you stop seeing him now."

"I don't want to," I insisted. "I wouldn't have come if I did." It was true. My lifetime of shames had knotted in my brain. I got lost behind them. I'd spent my life casting about, looking for someone to untie me, to show me myself. It took leaving Thad, whom I'd wanted the most, to finally see this mistake. My deceptions didn't need to be shameful covers for the things in my past I couldn't abide. My hiding didn't have to draw from fear. My lies could bring me closer to myself. If I used them well, for the first time, I could do something that mattered. Thad had said it the first day we met, when he looked into my face so I couldn't look away and said of my illegitimacy, *It must free you.* What I hadn't understood then was that for me, freedom would never be offered. I would have to steal it.

"I want to do what's right, Thad. But nothing I do will matter if you don't also do what's right. You need to promise that to me."

His voice was steady, but each word carried a heavy weight. "I can only promise to do my best, but you have my word on that."

"Can you stop this deal? Will the U.S. finally join the boycott?" My mind reeled.

"We won't bring down any governments, to be clear. Things are complicated. They take time, but"—

"But we'll help," I demanded.

He cupped my shoulder in his hand. My skin prickled under his palm. "We'll help," he said. "It won't be easy, but we'll help."

"Then, I promise you, too."

55

EVA

T had left me few instructions. "Hans trusts you," he'd said. "Do nothing to sacrifice that trust. Nothing can change between you. You're liberal so be liberal. You're smart, so be smart. You're just friends, so keep it that way. Brush him off now and then. Stay in charge. He'll follow. He always has."

It seemed too easy. From the beginning, my lies had manufactured Hans's affection. Since I'd created it, I could also control it. I was sure of it because he acted with me the way I used to with Thad. He would take what he could get, and it would be enough for him.

Playing dumb would never push Hans to share information. He measured himself through other people's eyes, so he wanted to impress. To impress, he had to be challenged. He had to earn the praise he needed so badly.

To get specific information about who was negotiating for the Jews, and whom they represented, I asked him the difference between international Jews, German Jews and Zionists. We were in front of the Ullstein publishing house, and I'd used it as a hook. With mathematical certainty, he said, "'The Jew' comes in many forms. This shape shifting explains his inexplicable survival after so many centuries of hatred and violence against him."

"You sound like Helldorf. Are they all practitioners of the dark arts?"

"They're more like Houdini. They're escape artists, fully explained by science."

I laughed. He was pleased. "Try again. Without the propaganda this time."

"You like facts."

"I like you to tell the truth."

"I always tell the truth."

"Do you?"

"To the best of my ability."

"Prove it."

"The Zionist and the so-called German Jew, because they are Jews, are inherently international, but the International Jew is not necessarily a Zionist or a German.

"Are the people who want to move all the Jews to Palestine of the German subset or the Zionist subset of the international Jews, or are they international but not Zionist or German at all?"

"You're making fun of me. This is why Joseph says we shouldn't talk politics with women."

"I forgot I was a woman. I apologize, Herr Lorenz. I won't ask you anything else." I clapped my hand over my mouth.

"Wait!" he said. I shook my head in an exaggerated no, still covering my mouth.

"Forget Joseph. I'll tell you," he said. "I want to tell you."

"Fine, but slowly and simply."

"I get away with nothing with you," he said, and went on to explain that the movement behind the deal was coming from Zionists in England and Palestine.

"So, who's their Pope? Who's the head Jew?"

He puzzled for a response. "There's no one person who's in charge. There's someone in Berlin now who refers to himself as their Foreign Minister, as if a title can make a man. He thinks he's on par with Joseph. He even asked to meet with him. I'd be surprised if he didn't try to get an appointment with the Führer, himself, his self-regard is so high."

It was Arlosoroff. It had to be. "You've done well!" I announced. "I believe you!"

A once attractive woman with rain-matted hair and dirty clothes stood under the awning of the bistro where we were eating dinner. Her eyes moved from Hans' fork to mine as we raised our food to our lips. She wasn't a lunatic. She seemed to be replaying memories of something good.

I buttered the bread in our basket and rose to give it to her. "Please," Hans said. "I'll take it." While she ate, he drew a map against his palm with his finger. He handed her some coins, and sent her off.

When he returned, his suit was splotched with rain. "She's a widow. She has children. She used to come to this restaurant all the time," he said.

"What did you tell her?"

"The only thing I could," he muttered. "That there's a soup kitchen in the basement of *Johanneskirche*." He tapped two fingers hard against the table, causing his knife blade to screech against his glass.

I moved the glass. "What is it, Hans?"

"This isn't how it should be."

"The economy's been bad for so long."

"But we said we would fix it!" he snapped, and coughed into his hand.

"You can't blame yourself. Isn't this something Finance or Labor should be responsible for?"

"They didn't make the promises, Eva! We did!" He coughed again.

"You'll make yourself sick."

"I never get sick."

"I didn't mean to offend you."

"I have a lot on my mind," he grunted, and gripped the arms of his chair. "I'm sorry to take it out on you."

I met his gaze. "I'm not upset."

He smirked, and put his hand on mine. "If only I could upset you."

I pulled my hand away. "I'm glad you don't."

"You know what I mean," he said.

"Let's talk about something else," I offered.

He pushed his chair back, loudly scraping the floor tiles. There was a nervous edge to his voice. "Industry is panicking. I'm inundated with their demands and their outrage, as if they've played no role in it. We're unusually susceptible to boycotts. Half our workforce is employed by two percent of our companies. People are losing jobs every day, which means they're losing faith. Like that woman." He pushed his plate to the side.

"It's still not your fault, Hans."

"Faith is our responsibility. Joseph is being blamed!"

"Are the companies attacking you the ones you meant when you talked about the Second Wave with that reporter?" I opened my eyes encouragingly wide.

I could feel a weight lifting from him. He seemed proud I put it together. "Yes, Eva, exactly yes. Them and more. The movement means nothing to them if they can't line their pockets."

"It must infuriate you."

"If you only knew," he exhaled.

My body hummed with excitement. I was getting close to something. "So, give me people to be angry at. Who do you want to be done with?"

He blinked rapidly.

"What?" I asked.

"Why did you say that?"

"I just"—

"It's not like you, all of a sudden, to be angry."

"I got caught up in your frustration. I'm sorry."

He shook his head. "I can't answer that question."

I sat on my hands to hide their tremor. "Then don't. I wasn't thinking."

The space between us darkened. "Look at you." His gaze leeched to my skin. "I've upset you, after all."

I had to turn this around. "You were rude," I said in a cowed hush.

"Rude?"

"Yes, rude," I replied, stronger.

"This is my fault?"

"You got me started. I was only standing up for you."

"You were?" He pulled back.

"What did you think I was doing?"

He eased back into himself and nodded slowly, not taking his eyes from mine. "That makes me happy."

I held up my hands. "That's all I wanted."

Thad was interested in the effects of the boycott and Hans' thoughts on the Second Wave, but he seemed more interested in Hans, himself. He would sit me down while he prepared drinks and plates of exquisite cheeses, *foie gras* or some sort of charcuterie he happened to get his hands on because someone at the office had just come back from Paris or Rome. Then he'd ask his litany of questions, nodding and clarifying. He made me repeat things over and over again. Even the most mundane details were interesting to him. What Hans was eating and drinking, what he was wearing, what made him angry and what made him laugh, all mattered. Did Hans *always* 'worship' Joseph or just sometimes? Did he ever question his 'faith' in the regime? Did he aspire to wealth? How much of his 'pride' in his success had to do with his apartment, his possessions? I answered them all.

"But what does he *want,* Eva?" Thad finally begged.

"Respect. Recognition," I replied. "He lives off others' approval."

Thad shook me off. "We all do that. The question is, why? What weakness explains it?"

"You mean what unfairness has the world inflicted on him to make him feel inferior?" I asked, repeating his words to me.

He held out his palm to concede the point.

There was only one thing that was always there for Hans. Every time I talked to him I could see it. "He's unloved, so he loves people fiercely, even blindly, just to experience what he imagines love is, even if he gets nothing back."

"Always remember that," he said, and moved on. I never once got tired of it. I could have recited the alphabet a thousand times and not tired of it because of the way he held onto my words. He repeated them back to me, referred to them days later. He barely blinked when I spoke. We were a good team, he said. And better, "We're doing good things."

For the first time since I'd known him, I didn't feel less than him, and I wanted it to go on forever.

56

EVA

Hans asked me to meet him at work. He'd invited me at the last minute to a mountain film at the Zoo Palast. The woman he was supposed to go with had a family emergency. He said her name was Viktoria Morelli, adding details as if I might have thought he was making her up.

"Will she mind that you're going with someone else?"

"We have an open relationship, like I have with you."

"You mean you're just friends?"

"I guess it's not exactly like I have with you."

"Then you can reassure her I'll do nothing to compromise you."

"I'm sure you won't," he said, and hung up the phone.

When I arrived, Hans was sitting at his desk, in front of a Nazi flag. "It was sanctified by the *blutfahne*," he said. "The flag stained with the blood of the martyrs of '23."

"Is that supposed to be good?"

"It's an honor."

Joseph pushed through the door. "Excuse me for interrupting, but your girl told me Fraulein Schmidt was here! I wanted to say hello."

He sat next to me. I smelled his cologne and prayed it wouldn't cause another coughing fit. I breathed through my mouth in the way Frau Pappenheim said made people look stupid.

"Magda says she brought you to the new house," Goebbels said.

"It will be beautiful," I replied.

"Magda has excellent taste. I leave it all to her."

"A wise decision, Joseph," Hans added.

Joseph rested his hands on his knees, and said, "There's excellent news! I can share it because it will be announced shortly by the Office of the Reichskanzler. We've been given control of foreign propaganda! Hitler took it out from under Foreign Minister von Neurath's nose! Finally, we can do it our way. We'll win the world the way we've won Germany!"

Hans beamed. "That's fantastic, Joseph. It's long overdue."

"We have a record of success. The Foreign Ministry has a record of failure. Am I correct, Fraulein?"

"It seems so," I replied.

"In the meantime, Hans, Hedda's getting Otto Meissner on the phone. I need you to listen in. It will only be a few minutes."

When the door closed behind them, I walked over to Hans' desk. It was pristine, except for a pad next to the phone on which he'd written *Dieter* in all capital letters. Beneath, he'd scrawled names of industries, with down arrows and their percentage decline. *Banks, Iron, Wine, Fur, Medical, Education, Tobacco, Toys,* all were down by large sums. Next to *Shipping* he wrote, *NEAR TOTAL FAIL,* and underlined it multiple times.

I ripped a sheet from the bottom of the pad and quickly copied the list.

Steps came toward the door. I dropped the pen, and flipped over my page as Joseph entered alone.

"You've moved," he said.

"I was looking at the flag," I sputtered. "I didn't touch it, though. I know it's"—I couldn't remember Hans' word—"special."

"You can touch it," Joseph said.

The imprint of my writing showed on the back of the paper. I moved from the desk. "Hans wouldn't like me to. He's very serious about it."

"As he should be, Fraulein, but he works for me, and I want you to touch it." He walked up to me. The thump and drag of his foot echoed in the base of my skull. "If you want to, that is." He put his hand on my back and turned me toward the flag.

"I don't." My voice came out breathless and weak. "Want to, I mean."

"I wouldn't have pegged you as one to quiver before the symbols of the Revolution, Fraulein."

Was it a test? Thad's words, *If you're liberal, be liberal,* played back in my head.

"I don't"—I looked down—"I'm just terrified of blood. Especially blood from dead people."

"This from the young thing who sliced and diced Count Helldorf in front of us all?" he cackled. "I thought you were afraid of nothing! Please, sit down." He gestured toward the sofa. "I don't care much for dead people's blood, either."

"Is Hans coming back?" I asked.

"That's what I came to tell you. He's gone to the washroom. He asked me to let you know on my way out. I'm sorry to leave you alone with that," he gestured to the flag, "but Magda insists I come home before Helge's bedtime."

He turned to go, but looked back with something like kindness, "The blood's symbolic, Eva. You have nothing to fear."

It was the first time he'd called me by my first name. When he was gone, I crumpled the paper into a ball, and shoved it into my purse. I heard Joseph say, "You scared the poor girl, Hans. Blood on the flag?"

57

HANS

"Your girl was trembling like a leaf in there. Remember our maxim: *there is no place for politics in relations with women, and there is no place for women in politics*," Joseph says as I walked him to the elevator. He lives by this mantra. He has separate pockets for Magda, his lovers, and his work. Contradictions and hypocrisies never bog him down.

Maybe I don't have as many pockets to put things in, or maybe my pockets have holes, but my work, my beliefs, and increasingly Eva, are with me everywhere I go. "Should I go back, Joseph? I didn't know I'd upset her."

"You've got this girl in your head. Get your work done, then take care of your woman." He's in a good mood, I know, because he's leaving so few scars.

He stuffs both hands into his suit pockets. His voice lowers. This is a conversation for my ears only. "I was going to wait to tell you this tomorrow when I tell the staff, but if you agree not to share it with Fraulein Schmidt, I'll tell you now."

"Of course," I say.

"Propaganda is officially the Reich's top foreign policy priority. I've selected excellent men from print and radio to carry out day to day operations. He listed six men including Friedrich Graff. Dread crept into my gut. I'd been left out.

"But," he continued, I want someone inside the Reichsminister's office to supervise. That will be you."

I swell up with happiness. I have more work than I can imagine already, but to be chosen by Joseph for this position makes me unspeakably proud. I will be the voice of Germany to the world. I want to shove it in Friedrich Graff's face. He won't dare call me Magda's handmaiden. He's reporting to me now.

"Foreign journalists are predators, Hans. They'll call you stupid, and a liar. One of our programs can be 99 percent effective, and they'll focus on the one percent that's not. To be against things is as easy as breathing! These people have never created something from nothing. They only know how to destroy."

He jabs his finger at the invisible throng. "The West won't understand us until they trust us. That's your job. You're the perfect fit, Hansi. You're trustworthy. Take all that nice of yours, and lather them up with it. They'll see we're fair to the Jews. They'll believe the Führer is committed to peace and disarmament. You'll make them believe it. It's your most important job."

I itch to get started. He says, "Now, go back to Eva. She's not one to keep waiting." When the elevator opens, he announces, loud enough for all to hear, "But don't neglect Magda, Hans. She favors you so."

58

HANS

My first day in my new role was a success. Hitler's Peace Speech was a hit abroad. War is "unlimited madness," he said. He announced Germany stands "perfectly ready to disband her entire military establishment and destroy the small amount of arms remaining to her if the neighboring countries will do the same."

German Intelligence reported Roosevelt loved it, and I leaked his enthusiastic embrace to the press. It made it into all the papers. The West lapped it up.

In the meantime, Joseph briefed me on our new, top-secret rearmament council. April 1, 1934 is the date set to publicly repudiate Versailles. We will conscript 200,000 men, and mobilize 240,000 plants, along with massively increasing synthetic oil production. Based on Roosevelt's buoyant reaction, it seems not a word of this has reached the American President. Perhaps my job won't be so hard, after all.

I decide to treat myself to a new suit. I'll get it at Eva's shop. Then I'll tell the foreign reporters, off the record, that I have my clothes made by a Jewish tailor. I'll even give them Perlstein's name, and say, 'He's the same quality but far cheaper than the shops in the West End.' They'll see we're not the animals they want to believe we are.

Eva stands at the counter, taping a brown paper package. The store is silent except for the crinkle of her wrapping and the metallic tick of a wall clock.

"It's good of you to come," she says, impressed. She thinks it's some sort of liberal stand. It's just as well, if it's what she wants. At least she'll see I have thoughts of my own, and I'm not a half-witted Party stooge, which she all but accused me of the other night.

I explain to her I need a new suit because I've been promoted. "I'm supervising our foreign propaganda operation."

"What an honor!"

"I'm proud to have Joseph's confidence. He says the international community will take me seriously because I'm trustworthy."

"Let's find you something trustworthy, then." She pulls out a few catalogs. "I'm the only one here, so pick the style you want while I finish these packages. Then we can discuss fabric and color."

I turn the yellowed pages until I land on double-breasted suits. This is Joseph's style. It will signal I carry his proxy. "How about this?" I ask, turning the catalog toward her.

She looks up from her wrapping. "Someone your size shouldn't wear double- breasted suits."

"You tell me what to get, then."

"Step back so I can see you," she commands, and I obey. I feel her eyes all over me.

"Do you want something French?" she asks.

"Not French," I say, both as a matter of principle and because I want her to keep studying me.

"Then, Viennese." She reaches for a different catalog and flips through the pages. Her hand skims across the drawings and photos.

Occasionally, she looks up to envision me in different designs. I blush. She asks, "Do you write press releases in your new job?"

Is it possible she thinks I'm a press assistant? "I run the whole shop. I have others who write press releases for me. I develop strategy, manage the operation."

"It sounds important." She pushes a catalog toward me. "How about this?" It's a three-button suit, narrow at the waist. The pants are wide, with a sharp crease.

"I like it."

She pulls up a box with fabric samples. I paw through it, though I know what I want: a wool and silk blend, charcoal with pinstripes. I tell her.

"You're too tall for stripes," she says, and points to a beige swatch. "For summer."

"If you like it, I'll get it."

"Come back to the mirror." She holds open a ragged curtain and I step into her workspace. She drapes a tape measure around her neck. "Take off your shoes and jacket." She looks at my reflection. Her face says she's done this for hundreds of other men.

She steps onto a low stool behind me. My body blocks her from my sight. I twitch with surprise when she touches the tape measure to my shoulder. A shiver passes through me as her fingers graze across my back. "What are you telling these foreign correspondents?" she asks, letting the tape measure fall so she can jot notes on a pad.

I can't help myself. "I was the one who leaked the story about Roosevelt's enthusiastic response to the peace speech. Did you read about it?"

"I did! It was in the headlines. Was the leak intentional?"

Now, she's moving the tape down my arm. Her finger rests on my hand. "The leak was entirely planned and entirely true. It came from a high-level source inside the US State Department. Europe will take our peace pledge seriously if they know the American President does."

She faces me, and wraps the tape around my waist. Her turquoise eyes catch mine. "So, Hitler will disarm? The pledge is true?" Her voice is like honey.

"Of course!"

"That's something new," she mumbles, like she doesn't believe me. Since the war, the German people have demanded greater, faster rearmament, if only for the honor of it. Even during the darkest days of the Republic, the *Reichswehr* was rebuilding.

"In this case, true and not true are one and the same."

"That means it's a lie."

"A lie for a higher purpose is not really a lie."

"It's a white lie," she adds.

"If that's what you want to call it, fine. The point is, yes. We want peace. But not on a grossly unequal playing field. We will disarm if our adversaries also disarm." The tape is around my hips. It tickles, and my thoughts jumble. "And, regardless of what Roosevelt says, they won't. Who would? We have no choice but to accelerate rearmament. Hitler has appointed a council of the best men from all the relevant agencies, including Joseph. They're making it happen. All will be clear by next spring. Then we'll negotiate"— my muscles tighten —"as equals."

Now she's kneeling to measure my legs. Her dark hair shines in the light. I want to reach for her, but I can't. "I thought rearmament wasn't permitted." I know her touching is meaningless. There's no intention in it. It's her job. I picture my desk, my papers, Joseph, anything to dull my urges. I repeat what I was ruminating on when I left the office. "Even the pissant Poles are five years ahead of us militarily. Our generals put the odds of invasion at 50 percent. What Western nation would tolerate that?"

She's done. I need to breathe. Her face is buried in her numbers. I'm not sure I should have said what I said. Some of the information was classified, but I trust her. She is the one who stands up for me. "Eva," I say. She's not paying attention. "This conversation must stay entirely between us."

Her face turns grave. "Of course, Hans. I would never say a word to anyone." She stands on her tiptoes, bringing her face toward mine. I think she wants to kiss me, but her head turns. She whispers, "It's my job to keep secrets. I've never betrayed anyone's confidence. I'll never betray yours."

I need air. "One minute," I say. "I think I left something on the counter."

When I push back the curtain, her boss, the old Jew, is standing stock-still. He's surprised. Did he hear what I said? "You need to be careful not to lurk behind curtains, old man," I tell him, smiling. "Someone might just step on you."

59

EVA

What Hans revealed in the shop was better than anything I'd brought to Thad before. I noted his words as exactly as I had his measurements, writing cryptic notes that only I would understand. I dropped the pad on Thad's ottoman.

"What is it?"

I repeated the conversation, emphasizing what I thought was important. *We must rearm . . . Hitler has appointed the best men from all the relevant agencies. They're making it happen . . . Poland five years ahead . . . 50 percent chance of invasion . . . All clear by next spring . . . True and not true are one and the same.*

He said nothing. "This must be important, Thad. Isn't it?"

My words broke his stare. "Yes, it helps. Thank you."

It was not the reaction I'd wanted, and my urgency evaporated. "That's it?"

He walked to the bar, then paced back. He said, "There's never one thing that's actionable, of course, but this is good evidence. I'll report it. People in Washington who don't always recognize the Nazis' duplicity. " He reached for my hand and squeezed it. "I'm proud of you, Eva. You're getting good at this."

I stared at the door, trying to tamp down my elation. He took both my hands in his, which surprised me. "Remember, if Hans told you this, he knows you know more than you should. You have to be careful. Do not lose his trust." His tone suggested that my moral courage was beyond the norm. It was what I'd waited to hear. I'd earned his respect.

I wanted to write to Frau Pappenheim, to Matthias, and announce that I, Eva Schmidt, was not only doing what they wanted, but I was doing it well. I was *helping*. I hung Thad's praise around my neck like a medal. Far better than his words, however, was the weight of his hand that lingered too long against the small of my back as he walked me to the elevator, and how it didn't shift, even as I pulled away from him to go.

60

HANS

It's the loose ends that drive me mad. They're little flashes of black in the corner of my eye, telling me I can't control how things will turn out. This flash is too big. The black moves from the periphery of my vision to its dead center. It pushes my breath back into my lungs.

It's a shame, because the old man had no intention of doing wrong. Many of them don't. This is what people mean when they say the *Eternal Jew*. They're the unending loose ends, the flashes of black that stalk your vision, raise your doubts, and never go away.

Our führer is right. Doubt weakens us. *Lukewarm we spit out.* Now, with Eva's boss, there will always be doubt. Did he hear?

Eva has said his language skills aren't top notch. He's old, maybe hard of hearing. He would have had to listen carefully to understand. And even if he did hear, how would he know I wasn't just expressing my opinions? They're ones held by the vast majority of the Fatherland. They're also the truth. We will renounce Versailles. Did I say that to Eva? I was distracted, so I wasn't paying attention. Did I say we fear the Poles, or we should fear them? Did I say we're rearming, or we need to rearm? Can the Russian Jew understand the difference? Would people believe him if he did?

Anyone else would have called the SD already. *He's a Communist.*
He spoke against the Party, is all I need to say and the poor shit will
be drowning in his own blood in a concentration camp. But I don't
want to do that. I don't like to hurt people. I don't want to do what
Eva despises. I would happily live with her way of doing things. It's
what makes me trustworthy.

Still, how can I live with the black?

61

EVA

"She has a headache," Ursula clipped.

"Please, tell her it's me," I said.

When Ursula returned, she pointed to the sanctuary. "I'm sure you can find your way, by now."

When I opened the door, the lights were out and the curtain was drawn. Magda's form emerged as my eyes adjusted to the dark. She lay on the couch with her arm across her face.

"Do you want me to stay?" I asked.

"Close the door. Don't turn on the light." The air was thick and stale. "Sit next to me," she breathed, as she sat up. "I have the most wicked migraine."

"I'm so sorry," I said. At that, her body shuddered. I moved to put my hand on her shoulder, as one might with a friend, but I pulled back, remembering who she was. "Please, tell me what's wrong. Let me help."

"I thought he would kill me," she finally said.

"Joseph?" I was unsure if I should have said it.

"I've lit a fire in him I can't put out. All I can think of is Helge. How will she live without me? And then, there's him. What will happen to him? I've never been so afraid."

"Who, Magda? Who's he?"

"Viktor!" she whispered, her voice hoarse with strain. My heart froze. "Viktor needs to know that I'm not, that he's not safe anymore. He has to leave Germany and never come back. He can never speak to me, or of me, again."

"Viktor is your"—

"Yes!" she rasped, as if she blamed me for making her speak the word. "He's my Jew. Is that what you want me to say? He's the one I loved."

I forgave her anger as soon as she said love. "Oh, Magda," was all I could say. I wanted to tell her everything would be fine, but the words would only gauze over a moment that required honesty. I knew what she'd sacrificed to open herself up to me. No one ever had told me anything so cherished. There was no part of me her secret, her need, didn't touch. I wanted to give her something back.

My truth raced through me, looking for an exit. If I let it out, she would know how well I understood her, because, like the love of her life, I was also a Jew.

I waited for her tears to stop. In the moment of stillness, after she had let everything out, when her body melted, exhausted, into the downy seat cushion, my mouth opened to speak. "Magda," I said. My voice caught on itself and there was a long silence. I tried again, "You need to know something." I was raw, as if I'd been turned inside out. I believed she could see my thoughts. They were in the way I said her name, the way I couldn't take my eyes from her. If she just looked at me, she would know what I wanted to tell her, and my words could fall out.

But she didn't look at me. Her breathing didn't change. She stood, and adjusted her skirt. She took three breaths, straightened her posture, and wiped mascara from under her eyes. "There," she said. "That's it." Her chin angled toward the door, and without looking back, she exited the sanctuary, leaving me teetering over the words I'd buried for so long, I'd lost the voice with which to express them.

Thad was untucked and unbuttoned, fumbling with a cufflink. "Close the door," I said. I moved to the couch, but I couldn't sit down. Viktor Arlosoroff would not be the first Jew to die at the hands of Joseph Goebbels. If I had counted the minutes I'd spent with Hans and Magda, it wouldn't exceed the number dead and disappeared since Hitler came to power. But I'd absorbed Magda's love for this one. This one I could protect.

"Tell me." His authority pulled the words from my mouth.

"Goebbels is going to assassinate Viktor Arlosoroff." Thad was skeptical. I had to give him more. "Magda told me."

His expression didn't change. I pressed him. "Magda's still in love with Arlosoroff. She's had contact with him recently, and she's reeling. Joseph knows all about it. He was so angry, she thought he would kill her, as well." Thad walked toward the window. "What will you do?" I asked, finally.

"This is what you will do," he said. "You will act as if everything is normal with all of them. You will accept you're wrong, which I assure you are, so this idea, what you say Magda told you, never crosses your mind or your lips again. Everything else we've discussed could have come from multiple sources, but this," he paused, "could only be from you. If anyone were to find out you even thought it"—

"But you'll help him, won't you?" I asked.

He pulled me to his chest. "I'll try," he murmured, more to himself than to me. "I always try."

I knew I wouldn't be able to resist what was coming next. I took his hand in mine and kissed his palm. My body lit up in the pause. My mouth fell open, trying to catch my breath, and he was kissing me. He kissed my neck, my chest, pulling me to the ground. He reached under my blouse and his hands were on my breasts. They came up my skirt and pulled down my underwear. His fingers were inside me and I couldn't wait. I rolled out from under him and pushed him onto his back. I stripped off his clothes and climbed on top of him, chasing the moment when there would be nothing between us, and our bodies could leave everything else behind.

62

EVA

Paulina planted her big hands on her hips. "I don't have all day," she said. "I need to deliver this to Frau Witt at 1:00." She tapped at her watch. "We have so few customers now, we really shouldn't keep them waiting."

"He's only been gone an hour. Maybe he couldn't get a cab in the rain."

"Why he insists on checking our work the way he does, I'll never know. I've gone five years without a customer complaint, but he still counts my pleats and measures my stitches as though I were that deaf, dumb Jewish girl." She pointed at Ruth's old machine. It had sat silent since Herr Perlstein let her go, three days after her family was evicted from their apartment. I'd heard nothing more since, so I back stitched and beaded, working to the memory of Ruth's rhythmic machine, never looking up to see she wasn't there.

"You know," Paulina continued, "by the end, he was paying her with his own money. He wouldn't do that for us, would he? Us, he makes wait." She tucked her chin and widened her eyes, as she always did preceding an announcement. "When I get my own shop, I won't need anyone else's say so."

I reached for my purse. "Sorry, but it's the end of my shift. I'm going, but I'm sure he'll come soon."

"It's your turn for the rubbish," she snipped. "That's the one reason it's too bad we lost the girl. We shouldn't have to do these chores."

I took the bins from under the workbenches and emptied them into a larger, wheeled barrel. When I pushed open the door to the alley, the rain had subsided, except for a few heavy drops that slid off the roof. The bored-looking manager of the Turkish teahouse leaned against the wall, flicking the ash of his cigarette onto the ground. Rotten vegetables and used napkins were crushed into the pavement, creased in dirt. I followed a trail of loose coffee grounds to the dumpster. The barrel rumbled across the fractured cobblestones, and flies buzzed erratically in my ear. I breathed through my mouth to block the garbage stench, and nearly stepped on a piece of glass. It was round, as though from eyeglasses, and was pocked with rain.

I discovered it was a lens, because when I dumped my bucket of tracing paper, stray pins and worn-down grease pencils into the dumpster, I saw its other half, still attached to its frame, dangling from an ear, right next to a mole, which was next to eyes that were unexpectedly small and spread wide apart.

63

EVA

I heard little of anything: Paulina's frantic muttering, the errant steps of the *staatspolizei* splashing through puddles, their low incantations too close to my face: *Did I see? Did I hear?*

All I could see was Herr Perlstein standing by the curtain as Hans walked out of the back room. All I could hear were my panicked questions boring into my brain. *Was it Hans? Was this my fault?* I couldn't answer the officers' questions because I couldn't bear to hear my own voice.

Brown shirts and black shirts, suits and dresses gathered under a forest of Romanesque sculptures. Giant, exaggeratedly muscled Aryans twisted and clawed, their faces struck with fire. Hans stood beneath the mauling limbs, mesmerized by a torso perched on a steel rod. His secretary had told me where to find him.

He brightened when he saw me. "I'm so glad you came! Today is the opening. Let me show you." He took my elbow. "It's Breker and Thorak, arranged by virtue: readiness here, then strength, militarism and loyalty."

"What have you done?" I asked, my voice quavering.

"Each one, every detail, is more perfect than the last. It reflects the best we can be. It's art that believes in us." He turned to a spear thrower and seemed to lose himself in its sinewy contours.

I raised my voice, unable to control the trembling. "What have you done?"

He turned back to me. "What's wrong?"

"Did you do it?"

He shook his head, confused. "I don't understand. Come outside."

We walked under the gallery's high archway to a darkened corner of the entrance hall. "What are you talking about?"

"Did you kill Herr Perlstein?" I choked on his name.

His fingers raked through his hair. "How could you say this? I would never—you have to know this." His eyes were glass. There was nothing behind them that didn't believe his own words.

"Then who? Why now?" I demanded.

He clutched my arms, pushing my elbows into my ribs. "It's terrible, but it could be anyone, any day. Herr Perlstein was probably denounced. The führer ordered an end to false denunciations. They hurt our cause, but people don't understand that. I'm sorry this happened to you, Eva. I'm sorry it happened to him. I know how much you cared for him."

My headache flared. I sat on a stone bench, letting its cold seep through me. He sat by my side. I moved farther away.

"Think about it," he pleaded. "My job is to explain to the West that we're not the savages their media say we are. Just yesterday, I referred a French reporter to Herr Perlstein's shop. You'll meet him; Beaulieu's his name. Why would I want another dead Jew on my hands? Why would I disobey the *Führer's* explicit orders?"

"Because you think he heard what you said. You threatened him."

Hans's eyes shifted as he remembered. "You mean when we were talking about work? I never threatened him, I only asked him to get out of my way. Your imagination is running wild. If he heard me, he only heard me restate popular opinions, nothing more. I can go in there right now and announce the very same things to the crowd. They'll carry me out on their shoulders."

"What about the leak?"

"The leak was brilliant. I want people to know about the leak."

"But he's dead." My voice caught and I couldn't say more.

Hans put his arms around me. "Eva, it's not your fault," he whispered into the top of my head. "You can be sad, but you can't blame yourself. It has nothing to do with us. I wish I'd known. I would have helped him, like I tried to help Matthias Altmann. It's what I do."

Slowly, my muscles relaxed. I could hear the hum from the opening. I could see the art. I could see Hans. What he said about the reporter was logical, and he really did try to help people. He wasn't hiding anything. He couldn't. He was too weak. I decided to believe him. I needed to, because if it was his fault it was also mine. As my fear and anger faded, it dawned on me for the first time since stumbling upon Herr Perlstein's body that the one person in Berlin who knew who I was had been buried under a pile of trash.

There was a rustling, a pop of a camera flash, then two. A photographer backed slowly into the lobby, followed by a woman as dominating as the statues she'd come to see. It was Magda. I no longer knew how to fit into her world outside her sanctuary. I didn't know how she would react to me, given the weight of the secrets she'd shared. I still carried her terror inside me. Not just for her, but for Viktor, the man who made her human, the man powerful enough to create a space where she and I could be friends.

I searched her for the pain she'd let fall into my lap, but there was nothing. She looked radiant.

Hans jerked to attention, and pulled me into the gaggle. A reporter peppered her with questions. The group turned toward the monumental warrior guarding the exhibit entrance. Its massive arms folded across its chest. Its maw thrust into space. Hans struck the same pose as we waited for Magda to notice us. The similarity was remarkable, except Hans would never have the face of an avenger. His transparency betrayed his hyper-masculine body. His naïveté could not be muscled over. I told myself he hadn't lied to me. He couldn't. I was the liar, not him. Never him.

"Bravo, Hans. It's smashing!" Magda exclaimed. "Let's get it on Joseph's schedule, shall we?"

"I will, Magda," Hans responded.

"You must be proud of Hans, Eva," she said. "He's put together something marvelous here."

I was unsure what to say. She knew I had no romantic interest in Hans. I had repeated it many times in the sanctuary.

"It is marvelous, Magda." My voice was hesitant. Hers was not.

"You're very lucky to have him," she added. "But I know you know that." I couldn't believe it was Magda speaking this way. She knew we weren't together. I'd been explicit. She caught Hans's eye, and he hers. He looked at me, eager for a response, which I wouldn't give.

"At least that's what you've been telling me," Magda's voice commanded. Nothing shifted in her face as she lied.

"He's a good friend." I couldn't feel betrayed by her. I wasn't eligible for betrayal. It would have meant she owed me something, and that was impossible. Rather, she'd written me into her outside script, where what we said in the sanctuary ceased to exist. She said it was sufficient for me to be Hans's companion. She said Hans would accept that. 'Everyone needs to show up places with a pretty girl on his arm,' she'd said. 'Especially men who are as attractive as Hans. If they don't, people start to wonder.'

A voice shouted, "Frau Goebbels!" Magda's arm reached for me, yanking me to her side. The camera flash shattered my vision and her voice hissed through the din, "Just smile."

64

HANS

I'd been caught in the cross-current of my arguments. If I was unsure of what I'd said that day, the old man had to be, too. There was a heavy curtain between us. His German wasn't good. Could he swear an oath that he'd heard what he claimed? Could he lay his hand on his Jewish bible and assert that what I'd said to Eva, within the confines of our private conversation, was anything more than my personal opinion? He wouldn't be stupid enough to go after me. Even if he did, no one would believe him, not in the new Germany. The old Jew had no chance against me. I was superior to him in every way.

It was my worrying which made me weak, not him. I'd been wringing my hands as if he was the one with the power, as if he could make me react in ways I didn't want to. I was a top aide to Reichsminister Joseph Goebbels. I had a right to deal with this situation as I pleased, without guilt or doubt. Doubt begets doubt.

I didn't kill him. I didn't kill him because I didn't want to kill him, and I don't have to do what I don't want to do. That's what the Revolution does for us.

65

EVA

I didn't cry until I got to Thad's. It was where Herr Perlstein's absence hit me, and hollowed me out. I had been so blinded by my own guilt, I let his loss slip through my fingers without honor or blessing.

Herr Perlstein had supported me when I'd arrived in Berlin, then guarded my deepest secret. I'd felt wronged by his coolness so I never acknowledged what he'd done for me. He protected me. He didn't try to shape me or change me. He let me live the life I wanted. All he said was the truth; he didn't know me. Now, he never would. Herr Perlstein was a good man. I would tell that to his family. I vowed to go to his *shiva* and tell them, *Zichrono Livrocho,* he is of blessed memory.

Thad lay with me in his bed. He said he was sorry. I said I couldn't take it anymore. Someone had to do something soon. He said, "That's why we're doing what we're doing. Everything will be alright. I'll help. I promise." He breathed the words into my ear, again and again. He held me without impatience, and when I asked, he made love to me.

After he got up, the weight of my release held me down. I lay bare and open to him. "Stay here," he said. "I need to go out for a bit, just to say hello to a Princeton friend who's in from London, but I won't be long. Please stay." I curled into a ball. He covered me, and watched me until I fell asleep.

When I woke up, the apartment was lit by the streetlamps' glow. Thad hadn't come home yet. I walked around his bedroom, feeling his carpet cushion my steps. I drew my hand across the back of his chair. The wood was cold. His work suit had fallen off the end of the bed. I took a hanger from his closet, folded the pants at the crease and slid them onto the brass locking bar. I put the jacket over the curved wood and buttoned the top button.

I brushed a piece of fuzz from the collar and imagined dressing him, caring for him. I refolded his towels, put his toothbrush back in its silver cup and washed its smudge from the sink top. I went into the hall and ran my fingers along its white walls, across the door jamb and against the always-closed door to his study. I felt the cool hardness of the knob in my palm, and knowing I shouldn't, I turned it.

Thad was asleep on the couch. A dim reading light framed his face. There was an empty brandy snifter on the floor. A pile of papers was strewn over his chest and across the rug. Even after all I'd done for him, I knew he wouldn't want me in his study.

My fear of waking him brought back the pained inequity we'd had before, where my moods and hopes depended on his favor. Yet, I still wanted him. He owned a part of me, and he could bring it to life at will.

I reached to turn off his light and something on one of the pages caught my eye. It was the word *moderation*. It was the perfect word for an American and the perfect word for Thad.

I loved him. He liked me. I would have married him. He would have dated me until he married someone else. I hated the Nazis. He didn't hate. It would be immoderate.

I picked up the page and read. It was a summary, written by Thad, for the Military Intelligence Division of the United States Army.

Interdepartmental consensus exists at the Embassy on key issues:

1. While the Nazi-led government uses terroristic methods to deal with Jews, Hineman and Rowan's report of 5 May is accurate re: Jewish and liberal manipulation of the Association of Foreign Press Correspondents, resulting in its overt hostility to the regime.

2. Any organized economic boycott of Germany is antithetical to US interests, viz. debt repayment, Communist threat and German rearmament. Chargé Gordon's effort to diffuse formal diplomatic protest among France, UK, et al. has been well received.

3. Intelligence suggesting direct negotiations between Zionist organizations and the regime is well founded. The negotiations represent a critical opportunity to end the international boycott. They should be exploited.

4. The regime maintains a highly exaggerated fear of Jewish power, and Jews' ability to impact the German economy through boycott. Agitation for boycott comes from labor unionists and Communists, many of whom are Jews. <u>It does not reflect the views of the more respectable elements of German Jewry</u>.

5. Gordon's view that Hitler represents the "reasonable center" of German *politics, and Wuest's argument that with "proper controls" by Göring and Goebbels, Hitler can be further hewn in, are sound, <u>including with respect to rearmament, which occurs apace</u>.*

<u>Conclusion</u>:
A show of goodwill by the US to the Reichschancellor, particularly regarding a boycott, will foster moderation and is in the best interests of the United States and her allies.

A deafening rumble grew inside me. I thought I would break apart. Amidst my madness was Thad's perfectly comfortable sleep. I couldn't piece together a reaction, and what I left unsaid spread poison through me. My spiritual mother's prophecy on my first train ride to Berlin flared in front of my eyes. Thad was my Alfonse. My scum procurer. With silk stockings and fake gold, with promises of work and running water, he crawled out of the shtetl's muck and shone his way into my trust. I didn't know what I'd done until I was abandoned to my bloody sheets, beyond redemption.

I was worse than a whore. I was bought only with praise. The words brave and strong and proud were my running water, my most basic need. Thad discovered my essential weakness, and he used it to make me trust him. He took my information and did the opposite of what I'd wanted. Then, he fucked me. And I gave it to him for nothing, because he was enough for me.

I opened the desk drawer and took out a marker and a piece of tape. I posted the memo on his door. Gripping the pen tightly in my fist so its ugly squeak rang in my ear, I drew a thick, black swastika over his words.

66

HANS

Eva's skin is washed out by the flash. There's a haunt to her concave cheeks. She's a wisp next to Magda, who steals the camera's focus. I'm standing in profile. My armband faces the camera and my eyes are trained on the women. I'd told the editor to use the photo, and I instructed him on how to phrase the caption. Eva Schmidt was a 'close confidante' of Reichsministerfrau Magda Goebbels, and was the 'special guest,' of Hans Lorenz, a 'top aide' to Reichsminister Joseph Goebbels.

Just to have Eva frozen like this, next to Magda, on the society page of *Der Angriff*, makes our connection real. It's not all in my head. Yesterday, when I was at the apartment, Magda finally spoke directly with me about Eva. She told me Eva had feelings for me. She told me she wanted us to be together, and Eva wanted it too, despite her dilly-dallying. Magda isn't one to part with good news easily. Nor is she one to lie to give heart to a tortured soul. I believed her. Finally, I'm getting somewhere with this girl.

I take the newspaper around to my colleagues. "This is my girl," I explain, "the one next to the *Reichsministerfrau*. They're very close."

"Nice, Hans," one says.

"Lucky man," replies another.

"She's too thin," says my secretary.

One of the radio guys invites us to go out with him and his pregnant wife. He wants to go to a Chinese place. He says spicy food induces labor, and his wife is the size of the Hindenburg. It worked for his other four children, he tells me. I'm hit by a jealous pang. His life is as it should be.

I remind myself that unlike Viktoria Morelli, who happily declined me just this morning, and despite Eva's intolerable indecision, she has never once said no to going out with me. Without asking her, I say yes.

67

EVA

It had laid waste to everything I'd done and everything I'd thought I'd become. Every block we'd ever walked, every dining room where we'd ever eaten, every government building I thought I was helping to dismantle insulted me as I passed. I'd wanted to stay in bed all day, but I'd vowed to go to Herr Perlstein's *shiva* to pay him respect.

I stood across the street from his flat, which was on the first floor of a stuccoed walk-up. A woman carrying a covered pot turned up the steps. Her hair was wrapped in a black scarf and her shoulders fell forward. Her husband held the door for her to enter. I had brought nothing but a tin of *pfeffernüsse*. I had no place to cook anything better.

Flashes of ladles and glints from white plates shone in the bow window. There would be pickled herring, chopped liver, and trays of smoked whitefish. Stuffed cabbage would be warming over a low flame. I imagined closer friends than I passing plates and filling teacups from a copper samovar. Six months ago, I might have been among them. Now, all I could do was enter, introduce myself, and speak the words I promised I would say. *Zichrono Livrocho,* He is of blessed memory.

At that, my doubts raced in. What if he'd gone home the day of my confession, tired and angry, and told his wife I'd asked him to lie for me? Would she remember my name? Would she whisper the story to the people sitting next to her? To think of her disdain left me cold. I imagined one of her girls gently, but firmly, guiding me out the door and out of their lives.

Worse than all of this was my terror that Herr Perlstein's departing soul might have witnessed my hideous relief when I remembered he was the last Berliner to know my past. I trembled to think he might have seen my soul's blackness as his returned to the light. His stinging words came back to me. *We shall operate as if I don't know you at all, Fraulein Schmidt.*

"*Zichrono Livrocho,*" I said to his window, and turned my back.

The *Perlstein* sign leaned face down against a metal chair. A man I didn't recognize rolled broad swaths of white paint across the walls. Herr Perlstein's abacus had disappeared, but the leather-bound pen cup still sat on the counter. The gray curtain separating the rooms was gone.

"I've come to get my things. I worked for Herr Perlstein," I said to the man, but he only grunted.

"Who's there?" came a voice from the other room. It stopped me. "Werner," it shouted. "Who is it?" Paulina appeared in the doorway and a grinding pain roared in my chest. "No," I breathed.

"What do you mean, no?"

"You denounced him!" I shouted.

"I did no such thing!" she snapped. "But someone else easily could have, with all his whispering into the phone, and closing the door to his office. He incriminated us every day we worked here and didn't report him. I came in one night, and he had five Jews, sitting around a bottle of slivovitz. Veterans, they said they were having a reunion. Plotting was more like it."

"Stop lying," I demanded.

Paulina's voice softened. "Even if he were denounced, I'm sure whoever did it never meant for him to wind up dead." Her blond eyebrows pushed into the folds of her forehead. "He didn't deserve that."

"Then, it was you!" I swung around to face her husband. He continued painting his slow rolls.

"You're one to talk, aren't you?" Paulina's wide hips sashayed toward me. "Werner, did you know there's a star in our midst?"

She held a copy of *Der Angriff* high in the air and slapped it onto the counter. I stared at the paper. I'd known it could happen once the picture was taken, but so many were taken, I told myself it was impossible for mine to be chosen. Yet, there I was, in black and white, on the society page of a Nazi newspaper. I stood next to Magda. Hans was to the side. The caption beneath the photo included my name, in case I tried to doubt it. *Eva Schmidt (right), close confidante of Reichsministerfrau Magda Goebbels (center), and special guest of Hans Lorenz (left), top aide to Reichsminister Joseph Goebbels.*

Paulina leaned with her hands on the counter. Her elbows jutted out like bat wings. "So, this is your secret, Eva. I knew it was something like this, with the way you talk, the way you act. Before the Nazis came, you were nothing more than a shop girl. You couldn't have nailed a clerk. But now look at you. I didn't want to keep you on, but I see I'm stuck with you. You've got your lover's protection."

"I would never work for you," I seethed.

She threw her head back and cackled, "Look who's too good for us now, Werner?"

68

HANS

"All hail Caesar!" the boys in the office shout when Joseph enters. "Conqueror of Rome!"

Joseph pops the cork to a bottle of *Asti Spumante*, and lets the bubbles roll over his hand. We rush forward with our cups to catch the precious drops. Rome was the most successful trip I've organized for Joseph in years, and it came just at the time things are most bleak internationally. It took only a few days before he had *il Duce* proclaiming the German Revolution to be the greatest in the history of the world!

One thing is certain, without the filter of the Jewish press, Joseph can persuade anyone, anywhere, of anything. We in the Ministry are measured by his success, and tonight we're geniuses.

"How did you do it, Herr Doktor?" I hear from behind me. *Tell us!* and *Yes!* volley forth.

Joseph thinks for a moment, and says, "I persuaded him of our end game."

One of the new pressmen holds his glass high. "To the master of our game!"

I know before Joseph's face darkens that the soft-soaping sap has taken it too far. He doesn't know he's done anything wrong. He never will. He also never will get another promotion at the Ministry. He doesn't know that Joseph doesn't believe in good intentions. It's why he works so hard to mold people's thoughts. The pressman has committed the sin of over-praise, and as fast as he does it, Joseph decides he's a liar.

As the room clears out, Joseph approaches. Aside from the secretaries cleaning up, it's just the two of us. The linings of the ladies' skirts swoosh against their stockings. Their brisk paces tell us they're paying us no mind. I love the sound of women's work. I wonder what it would be like to be mindless like that, to be made happy by putting things back in drawers, disposing of trash, and restoring order.

"Magda was fantastic with Mussolini, Hansi. You should have seen her," Joseph says.

"Magda's a force, Joseph. *Il Duce* is wise to appreciate her."

"*Il Duce* finds ways to appreciate all sorts of women."

"Then *Il Duce* is wise about a lot of things."

I walk with him back to his office. He says, "We did well this week. I'm celebrating with Hela. What are your plans?"

"I hope to see Eva."

"You will see Eva, then." Joseph's voice is generous. Things must have improved with Magda. I wonder how he dispensed with the Arlosoroff matter.

"I know what it's like to be in love with an intelligent woman, Hans. I see a lot of Magda in your girl. She's hard on you. She uses her brain. I'm sure that's why Magda likes her so much."

"I'm glad Magda likes Eva. She doesn't suffer fools."

Joseph laughs. "Listen to me, Hans. If there's one thing I've learned about love, it's the more intelligent your woman is, the more you need to direct her. It's easier to be with an idiot, but we don't want that, do we? We're addicted to the challenge."

I'm stunned he's comparing us. Eva's like a moth, made frantic by light. The conversation with Magda at the opening was no exception. I couldn't pin her down. Not even Magda could. To resist is as natural as breathing for her. I expect she's far more left wing than she lets me know. Magda is, too, I'm sure. Maybe it's why Eva can't commit, despite what Magda says are her true feelings.

"What do you do about it, Joseph?"

"Believe me, no matter what feminist spew she throws your way, no woman wants to have too much power. The second she thinks she owns you, she'll drop you like last year's dress. Truly strong women want their men to be even stronger."

I don't know what strength to show Eva to make her love me. I could start by not asking her to tell me what my future holds. She probably thinks I'm no better than the Slavic slobs she sees every night at the bar.

"I've been stupid," I blurt out.

"You're doing it again," he tutted. "You're taking the back seat. Man is the organizer of life, woman is his helper and his executive agent."

"I know, Joseph. You're one hundred percent correct."

He wasn't through with me. "Let her know how you see things. Explain to her what's meant to be, and," he shoves the flat of his hand against my chest. "Show her you will destroy anyone or anything that steps in your way."

69

EVA

Gnats and moths swirled around the muted yellow light above the door to the *klub*. Zara prattled on about how the university had changed the curriculum. "We're to study 'German knowledge' now. It's different from the 'knowledge' we used to 'know.' We won't teach physics. That's Jewish." She puffed her chest in imitation. "Physics is 'the diseased product of poisoned minds.'"

"Instead, the men will teach boys 'German physics,' and 'German biology.' The women will teach girls nothing but how to set a table and change a diaper in the German way, of course. *Kinder! Küche! Kirche!* Children! Kitchen! Church!" She took a long drag on her cigarette and exhaled a spiral plume.

I had no interest in engaging with her. I went back inside. I wanted to shout to everyone in the bar what Paulina had done, but I couldn't take a big enough breath, so I sat at Salomé's table, watching Shmuel's mop circle across the floor.

It wasn't long before the peddler of German physics himself entered the *klub*. His presence clogged my throat. He had no idea how thoroughly Thad's deception had degraded him in my eyes. He was useless. We both had been eviscerated of value. We were left with only our venality, and I hated us.

He came straight for me and held out his hand. "What do you see?"

I saw filth. It made me sick. "Why are you here?"

He shrugged. "I was telling my friends about you. I didn't have answers to their questions. I was embarrassed. We were in the paper together. I have the right to know something about what makes you who you are."

Magda was the one who gave him the confidence to claim a right to me, not the newspaper. And, he did have the right, because I was no better than he was anymore. "I'm at work. You'll get me in trouble."

"I'll pay you, then. Just start. We don't have to finish today."

"I'm an orphan, Hans. I have no past."

"Where was your orphanage?"

He was too ill-bred to understand it was rude to ask these questions. It was rude to acknowledge anything about my past. "Can't you see I don't want to talk about it?"

"What I see is a woman who faces a world where there's no more need for shame, and yet, she insists on it. I won't judge you, Eva, even if you judge yourself. We're lucky to be alive at this time."

"You're lucky, Hans. You're not dead in a dumpster."

"There's something wrong with you tonight. You're not yourself." He tapped the table three times. Thad's warning came back to me. *Hans knows you know more than you should. Be careful. He has to trust you.*

"Look at me," he insisted. My father's a madman and my mother was forced to patch together a living off her lovers' charity. I wouldn't call either of us very lucky on our way up. It's to our credit that we've come out so well."

I was balancing on constantly shifting earth in order not to be buried, and this absurdity was just another pile of dirt that had turned upside-down. I surrendered. "I was abandoned."

"How old were you?"

"A baby."

"An infant?"

"I was left in a cardboard box on the doorstep of a convent, starving, without the strength even to cry," I lied. The words came easily because they fit me so well. "Now you know. I hope it's interesting enough for you to tell your friends."

"I would like to meet the nuns who created such a woman out of a baby in a box."

"You and the nuns don't have the same taste."

"And, you have to learn to accept compliments."

I looked away. "Please, you need to let me get back to work."

"I'll take you to the nuns. They'll see the woman you've become."

"Stop!" I begged. "I work in a bar. I tell fortunes. It's hardly the life of a good Catholic girl."

He shook his head slowly, then looked at me. His eyes were bright, his smile, wide-open. "It's not what is, it's what will be that matters. With me, you will have respect. Why can't you see what's right in front of you? These nuns will be proud of you."

My heart beat faster. This had gone too far. *Never lie* beat against my temples. I had to end it. "I won't go. I don't want to. I don't care what they think. They were just a couple of mean, old nuns. I don't know what's become of them," I moaned.

"And where did you live with these mean, old nuns whom you never want to see again?"

"Frankfurt. Now, please." I glanced in the direction of the bar, but Rudi paid us no mind. "You have to leave."

"So, that's what you're hiding. You were raised in the shadows of Goethe University, the Institute for Social Research, perhaps. It explains your liberal side."

A piercing ring started in my ear. Frau Pappenheim had taught us about this 'so-called Institute for Social Research.' It was run by wealthy Frankfurt Jews who used their abundant intellectual gifts in the service of Karl Marx. She said they brought shame on us all.

He ran his fingers down my cheek to my jaw, then lifted my face toward his. His heat assaulted me. "Are you afraid to tell me you used to sneak out for *kaffee und kuchen* with Communists and Jews from the University?"

He turned my hair between his fingers. "Did you catch this black hair from your Jews?"

The ringing in my ear turned to a howl. I pounded my fist on the table. "How dare you say that?"

He jerked back, then leaned so close to me, I could map the pores of his skin.

He ran his hand down the back of my head, catching his finger in a knot of my Jewish hair. He yanked through it. The pain caused my eyes to water. His breath covered my face. I thought I would collapse under my own weight.

A laugh started in the shake of his shoulders. When the sound finally came out, he said, "What a good Nazi you've become."

70

EVA

My room was inhumanly hot. My bed felt like it was covered with bugs. I jumped up and opened the window. I leaned out, desperate for air. There was none. I took off my clothes, and paced naked. Sleep wouldn't come. If I lay down, my thoughts raced, and I had to get up; and if I stood up, I was so overwhelmingly tired, I had to lie down.

Hans was circling me. It wouldn't be long before he figured things out. How could he not? I was floating above my life with no place to land.

I thought about fleeing, but I had no false papers, and I couldn't pay to get any. I'd burned my real papers. If I replaced them, I would have to hand my true identity to a Nazi agency. If nobody followed up on that, and I got a passport, I would still need police permission for an exit visa. How long would it take? Where would it lead? Would they trace me back to Hans, Magda or even Thad? If the police put me on a list, if they saw the *Der Angriff* photo, if they refused to let me go . . .. The *ifs* closed in on me, each one a knife cut to my brain, driving me mad.

I wanted a sanctuary like Magda's, where nothing was real, but everything was true.

330 / Jill Morningstar

When the first light appeared over the rooftops, I dressed. I passed Zara's door. She'd met a party member at school. His muffled voice, and her delighted, careless laughter chased me down the steps. So much for what our landlady would do if we brought a man up to our rooms. Party members probably didn't count as threats anymore, at least if they didn't want to be.

I wanted Matthias. I wanted Frau Pappenheim. I wanted everyone I couldn't have. I wanted the ones I loved.

The owner of the newsstand down my street unlocked the padlock to his kiosk and swung its green doors open wide. He dragged a stack of newspapers from the back of an idling truck, waving when he saw me. "You're so early today," he said, in his Italian accented German.

"I lost my job."

"I can't believe it. You work so hard."

"My boss was a Jew."

He shook his head. "It's a terrible thing. I'm so sorry for you. You want the usual?" I handed him my money, but he waved it away, and cut the cord from a stack of *Berliner Tageblatts*.

I looked around, distracted. Papers from the day before were still on the racks, and a black and white face on the front page of the *Jüdische Rundschau* caught my attention. It was a headshot of a solemn man with hooded, sensitive eyes and soft cheeks. I stopped breathing. *Chaim Arlosoroff Murdered.*

I took it, leaving the *Tageblatt* behind. I read the article three times, unable to stop seeing Viktor's death as the reporter described it: the Mediterranean sky washed over in silver moonlight, Arlosoroff, so mythic in my mind, failing as his blood spilled into the sand, his widow, desperately calling for help as the killers escaped over the dunes. Right-wing, Revisionist Jews were suspected, followers of a man named Ze'ev Jabotinsky. They were enraged a Jew would negotiate with the enemies of Zion. When my shock broke, I ran to Magda.

No one answered the door to the apartment so I went to the residence. Ursula said Magda was not to be bothered. My heart sank. I wanted to help her. I wanted to attach my sadness to hers. I don't know where my boldness came from, but I said with force, "She'll want to see me. It's important." Ursula hesitated. "We've been through this before, Ursula," I demanded.

"Very well, then," she snipped, and led me to the sanctuary. "Fraulein Schmidt for you, Madam," she said to the closed door.

A weak 'fine' came back.

The silence hung heavily over the room. Magda sat on the couch, her back straight, her knees pinned tight together. She stared out the French doors with blank eyes. I sat, mimicking her stillness, guarding the sacred.

After a minute, she twitched. She hummed. She continued in spurts, back and forth, as if she was negotiating with herself.

I reached toward her, but she slapped at my hands. "No!" she shouted.

My heart ached for her. "It wasn't your fault," I said. "There was nothing you could do."

She looked up, her face filled with rage, and said, "You think it was Joseph. You think Joseph killed him because of me." It was a command, not a statement, as if she were directing my thoughts, staving off any other conclusion before I had it. She couldn't carry her fears alone, I thought. She needed me to believe her, and I did.

71

HANS

Magda stands at the end of the hallway, talking quietly into the telephone. She's wearing a form-fitting, sleeveless dress that cuts in a V at her chest. She's too beautiful, and I don't trust my eyes. She should put on her jacket, as befitting a First Lady.

I never know how to appreciate Magda's looks, particularly around Joseph. He loves her most when she's in the spotlight. For her, it's the same. They have a way of seeing each other through the eyes of the third person in the room. But if I were to appreciate her too much, he would hammer nails into my eyes.

It's different for me and Eva. It's only the two of us. Of course, I'm pleased that Joseph and Magda have blessed her, but I like that I've discovered her less than obvious beauty myself. It's as if I created it. I'm losing myself in this thought when the phone lands hard in its cradle.

The V of Magda's neckline comes toward me too fast. I see the edge of her brassiere. She doesn't care that I'm blushing, that I want to crawl behind the radiator and not come out until she's gone. She has no airs today.

"Was it him?" Her voice grinds from its force. "Tell me he did it."

"I don't understand, Magda," I protest, although I know too well what she's asking. Even I wondered when I heard about Arlosoroff's murder. But a British subject on British soil? It's impossible, even for Joseph.

"I hear things, Hans."

"About what?" I sound like an idiot.

She claws my arm. "I know about the agents. I know Joseph sent them to Palestine. What business does Joseph have in Palestine?" Her eyes search me, their blue manically shifting along her lower lids.

My heart pounds as I catch up. "He sent them to repossess German gold, to keep it from the British."

"But they returned without it. Why would Joseph have anything to do with lost gold, anyway?"

"It's not our affair, Magda."

"He sent them to hire assassins. You know he did."

It would be so much easier if I could hold her and ease away these questions, just like I did with Eva at the museum. But, it's not despair she's feeling. She's too hot. Her fuse is lit. She tastes something in me she's desperate to hear.

"There are a hundred reasons for German agents to find themselves in Palestine. We have a settlement in Sarona, to start." The answer calms me. "I assure you, if you're thinking something nefarious"—

Now she's leering, as if she might spit on me. "You're a lying fool."

I wasn't lying. I don't believe Joseph did this murder. Even the Jewish press said the man was killed by one of his own. Still, when I think back, Joseph was so kind about Eva after the celebration. He's only kind when he comes from a position of strength. I hadn't stopped to think what put him there. He's had other rivals for Magda's affection. Hitler stands at the top of the list. Joseph can do nothing about the boss, as much as he wishes he could. It's in the order of things for women to worship him the most. Magda's special relationship with Hitler benefits Joseph tremendously. It protects, and enhances him. They're a strange, interdependent trio.

On the other hand, of all her former lovers, Arlosoroff is the open sore. His mere existence would have nagged at Joseph like a buzzing fly until he could think of nothing else. He had no choice but to smash him into oblivion.

None of this is to mention the recent imprisonment of Magda's ex-husband, Gunther Quandt. Quandt is one of the wealthiest men in the Reich, yet he sits in a jail cell on dubious charges, something about taxes.

Perhaps it's also a coincidence, but there's the unexplained appearance of a man named Richard Friedlander at the Ministry a few weeks ago. This is the name of Magda's Jewish stepfather. I don't know if he met with Joseph or someone else, but he was escorted out of the building by black shirts.

Are these the lengths to which Joseph will go to tame his woman? Is this what he was explaining to me the other night? Were these conquests what gave him the strength to be kind?

I'm playing into the lady's madness. How pleased she would be to know.

72

EVA

A crowd of black spilled down the stone steps of the Philharmo-
nie for Viktor Arlosoroff's memorial service. The Great Hall
was full well before the start, and I stood in the lobby. I'd come for
Magda, whom I knew could never come. I thought she would want
me to be there. I wondered if she had dressed as these women had,
in neat black. I pictured her in the sanctuary, immobilized by grief.

I'd never mourned anyone before. Not having to rip your clothes
in anguish was one asset orphans could claim. I'd told myself I was
immune to this kind of sorrow. Still, Herr Perlstein and Arlosoroff's
deaths both hinted at parts of me that could be shaken by loss.

"Die Jews!" burst through the open doors. A throng of
brownshirts and the raging mob that followed them had gathered
around the steps. The *Staatspolizei* separated them, but the
screaming didn't stop. "Parasites!" "Demons!" rang out.

A Nordic-looking man was next to me. Like me, he stood
straight, without tears. His eyes closed to the madness behind us. I
was grateful not to be the only presumed aryan inside. There were
several, by my count. His eyes opened. Without turning to me, he
asked, "Did you know him?"

I wished I could have said yes. I didn't deserve the sadness I felt from his death. It was too big for my tiny connection to him. "Through a friend," I said. "And you?"

"He was my student. One of the best I've ever taught." He clasped his hands in front of him and we stood together in silence.

The sounds of the service carried to the lobby, but the audio speakers swallowed many of the words. A few popped out clearly. I would take them back to Magda: *true visionary, accomplished author, married a doctor, economics, homeland, mother, Ukraine, genius, Viktor, Chaim, Chaim, Viktor.*

It seemed the others understood something I didn't. They nodded, occasionally laughed, and shared meaningful glances. Some cried, always at what seemed like the right moments.

Near the end, there was a silence, fractured only by the sound of shuffled papers and the harsh bang of an inadvertent brush against the microphone. Then, silence again. When it broke, I heard every word. Inside the Hall and outside, unabashed and unrelenting, the people recited the *Kaddish. V'yiskadal, V'yiskadash, shmei raba,* May His great name be exalted and sanctified. It was the Jewish prayer for the dead, an assertion of God's presence, a steadying force during the worst of times.

The Aryan stared solemnly into the distance, taller than the voices, breathing different air. His jaw was clamped shut, a mirror of mine.

Oseh Shalom bimromav, hu oseh shalom . . . May He who makes peace on high, make peace . . .

The words sat like lead on my tongue, my silence suffocating me.

I went straight to Magda. I needed her to know the depth of the mourning in the hall, in those voices, of those people who shared her love. I considered telling her what happened to Herr Perlstein.

Maybe we could cry together. Maybe she wouldn't feel so very much alone.

Magda herself answered the door. She wore a cream-colored summer suit trimmed with thick, black grosgrain. When we got to the sanctuary, I waited for her façade to crumble, but she remained strong.

"I went to the service, Magda, but I couldn't get into the Hall. That's how many people were there."

She was touched by my words. "Tell me about it. I want so much to know." She turned her knees toward me on the sofa, resting her shoulder against the cushion. There was no sign of the brittle, emptied woman with whom I'd sat only a few days before.

"There were thousands of people there. So many young people, too. They all came out for Viktor." In the sanctuary, I could call him by his first name.

"Yes," she urged.

"Nazis were there. They shouted the most horrible things. 'Die Jews! Demons!' It was awful!" I couldn't believe I'd said it, but I needed her to sympathize with these Jews, whom she had once embraced as her own, who were free to weep for her love.

Magda stared out the French doors, nodding slowly, without surprise.

"But it didn't stop the service. Not for one second. Every speaker talked about his brilliance"—

"He was the most brilliant. He wrote books." Now, her eyes sparkled.

"They called him a visionary."

"He could solve any problem. I'm so pleased you were there. I've wanted you to understand what I had with him."

"People adored him, Magda. You would have been proud."

"He was one of the greatest," she said, hugging her arms to herself. Her face warmed with far away thoughts. "I was lucky to have had such a great man."

"You were, Magda," I said with all honesty. "You were very"—

"I know," she interrupted. Her hand reached for my knee, and as quickly, fell off. "But things have become so much clearer." Her eyes set on me. They were like topaz, ice blue over a white-hot flame. I braced for her outburst. I wanted her rage to hammer at the walls of the sanctuary, to sprout cracks through the stone. The angels of her truth: Viktor, the Buddha, her stepfather Friedlander, little Helge, George Gershwin, and I waited for her lead.

"Tell me, Magda," I begged.

Her breath filled her chest. "Joseph is greater."

I mined her inscrutable glow for what she could have meant. She looked at me similarly, not understanding what I didn't understand.

"My world was smaller then, small enough to be filled by someone like Viktor. I couldn't imagine past him. I almost gave up on myself."

"You were in love."

"But now I see Joseph is capable of something far greater. It will submit to no one, obey no rule.

"With all of his ideas and his people, Viktor would have conquered nothing for me. He lived for them. Joseph has proved he'll take me to the summit." She had risen above me, carried by her vision.

"Don't you see? From the top, the fall will hold no fear. I will have had everything I ever wanted. That's Joseph's power. He's the one."

"Magda," I begged. "We're in the sanctuary. You can tell the truth here."

She walked to the French doors and opened them wide. "And the truth is finally good."

I had thought Magda and I were the same, empty. I'd believed we were vessels, waiting to be filled by someone else. I'd pitied us because we'd not realized until too late that as easily as we could be saved by someone great, we could be destroyed by someone evil.

I believed Magda had been filled so fast and so fully by Joseph, by the time she realized it, she was drowning in him. I saw strength in her struggle for air, in her getting through each day, making no mistakes so she could stay alive long enough to be there when her soul returned. She was I. I was she. Our souls were united in their absence.

But sitting in her sanctuary, her place of truth, I knew the light in her eyes was rapture. In the burning, I saw I'd been tragically wrong. Magda was my opposite. I was taken by others. I was erased. She never once was taken. There were no stories or lives beyond her own. Hers was the face that launched a thousand ships. She was made more god-like by each body that fell in her wake. She stole people. She stole Viktor. She stole me.

I undressed and lay on my metal bed, motionless in the heat. I was suspended in time, unable to face what I'd let myself fall into. I'd lost Herr Perlstein and Matthias. I'd lost my dreams of Thad and Magda. I was left with a Nazi puppet, and I deserved it all.

After Magda had come down from her high, she snapped, "Now, tell me how you and Hans are getting on."

"I think I've told you, Magda"—

My voice faded into doubt, and she leapt into the pause. "You'll work it out soon enough. He's good for you. I want you to have what's good for you."

She was plotting my role in her ascent. I was to play the faithful friend, more than a bit part, less than a star. I didn't know how to write myself out of it. The tension notched with each silent note I let hang between us. "That's kind of you, Magda," I said.

Her nose twitched in irritation. "Take what you're given, Eva. Kind has nothing to do with it."

73

EVA

I hadn't known I was crying until Hans came to my door. He'd left a note earlier saying he would be by to take me to a movie. He was stunned to see me so sad. He stroked my hair and wiped my tears. "Please," I kept saying. "Please, let's just go to the movie. It's not important."

"If you'd just tell me," he said. "I could fix it."

"There's nothing to fix, Hans. It's about a friend, a woman. You wouldn't understand." This, he could allow. Eventually we walked. We entered the theater as the music started. It was *Scarface,* starring Paul Muni, a veteran of Yiddish theater.

The smoke and shadows, the back-lit, frosted glass blended into a gray haze. "I don't know nuttin', I don't see nuttin', and I don't hear nuttin'," Camonte said, and my mind was gone.

To the shriek of car wheels and the endless pop of guns, I contemplated what I believed was true. Joseph Goebbels had ordered the assassination of Viktor Arlosoroff. Magda had all but admitted it to me. One of the highest-ranking Nazi officials had killed not only a leading Zionist, but a British subject on British soil. Viktor Arlosoroff was not just a simple tailor on Oranienburgerstrasse. This would move people.

I wanted to punish Thad with the truth. I would scream until he admitted he was horribly, totally wrong. I needed, at least once, to be right, or I couldn't live with myself.

Hans was laughing at Tony's mother pleading with her daughter. "What for you take that money? . . . Tony no love you like he make you believe." Hans reached for my hand. I excused myself, and didn't come back.

My head was buzzing. At the cafés on the Ku'damm, people reveled in the late setting sun. Strings of bulbs hung over empty wine bottles and pitchers of beer, their filaments drawing bright orange lines against the still light sky.

"Eva!" someone might have shouted from one of the patios, but it didn't occur to me to stop. The voice came again, louder and more intentional. "It's the *parvenu*, lady and gentlemen!"

I turned to see Christopher, Katharina, and the two Anglophiles crowded around a café table that was too small for all they'd ordered. Christopher stood, nearly knocking over a board of blood sausage and limburger cheese. He kissed my cheeks. "We've missed you Eva, but I see you've blown with the Teutonic winds. I never would have put you with a Goebbels man."

"I'm not with him, Christopher."

"And the *Reichsministerfrau*? We couldn't believe it, but as I told Katharina, 'She's on her own. She has to be practical!'"

"He's only defending his *kamerade*, Eva," Katharina said. "Thad's so rarely passed over, all these boys are worried they might be next!"

"And, by all these boys, she means me," Christopher said.

"I'm quite sure you'll survive the shock," I muttered.

"Not so. Our friend hasn't been himself since you left him. Despite what we all thought we knew about him, it seems he's been wounded."

"We've tried to set him up, give him a boost, but you should hear him," Anglophile One interjected. "This girl's too lazy, that one's too boring, the other's too stupid."

"Eva!" Thad's voice came from behind me.

I spun around to see him jogging across the street.

"I was right!" I seethed.

His eyes warned me not to speak, but I didn't care.

"It was true."

"Come with me," he gripped my wrist and pulled me away.

"I told you there was more to this story," Anglophile Two crowed.

"The only more to this story is that he's in love with her, and he didn't know it until it was too late," Christopher added.

"He *knew* it, Darling, he just didn't know what to *do* about it." Katharina's voice faded as I followed Thad into an alley.

"What are you thinking, making a scene like that? You've been in the paper!"

"I don't care."

"You care too much."

"You don't know what that means."

"You're not hearing me," Thad scolded, then his face turned grave. "You're going to give yourself away."

"Why didn't you listen to me about Arlosoroff?" I asked.

"I did. I thought you were wrong. I still do."

"Magda told me he did it!"

"Then she's wrong, too."

"It made her love Joseph all over again."

"All the evidence points to rival Jews."

"She wouldn't be so happy if anyone else had done it."

"Stop," he said.

"He offered her a human sacrifice."

"Stop, now!"

"Why stop? Why is it always stop?"

"Because!" His voice grew fierce. "Even if you're right, which I'm certain you're not," he paused, "no one would care."

"You mean you don't care."

"I mean no one cares. You're chasing something that will never happen."

I stumbled back against the building. He reached for my hand, catching my fingers between his.

"I understand why you're angry. You should be. But I didn't lie. Not exactly. Everything is far more complicated than you know. Things will get better. It just takes a long time."

"Do you believe what you wrote?"

"I believe that no good will come to my country, or yours, if we further isolate Germany."

"Right. The debt! The Reds!" I gripped his hand hard enough to hurt him.

"Let's not"—

"If they knew how bad it is. If you'd told them the half of it!"

"They know."

"How could you not"—

"It's not what's important."

I ripped my hand out of his. "Why did you make me spy, if nothing I told you is important?"

A mix of sympathy and surrender clouded his eyes. "It's not what you told me," he said.

"You'll have to do better than that."

He shifted his weight. "It's not what Hans said, it's that he said it, and he said it to you." He circled his finger as if there was an obvious answer I should have been able to guess. I couldn't.

"You weren't the spy, Eva."

"What was I, then? Why did you do this to me?"

"You provided access. We're close now. What you did was excellent."

"Close to what?"

"To Hans!" he snapped, but quickly collected himself. "Nothing happens anymore without Goebbels' fingerprints all over it. Hans can give us eyes and ears at the highest levels of government."

It took my breath. "He's the one you always wanted."

Thad's body sagged. "And you, Eva. I wanted you, too." He ran his hand up and down my shoulder.

"Don't touch," I said.

"It's gone too far. I thought I could keep things separate. It didn't work. Get out of Berlin for a while. I'll help you. We'll figure things out."

"I hate you." My voice was so tight with anger, it hurt to speak.

"I've missed you. I know I was stupid, selfish. I don't want to be in Berlin without you. In a while, we can try again, without all the complications. Just us."

His words were all I'd ever wanted to hear. "I hate you too much."

"Where were you?" Hans was waiting by my front door. He seemed taller than he was as he approached. "I was sick," I said. "I threw up in the bathroom, I couldn't come back to the theater."

"Where did you go after that?"

"I stopped to get tonic and I walked. I needed fresh air."

"You look well now," he said.

"It did help."

"You could have told me. You had to know I'd be worried."

"I didn't want you to miss the film. You were enjoying it. I assumed you would figure"—

"It out," he asserted. "You assumed I would know you were sick in the bathroom, then got tonic, then went for a walk, all while you were supposed to be on a date with me."

"Maybe it was stupid, but yes. That's what I thought."

"How could you be vomiting, buying tonic, getting fresh air, and be on a date with me, all at the same time?"

"I suppose our date ended when I vomited, went to get tonic and got fresh air."

"You walked out on me."

My patience abandoned me. "Truthfully, it wasn't a date. I've told you we're not dating. I've always been honest with you."

He reached his hand to my face and, with his thumb, drew a line from my left eye down the side of my cheek. It was harsher than a teardrop, but more gentle than a scratch. He breathed heavily. "And this thing that just a few hours ago had you crying in my arms is what keeps you from me?"

My nerves were so frayed I couldn't hold anything back. "It's you, Hans. You're what keeps me from you. You make me cry."

74

EVA

A stranger named Franz Berger sent me a card. He wrote he had a timely message for me from an old friend in Frankfurt. I was to go to the Adlon Hotel at 1:00, find the house phone, and ask for him by name, in the concierge office.

My heart seized. My only old friend was Frau Pappenheim, and she had never approached me in this way. There had to be something wrong. She had to be in trouble for this man to be so secretive.

When I made my call, the lobby was full. People milled around me, and luggage carts rolled by. An English woman, with her face buried in a street map, almost walked into me. There was no trouble to be seen. *Everything is fine*, I said to myself. *There couldn't be anything wrong with Frau Pappenheim, because there never is anything wrong with Frau Pappenheim. It's impossible.*

Herr Berger walked toward me carrying a black canvas tote. He had wire-rimmed glasses and a full head of neatly combed, gray hair. He was attractive, even graceful, as he swerved through the crowd. "Fraulein Schmidt," he said without breaking his stride. "Please, follow me."

He led me outside, toward Brandenburg Gate. When we entered the Tiergarten, I said, "Please, tell me what you need from me, Herr Berger. I don't understand."

"We just need a quiet spot," he replied.

There was no way my spiritual mother would have told a strange man to take me to a quiet spot in the Tiergarten, even if he was a concierge at the Adlon. I could only think Hans was behind this, that he had searched for my nuns.

I stopped short, then side-stepped under a weeping willow. Its drooping branches obscured his face. "How about this?"

"Forgive me, Fraulein," he smiled. "Frau Pappenheim sent me. We've known each other for many years."

"Is she alright?" I demanded from behind the leaves.

"She's quite fine. It's just a bit farther." We walked in silence, except for the rush of a distant fountain and the clop of hooves on dirt. He led me to a path that cut through a rhododendron copse, and we sat on a bench. Dead blossoms were strewn at our feet. A light breeze tickled the space between my ear and jaw, making me irrationally cold.

Finally, he said, "Frau Pappenheim sent these books for you."

I stared at the bag. "Why didn't she just send them to me directly?"

"Because they require explanation. She wants to be sure you understand her intent."

"So, why didn't she write?"

"She feared the censor, of course. If you'll let me explain, you'll understand." He handed me the bag. "Please, don't open it until I finish."

I nodded. I didn't know what could be so dangerous about a bag of books.

"Inside one of these books is an envelope. It holds your papers. They won't say what you expect." Footsteps ground in the path behind us. When they fell silent, he continued.

"They say your name is Evangeline Schmidt and you are a baptized Catholic, born to and abandoned by Anja Schmidt, father unknown. You were raised by nuns in the old Santa Maria convent in Sachsenhausen. The documents are authentic, attested to by Sister Adela Bauer.

"The convent closed last year and the nuns dispersed, so your story won't be easily verified." He pointed to the bag. "In the meantime, you're to study these books, the New Testament and the Catechism, so you have something to say for your years there. Sister Adela has enclosed information and photographs of the convent, should you ever need to prove yourself to someone."

I looked into the bag. The books were used. The red dye on the edges was splotched with water stains. The leather was worn at the corners, and the satin bookmark was frayed. My spiritual mother had thought of every detail.

"Frau Pappenheim trusts Sister Adela, and she's confident the Sister will vouch for you if it comes to that, but you must do everything to avoid it coming to that. This woman has risked a great deal for you."

I couldn't catch up. Frau Pappenheim wanted me to sever my connection to everything she believed. She was asking me to lie, to hide, to deny our faith and to renounce our people. She was giving me the freedom I'd sought for so long, and it was breaking my heart.

"Did she do this for all the girls?"

"She's sending the young ones to Scotland, but there's little she can do for most of the older ones. They're foreign-born. They have accents. Their names will give them away. They've married Jews and have Jewish children. They can't hide. You and a few others are the only ones she can help."

I pieced the story together several steps behind. When we were young, for us to take such a path would have been as good as dying in her eyes. Now, in this death, for a second time, she was giving me life.

"I don't deserve this," I said to Herr Berger. "I've done too much wrong. She doesn't know that."

"And the rest of us?" With a look of regret, he turned toward the tips of monuments poking above the trees, and then back at me. "She insisted I tell you these words exactly." As if they were his own, he said, "These papers lie. Never forget that."

I could only nod.

"Please, answer. She wants to know."

"I swear. I'll never forget."

"Thank you," he said.

He stood up. I couldn't stand, so I looked up to his shadow-darkened face. "She needs to break contact with you. This will be the last time you hear from her. There can be no connection between you if this is to work."

"I can't do that!" I stammered.

His face softened, and he took my hand in his. I wanted him to be her, and I wanted him to hug me. "She also said this, 'I love you, and I will miss you every day.'"

The words took my breath. By the time I came back to life, he was gone.

The books weighed on my lap. I was afraid to open them, afraid of achieving what I'd for so long tried to make real. When our tiny corner of the Tiergarten was washed in shadow and cold, I vowed I would come back here if I ever forgot who I was. Without Frau Pappenheim in my life, only the bushes, the peeling bench and the flecks of quartz shining from the rocky path were left to share the memory of who I'd been and what she'd done for me. And if all those were gone, I would dig it up from the packed dirt beneath my feet.

75

HANS

"Hansi!" Joseph's voice shoots into my office. He appears in the doorway. "Magda wants you and your gypsy to come to supper tomorrow before she leaves for Bad Heiligendamm. It's just the four of us. She's decided on your match, so it's time to move things along. How about it?"

The cursed red flares on my neck. What to tell Joseph? That I've failed again? That the gypsy is beyond my grasp?

My anger returns hard and fast. After giving Eva every ounce of patience and kindness I have, all she has to say in return is I make her cry. And her defense? She was always honest with me. Every cruelty can be justified by honesty.

All her reading has taught her to glamorize her own misery. She's been told not to trust men, not to trust love and not to trust happiness. She's her own worst enemy, only wanting what she can't have.

No matter what I tell her, she'll never accept she's not a victim. She's her own worst enemy. She suffers by choice, when choices are made by greater men than us. Our leaders create order. Things snap firmly together if they're put in the right place. Why can't she see it?

I have to brighten up for Joseph. He is ebullient after a rally this morning. Nothing makes him happier than to win the admiration of the faceless and nameless. They give him no reason to doubt himself because he'll never see them again. He can just flash them his power, lull them with his words, stamp his greatness on them, and walk away, leaving behind a divine impression, an unchecked memory.

I want the opposite with Eva. I want to know her and for her to know me. I'm too entwined in the relationship; I care too much. She makes me doubt myself every day, and she knows it. How could she not question me when I question myself? I've done everything wrong. I need to flash like Joseph. I need to leave no doubt.

This dinner must happen because Joseph, the one who doesn't care a thing for love, is the only one who can teach Eva not to fear it. He will snap us firmly together, put us in our right place.

"Thank you, Joseph," I say. "We'll be there."

I send my secretary to leave Eva my note. *Magda and Joseph expect us at dinner tomorrow. I'll send a car at 7:00. Neither of us is in a position to decline.*

76

EVA

Having passed for more than three years undetected, any rational person would have said I didn't need to change anything to continue the ruse. But if there was one thing I learned, it was that Evangeline would never settle for being like me. Evangeline was raised in freedom. If I were to become her, I had to replace huge amounts of myself with something bigger, brighter, and stronger. I had to be so much more than I was.

I examined the way I always walked, always stood, always smiled. It was not at all right. I was too small, too protected. I needed to float more, to think less. I couldn't let troubles stick to me. I needed less weight.

I smiled like Zara, wide and glowing. When that didn't work, I tried Katharina, smart and amused. I practiced laughing lightly, leaning toward instead of away. I lifted my chin, straightened my back, lowered my voice, and then raised it again.

None of it would have mattered if I only could have made myself believe I could be like Evangeline. If I could trust myself, I could be brave. This was the reason I forced myself not to panic at the sight of Hans' card in my box. Evangeline could handle Hans. She would be the one to dispense with him once and for all. She could do it because she'd never had to defend her existence. She hadn't lied. She hadn't been irrevocably diminished by fear.

77

HANS

I bought a four by six oil painting of the Parthenon and it hangs where the Jew's Cubist knock-off used to be. The living room is finished, and I have a mahogany *fin de siècle* set coming for the dining room. Joseph and Magda gave me an alabaster bust of Ares as a house-warming gift. I put it on the entryway credenza. When I showed the apartment to Viktoria Morelli, who I actually might enjoy if she weren't so mean, she said, 'It's full of niggling reminders of your new money. Did you buy them from the *I Am Rich* store?'

Eva would never say that, but Eva's not a bitch. For all she sees in others, she knows nothing about herself. She needs clarity, and I haven't been clear. I should have told her at the start that I love her and my love will make things right. I should have explained that because this love is true, it deserves to happen.

I switch the Ares bust with a vase of two dozen white roses I bought for her visit. No doubts, I remind myself, and switch them back. The knock comes. The driver announces, "Fraulein Schmidt." She's in a modest dress a woman might wear to lunch at a hotel café.

I told her to be ready at 7:00, though the dinner is called for 8:30. I sent a driver for her. We'll have a drink. She'll see my Tiergarten address, my niggling reminders, and she'll know I'm worthy to care for her; she'll know she is safe with me.

"Don't we need to go?" she asks, making her voice light.

"I thought we'd have a drink first. Dinner's not until later."

She's nervous. I hate that because I would never hurt her. Aside from Joseph, I don't think I've ever met anyone with as little trust as Eva. I lead her into the living room and pour her an Islay single malt, which I know she'll love. I pour myself a brandy and swirl it in the snifter. Its warmth relaxes me. I motion for her to sit on the couch. I stand by the mantelpiece, next to its carved lion's head, under a portrait of Adolph Hitler.

"I don't like how we left things, Eva. You make me happy. We're happy when we're together. It's wrong that I make you sad. It's an excuse to blame me for whatever your problem really is."

"I don't think so, Hans. I'm sorry."

"Please, let me finish. Without a father, you never learned what a relationship with a man should be. You can't recognize love because you've never seen it before."

"It has nothing to do with that." Her voice is sharp.

I've affected her, so I push on. "I'm not blaming you. Your past isn't your fault, but you're letting it stand in your way."

She puts her drink down. "No, Hans."

Except for Magda, Joseph, and Viktoria Morelli, it's rare for someone to so flatly contradict me. There's a ticking in my shoulder. "I've given this a tremendous amount of thought." I pause so she will take in every word. "I believe in this."

"You want love, Hans, and you think this is it, but it's not. You're in love with something in your imagination."

Is it possible she's telling me I don't know my own feelings? This, from the woman who understands her emotions about as well as she understands astrophysics? I stop listening, but she keeps talking. She can't stop saying the wrong thing. She can't stop being wrong.

"I'm not listening, so stop talking!" I say, louder than I like. If she doesn't love me, at least she can show me a modicum of respect, after all I've done for her.

Her mouth is still moving. She gets up. Fissures open in my chest. "Shut your mouth!" I shout.

I don't recognize her expression. She seems angry. "You have no right to look at me like that! I've given you everything. I love you. Nothing else matters!" My voice is so loud it scrapes my throat. My eyes burn. The face I love, her beautiful face, is shocked.

"I don't know what to say, Hans," she says, more calmly, and I calm down, too.

"You don't need to say anything. You don't need to do anything. Just be." I say each word with more power than I knew I had.

Her silence crushes me. Finally, her voice says, "No." She turns her back. She's walking to the door.

My panic flares. "No!" I shout. "No! No! No!"

Now I've got her. She screams. Her legs kick. But I'm too strong. "See!" I say in her ear as I carry her. "See!" I say again as she fights me. She's saying that awful word again, so I clamp my hand on her mouth. "I love you," I say. "I love you."

I have her on my bed. She tries to escape. I sit on her. Her hips push into the inside of my thighs. "Get off," she begs. "Get off and we can talk." Her voice is soft. It wraps around me, sending a bolt through me.

"Please, Hans. You're a kind man, please," she says. "You're better than them." A tear falls down the side of her cheek. She needs to stop that now. It will make me come too soon. I turn her over and push her face into the pillow so I don't have to see her or hear her. Everything has to be slower. I want to know every part of her before I enter her. That's what good couples do. I put my other hand around the front of her neck. I squeeze, but only to show her I can do that if I want to. I would never hurt her. This is about trust.

I reach beneath her and feel her soft, full breasts. I want to kiss them, but I force myself to wait. I let her breathe. "Please," she says. I'm getting what I want. I grab her waist. It's smaller than the span of my hand. I push it into the mattress. She's trying to get away. I pull up her head and she gasps, more than before, then I put her face back down and reach inside of her. Her body tenses and I whisper in her ear, "Everything's fine now. I love you. This is how it should be."

When I flip her over, I know I've won because she doesn't fight anymore. Her face is beautifully empty. Her body is like wood. She lets me spread her legs. She lets me kiss her lips, her neck. She has surrendered.

Electricity rolls through me. I'm flying. I ram into her. I can't control it. I do it again and again. There is no part of me that isn't owned by this moment. This is real. This is perfection. I let everything go, I give her my whole being, all my feeling, and I'm weightless. She accepts me without a word.

78

EVA

If memory tells a story, I was without memory. There were snap shots. There was a woman who was so small she was almost crushed by a monster, a woman pathetically gasping for air, waiting to die, a woman who could have been split in half from his force. But the woman wasn't me. The woman repulsed me.

Memory started when he collapsed on top of me. His shoulder jammed under my chin, hard as iron, thrusting my neck back in a painful arch. His sweat smell pressed into my skin, leaving a permanent scar. But it was his hot breaths through my hair, spreading a film on my scalp, which woke me from my shock and drove me mad.

A desperate urge to rip his eyes out, to crush them between my fingers, consumed me. I needed to claw at his face until I shredded his skin. I had to get on top of him, and force my fist down his throat until he could no longer breathe, then light his cock on fire and watch him scream.

But my need couldn't get him off me. It couldn't free my arms. With no outlet, it lay waste to every corner of my brain and heart, until I choked on the weight of my powerless hate.

It was the hate that discovered my weapon. It had poisoned everything I could see and feel. The only thing left was the one part of me Hans hadn't desecrated, the part he'd never known. It was pure and shining, and it would kill us both. I didn't care if it did because the only reason I wanted to take another breath was to inflict on him unimaginable pain.

Without any emotion, without any fight, with my body caged beneath him, I lit my match. I whispered in his ear, just loud enough for him to hear, "I'm a Jew."

His body pulled taut. It quivered with strain. The tension lifted him enough for me to slide out from under him. He didn't turn. He said nothing. He lay face down in the sheets. I waited for the explosion. I deserved to see his destruction. I needed to be sure of it. But the air stayed dead. I hadn't lit a match after all. I'd inflicted a slow rot, an infection, just as he would have imagined. It was unsatisfying, until I saw in his face the desperation of a man who hated himself the most.

I put on my underwear and tucked in my blouse. I picked up my purse. When I closed his door, there was a wail. It was abject, without strength or rage. It collapsed in defeat. I knew, because I knew too well the sound of nothing.

79

EVA

The last of the sun covered the city in a heavy orange glaze, but I couldn't get warm. Panic squeezed my chest and pushed a knot into my throat that tore through my breaths. I remembered what people did when they were in trouble with the regime. They ran. Without thinking beyond that, I went to the American Embassy.

Limousines with little flags idled, waiting to unload at the gate. I stared through the iron bars. A banner with swirling script read *Happy Fourth of July!*

The Anglophiles rocked back on their heels, toasting with German officials in Swastika armbands. Tuxedoed waiters wandered between cocktail tables festooned with stars and stripes. Decorated *Reichswehr* and SS officers danced with pretty girls. The guests watched the bar, the band, each other. They looked at the sky and back at the embassy. No one saw beyond the gates.

It was as though I was staring through the reverse end of binoculars. The people, the scene, were far, far away. They were little wax figures on top of a cake. There was Katharina kissing an SS man's cheek. There was Christopher shaking his hand. I knew I knew them. And then there was Thad carrying drinks. I knew I knew him, too.

I pieced together what to do to save myself. I had to shout to Thad, then make him bring me inside. I had to refuse to leave until Christopher opened the floodgates one more time to get me to America. I held Thad's name in my throat and I waited for the moment these people became real, when the binoculars turned back around, and we could inhabit the same space.

Thad's waxy miniature saw me. It moved around Christopher and came toward me. But it wasn't I and it wasn't he. He was a cake piece, or maybe I was the cake piece and he was the human. My head swam with confusion. My breaths outpaced his steps. He remained far away even when he stood in front of me.

"What happened?" he asked, taken aback by my shaking hands, and unkempt hair.

The air was too big, too much.

"Say something," he demanded.

The only words I had left whispered from me. "I'm a Jew."

"Right," Thad replied. The dip in his voice suggested he already knew.

"You knew," I said.

"I assumed," he replied.

I stepped back from the bars. "It's how you knew I would do what you asked." My shaking words fell out one at a time. "You knew, and you pushed me on him, anyway."

"Tell me who knows, right now."

My eyes brimmed with tears.

"Eva!" he snapped. "Who knows?"

"Hans."

Thad's stony gaze cracked. His words slipped from him, almost without sound. "What did he do to you?"

A sob rose in my throat, and I shuddered violently to hold it down. "After he did it. . ." I slapped my forehead to block the memory. "It was all there was left," I pleaded. "It was all I had that could hurt him."

He had a look I'd never seen before. It was close to shame. A siren blared in the distance. "I'm coming to get you," he commanded.

I turned my back and waved him away.

"It's too dangerous, Eva," he begged. "I'll help you."

I staggered between two limousines and nearly fell into the traffic.

"Eva," he called, "Don't go!"

Cars swerved to avoid hitting me, and the blast of horns drowned out his voice. I fought my way through the pedestrian rush, the dings of bicycle bells and the high-pitched rants of Hitler Youth leafleting on opposing corners.

When I reached Potsdamer Bahnhof, the city was shrouded in a darkened, dirty haze that clung to my neck, unrelenting until I boarded the overnight train to Frankfurt. I was going home.

80

EVA

She didn't say a word. She just looked. We stood on the threshold, facing each other, not moving, not speaking, showing nothing until she took my hand. I sat on her couch. She closed the drapes. She opened a closet. She handed me a blanket. She left the room and brought back tea and biscuits. She set the tray on a cocktail table between us and poured. I watched as the steam disappeared from my cup. The water turned from rust to brown to thick, cold black.

Her hands were in her lap. The grandfather clock ticked. At some point, it gonged.

"I can't," I said.

"That's fine," she said. She waited longer. My shaking came back. I thought I heard her breath catch. Her hands turned up to me. They were reluctant, but they were open, and I told her. I told her everything until there was nothing left to tell.

When I stopped, she leaned toward me. She waited for me to look at her. "I understand," she said.

She left. She ran a bath. She came back to get me. She took my clothes away.

I sat in the tub. I hugged my knees. I felt the waterline against my back and thighs. I wanted it to cover me, but I couldn't uncurl myself.

"Let me." She took the hand-held shower and felt the water. She turned its warmth on me, letting it roll over my skin, until I let go of myself. I lay back. She held my head. She washed my hair. A thin tear rolled from the corner of my eye. She wiped it away with the edge of her palm.

The next morning Frau Pappenheim was at the dining room table. Her face was tired, but I knew her brain had not stopped since she put me to bed the night before. She spoke to me as if I'd been part of her mental conversation the whole time. "You have to go now," she paused, "before things catch up to you. There's no other way."

My place was already set. "Sit down. Eat," she commanded, then poured me tea. She placed a silver rack with blackened toast tips in front of me, and used eagle-claw tongs to put two butter pats on the side of my plate. She let me eat in silence, knowing I needed to eat before I could hear.

When she finally spoke, she said, "I've talked with my friend, Madame Rappaport, in Paris. Tonight, she'll cable your boss at the nightclub and your landlady. Give me their full names and addresses." She passed me a pad and pencil. As I wrote, she explained, "The cable will be from you. It will say you've arrived in Paris and have decided to remain for the indefinite future. That should give us time to sort things out."

I didn't want to make choices. I wanted everything to stop. I wanted to stay with her and never leave. By the time I could thank her, she had already moved on. Only bits of what she said broke through my fog. *New name . . . exit visa . . . Austria's becoming as bad as here . . . France . . . language problem . . . Switzerland . . . no means of support.*

When she spoke of America, I paid attention. "The Embassy says they've reached their quotas, but they're lying. It's their policy to lie.

There are many more slots. We could talk to Colonel Cartwright. He told you he wanted to help. We need to be absolutely certain he's sincere."

"I think I believe him, but I've believed him before. He was upset, for me this time, not for him. How can I be sure?"

"We can't go to him if you're not sure."

I was angry she was insisting on this trust, and humiliated by the impossibility of it. I wanted to stay with her. I told her. She smiled, and I felt myself dissolve. "Please," I cried, gripping my knife. "It's all I want. It's all I've ever wanted."

She shook her head. "I want," her voice splintered. "What I want can't be."

I shouted, trying to make myself bigger, but I only got smaller. "I don't care if they find me!" I sobbed into my hands. "You said you were my spiritual mother. You can't push me out." My begging only added to my misery. It burned through my restraint, and I turned on her.

"You were never *my* spiritual mother. You were *our* spiritual mother. It wasn't *Ich liebe dich,* I love you. It was *Ich liebe euch,* I love you all. It was always plural. That's not what a mother says. It's what we settled for.

"You loved our part in your cause, but now, your cause is dead. We failed you. We couldn't make the Gentiles like us. We're only as good as *They* say we are, and *They* say we're demons. That's how you see me, now! That's why you're abandoning me!

She put her arm around my shoulder and pulled me to her. She chased down my gaze. She spoke over her hurt. "I love *you*, Eva Schmidt. *You* are going to make it. I am *your* spiritual mother. I always was and I always will be. But I wouldn't be if I let you stay. I can't be if you are here."

Frau Pappenheim didn't allow me to go out, answer the phone or even stand near the window of the house. When she was in the apartment, I was up, cleaning and re-cleaning things the maid had already scoured. I wanted her to admire my tenacity. But when she left, and I didn't have to be humiliated, I crawled into bed and didn't come out.

There were times when I thought I would suffocate in the dark, among her fine things. She had the same Imari tea set as Magda, and a Biedermeier sideboard similar to Hans'. I wanted to open the windows so people could witness the display. *See!* I would shout. *This is what you're afraid of!*

Other times, I wanted to tell her she was a fool for possessing such tainted items. I wanted to excoriate her for teaching us to admire these things, for saying we were the same as *Them.*

Hans arrived in disjointed flashes that attacked at will, erasing the hours, then days that had passed. I had to bite my arm to keep from screaming. His sheets were still in my mouth. His weight was still on me. His breath was still in my hair. His words that said he loved me still screamed in my ears. I couldn't free myself from them because what he actually was saying was I had allowed this. It was my fault, and I was inescapably trapped inside myself.

It wasn't long before Frau Pappenheim's efforts bore fruit. Bella Glaz, a piano player with whom I'd grown up, had married a renowned violinist, Artur Zich, while studying in Vienna. Herr Zich had taken her with him to Krakow, where she took his name and his Polish citizenship. Frau Pappenheim still had Bella's papers in a file in the orphanage, and when contacted, Bella was more than happy to give them to me.

She was two years older than I, and she remembered me fondly. She had lived in the orphanage since she was three. Her father had died from an oral abscess, leaving her mother in Minsk without the means to provide for her. Bella could remember nothing from that time or place, so along with her papers, she passed on a blank slate. I wouldn't need to make up a past or a language I didn't already know. Her memories were my own.

In the moments when all I could feel was his weight, his breath, his words, and I needed to erase myself, the person he'd chosen, the person who'd chosen Magda, I wanted to become Bella Glaz. She took away time.

81

EVA

The rush of the kitchen faucet drowned out the man's knock. I heard the door to Frau Pappenheim's study open, followed by muffled voices. Hers was low, yet it controlled the conversation. His was softer, responding. I had never heard a man's voice in her apartment, unless it was a maintenance worker. This voice was not there to repair things. Their conversation was long, with much back and forth. Her voice raised and hardened at times, like a quick slap; his was steady throughout. My imagination drove my fear. What if it was Hans, or someone he'd sent? What if it was someone Magda or Joseph had sent?

The heat in the room pressed in on me. I stared at the distance from the kitchen window to the ground, wondering if I could survive the jump.

Frau Pappenheim's footsteps came quickly. She was alone. My back was to the sink. A wet sponge shook in my hand. Water snaked down my wrist and into my sleeve.

"Colonel Cartwright is here. He would like to speak with you," she said.

"Did you contact him?"

"He found you. He wants to help. You can be certain."

He was waiting in the parlor. He stood when I entered. I felt the same shyness I used to have with him, but this time he was shy, too. He didn't touch me, as though he thought I might break if he did.

"How did you know where to find me?"

"It wasn't hard. Frau Pappenheim is well known to the Embassy, and to Christopher, in particular. Several years ago, she accused the consulate of turning a blind eye to the white slave trade. Christopher found her difficult to deal with, and he told her he didn't need to justify himself to a woman like her.

She had powerful members of her American family lobby the Secretary of State directly. It fell to Christopher to remedy the mess. He came out of his meeting with her looking like he'd been knocked around by a prize fighter. To satisfy her was a Sisyphean task, and one none of us will soon forget."

"But how did you connect us?"

"You talked about the social worker in Frankfurt who was from Vienna, who taught you Schiller, Bach and English. I couldn't help but contemplate a connection. And you were overly defensive about certain things. I suppose you cared more than was normal for a typical German. You all but told me directly that day at Luna Park"—

"And that's how you got me to help you?"

"I wish I hadn't but, yes. You held your secret so close, you couldn't get beyond it. I figured you would do almost anything, just to do something."

"Except be it," I whispered to myself. To him, I said, "Why didn't you ask me?"

"I didn't think it was anything anybody needed to know, especially now. You had a practical solution to a difficult problem. I don't believe you should have to be what you don't want to be."

"I used to believe that."

"I still believe that."

"You didn't have to come."

"If I can find you, Hans Lorenz can find you. Magda can find you. I have a place for you to stay until we get everything straightened out. It's with an American couple. They can be trusted.

"It will take a favor from someone inside the German government to get you an exit visa, but once we have it, we'll get you into the United States. You'll have to go as Bella Glaz. These are the forms you need. When we get to the apartment, we'll fill them out."

"I thought America stopped taking Jews."

"You're different. There are exceptions."

"I don't want to be an exception anymore."

"It's far too late for that." He sat down. I remained standing. He bowed his head and said, "I don't want to say goodbye."

I waited for him to look up before I spoke. "It's also far too late for that."

"I'll find you when I'm through here. Who knows what might happen?"

"I know. So do you."

"I don't want to lose you."

"That's not the same as loving someone, is it?"

"I wish I knew. I don't know how to know." He said nothing for a long time. I put my hand on the doorknob. It brought him out of his trance. "I never lied about you, Eva. I was amazed by you. I still am. I hope you can believe that."

"Then how could you do what you did?" my voice rasped.

His face reddened. He covered his eyes with the heels of his palms and drew them behind his ears. "I was afraid to choose. I wanted it all. I was wrong. I wish"—

I held up my hand. I'd reached the end of wishing.

His face opened and his voice held unmitigated regret. "I'm just so very sorry."

I agreed to go to the Americans' apartment. Frau Pappenheim came to see me every day. When she wasn't there, I missed her terribly. She pushed me to go to America. She would give me the contacts I needed. A job would be waiting for me once I arrived. Thad was handling everything else. It was all but done. People would kill for my visa.

"Then it should go to them," I said.

"Now's not the time for guilt. You will do what you have to do to get out. It's not ours to decide what people deserve." She was impatient with me for the first time since I'd come to Frankfurt.

"I'll owe him too much. I'll never move on."

"You will. Of course, you will. Things like this always take time. You're too young to know, but I do. I know much more than you think."

"I need to do it by myself," I said, and I proceeded to give her the same speech I'd delivered before I left the orphanage for Berlin. This time, it was laden with sorrow. I said I could no longer sit among damaged things, waiting to be found. I wanted to be new.

My spiritual mother remembered, and as she had that day, she said, "I didn't raise you to be found." She held up her hands and moved neither toward me, nor away. "Go Eva. I raised you to go." With that, she cut me loose.

Viktor Arlosoroff saved my life. The agreement he'd come to Germany to negotiate, called the Transfer Agreement, or in Hebrew, *Ha'avara*, won me my freedom. Frau Pappenheim gifted me the 1,000 pounds I would pay to the British Mandate for my life. In addition, she paid me another 1,000 pounds, an absurd amount for the little bit of housework I did while I'd stayed in her apartment. It was sent to a trust company, which would use it to purchase German goods for Palestine, thus violating the international Jewish boycott of Germany. In turn, the Germans allowed Bella Glaz to leave the Reich. It was the plainness of the whole thing that stunned me, its bureaucratic regularity. Even its name, Transfer, was as mundane as the scrap of newsprint used to change buses without paying. This, after so much was paid.

The Transfer Agreement was what brought Viktor Arlosoroff back to Germany, and what may have killed him, whether at the hands of Joseph Goebbels or his Revisionist enemies. It was what drew me back to Thad, and what inspired me to steal Hans's secrets. I'd believed the agreement would guarantee our abandonment by the West. I believed it was grossly immoral. But, in the end, it saved me, along with 60,000 others.

On the day my papers came through, Frau Pappenheim hired her trusted driver and brought me to the train station. I carried a small suitcase with my most essential possessions: a few outfits, toiletries, and a sepia photograph of Frau Pappenheim that was peeling and cracked along the edges. I thought back to the day over three years before, when we had gone to the station with this same driver. Frau Pappenheim was off to save the world, and I, to save myself. This time, she could do nothing for the world. This time she could save only me.

She handed me a letter, which I slid into my purse, unopened. Then she held my hand and we walked down the platform. I could still feel her grasp as the train pulled away and I watched her wave through the scratched glass.

82

HANS

I've committed the crime of *rassenschande*. I'm a race defiler. We can kill them. We can beat them. We can steal from them. We can shatter their windows, burn their books and ban their art, but we cannot put any part of ourselves inside of them. I am a criminal. Not yet in the eyes of the state, but in the eyes of the Party, and in my eyes.

I'll have a good many defenders. They'll say it wasn't my fault. The girl lied. I didn't know. No one knew. Not Joseph, not Magda, not anyone who saw her or talked to her. They'll say I deserve forgiveness. But they'll be wrong, because I should have known, and sometimes, I think I did know. Not because of the way she looks, or the way she talks, though there are hints of it, to be sure, but because I wanted her. I wanted her because I saw in her what others didn't see. It's what made her mine, alone. I was attracted to her dark places, to the things about her I couldn't name.

She was my exception, and it's in our exceptions that we find ourselves. They're our bits of freedom. I loved her for giving me that. That's what's criminal. That's what's wrong with me. It's pathological. I know it is, because I'm uncured. I love her, still.

When the nighttime knock comes, I'm not surprised. I can imagine what happened. Eva told Magda, who is no cleaner than me when it comes to loving Jews, and Magda, out of spite, boredom or the need to redeem herself, told Joseph. I can see his reaction, exactly. Only his nostrils move at first. They flare, just a little. His irises reflect light as he considers my punishment. In a crisp motion, his hand reaches for the phone.

I walk to the door. I don't need to open it to see the blackshirts, the lightning bolts flashing on their collars. I have no beef with them. They're doing their jobs.

I look through my peephole, but there are no SS there. It's the American from the Excelsior bar, the assistant military attaché. Through the odd angle of the glass, his upper body is outsized. He looks like a genie coming out of a bottle. Cartwright is his name, Colonel Thad Cartwright.

I let him in before it occurs to me that it makes no sense for him to be here.

"To what do I owe the pleasure, Colonel Cartwright?" I ask. I wonder if he hears the sickness in my conviviality, or smells my decay in the gagging stench of the dead roses I'd bought to impress Eva.

He looks at the bust of Ares, then takes in my poor contrast. "I have information of value to you, Herr Lorenz. May I have a moment?"

This is good. There are many in the American Embassy who want to help us. Maybe he's among them. "Please. Sit down. What can I offer you?"

"Whatever you're pouring."

"*Weinbrand*," I say. German Brandy. I hand him his drink and he waits for me to pour one for myself. I raise my glass to him, and he reciprocates, though he doesn't drink. For the briefest second, his face falls flat. It takes the air out of the room. Soon enough, his smile returns and he says, with encouragement, "I've been following your career, Herr Lorenz."

"I find that hard to believe."

"I've read your columns. I've seen you speak. You're a man of faith."

This is a fair assessment. Some Americans easily understand us, those of the better sort, anyway. "That's true. Nazism has saved me. I believe it can save Germany."

He searches the air for his memory. "If Germany is no longer crippled by the twin diseases of intellect and reason, which spawn only weakness."

"You were at the Charlottenburg speech."

"That, and the one in Spandau, although in Spandau, I believe you said 'depravity' instead of 'weakness.'"

"I'm impressed."

"It's my job, Herr Lorenz. Not my pleasure."

All warmth is gone. It takes a few seconds for me to understand. Thad Cartwright isn't here to help me. He's an intelligence officer in the United States Army. We've been trained to expect this. I stop him before he starts. "You must know, Colonel, that as a man of faith, I can't be bought. There's no price you could pay to turn me against my country, or to compel me to act in the service of another."

"I have no intention of paying you anything, Herr Lorenz." He runs his fingers along the gooseneck of my reading lamp.

"Then, what is it you want?"

"What I want is irrelevant." He walks slowly toward me, placing his glass on the mantel, next to a coaster. It will leave a ring. "Because what I actually want is to kill you."

"Tell me what you're after, Herr Cartwright. The Security Services can be here in minutes."

"I'm after you, Herr Lorenz, because of what you did to my close friend. I'm certain you remember her."

My mind flashes back to the blue light of the Excelsior bar, to Eva's strange behavior upon seeing this man. I smile foolishly. The picture slowly becomes clear. He knows what happened between me and Eva that caused her to act so hatefully toward me. He didn't divine it from any smell or sight or sound, as Eva would have done. She told him. And why would she tell him? Why would he care so much about her that I now find him in my apartment? Because he is the one who kept her from me. He is the one she loved.

"I'm sure you understand," he continues. "If I were to kill you, it would be an act of faith. I would believe in it."

Every one of my muscles wants to tear him apart. I'm far stronger than he is. I could kill him with my bare hands, right now.

He touches his hand to his breast pocket, indicating a side arm under his suit jacket. Mine is in the bedroom armoire. Picturing it under a pile of sweaters gnaws at the base of my skull. It blunts my reflexes. He waits. I wait. His smile returns.

"You'll be relieved to know, in this case, both reason and intellect require me to act against my beliefs."

He would be surprised to know I'm not at all relieved. One of Joseph's favorite aphorisms tempts me. *Perhaps we Germans do not know how to live, but we certainly know how to die spectacularly.* To have my shame cut short, to be martyred by the enemy in my own home, left to bleed out under a portrait of Adolph Hitler, is far more than I deserve. It's the stuff of which legends are made, songs are written. If only I had the courage to go ahead with it. "What is it you expect from me?"

"Nothing now. You can go about your business. I'll tell you as it unfolds, but you will meet with me when I ask, where I ask. You will do as I say. You will have no control. I'll be the only one you care about, the only one you need, because given how thoroughly you've betrayed your cause, I'm the only one who can save you."

This arrogance is too much. "You assume Dr. Goebbels will care about what's happened with Eva. I'll confess to him myself. Shall I call right now? He's having dinner with his wife."

"If your so-called race defilement was your only offense, you might be right. It's a well-trodden path, one blazed by both Dr. Goebbels and his wife. The difference is, you exposed these hypocrisies to your Jew, the same Jew who was acting as my agent. You know better than anyone what becomes of people who spread malicious rumors about the Reichsminister's wife."

I try to catch up. Now, he's not waiting.

"You told Fraulein Schmidt about Frau Goebbels' liaison with her former lover, Viktor—I mean Chaim—Arlosoroff, and how she, through you, came to his aid. You told her of what were then highly classified negotiations with the Zionists to grant a currency exemption to Jewish émigrés to Palestine. You outlined, in significant detail, the true impact of the international boycott on Germany's economy, which is information about which you and your government deceive the public daily. If that's not sufficiently disconcerting, you assessed the Reich's military disadvantage vis à vis its neighbors, told her of your government's violations of the Versailles Treaty, and informed her of Hitler's secret rearmament council. Shall I go on? Perhaps about Herrdoktor's plans for your so-called 'Second Wave'?"

His words burst in a rat-a-tat of rifle fire. I am sick to hear them, sick that Eva betrayed me after I gave her my trust.

"What did you threaten her with to make her turn against me? Were you going to expose her, or did you just fuck her into it?"

"My God, she's right. You really aren't very bright." He slashes the air between us with the side of his hand. "I didn't turn her."

Slash. "She's a Jew." Slash. "She hated you. She hated everything you do. There wasn't a moment she wanted to be with you. She wanted to do what's right. She's a good German." Slash. Slash. Slash.

His emotion betrays him. I'm not dead, yet. He thinks I'm not very bright? He doesn't know I know he's bluffing. He's neither rational, nor faithful. He's in love. Only one who shares the same love can see it so clearly in another. Eva will be my savior, after all.

"It's a good try, Colonel. But if you reveal any of this to anyone, you'll write Eva's death sentence. They will find her, and they will kill her. I suspect that's something you can't abide."

Is it pity or amusement on his face? I'm not like Joseph. I don't see inside other people's thoughts.

"They'll never find her, Herr Lorenz. She's left the Reich. They can't touch her. They never will."

Holes open in my stomach. How perfect that Eva was my last resort and she's left me with nothing. I'm plummeting to what I was before Joseph, when I had no options or hope, when I cared only for myself, when my world was small and my life was a constant reaction.

I need something to hold onto. This American is all there is. "What is it you would like me to tell you?"

"It's easy, Herr Lorenz. I only ask that you tell me the truth of what you see and hear."

My laugh bursts out. It's a quick bark, as though he whacked my back and I choked up vomit. "I'll try, Colonel, but you've said it yourself. I'm stupid. I see what I want to see, hear what I want to hear. I don't recognize truth. None of us do. Truth is what we wish it to be. We believe in that. And, I am a man of faith."

The movement of the street passes as if it's a newsreel playing on giant screens. I can't stop it and I can't step into it, so I walk next to it, making my way to Reichskanzlerplatz. One last option has presented itself to me. It grows more brilliant with each of my steps. When I piece together my plan, my pride swells. I feel like a parade balloon, an oversized version of myself, looking down on the world.

"They're eating," Ursula swipes when she opens the door.

"I wouldn't interrupt them if it weren't urgent," I insist. She pads toward the dining room with her usual sullenness, opens the door, waits, then gestures for me to enter.

Joseph sits at the head of the table. He holds his fork over his plate. The bowl of Magda's wineglass rests between her fingers. She's put out by me. There's still daylight, and the chandelier is off. The dim room flickers with candlelight. I stand at attention, facing Joseph. I announce, "I've learned that Eva didn't go off to tend to one of her dying nuns, as I previously thought." I'm too urgent. I need to calm down. "That's not why she's been away."

"Is it possible you're interrupting our dinner to discuss the whereabouts of your girlfriend, Hans?" Magda jabs.

My voice gets louder. "I came to tell you, to my shame, that for as long as I've known her, for as long as you've held her in your confidence, Frau Goebbels, Eva was lying to both of us. She's a Jew." I feed the last part directly to Magda, forcing the poison down her throat.

Her expression remains the same. It appears I'm telling her something she already knew.

"I'll repeat the question, Hans. Is it possible you're interrupting our dinner to tell us about your girlfriend?"

Joseph saws at his meat with exaggerated cuts. His cheeks are concave, drawing his chin into an ugly point. Ursula enters with a steaming kettle, and walks to the sideboard to fill the teapot. Joseph says, "Just put the kettle down, Ursula." She complies, and he flicks her away with the back of his hand.

When she's gone, I say, "There's more. An American intelligence officer has come into possession of this information. Tonight, he attempted to blackmail me with it. He wants me to share secrets in exchange for keeping silent about Eva. He says he will tell you not just about Eva's regrettable past, but that I told her classified information. Of course, this is an outright lie. If she obtained any information, I swear on my life it didn't come from me." I pause to let this sink in. "As I think on it, I'm worried the American might find his way to you, Frau Goebbels. You and Eva were very close, after all."

I try to make eye contact with her, but she's looking at Joseph. I wonder if he didn't hear me because still, he says nothing. An imploding fear squeezes my chest. "I've come to you instantly, Joseph. I want to use this connection to serve the Reich," I say. "I'll feed the Americans misinformation, anything you want. I'll tell you everything he asks. I'll be a double agent."

Magda looks back and forth between us. She takes a sip of wine. Joseph rises and limps in my direction, each step a drawn out torture. But he brushes past me and lumbers toward her. I can't testify to it, but I believe she's amused. Doesn't she see this can be put on her as easily as it can be put on me?

She starts to stand, reaching for Joseph's cheek, as if to pat away a child's hurt feelings. "*Engelchen*, you can't possibly think"—

He pushes her back down into the chair. Pleasure seeps through me. Her jaw drops open.

Joseph grabs her wrist and slams the back of her hand flat against the table, causing her wine glass to fall onto her plate. The dark liquid sprays tracks across her blouse. Her palm, the palm Eva so closely analyzed with its branches and cracks, lies open to him. He takes the kettle with his free hand. Steam shoots from it as he lets the boiling water roll down. Her fingers pull and claw under the scalding rush. With a chemist's precision, he pours until the last drop hits its mark. When her hand twitches, and the agony on her face lapses into shock, my intoxication breaks.

He turns back to me and drags his way over. I can't get the words out fast enough. "Whatever you say, Joseph. This is why I came to you."

He pats my cheek as he passes. "Of course, you will, Hansi. That's why I like you. You're so very trustworthy."

We three share a secret. Magda, Joseph and I are now an interdependent trio. If one of us goes down, we all go down. We have to trust each other. Joseph thinks so, too. He said he trusts me. Now, I can be a hero.

On cue, a black car pulls up, and two SS men step out. The first one, I recognize as the man who drove me to Magda's bedside after her miscarriage. His name is Ludwig. The second one, I don't know. "Herr Lorenz," Ludwig says. "You must come with us." He helps me into the back seat, then gets in the front. The second man drives.

"Thank you," I say. "I'm ready to be debriefed." I prepare to sit at a bare table, kept alert with coffee and cigarettes while they drain every ounce of intelligence out of me. I try to remember everything about Colonel Cartwright, what he wore, what he drank, what he said. I point in the direction of Prinz-Albrecht-Strasse, where SS headquarters are. "Why didn't you turn?" I ask. They say nothing.

We're long past it now. A rock sinks in my stomach. I'm to be punished. It seems the Reich needs Joseph and Magda to be together. It does not need Joseph, Magda and Hans to be together. But that's wrong! I fix them. No one else can do that. We're a trio. Do these men know this? I'm indispensable!

"Tell me where you're taking me," I demand. "The headquarters is back there!"

The driver raises the glass divider between us, then rolls down his window. Ludwig does the same. He lights a cigarette, then dangles his arm in the evening breeze. It's hotter than usual. The driver adjusts his mirror. He lets the air blow through his fingers. I know what they think: *Lorenz deserves what he gets. I can't be worried about this one or that one.*

Sweat rolls down the middle of my chest. It's getting hotter by the second. This will be done off the books. There will be no trial, no statutorily established prison term, no uniform, and no visitors. I look everywhere for an opening. I'm trapped by glass, bathed in sweat. They have me in a fucking swamp. My breath skims my lungs. My eyes lose focus. I see chains, truncheons. I picture my dirty, sick blood on my seat, on the sidewalk, against the windows I can't open.

We drive north and east, all the way into Prenzlauer Berg. It's where I grew up. It's where my catatonic father and cheating mother live. We're on Pankower Chaussee. We pass the Jewish cemetery with its crooked graves, jammed into rows. We pass the shop where I used to buy potatoes for dinner and the petrol station where I worked after school. I wonder if the barracks are here. Maybe they're in the basement of the Communist Party offices I shut down in February. At least they can spare me the indignity of breaking my bones in the slum where I was born.

The car turns left and then right. It comes to a stop in front of my parents' basement flat. The glass divider rolls down and cooler air hits me. I gasp for it. "We're here," Ludwig says.

"I don't understand. What's happening?"

Ludwig gets out, and I do the same. He holds out his hand, as if to welcome me into my own family's house.

My heart flutters and I can't stop it. "Where are the barracks?"

He looks at me like I'm a lunatic. "There are no barracks."

Was I paranoid? Is this about my parents? One of them must be ill. Joseph is treating me with kindness. He accepted my proposal!

I open the door to the crumble and crack of broken tile under my father's rocking chair.

"Step in," Ludwig says. "Please."

My father's face is baggy, close to white. He shakes his head like an itchy dog. Then he goes back to rocking. "So much to do," he says. "Let them pass."

My mother is nowhere. Could she be dead?

"Where's Mutter?" I bark at him, though I know he won't answer.

"Perhaps she's on holiday with one of her boyfriends," Ludwig mocks. Apparently, Joseph has shared my dossier with him.

"What is this, then?" I demand.

"Dr. Goebbels asked us to take you home."

"I live on Tiergartenstrasse," I say.

"So busy," my father squawks.

Ludwig adjusts his black tie. "According to Dr. Goebbels, this is where you live."

Now, I understand. Joseph isn't going to have someone else torture me. He's doing it himself. He's taking my life from me, piece by piece. He's taking my home and my job. He's banishing me from the Party, so I can never work again. He's forcing me to watch from this shit hole as the 1,000 year Reich soars. How pleased he must be with himself. How well he has picked my poison. It is the one that keeps the body alive, but destroys the spirit. He doesn't know that the woman I love has beaten him at this cruel game. My soul is already dead.

The driver enters and stands behind me. He shifts from foot to foot. I don't turn because I don't want to see him as he sees the depths of my disgrace.

"Let them pass," my father says again.

"That means hello," I say.

The driver chuckles.

Now it's my turn to chuckle. I hold out my hands to display my newfound dungeon. "What more could he possibly add?"

"He says it's a shame. Your body is of the Gods of Antiquity"—

My father raises his voice. "So busy. So busy."

— "but you are just too"—

Air rushes above me. A shining shaft of silver wings toward my neck.

— "stupid."

83

EVA

I had traveled through six countries and crossed a sea before I was brave enough to take Frau Pappenheim's letter out of my bag and break the envelope's seal. People were gathering on the deck, leaning and pointing toward the landmass ahead of us. Free to hope for the first time in months, the crowd hushed. "We'll make it," someone said with awe.

I followed the golden sky back over my head to the West, turning my back to the crowd, away from the silhouette of land that would be my home. The red flame of the sun plunged beneath the water behind us, and when it was gone, and the sea turned black, I read.

Dearest Eva,

I could not say this to you for fear of not saying it well. Not knowing what the future holds and being forced to question all I have thought, done and imparted to you, I write to explain myself.

For me, we were always a family. I felt it. You girls did not. When one tried to impress me, when another didn't reach for my hand, it was because she felt a difference. What I did and said to persuade her couldn't erase what she'd lost. This girl could learn from me. That one could need me. But no one could ever forgive me for not being what she wanted the most.

Even if I were to coo Yiddish lullabies through tin teeth and extol their every scribble as genius, even if I wrapped my hair in a scarf and wore dresses scented with herring, even if I were dead, I would not have been their mother.

It's too much to ask someone to love what she can't forgive, so I never asked any of you to love me.

I thought it might be different with you, Eva. You never knew your mother. When you grew up, I hoped you would see yourself as a daughter to me. But you never escaped the shadow of your illegitimacy; you never thought you deserved a mother. I knew this because I, too, have held onto the shames of my past with a clenched fist. They are greater and more abundant than yours, without doubt, and I suppose I never believed I deserved a daughter.

I didn't do enough to disabuse you of your view. That was my mistake. I didn't want to show favoritism, or to make you feel different. Maybe I feared I could never get through to you, and it would break my heart if I tried.

When you closed the door to your apartment in that ramshackle building in Berlin almost four years ago, I saw the turn of a smile on your face, and I knew you were gone.

I meant as much to you all for what I was not, as for what I was. How could it be any other way? I lived behind the permanent shade of your memories and your imaginations.

Please, remember this. From that colder place, I still love you. You are my spiritual daughter. We are a family, even though you need to look through dark to see it.

Love,
 Frau Pappenheim

I crawled back into my berth. I read her words again and again until I could repeat them, and then, as I'd done in the orphanage, envying the tears of my roommates, I lay on my flattened pillow and looked for shapes hidden in the cracks of the ceiling. When the night fell silent, I wept for the mother I'd finally lost.

We didn't disembark until the morning, and the sun was already beating down from above the hill that guarded the port. The streets and buildings were made from the same light, rough-hewn stone. Its bleached dust left an itchy coat over my ankles. Cypress trees poked holes into the shocking blue sky. There was no shade, no haze, no gray. A bright white banner twitched in the breeze, *Welcome to the Port of Haifa.*

It was a city that was more like a small town. Peddlers' bells and the slow drag of sandals over gravel hung in the air. The open and close of metal shutters and the pull of a clothesline along a rusty reel rang in my ear. Men drank coffee and read Arabic newspapers on benches next to the dock.

A British officer paced our line, and shouted dully, "You will need to have your passports and visas ready for inspection."

The man in front of me was nervous, sweating. "What's he saying? I don't want to make a mistake." I translated for him.

We got closer to the front where another British officer sat at a card table under a square, white awning. A metal fan rattled in front of him. Its breeze rustled a stack of papers that I assumed validated our documents. Every once in a while, a page took flight, causing my heart to skip. Without shifting his focus, the man smashed it back down again. The startling bangs sent currents of anxiety through the line. The man in front of me looked sick.

"What's your name?" I asked.

"Gunther Hirsch," he said. "But that name is dead. I'll have a new name now, a Hebrew name."

"What is it?"

He shook his head. "Not yet."

I asked him where he'd lived in Germany. "Munich," he grunted. "The worst place on earth." Then he turned back to the sea, as if to be sure of the vastness of the distance from where he'd come.

"You need a new name," he said to me, after a while. "You will be Yaffa Schachar, beautiful dawn. It suits you well."

I smiled in thanks, then looked away. Low-slung, flat-roofed buildings crawled up the hill like decrepit steps, but in the sun, their stone shone boldly against the flat, hard sky. I couldn't believe that any dawn had ever brought this much light. "It's a beautiful name," I said to my new friend.

Wild cats crept cautiously in front of us. Their fur was matted with mud and dust and they smelled of fish. Herr Hirsch knelt. He fed them bits of old bread from his hand.

An English voice barked, "Next!" It broke his reverie and jolted him to the table. "Papers!" came the voice. I could see Herr Hirsch's hands shake as the officer inspected his documents, eyebrows raised over black reading glasses. His torturous silence finally ended and he shifted his stare to Herr Hirsch, then back to the papers. "What will you be called in Palestine?" he asked.

Herr Hirsch announced, "Avraham Harel." Then he turned back to me and smiled.

"Spell it. Hebrew and English, please," the officer grunted.

"*Aleph, bet* . . ."

The guard shook his head and grumbled under his breath as he wrote. Then he said, "Very well, Mr. Mountain of God. Follow the Son of the Lion to the blue bus. You're going to a kibbutz near

Nahariya. I hope you like socialists and bananas, because that's all they've got."

Herr Harel, nee Hirsch, clucked for the cats and left his pile of bread at the foot of a tent pole. When he was sure they had it, he grabbed his suitcase and ran for the bus.

"Next!"

I stepped before him. "Papers!"

I handed them over, my chest fluttering. I watched the cats devour their breakfast, afraid to see the officer as he read. "Is Bella Glaz the name you would like to record?"

I looked past the waiting buses, up the mountainside and straight into the sun. When I turned back, my eyes danced with its brightness. I said, "My name is Eva Schmidt."

EPILOGUE

Bet Hakerem, Jerusalem, 1954

When the pink over the desert fades and the black comes, it steals the last hint of warmth from the day, dropping a silence that stops my heart. The sounds that fill me, my husband Aron's feet coming up the stairs from work, children playing in the street, car engines turning over, are erased, and the world goes blank. It is into this blank that I say their names: Herr Lieb Perlstein, Ruth Paretsky, Shmuel Rosenstein, Bella Glaz Zich, Helene Rothenberg, and all but two of the girls with whom I was raised. They weren't enough to me then. That was my crime. I made them small. Now, in the blank, they can be impossibly big. They're all there is in the world.

My husband, Aron is a doctor from Bialystok. His wounds run deeper than mine. He gave more and lost more. I say his names, too. Zelman, Esther, Yitzchak, Aizik, Feschke and Lena Fejnsod. I never knew his family. I never will, but in the dark, they, too, can be everything. They can be as bright as the infinite stars.

The two to whom I surrendered all have no place in the blank. They come at me in the daytime, as though they are of me. He sits on the *Egged* bus, two rows ahead. When the radio dings to announce the news, and the voice intones, *Kol Yisrael, Shalom,* he doesn't turn his head or pay attention, as the rest of us do. Sometimes, he stands behind me at the *shuk* as I spoon turmeric, zaatar and cumin into little bags tied with wire. I know he's not really there, lurking behind a jasmine bush, or drinking tea from a glass on a dusty patio in Emek Refaim. Often, he's just a flash, gone before I recognize him, leaving the imprint of dread in a low ache on the side of my neck.

She is different. She, who played cards after murdering her six children, sweet Helge among them. She, who killed herself rather than answer to the world she bled until there was no more to take. She sends hot jolts through me that cause me to twitch in shame.

I know nothing of what happened to my friends in Berlin except for Matthias and Thad. Matthias, who always knew the truth of things, got out of Germany in 1934, far in advance of most Jewish exiles. I stumbled upon his emigration in 1935, in the dark of the Zion Cinema on Kikar Zion. I'd seen *Liliom*, a less than enthralling French film by none other than Fritz Lang. When the credits rolled, I got up to go. As I pushed open the door to the lobby, I caught the words, *Assistant to the Editor . . . . Matthias Altmann*, in white against black. I thought I'd imagined it, so I sat back down and watched the movie again. When his name passed, my relief and joy burst inside of me and I sobbed all the way home.

After the war, I searched for him first on the lists of refugees, and then on the far longer lists of the dead. Matthias's only mistake was that he hadn't gone far enough. He was taken from Paris in the Vel' d'hiv roundup on July 16, 1942 and later was recorded among the dead at Auschwitz.

I take comfort thinking of him in his final years. I imagine him debating art and literature with the likes of Chagall, Soutine and Döblin. I picture him drinking coffee and sipping wine in the cafés of Montparnasse. Mostly, I see him the day the credits first rolled, with his unvanquished pride, walking free in Paris's dreamy light, believing, without cynicism, that he had discovered heaven on earth.

Thad was repatriated shortly after I left Germany. He spent the war in Army Intelligence. I know this because he visited Israel in

1950 as a Congressman from Pittsburgh, serving on the Armed Services Committee. He was able to locate me without difficulty.

He was still too thin, but he remained handsome. White strands lightened his hair, and deep-set wrinkles on his forehead made him look older than he was.

We had drinks on the veranda of the King David Hotel, overlooking the Old City. Its crenelated walls were haunted against the blue and black of the night sky. Because there was too much to say, I said little. I told him I was relieved he came through the war, and that I wondered about him often, hoping for his survival. He said the same of me. I talked to him about Aron, and about the work we shared. But I was far more interested to hear his news.

He reported that both the Anglophiles were killed in action: the first outside Florence, and the second at Okinawa. Christopher, though, was in top form, having spent the war at the State Department due to his father's intervention. In 1939, when the US Embassy staff was recalled from Berlin, he proposed to Katharina. She declined, saying things weren't yet bad enough to justify America. She survived the bombings holed up in her parents' Brandenburg estate on a diet of root vegetables and hard bread, though it never came to rats and squirrels, she always boasted.

Not willing to concede defeat, Christopher flew back to Germany after the war. With ungodly sums, he bribed his way into the Soviet zone, and again asked Katharina to marry him. The second time was a charm, but, as she put it, only because she was nothing if not practical.

As for himself, Thad said somewhat sheepishly that he had married Christopher's cousin, Betsy, and they were happy together. He thought I would like her very much. She was a reader, and was raising their two boys to be, as well. They divided their time between Pittsburgh and Washington. It was difficult with the boys, but they planned to send them to the same boarding school he and Christopher attended, so things would get easier. All in all, he thought things had turned out as well as they possibly could, given the times in which we lived.

For several minutes, we said nothing at all, entranced by the passage of time. He'd brought back memories I'd forgotten I had, and they swirled inside me, drilling down to my deepest fears and shames. As they gained power, I announced I had to go home. Aron would be expecting me. I gathered my purse, and said how truly glad I was to learn of his happiness.

He reached into his suit pocket and pulled out a yellowed page that had been torn from the *Berliner Tageblatt*. The printed German caused my nerves to prickle. I had to put my arms around it to hide it from anyone sitting near us who would be wounded by the sight.

"I've saved this for you since '33," he said. "I wanted to give it to you myself."

I couldn't imagine what horror he was yet to reveal, and my hands shook as I unfolded the paper. It was a full-page spread summarizing the Four Power Pact. "I don't understand," I said.

"The bottom right."

I saw a short article, tucked into the corner of the page:

PRENZLAUER BERG MURDER

The Ministry of Information and Public Enlightenment has identified the decapitated body discovered in a Prenzlauer Berg basement as that of Ministry employee, Hans Lorenz. Police believe Lorenz's throat was slashed after he interrupted a robbery in progress. Lorenz was living in the apartment with his mother, who was not home at the time of the murder, and his father, an invalid, who, though unharmed, was unable to serve as a reliable witness to the crime. The number of home

invasions in Prenzlauer Berg, a heavily working-class district,
is on the rise this year, and is among the highest in Berlin.

I read it twice. Its cold anonymity satisfied my sense of justice, but it gave me no happiness. I suppose if I'd maintained any stake in Hans's fate, it would have breathed life into the ghost who still followed me, just far enough away. I could give him no more of myself than he'd already taken.

The waiter interrupted to ask if we wanted another round, but Thad signaled for the check.

"He didn't live with his parents, you remember," I said. "He had an apartment on Tiergartenstrasse."

"Maybe it's a reporting error," Thad replied, fumbling in his pocket for his wallet.

I stood to go. "Was it you?"

"No."

"But you had something to do with it."

"No."

I laughed. "How could you have? He's the one you wanted the whole time."

"And you, Eva. I wanted you, too."

"Open your palm," I said, grabbing his wrist. After 17 years, I still remembered its bony mounts and deep-set lines. Looking straight into his eyes, I said, "I believe you."

Before we were married, I told my story to Aron, but only once. He heard every word. His perfect stillness protected each part of it. He sought no comfort for himself, neither asking for, nor providing any justification for all I had done. He took my truth whole, with love. I did the same for him.

We rarely revisit our pasts, except by vague allusion, an intentional glance or a touch that carries the full weight of what we know, unforgotten and undiminished, in our hearts.

When I got home that night, he was at his desk, reviewing his patients' charts. I dropped the page from the *Tageblatt* in front of him, pointing to the article.

He held it under a cone of lamplight. His expression grew serious as his eyes moved over the words. Like me, he read it twice. When he finished, he let it fall onto his desk. But for the clench in his jaw, his expression didn't change. His soft brown eyes held mine. "It's good," he said.

He brought me into our bed and pulled me to him. We slept like that, through the night, our slow breaths rising and falling as one.

I started to talk to you on May 29, 1936. It was the day I read your obituary in *Ha'aretz*. You died of cancer. You were 77 years old.

I had known it was coming, but the news still ripped me apart. I didn't know what I would do without your letters, which were usually brief admonitions to stay out of the sun, to resist the boorish acculturation inevitable among Jewish émigrés to Palestine, and most important, to look out for this one or that one whom you'd helped get from there to here. I cherished whatever you wrote because beneath the mundane sentences, next to the Gmund watermark, you offered me your name with love.

Now, I'm grateful you died when you did. You didn't see the *Judischer Frauenbund* banned. You didn't hear the children's cries as the Neu Isenberg house was torched on *Kristallnacht*. You didn't watch as the ones to whom you gave your life were forced back to the East to be gassed and burned, their bodies dissected and destroyed by the countrymen you so deeply honored. The words Auschwitz-Birkenau, Sobibor, Treblinka and Bergen-Belsen never entered your consciousness or crossed your lips. You never knew the truth of evil; you never saw its absolute and unending darkness. You made it to the light before it could touch you.

Last year, your story became public. Over the protests of your family, a man you would have despised by the name of Ernest Jones revealed to the world the thing in your past that brought you your shame. It was the shame about which you wrote to me when I left you for the last time. It was what made you believe you didn't deserve a daughter, as I believed I didn't deserve a mother.

He told all who would listen, all who would read, that you were Anna O, the brilliant hysteric, the mad patient of Breuer, the iconic case study of Freud, the star of the great doctor's career.

It was a story about which you never spoke. Yet, I'm certain it is what gave you the compassion to save us. You did not want us to live haunted by our pasts. I hate Ernest Jones for stealing your secrets and sharing them with the world. But you must understand that knowing your truth fills me with more love for you than I'd ever thought possible. It makes me stronger, as I know it did you.

This year, the West German government put you on a postage stamp as a 'Helper of Humanity.' I wonder if you would have accepted this honor, had you lived through the war to see it.

After all your accomplishments, you once said, 'the very best a woman can do is to mean something to someone, and I am happy if I feel sometimes that I will not die without having warmed someone at my small fire.'

Frau Pappenheim, I am warm. This year I will pay you the only honor you ever asked of those for whom you lit your flame. I will do what I vowed never to do. To the horror and outrage of my neighbors and friends, I will return to Germany. I will place a pebble atop your grave in the Old Jewish Cemetery in Frankfurt. But my stone will carry the fire of these desert hills, and with it, I will bring

36 more, one for each of the children Aron and I have raised in our orphanage. They've patched our hearts with the shattered pieces of their own, and they filled us with love.

We lost two in the War for Independence, and one succumbed to his ghosts on his eighteenth birthday. Every day we live, we are blessed with their memories. Every day, our hearts break for them anew.

Many others have reached adulthood. We have two *Kibbutzniks*—please, don't be upset—two PhD students (English and biology), a librarian, a waiter, a shop clerk, a botanist and a deeply frustrated artist. Thanks to Aron, we have three in medical school, two of whom are women; and, thanks to my memory of Herr Perlstein, there is also a dressmaker. Between them, they already have 18 children of their own.

Our children visit us with their babies. They say when we sat by their bedsides while they cried at night, when they felt the warmth of our fire, they knew we were a family.

As I think of their words, I picture the 36 extra stones I will place atop your grave. I feel their weight. I see their scars. I smell the dirt that sits in their crevices. I say to myself what I've said so many times to my children. We never could have been a family if I had not had one of my own.

Printed in the USA
CPSIA information can be obtained
at www.ICGtesting.com
JSHW020944131124
73503JS00002B/8